Variable
Star

Books by Robert A. Heinlein

Books by Spider Robinson

Variable Star

Robert A. Heinlein

and

Spider Robinson

A Tom Doherty Associates Book
New York

VARIABLE STAR

Copyright © 2006 by The Robert A. & Virginia Heinlein Prize Trust and Spider Robinson

A Tor Book
Published by Tom Doherty Associates, LLC
175 Fifth Avenue
New York, NY 10010

www.tor.com

Tor® is a registered trademark of Tom Doherty Associates, LLC.

ISBN-13: 978-0-7653-5168-5
ISBN-10: 0-7653-5168-4

First Edition: September 2006
First Mass Market Edition: December 2007

Printed in the United States of America

0   9   8   7   6   5   4   3   2   1

For the women without whom
none of this would have been necessary:
Bam, Evelyn, Ginny, Jeanne, Amy, Terri Luanna,
Ruth, Kate, and Eleanor

Editor's Preface

In Robert A. Heinlein's *Stranger in a Strange Land* there is a story about a Martian artist so focused on his work that he fails to notice his own death, and completes the piece anyway. To Martians, who don't go anywhere when they die but simply become Old Ones, the burning question was: should this work be judged by the standards used for art by the living, or for art by the dead?

A similar situation occurs here for one of the first times on this planet. This book is a posthumous collaboration, begun when one of its collaborators was seven, and completed when the other was seventeen-years-dead. Spider Robinson discusses this at length in his Afterword, but a brief explanation at the start may help readers to better appreciate what they're reading, and to decide by what standards they should evaluate it.

After the passing of Robert Heinlein's widow, Virginia, in 2003, his archivist/biographer discovered a detailed outline and notes for a novel the Grand Master had plotted in 1955, but had never gotten around to writing, tentatively titled *The Stars Are a Clock*. Heinlein's estate executor and literary agent decided the book deserved to be written and read, and agreed that Spider Robinson was the only logical choice to complete it.

First called "the new Robert Heinlein" by the *New York Times Book Review* in 1982, Robinson has been linked with him in the reviews of most of his own thirty-two award-winning books. The two were close friends. Spider penned a famous essay demolishing his mentor's detractors called "Rah, Rah, R.A.H.!," and contributed the introduction to Heinlein's recently-discovered 1939 first book, *For Us, the Living*.

It was a pairing as fortuitous as McCartney and Lennon. You are about to read something genuinely unique and quite special: a classic novel fifty years in the making, conceived in the Golden Age of SF by its first Grand Master, and completed in the Age of Cyberspace by one of his greatest students. *Variable Star* is Robert A. Heinlein's only collaborative novel—and we believe he would be as proud of it as Spider Robinson is, and as we at Tor are to publish it.

—Cordwainer LoBrutto,
Senior Editor

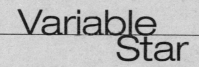

1

**For it was in the golden prime
Of good Harun Alrashid ...**

—Alfred, Lord Tennyson,
Recollections of the Arabian Nights

I thought I wanted to get married in the worst way. Then that's pretty much what I was offered, so I ended up going trillions of kilometers out of my way instead. A great many trillions of kilometers, and quite a few years—which turns out to be much the greater distance.

It began this way:

Jinny Hamilton and I were dancing.

This was something of an accomplishment for me, in and of itself—I was born on Ganymede, and I had only been Earthside a few years, then. If you've never experienced three times the gravity you consider normal, imagine doing your favorite dance ... with somebody your own weight sitting on each of your shoulders, on a pedestal a few meters above concrete. Broken bones, torn ligaments, and concussions are hazards you simply learn to accept.

But some people play water polo, voluntarily. Jinny and I had been going out together for most of a year, and dancing was one of her favorite recreations, so by now I had not only made myself learn how to dance, I'd actually become halfway decent at it. Enough to dimly understand how someone with muscles of steel and infinite wind might consider it fun, anyway.

But that night was something else.

Part of it was the setting, I guess. Your prom is *supposed* to be a magical time. It was still quite early in the evening,

but the Hotel Vancouver ballroom was appropriately decorated and lit, and the band was excellent, especially the
singer. Jinny was both the most beautiful and the most interesting person I had ever met. She and I were both finally
done with Fermi Junior College, in Surrey, British Columbia. Class of 2286 (Restored Gregorian), huzzah—go, Lep-
tons! In the fall we'd be going off to university together at
Stony Brook, on the opposite coast of North America—*if*
my scholarship came through, anyway—and in the meantime we were young, healthy, and hetero. The song being
played was one I liked a lot, an ancient old ballad called "On
the Road to the Stars," that always brought a lump to my
throat because it was one of my father's favorites.

> *It's the reason we came from the mud, don't you know*
> *'cause we wanted to climb to the stars,*
>
> *In our flesh and our bone and our blood we all know*
> *we were meant to return to the stars,*
>
> *Ask anyone which way is God, and you know*
> *he will probably point to the stars . . .*

None of that explained the way Jinny danced that night. I
knew her as a good dancer, but that night it was almost as if
she were possessed by the ghost of Gillis. It wasn't even just
her own dancing, though that was inspired. She did some
moves that startled me, phrases so impressive she started to
draw attention even on a crowded dance floor. Couples
around us kept dancing, but began watching her. Her long
red hair swirled through the room like the cape of an inspired toreador, and for a while I could only follow like a
mesmerized bull. But then her eyes met mine, and *flashed*,
and the next thing I knew I was attempting a combination I
had never even thought of before; one that I knew as I began
was way beyond my abilities—and I nailed it. She sent me a
grin that felt like it started a sunburn, and offered me an intriguing move, and I thought of something to do with it, and
she lobbed it back with a twist, and we got through five fairly

complex phrases without a train wreck and out the other side as smoothly as if we'd been rehearsing for weeks. Some people had stopped dancing to watch, now.

On the way to the stars—
every molecule in you was born in the heart of a star.
On the way to the stars—
in the dead of the night they're the light that'll show
where you are
yes they are
from so far . . .

In the back of my head were a few half-formed, half-baked layman's ideas for dance steps that I wasn't even sure were physically possible in a one-gee field. I'd never had the nerve to actually try any of them with a partner, in any gravity; I really hate looking ridiculous. But Jinny lifted an eyebrow—*what have you got?*—and before I knew it I was trying one, even though there was no way she could know what her response was supposed to be. Only she did, somehow, and made it—or rather, an improved variation of what I'd thought of—and not only was the result successful enough to draw applause, by luck it happened to offer a perfect lead-in to another of my ideas, which also turned out to work, and suggested something to her—

We flew.

We'll be through if the day ever comes when we no
longer yearn to return to the stars.

I can't prove it's so, but I'm certain: I know
that our ancestors came from the stars.

It would not be so lonely to die if I knew
I had died on the way to the stars.

Talking about dance is as silly as dancing about architecture. I don't know how to convey exactly how we danced that night, or what was so remarkable about it. I can barely manage to believe we did it. Just let it stand that we deserved the applause we received when the music finally ended and we went into our closing clinch. It was probably the first time since I'd come to Terra that I didn't feel heavy and weak and fragile. I felt strong . . . graceful . . . manly. . . .

"After dancing like that, Stinky, a couple really ought to get married," Jinny said about two hundred millimeters below my ear.

I felt fourteen. "Damn it, Jinny—" I said, and pulled away from her. I reached down for her hands, trying to make it into a dance move, but she eluded me. Instead she curtsied, blew me a kiss, turned on her heel, and left at high speed, to spirited applause.

It increased when I ran after her.

Jinny was 178 centimeters tall, not especially tall for a Terran, and I was a Ganymedean beanpole two full meters high, so her legs were considerably shorter than mine. But they were also adapted from birth to a one-gee field—to *sports* in a one-gee field. I didn't catch up with her until we'd reached the parking lot, and then only because she decided to let me.

So we'd each had time to work on our lines.

Ginny went with, "Joel Johnston, if you don't want to marry me—"

"Jinny, you know perfectly well I'm going to marry you—"

"In five more frimpin' years! My God, Stinky, I'll be an old, old woman by then—"

"Skinny, you'll *never* be an old woman," I said, and that shut her up for a second. Every so often a good one comes to me like that. Not often enough. "Look, don't be like this. I can't marry you right now. You know I can't."

"I don't know anything of the sort. I know you *won't*. But I see nothing preventing you. You don't even have to worry about parental consent."

"What does that have to do with it? Neither do you. And we wouldn't let parental disapproval stand in our way if we *did* want to get married."

"You see? I was right—you *don't* want to!"

I was becoming alarmed. I had always thought of Jinny as

unusually rational, for a girl. Could this be one of those hormonal storms I had read about? I hoped not—all authorities seemed to agree the only thing a man could do in such weather was lash himself to the mast and pray. I made a last stubborn attempt to pour logic on the troubled waters. "Jinny, please—be reasonable! I am not going to let you marry a dole bludger. Not even if he's me."

"But—"

"I intend to be a composer. You know that. That means it's going to take me at least a few years to even start to get established. You knew that when we started dating. If, I say 'if,' all those bullocks I sacrificed to Zeus pay off and I actually win a Kallikanzaros Scholarship, it will be my great privilege to spend the next four years living on dishrag soup and scraped fridge, too poor to support a cat. If, and I say 'if,' I am as smart as I think I am, and luckier than I usually am, I'll come out the other end with credentials that *might*, in only another year or two, leave me in a position to offer you something more than half of a motel cubicle. Meanwhile, you have your own scholarships and your law degree to worry about, so that once my music starts making serious money, nobody will weasel it away from us."

"Stinky, do you think I care about *money*?" She said that last word as if it were a synonym for stale excrement.

I sighed. Definitely a hormonal storm. "Reboot and start over. What is the purpose of getting married?"

"What a romantic question!" She turned away and quested for her car. I didn't move.

"Quit dodging, I'm serious. Why don't we just live together if we want to be romantic? What is marriage *for*?"

The car told her she was heading the wrong way; she reversed direction and came back past me toward its voice and pulsing beacon. "Babies, obviously."

I followed her. "Bingo. Marriage is for making jolly babies, raising them up into successful predators, and then admiring them until they're old enough to reward you with grandchildren to spoil."

She'd acquired the car by now; she safed and unlocked it. "My baby-making equipment is at its peak *right now*," she said, and got in the car. "It's going to start declining any minute." She closed, but did not slam, the door.

I got in my side and strapped in. "And the decline will take decades to become significant," I pointed out logically. "Your baby-making gear may be at its hypothetical optimum efficiency today—but my baby-*raising* equipment isn't even operational yet."

"So what?"

"Jinny, are you seriously proposing that we raise a child as extraordinary and gifted as ours on *credit*?" We both shared a most uncommon aversion to being in debt. Orphans spend too much of their childhood in debt to others—debt that cannot be repaid.

"*Nobody* seems to be seriously proposing around here," she said bitterly.

Hormonal hurricane, maybe. A long time ago they used to name all hurricanes after women. On Ganymede, we still named all groundquakes after them. "Look—"

She interrupted, "Silver: my home, no hurry." The car said, "Yes, Jinny," and came alive, preparing for takeoff.

I wondered as always why she'd named her car that—if you were going to pick an element, I thought, why not hydrogen? I failed to notice the slight change in address protocol. Despite our low priority, we didn't have to wait long, since nobody else had left the prom yet and the system was between rush hours; Silver rose nearly at once and entered the system with minimal huhu. That early in the evening, most of the traffic was still in the other direction, into Greater Vancouver. Once our speed steadied, Jinny opaqued the windows, swiveled her seat to face me, and folded her arms. I'm sure it was quite coincidental that this drew my attention to the area immediately above them. I believe in the Tooth Fairy, too. "Pardon me for interrupting you," she said.

She looked awfully good. Her prom dress was more of a spell than a garment. The soft warm interior lighting was very good to her. Of course, it was her car.

That was the hell of it. I wanted to marry her at least as much as she wanted to marry me. Just looking at her made my breath catch in my throat. I wished with all my heart, and not for the first time, that we lived back when unmarried people could live together openly. They said a stable society was impossible, back then. But even if they were right, what's so great about a stable society?

My pop used to say, "Joel, never pass up a chance to shut up." Well, some men learn by listening, some read, some observe and analyze—and some of us just have to pee on the electric fence. "Jinny, you know I'm a backward colonial when it comes to debt."

"And you know I feel the same way about it that you do!"

I blinked. "That's true. We've talked about it. I don't care what anybody says; becoming the indentured servant of something as compassionate and merciful as a bank or credit union simply isn't rational."

"Absolutely."

I spread my hands. "What am I missing? Raising a child takes money—packets and crates of the stuff. I haven't got it. I can't earn it. I won't borrow it. And I'm too chicken to steal it."

She broke eye contact. "Those aren't the only ways to get it," she muttered. Silver gave its vector-change warning *peep*, slowed slightly, and banked left to follow the Second Narrows Bridge across Burrard Inlet.

"So? I suppose I could go to Vegas and turn a two-credit bit into a megasolar at the roulette wheel."

"Blackjack," she said. "The other games are for suckers."

"My tenants back home on the Rock might strike ice. In the next ten minutes I could get an idea for a faster-than-light star drive that can be demonstrated without capital. I can always stand at stud, but that would kick me up a couple of tax brackets. Nothing else comes to mind."

She said nothing, very loudly. Silver peeped, turned left again, and increased speed, heading for the coast.

"Look, Spice," I said, "you know I don't share contemporary Terran prejudices any more than you do—I don't insist that I be the one to support us. But somebody has to. If you can find a part-time job for either of us that pays well enough to support a family, we'll get married tomorrow."

No response. We both knew the suggestion was rhetorical. Two *full-time* jobs would barely support a growing family in the present economy.

"Come on," I said, "we already had this conversation once. Remember? That night on Luckout Hill?" The official name is Lookout Hill, because it looks out over the ocean, but it's such a romantic spot, many a young man has indeed lucked out there. Not me, unfortunately. "We said—"

"I remember what we said!"

Well, then, maybe I didn't. To settle it, I summoned that conversation up in my mind—or at least fast-forwarded through the storyboard version in the master index. And partway through, I began to grow excited. There was indeed one contingency we had discussed that night on Luckout Hill, one that I hadn't really thought of again, since I couldn't really picture Jinny opting for it. I wasn't sure she was suggesting it now . . . but if she wasn't, I would.

"See here, Skinny, you really want to change your name from Hamilton to Johnston right away? Then let's do it tomorrow morning—and ship out on the *Sheffield*!" Her jaw dropped; I pressed on. "If we're going to start our marriage broke, then let's do it somewhere where being broke isn't a handicap, or even a stigma—out there around a new star, on some new world eighty light-years away, not here on Terra. What do you say? You say you're an old-fashioned girl—will you homestead with me?"

A look passed across her face I'd seen only once before—on Aunt Tula's face, when they told us my father was gone. Sadness unspeakable. "I can't, Joel."

How had I screwed up so badly? "Sure you could—"

"No. I *can't.*" She swiveled away from me.

The sorrow on her face upset me so much, I shut up and began replaying everything since our dance, trying to locate the point at which my orbit had begun to decay. Outside the car, kilometers flicked by unseen. On the third pass, I finally remembered a technique that had worked for me more than once with women in the past: quit analyzing every word I'd said and instead, consider words I had *not* said.

Light began to dawn, or at least a milder darkness. I swiveled her seat back to face me, and sought her eyes. They were huge.

I dove right in. "Jinny, listen to me. I *want* to marry you. I ache to marry you. You're the one. Not since that first moment when I caught you looking at me have I ever doubted for an instant that you are my other half, the person I want to spend the rest of my life with. Okay?"

"Oh." Her voice was barely audible.

"You give me what I need, and you need what I can give. I want the whole deal, just like you've told me you want it— old-fashioned death do us part, better or worse monogamy, like my parents. None of this term marriage business, no prenup nonsense, fifty-fifty, mine is thine, down the line, and I don't care if we live to be a hundred. I want to marry you so bad, my teeth hurt. So bad my *hair* hurts. If you would come with me, I would be happy to *walk* to Boötes, carrying you on my back, towing a suitcase. My eyeballs keep drying out every time I look at you. Then when you're out of their field of vision, they start to tear up."

Her eyes started to tear up. "Oh, Joel—you *do* want to marry me." Her smile was glorious.

"Of course I do, Skinny you ninny. How could you not know that?"

"So it's just—"

"Just a matter of financing. Nothing else. We'll get married the day we can afford to." I loosened my seat belt, so I'd be ready for the embrace I was sure was coming.

Her smile got even wider. Then it fell apart, and she turned away, but not before I could see she was crying.

What the hell had I said *now*?

Of course, that's the one question you mustn't ask. Bad enough to make a woman cry; to not even know how you managed it is despicable. But no matter how carefully I reviewed the last few sentences I'd spoken, in my opinion they neither said anything nor failed to say anything that constituted a reason to cry.

Silver slowed slightly, signaling that we were crossing the

Georgia Strait. We'd be at Jinny's little apartment on Lasqueti Island, soon. I didn't know what to apologize *for*. But then, did I need to? "Jinny, I'm sorry. I really—"

She spoke up at once, cutting me off. "Joel, suppose you knew for sure you had your scholarship in the bag? The whole ride?" She swiveled her seat halfway back around, not quite enough to be facing me, but enough so that I was clearly in her peripheral vision.

I frowned, puzzled by the non sequitur. "What, have you heard something?" As far as I knew, the decisions wouldn't even be made for another few weeks.

"Damn it, Stinky, I'm just saying: Suppose you knew for a fact that you're among this year's Kallikanzaros winners."

"Well . . . that'd be great. Right?"

She turned the rest of the way back around, so that she could glare at me more effectively. "I'm asking you: If that happened, how would it affect your marriage plans?"

"Oh." I still didn't see where she was going with this. "Uh, it'd take a lot of the pressure off. We'd know *for sure* that we're going to be able to get married in as little as four years. Well, nothing's for sure, but we'd be a whole lot more . . ."

I trailed off because I could see what I was saying wasn't what she wanted to hear. I had to shift my weight slightly as Silver went into a wide right turn. I didn't have a clue what she did want to hear, and her face wasn't giving me enough clues. Maybe I ought to—

Wide right turn?

I cleared my side window. Sure enough, we were heading north; almost due north, it looked like. But that was wrong: we couldn't be that far south of Lasqueti. "Jinny, I—"

She was sobbing outright, now.

Oh, God. As calmly as I could, I said, "Honey, you're going to have to take manual control: Silver has gone insane."

She waved no-no and kept sobbing.

For a second I nearly panicked, thinking . . . I don't know what I was thinking. "Jinny, what's *wrong*?"

Her weeping intensified. "Oh, Jo-ho-ho-ho—"

I unbuckled, leaned in, and held her. "Damn it, talk to me! Whatever it is, we'll fix it, I know we will. Just tell me."

"Oh, God, I-hi-hi'm sorry . . . I screwed it all up-hup-hup-hup . . ." She clutched me back fiercely.

I was alarmed. I'd seen Jinny cry. This was hooting with sorrow, rocking with grief. Something was seriously wrong. "Whatever it is, it's okay, you hear me? Whatever it is."

She writhed in my arms. "Joel, I lie-hi-hi-hi-hied . . . I'm so stu-hoo-*hupid* . . ."

Ice formed on the floor of my heart. I did not break our embrace, but I felt an impulse to, and I'm sure she felt it kinesthetically. She cried twice as hard. Well, much harder.

It took her several minutes to get back under control. During those minutes, I didn't breathe or think or move or digest food or do anything at all except wait to learn what my Jinny had lied about. Then, when she took in a deep breath and pulled away from my arms, suddenly I didn't want to know. So I thought of a different question she could answer instead. "Where are we going?"

Her eyes began to slide away from mine, then came back and locked. "To my home."

This time I caught the subtle change. Usually the instruction she gave Silver was "my *place*."

"So? And it's north?"

She nodded.

"How far?"

"Silver: step on it," she said. The car acknowledged. Then to me, as Silver faced our chairs forward and pressed us back into them with acceleration, she said, "About twenty minutes, now."

I consulted a mental map and glanced out the window—with difficulty, as we were now pulling serious gees. Jinny's car was exceedingly well loved, but nonetheless it was just short of an antique. There was simply no way it could go anywhere near this fast. I made myself breathe slowly. This just kept getting better and better.

Twenty minutes north of Lasqueti at this speed would, it seemed to me, put us smack in the middle of a glacier some-

where, just below the border with Yukon Province. I was
dressed for a ballroom, didn't have so much as a toothbrush.
Not that it mattered, because we were doing at least four
times the provincial exurban speed limit; long before we
reached that glacier the Mounties (local cops) were going to
cut our power and set us down to await the Proctors . . .
probably in raw forest. Unless, of course, Silver tore himself
apart first, traveling at four times the best speed he'd been
capable of the day he left the factory.

Less than half an hour before, I'd been as perfectly happy
as I'd ever been in my life, dancing with my Jinny. I opaqued
my window, surrendered to the gee forces, and stared straight
ahead at nothing. To my intense annoyance, she let me.

Life is going to continue to suck until somebody finds the
Undo key.

2

Howe'er it be, it seems to me
'Tis only noble to be good.
Kind hearts are more than coronets,
And simple faith than Norman blood.

—Alfred, Lord Tennyson,
Lady Clara Vere de Vere

The engine did not explode. It didn't even sound any
louder than usual. The Mounties somehow failed to notice us blazing across their radar, or to log any complaints
about shattered windows; we crossed the province unmo-
lested. For most of the trip we were above atmosphere, so
high that the horizon showed a distinct curve—we pretty
much had to be at that speed, I think—but if the Peace
Forces satellites noticed us, they kept it to themselves. Nineteen minutes later, the car finished decelerating, came to a

dead stop, and went into hover mode, glowing softly from the heat of our passage and reentry into atmosphere.

"Wait," Jinny said—whether to Silver or to me, I was unsure.

I glanced at her, then turned to my side window once again and looked down. Sure enough, what lay some three thousand meters below us was a nearly featureless glacier. There was a big rill to the east, and a shadowy crevasse almost directly below that was much smaller, but still large enough to conceal several dozen cars the size of Silver. I looked back to Jinny. She was staring straight ahead at the windshield, which was still opaque.

Keeping my mouth shut was easy this time. I not only didn't know how I felt, I didn't even know what I felt it *about*. I couldn't have been more clueless if I'd had my head in a sack. Anything I said was likely to sound stupid in retrospect, and there are few things I hate more.

"I rehearsed this a hundred times," she said finally. "Now I've screwed it up completely."

I suspected this was true, but kept my mouth shut.

She swiveled my way and unbuckled her crash harness, though we were still three klicks above hard ice. It gave her enough freedom of movement to lean forward and take one of my hands in both of hers. I noted absently that the skin of her palm was remarkably hot. "Have you ever heard of Harun al-Rashid?" she asked me.

"Plays defense for the Tachyons?"

"Close," she said. "You're only off by, let me see, a little more than a millennium and a half. Fifteen hundred and some years."

"But he does play defense."

"Stinky, please shut up! He was a rich kid, from a powerful military family in ancient Persia. His father was a Caliph, roughly equivalent to premier of a province today, a man so tough he invaded the Eastern Roman Empire, which was then ruled by the Empress Irene."

"You're making this up," I charged.

Her eyes flashed. "I *said* 'please,' Joel."

I drew an invisible zipper across my lips.

"Harun became Caliph himself in the year 786." Over a thousand years before man could even travel *anywhere*. "He was probably as wealthy and powerful as anybody in living memory had ever been. Yet somehow, he was not an ignorant idiot."

"Amazing," I said, trying to be helpful.

Go try to be helpful to a woman who's talking. "He had the odd idea it was important to know what his people were really thinking and feeling about things," she went on as if I had not spoken. "He wanted more than just the sanitized, politically safe version they would give to him or to anyone he could send to talk to them. He understood that his wealth and power distorted just about everything in his relations with others, made it difficult if not impossible for truth to pass between them. You can see how that would be, right?"

"Sure. Everybody lies to the boss."

"Yes!" Finally, I'd gotten one right. "Then one day he overheard one of his generals say that nobody knows a city as well as an enemy spy. It gave him an idea.

"That night he disguised himself as a beggar, sneaked out of his palace alone, and wandered the streets of Baghdad, a spy in his own capital. Everywhere he went, he listened to conversations, and sometimes he asked innocent questions, and because he was thought a beggar, no one bothered to lie to him. He got drunk on it. He started to do it whenever he could sneak away."

Her eyes were locked on mine, now. It was important that I get this.

"Do you see, Joel? For the first time in his life Harun got an accurate picture of what the common people honestly thought . . . more than just what they thought, he experienced firsthand what life was really *like* for them, came to understand the things they didn't even think about because they simply assumed them . . . and their perspective informed and improved his own thinking from then on. He became one of the most beloved rulers in history—his name means Aaron the Just, and how many rulers do you suppose have ever been called that? One time fifteen thousand men followed him into battle against one hundred twenty-five thousand—and whipped them, left forty thousand legionaries dead on the ground and the rest running for their lives. He lived to a ripe old age, and when he died the whole Muslim world mourned. Okay?"

I was nodding. I understood every word she said. I had no idea what she was driving at.

She took a deep breath. "Okay. Now, imagine you're a young Persian girl in Baghdad. I see your mouth opening, and so help me God, if a wisecrack should come out of it . . . that's better. You're a poor-but-decent young Persian girl, working hard at some menial trade, struggling to better yourself, and so is—"

A strange alto voice suddenly spoke, seemingly from the empty space between Jinny and me, just a little too loudly. I was so startled I nearly jumped out of my seat. "Your vehicle's hull temperature has dropped sufficiently to permit safe debarking now, Miss Jinny."

If I was startled, Jinny was furious. I could tell because her face became utterly smooth, and her voice became softer in pitch and tone and slower in speed as she said, "There are only four letters in the word 'wait,' Smithers. There seems little room for ambiguity."

"I'm sorry, Miss Jinny," Smithers said at once, and although there was no noticeable cessation of any background hiss or power hum, somehow I knew he was *gone*.

"And so," she went on before I could ask who Smithers was, "is your boyfriend . . . call him Jelal. The two of you are very much in love, and want to get married, but you just don't have the means. And then one day—"

"Wait," I said, "I think I see where this is going . . . sort of. One day the beggar who lives next door comes over, right, and it turns out he's incredibly rich and he says he's been eavesdropping and he understands our problem and he offers Jelal a—"

I stopped talking. The penny had just dropped. All of sudden, I actually *did* see where this was going, at least in general terms. "Oh . . . my . . . God . . ." I breathed. "I've got it just backward, don't I?"

Her eyes told me I was right. "There wasn't any other way, do you see? Once I met you as Jinny Hamilton, I *couldn't* tell you. And anyway, the whole point was to—"

"*You're* Harun al-Rashid!"

"Well, his granddaughter," she said miserably.

I was stunned. "You're rich."

She nodded sadly. "Very."

Tumblers began to click into place. I tried to think it through. "You're not even an orphan, are you?"

Headshake. "I couldn't let anyone at Fermi meet my parents. They're . . . pretty well known. Hiring a pair of Potemkin parents for social purposes seemed grotesque."

"And you came to Fermi, instead of Lawrence Campbell or one of the other top prep schools, so you could—what? See how the other half lives?"

"Well . . . in part."

I was ranging back through my memories, adding things up with the benefit of hindsight, understanding little things that had puzzled me. Silver's previously unsuspected power. Jinny's extraordinary confidence and poise, so unexpected in an orphan. How, whenever someone brought up one of the really fabulous vacation destinations—Tuva, or the Ice Caves of Queen Maud Land in the Antarctic, or Harriman City on Luna—Jinny always seemed to have seen a good documentary about it recently. The way, when we ate pistachios, she always threw away the ones that were any trouble at all to open—

I became aware that Jinny was absolutely still and silent, studying my face intently for clues to what I was thinking. It seemed like a good idea; maybe I should get a mirror and try it. I thought about banging my head against the dashboard to reboot my brain.

Instead I looked at her and spread my hands. "I'm going to need some time to process this," I admitted.

"Of course," she said at once. "Sleep on it. There's no hurry. Tomorrow I'll introduce you to my real father. And meantime I'll answer any questions you have—no more evasions, no more white lies."

I didn't feel as though I knew enough to formulate a coherent question yet. No, wait, I did have one—purely for form's sake; I didn't see how the answer could help me. Still—

"What is it *really*?"

She blinked. "Crave pardon?"

"You said, 'Once I met you as Jinny Hamilton . . .' So that's not your real name. Okay, I'll bite. What is?"

"Oh, dear," she said.

" 'Jinny Oh.' Chinese, dear?"

Not amused. "Joel—"

"Come on, how bad could it be? Look, let's meet for the first time all over again. Hi there, I'm Joel Johnston, of Ganymede. And you are—?"

She stared at me, blank-faced, for so long I actually began to wonder whether she was going to tell me. I couldn't recall ever seeing her hesitate about anything before, much less this long. One of the many things I liked about her was that she always knew what she wanted to be doing next. Finally she closed her eyes, took in a long breath, released it . . . squared her shoulders and opened her eyes and looked me right in the eye.

"I'm very pleased to meet you, Mr. Johnston. I'm Jinny Conrad."

For a second or two nothing happened. Then my eyebrows and my pulse both rose sharply. It couldn't be. "Not—"

"Of Conrad," she confirmed.

It *couldn't* be.

"It's true," she said. "My father is Albert Conrad. Richard Conrad's third son."

"You're Jinnia Conrad of Conrad," I said.

She nodded once.

I didn't quite faint—but it was good that I was sitting down, and strapped in. My head drained like a sink; all the blood and most of the brain matter dropped at once to my feet.

V*ERY RICH*, SHE'D said. Yeah, and the Milky Way is rather roomy!

The Conrad industrial/informational empire was larger than the Rothschild family, the Hanseatic League, Kinetic

Sciences Interplanetary, and Rolls-Daiwoo combined, and only slightly smaller than the Solar System. Nothing like it could have existed before the advent of space travel—and perhaps it became inevitable in the first minute of Year One, as Leslie LeCroix was still shutting down the *Pioneer*'s engine on the virgin surface of Luna. The Conrads were a 150-year dynasty, every member of whom wielded wealth, power, and influence comparable to that of the Hudson's Bay Company or Harriman Enterprises in their day. Their combined interests ranged from the scientific outpost on Mercury, to Oort Cloud harvest—to interstellar exploration as far as sixty-five light-years away. At that time there were well over a dozen starships either outgoing or incoming, and eight had already returned safely (out of a hoped-for eighteen), five of them bearing the riches of Croesus in one form or another. Three of those big winners had been Conrad ships.

SHE GAVE ME a minute—well, some indeterminate period. Finally she said, "Look, I have to land, now. Smithers wasn't completely out of line to remind me. We . . . don't like to hover, here. It's just a bit conspicuous."

"Okay," I said, to be saying something. "Where's here?"

"In a minute. Silver: I relieve you."

"Yes, Jinny." She took the stick and we dropped three thousand meters rapidly enough to give me heart palpitations.

Which nearly became cardiac arrest when the ground came rushing up, and she failed to decelerate hard enough to stop in time! We were going to crash—

—right through the imaginary glacier—

—and into a deep valley, its floor lush and green and inviting and, best of all, still hundreds of meters below us. She landed us, without a bump, in a small clearing that from the air had looked indistinguishable from dozens of others, to me at least. But the moment she shut down, hoses and cables sprouted from the forest floor and began nurturing Silver. Ahead of us was a huge boulder, the size of a truck; as I watched, a large doorway appeared in it, facing us.

"We're here," she said.

"I ask again: Where is here?"

She shook her head. "It isn't."

"Isn't what?"

"Isn't anywhere."

I turned my head just enough to be looking at her out of the corner of my eye. "Here isn't anywhere."

"Right."

I closed my eyes. If I had just stayed back home on the farm, by now I might have been making enough of a crop to afford a hired man. That would have freed me up to do some courting—in a frontier society with considerably looser rules about premarital experimentation than contemporary Terra.

But I knew for a fact there was no one remotely like Jinny anywhere on Ganymede. *Had* known it for a fact, that is, even *before* learning that she was more well off than the Secretary General. . . .

No, I couldn't take that in just yet. "I really really wish I could think of something more intelligent to say than, 'What do you mean, "here isn't anywhere"?' "

She shrugged. "You tell me. If a place does not appear on any map, anywhere . . . if it doesn't show in even the finest-grain satellite photos . . . if no wires or roads or paths run to it, no government takes mail to it or taxes from it, and nobody is from there . . . in what sense does it exist? There *is* no here. Just us."

"Here."

"Exactly."

I nodded and dismissed the matter. "And this is your home?"

"One of them."

I nodded. "And your apartment on Lasqueti, of course. It must be weird having two homes."

She didn't say a word or move a muscle.

I turned to look at her. "More than two?"

Silence. Stillness.

"How many homes do you have, Jinny?"

In a very small voice, she said, "Eight. *Not* counting the Lasqueti place."

"So?"

"But three of them are off-planet!"

"Naturally," I agreed. "One winters in space."

"Oh, Joel, don't be that way."

"Okay. Let's go in."

She looked distressed. "Uh . . . if you are going to be that way, maybe it might be better to do it out here, before we go in."

I nodded again. Mr. Agreeable. "Sure. That makes sense. Okay." Then, big: *"How could you do this to me, Jinny?"*

She didn't flinch or cringe or duck. "Think it through, Joel. Sleep on it. Tomorrow morning, you tell me: How could I have *not* done it?"

I began an angry retort, and swallowed it. I had to admit I had not begun to think this thing through yet, and Dad always drilled into me that the time to open your mouth came *after* that. Besides, I already had a glimmering of what she meant. I filled my lungs, emptied them slowly and fully, and said, "You're right. Okay, I'm prepared to be polite, now. Let's go inside."

"You won't have to be," she said. "I promise you won't see any family at all until tomorrow morning. I made them guarantee that. This is our Prom Night."

I frowned. "I wish I had an overnight bag. Change of socks, fresh shirt, my razor—"

"Don't worry about it," she said, and unlocked the doors.

I let it go. Probably the contents of the slop chest here were finer than anything I owned. "All right. Invite me up to your place."

"Down, actually."

We opened our doors and got out. The roof of imaginary glacier did not exist from its underside; the moon and stars shone unimpeded overhead, a neat trick. But this was definitely not a natural ecology. The air was skin temperature, with an occasional breeze just slightly warmer. It smelled of dirt and green growing things, with just a little ozone tingle as if it had rained recently, though it had not. The loamy earth beneath my feet was rich, almost quivering with life;

any farmer I knew back on Ganymede would have desperately envied it. Acres of it, at least a meter deep: wild, uncultivated, supporting nothing but trees, scrub, and inedible berries. Just *lying* there. Conspicuous nonconsumption. *Start getting used to it, old son.* I thought of saying something, but I knew Jinny would never understand. It's funny: the very *word* "Terra" means "dirt"—and not one hungry terrestrial in a thousand has a clue how important, how precious it is. I shook my head.

The door in that huge rock ahead of the car was indeed an elevator. Back when I was four I'd been in an elevator that nice. In Stockholm, when Dad came Earthside to pick up the Nobel. Like that one, this elevator had a live human operator, of advanced age and singular ugliness, who made it a point of pride to remain unaware of our existence: he happened to be leaving as we stepped in, and took us down a good fifty meters with him. The car descended with unhurried elegance. It gave me time to think about the kind of people who would live deep underground, in a place that did not exist . . . and still feel the need to pull the sky over them like a blanket. "Paranoid" didn't seem to cover it.

By happy chance the operator decided to pause and check the operation of the doors just as he was passing the floor we wanted; so intent was his inspection, we were able to escape unnoticed. This left us in a kind of reception room, so lavish as to remind me of the lobby of that hotel back in Stockholm. The carpet was grass. But I didn't get time to study the room; nearly at once I felt a tugging and turned to see a man older and uglier than the elevator operator trying to take my cloak. With some misgivings I let him have it, and that seemed to have been a mistake, for he simply handed it off to a small boy who suddenly appeared in my peripheral vision, and then literally threw himself at my feet and began loosening my shoes. I . . . reacted. If we'd been under normal gravity, on Ganymede or Mars, I think I'd have kicked his teeth in; as it was he went sprawling. But he took a shoe with him as he went, a trick I admired as much as I resented it. Jinny giggled. I recovered, removed the other shoe myself with as much dignity as I could muster, and handed it to him as he approached again. He reunited it with its twin, bowed deeply, and backed away.

I turned to Jinny and forgot whatever I'd been about to say. Her own cloak and shoes had been magicked away by tall elves, and she looked . . . how do girls do that, anyway? One minute just be there, and the next, *be there*. They can do it without moving a muscle, somehow.

"Good evening, Miss Jinny," said a baritone voice from across the room. "Welcome home."

Standing just inside a door I had failed to notice was a man nearly as tall as me with a shaved head, wearing a suit that cost more than my tuition at Fermi Junior. Like us, and the various elves I'd seen, he wore no shoes. Presumably they would cobble us all new ones in the night.

"Thank you, Smithers. This is—damn. Excuse me." She lifted her phone-finger to her ear, listened for a few moments, frowned, said "Yes," and broke the connection. "I've got to go, for just a few minutes. Get Joel situated, would you please, Smithers? I'm sorry, Joel—I'll be back as soon as I can."

"Okay."

She was gone.

Somehow he was at my side, without having covered the intervening distance. "Good evening, Mr. Johnston. I'm Alex Rennick, master of the house at present. Welcome to the North Keep. Let me show you to your room, first, and then perhaps I can give you the ten-credit tour."

His eyes were gray, almost mauve. His head wasn't shaved, it was depilated. Despite his height, a dozen subconscious cues told me he was earthborn. He was fit, and had an air of great competence and great confidence. I'm pretty good at guessing ages, given that everybody looks alike now, and I couldn't pin him down any closer than the thirty-to-sixty zone. I found it interesting that he knew my last name without having been given it.

"Thank you, Mr. Rennick. You are most kind. Please call me Joel."

"And I am Alex. Will you come this way, Joel?"

I thought of an ancient joke, put it out of my mind, and followed him from the room. As I did I promised myself, solemnly, that no matter what wonders I was shown here, I would not boggle. No matter how staggeringly opulent the place proved to be, I would not let it make me feel inferior. My father had been a Nobel laureate, and my mother a great composer—how many of these people could say as much?

"Do you have any questions to start?" he asked as we went.

"Yes, Alex," I said, memorizing the route we were taking. "Why does Jinny call you Smithers?"

"I have no idea." His tone was absolutely neutral, but somehow I knew I'd touched a sore spot. Either it bothered him not to know—or the answer was humiliating.

"Ah," I said, lowering my pitch. "To drive you crazy, then." I was curious to see how he'd respond to an invitation to a jocular, between-us-men discussion of his mistress—whom I personally knew to be a handful and a half.

He sidestepped effortlessly. "That would be redundant, I'm afraid."

"Have you worked here long?"

"Yes."

I see. "How many people live here in . . . the North Keep, you said?"

"The number varies."

His stinginess with information was beginning to mildly irritate me. "No doubt. But surely as master of the house you know its current value."

I halfway expected him to say "Yes, I do," and clam up. But he wasn't that kind of childish. Instead he used jujitsu. "There are eighty-four persons resident in the North Keep at the moment. By midnight the number will be ninety-two, and shortly before breakfast time tomorrow it is expected to drop back to eighty-nine."

"Ah." I hesitated in phrasing my next question. "And how many of those are employees?"

"All but four. Five tomorrow." Yipes! Yes, Conrads lived here, all right. "Here we are." He stopped before a door that looked no different from any of several dozen we'd passed along the way, and tapped the button which on Terra is for some reason always called a knob.

The door dilated to reveal a room full of thick pink smoke. At least it looked like smoke, and behaved like it, roiling and billowing—with the single exception that it declined to spill out of the open door into the corridor. I reminded myself I'd promised myself not to boggle, and with only what I hoped was an imperceptible hesitation, I walked right into the pink smoke, came out the other side—

—and boggled. Worse; I actually yelped.

I was on Ganymede.

Look, I admit I'm a hick. But I *had* experienced Sim walls, by that point in my life, even if I couldn't afford them yet. Even good ones didn't really fool you; you could tell they were not-real, just rectangular windows into worlds that you never really forgot were virtual. I'd even experienced six-wall Sim, 360-degree surround, and even then you had to voluntarily cooperate with the illusion for it to work: it never *quite* got the rounding correction perfect at the corners. But it was pretty good.

This was *real*. I was back home on Ganymede—so convincingly that for just a startled moment, two-thirds of my weight seemed to leave me. I realized with astonishment that the air even *smelled* like Ganymede air, tasted like it, different from terrestrial air in ways subtle but unmistakable. I was standing in the middle of a newly made field, the soil only just coming to life. Beneath my feet, earthworms were shaking off the grogginess of cold sleep and beginning to realize they weren't on Terra anymore. On the edge of the field, fifteen or twenty meters away, was a new-built farmhouse, smoke spiraling from its chimney. Try and build a fire anywhere else on Terra and they'd fine you the equivalent of two months' tuition—for a first offense. Until today, I hadn't seen a square meter of naked soil since I'd landed on its namesake. I felt my eyes begin to sting and water, and with no further warning a tidal wave of homesickness broke over me.

I spun around in time to see Rennick come through the doorway. From this side too it looked like it was full of pink smoke. But it was no longer a door *in* anything: it just stood by itself in the middle of the field, a rectangle of pink smoke without any wall to be a hole in. I turned my back on hole and house master alike.

"Miss Jinny thought you'd find this congenial," he said from just behind me.

I nodded.

"Follow me please."

That didn't require an answer either. We walked to the farmhouse and went inside. "The 'fresher and entertainment center are in the obvious places. You'll find clothing in that closet, Unlimited Access at that desk. If you want anything—anything whatsoever—state your wishes to the house server. His name is Leo."

I had the homesickness under control now, enough that I trusted myself to speak at least. "Leo is listening at all times?"

"Leo listens at all times," he agreed. "But he cannot *hear* anything unless he is addressed. Your privacy and security as a guest are unconditionally guaranteed."

"Of course," I said as if I believed him. I idly opened the closet he'd indicated, and found all my own clothing. Boggle.

On closer inspection it proved to be *copies* of nearly every piece of clothing I owned—all the ones Jinny had seen. They were not quite identical copies. For one thing, in nearly every case the quality of the copy was slightly better than that of the original.

Suddenly I felt vastly tired. I didn't feel like boggling anymore, or struggling not to. "Mr. Rennick—Alex—I thank you for your offer of a tour of the North Keep, but I believe I will pass, at least for tonight."

"Certainly, Joel. If there's nothing further I can do for you now, I'll leave you to rest."

"I'm fine. Thank you."

"Good night." He left. I watched through a window as he walked across the field and through the pink smoke of the door-without-a-wall. I looked around the "farmhouse," then back out the window at a sky with two moons, and thought about bursting into tears, but I decided I was too manly.

"Leo?"

"Yes, Mr. Johnston?"

"Can I get a cup of coffee?"

"On the desk, sir."

I blinked, looked—a steaming cup of coffee sat on the desk beside me. It hadn't been there a moment ago, but I hadn't noticed it arrive. Without a word I picked it up and tried it. The superbness of the coffee was no surprise at all. The *perfect* drinking temperature was only a mild one. But the cream and two sugars—

"Did Jinny tell you how I like my *coffee*, Leo?"

"Miss Jinny has told me many things about you, Mr. Johnston."

"Call me Joel."

"Yes, Mr. Joel."

I opened my mouth, then closed it. There must be something sillier than arguing with software, but I can't think offhand what it would be. I sat down on a rocking chair that creaked authentically, put my feet up on a hassock, and began to dismiss Leo from my mind, to prepare for the upcoming conversation with Jinny. Then a thought occurred. Carefully not addressing him by name I asked, "How long do you keep listening after I stop speaking, before you conclude I'm done and stop listening again?"

Answer came there none. Which answered me: somewhere between five and ten seconds. Useful datum.

"Leo?"

"Yes, Mr. Joel?"

"Can you let me know just before Miss Jinny arrives here?"

"No," she said from the doorway. "He can't."

WE WERE BOTH tired, and both emotionally upset. But we both knew there was more to be said before we could sleep. I took my feet down off the hassock, and she came and sat before me on it, and took both my hands in hers.

"No more ducking and weaving. Spell it out for me," I said. "In words of one sound bit, what's the deal?"

She was through dodging. "I'm proposing marriage, Joel. Just as we've discussed: lifetime, exclusive, old-fashioned matrimony. And I'm offering to support us . . . uh, at least until you get your degree and start to become established as a composer and start earning. I can afford it. I'm quite sure you'll get that Kallikanzaros Scholarship—but if you don't, it won't matter. And best of all, we can start our first baby *right away*—tomorrow night, if you want."

"Huh? Skinny, what about *your* degree—your career?"

"My second career, you mean. It'll keep. I've always known what my first career has to be." She tightened her grip on my hands and leaned slightly closer. "Stinky, maybe now you'll understand why I've been so . . ." She blushed suddenly. "So frimpin' stingy. So square, even for a Terran girl. Why I don't park, or pet, or sneak out after curfew, and why our clinches never got out of hand—or even into it, so to speak. I think you know I haven't wanted to be that way. But I had no choice. It may be all right for some other girls to bend the rules and take risks, but me, I've had it beaten into my head since I was three that I have responsibilities."

"The family name."

"The family name my left foot! The family *genes*. Stinky, I'm a female human animal; my number one job is to get married and make babies. And because I'm who I am, a member of a powerful dynasty, it makes all the difference in the world what baby I have—and who its father is." She let go of my hands and sat up straight. "You're it. This is not a snap decision."

It began to dawn on me that I was not merely being offered acceptance into the fringes of the Conrad family. I was being asked to father its heirs.

On Ganymede I'd grown up seeing stud bulls brought in and put to work. They were always treated with great care and respect, very well fed, and certainly got all the healthy exercise a male animal could possibly want. Their DNA was vastly more successful than that of most other bulls, and their own lives vastly longer. Nobody made jokes about them in their hearing.

But I couldn't recall one who had looked very happy about the business.

"Don't look so worried, Stinky. It's going to work out fine. You *do* want to marry me, we settled that, right?"

I opened my mouth—realized I was harpooned, and closed it again. I had stated that only money prevented me from proposing; I didn't have a leg to stand on.

Nevertheless I found myself on my feet and being embraced. I had to admit it was a very nice embrace, warm and close and fragrant. "Then it's all really very simple. All you need is a nice long chat with Gran'ther Richard. You'll love him, really. And I know he'll love you."

I stiffened in her arms, and fought with the impulse to faint. Good old Grandpa Richard. Known to the rest of the Solar System as Conrad of Conrad. The patriarch. The Chairman. I'd heard he had broken premiers. But perhaps the most awesome thing about his wealth was that, when I thought about it, I didn't actually know a single fact about him, save his name and exalted position. I'd never read an article about him, or viewed a bio, or even seen a picture of his face. For all I knew he had taken my cloak when I arrived. Harun el-Hatchek.

She released me and stepped back. "You'll see him first thing tomorrow. He'll explain things. And then afterward you and I will have breakfast together and start to make some plans. Good night, Stinky."

We parted without a kiss. She didn't offer, and I didn't try. I was starting to feel resentment at having been played for so long—and also I flatly did not believe there were no cameras on us.

After she was gone, I thought about firing up that Universal Access Rennick/Smithers had mentioned, and researching the size and scope of the Conrad empire. But I knew if I did so here, now, on this computer system, Gran'ther Richard would know about it. It just smelled ripe to me. Milady brings home a handsome hick, and the first thing he does is start pricing the furniture. The thought made my cheeks burn.

Instead I used that UA to google around until I had figured out the "Smithers" gag. It turned out to be just as well Rennick didn't know the reference—if in fact he really didn't. Jinny was comparing him to an ancient cartoon character who was a cringing bootlicker, a toady, a completely repressed monosexual, and an unrequited lover. I wondered how much of that was accurate and how much libel. And just how far the analogy was meant to go: Smithers's employer in the cartoon, a Mr. Burns, was vastly rich, impossibly old, and in every imaginable way a monster. Did he represent Jinny's grandfather? Or father?

Well, I would find out in the morning. Or maybe I would get lucky and be struck by a meteorite first.

The bed turned out to be just like mine back at the dorm, except the mattress was better, the sheets were infinitely softer and lighter, and the pillow was gooshier. Was I hallucinating, or did the pillowcase really smell faintly of Jinny's shampoo? It certainly did put a different perspective on things. It might be nice to smell that on my pillow *every* night from now on. And every morning. If in fact I was really smelling it now. While I was wondering, I fell asleep.

3

J oel. It's time to wake up, dear."

Yes, that was definitely her hair I smelled.

I had heard Jinny say just those words, in much that low throaty tone of voice, at the start of more than one pleasant dream. It was a novel experience to hear them at the end of one. Now if only everything else would continue to unfold as it usually did in the dream. . . .

I opened my eyes and she was not there. The scent was either vestigial or imagined. *Drat*.

"You really need to wake up now, Joel," she murmured insistently from somewhere nearby.

"Okay," I said.

"Wake up, Joel. It's time t—"

I sat up, and she chopped off in midword. She wasn't there. Anywhere.

I wake up *hard*. I had to sit there, blinking, for a few seconds before I had it worked out. The speaker was not Jinny but Leo the AI server, perfectly imitating her voice while acting as an alarm clock. Doing the job well, too: I could fool my own alarm at the dorm by simply telling it I was getting up. Leo was programmed to accept nothing less than verticality as proof of compliance.

Why did I need to get up now? I could tell I had not had eight hours' sleep. I had graduated, for Pete's sake—what was so urgent?

It all came back to me at once. Oh, yes. That's right. Today I was going to have a personal interview with one of the most powerful men in the Solar System. Had I supposed it would be scheduled for *my* convenience? A man like Conrad of Conrad would doubtless want to dispose of matters as trivial as meeting his grandchild's fiancé as early as possible in the business day.

"How soon am I expected?" I asked.

"In half an hour, Mr. Joel," Leo said in his own voice.

"How do I get breakfast?"

"I can take your order, sir."

I started to say scrambled on toast, bucket of black coffee, liter of OJ. Then I thought to myself, this morning you are going to have a personal interview with one of the most powerful men in the Solar System. "Eggs Benedict, home fries, Tanzanian coffee—French Press, please, two sugars and eighteen percent cream, keep it coming—and squeeze a dozen oranges."

Leo returned the serve. "Very good, Mr. Joel. Do you prefer peaberry or the normal bean?"

"The peaberry, I think," I managed.

There was a scratching sound at the door. It opened, and a servant entered, pushing a tray ahead of him at shoulder height with two fingers. He was easily as old and as ugly as the servants I'd seen the night before, but nowhere near as surly. Maybe day shift was better.

"What's that?" I asked.

He steered the tray to a table near the bed, and somehow persuaded it to sit down. "Eggs Benedict, potatoes, coffee, fresh orange juice, and this morning's news, sir," he said, pointing to each item as he named it. Nothing in his manner suggested that only an idiot would need these things named.

I promised myself that just as soon as I had the time, I would wonder, very hard, about how any of those items could have been produced instantly, much less all of them at once. But meanwhile, there was no sense pretending they had not caught me by surprise. "If I'd known how fast the service is here, I'd have asked them to wait ten minutes, while I used the 'fresher," I said with a rueful grin.

He turned to the tray, made some sort of mystic gesture. The food became obscured by a hemisphere of . . . well, it looked like shimmery air. "Take as long as you like, sir. Everything will be the same temperature and consistency when you get back out."

Oh. Of course. I wondered how the hell I would get the air to stop shimmering, but I was determined not to ask. I'd figure it out somehow.

"Just reach right through it, whenever you're ready, sir," he volunteered. "That collapses the field."

I opened my mouth to ask what kind of field, how was it generated, what were its properties—and stifled myself. There would be time for that later. "What is your name?"

"Nakamura, sir."

"Thank you, Mr. Nakamura. You're very kind."

"You're welcome, sir. And thank you." Somehow he was gone instantly, without hurrying.

I started to get out of bed . . . and the damned thing *helped* me. The part right under my knees dropped away, and the part under my butt rose, and I was on my feet. I reacted pretty much as if I'd been goosed—the physical sensations were not dissimilar. I said the word "Whoa!" louder and an octave higher than I might have wished, leaped forward a meter or so, and spun around to glare accusingly at the bed.

"Is something wrong, Mr. Joel?" Leo asked.

I took a deep breath. And then another. "Not yet," I stated cautiously.

On the way to the 'fresher, I passed close to the tray of food. I could see a cup of coffee in there, and wanted it so badly it brought tears to my eyes. But I knew if I "collapsed the field" now, I probably wouldn't be able to re-create it again. And besides, there was the question of making *room* for the coffee.

So okay, I would hurry and be out of the 'fresher in five minutes instead of ten. I stepped in. . . .

On Ganymede we're more reticent about such matters than Terrans—for complex sociocultural reasons I'd be perfectly happy to explain any time you have an hour to kill listening to a guy who doesn't know what the hell he's talking about. So I'll just say that this 'fresher was about ten times better equipped and programmed than I had ever imagined possible, and let it go at that. It was more like fifteen minutes before I was able to make myself end the sybaritic cycle.

When I came out, my clothes were gone.

I remarked on this, as casually as I could manage. Leo explained that they had been taken away for laundering. He invited me to wear any of the fakes in the closet that pleased me, and assured me, unnecessarily, that they would all fit me perfectly.

I was not at all happy about this, but I could see my wallet, phone, and keys on the bedside table, so I postponed the matter until after coffee.

By the end of the first cup, I had no strong objection to anything short of disembowelment or denial of a second cup. If you are ever given the choice, insist on the peaberry. Trust me.

When I was ready to dress, I automatically reached for the copy of my best suit, comforting myself as best I could with the guess that this version of it, at least, would be freshly cleaned, and would not be worn nearly through in spots. But as I took it from the closet, I noticed an item hanging just behind it that certainly was not a copy of any garment I owned. It was a J. L. Fong suit. Top of the line, of the latest cut and style. In a color, I noticed, that would complement Jinny's hair. It was worth more than my entire wardrobe—more than my passage to Earth had cost. The tights were just a bit daring, but I decided I had the calves to carry them off. I was unsurprised to find suitable underwear and other necessary accessories in drawers, tucked in among my own trash.

The moment I put it on, that suit became an old, familiar, and valued friend—and I became taller and wider across the shoulders. It could not have fit better if it had been made on my body. It knew things about me I wouldn't learn for years yet, and approved of them all. Wearing a suit like that, you could break up a knife fight with an admonishment, secure a million-dollar loan without being troubled for a signature, walk away from a crime scene, or obtain illicit drugs on credit. I examined the effect in the 'fresher room mirror, and decided that on me, it looked good. Perhaps, I felt, I could even survive an interview with Conrad of Conrad without soiling it. If it was a brief interview.

"Will Jinny be present at this meeting, do you know?" I asked Leo.

"No, Mr. Joel. Only Mr. Conrad, Mr. Albert, and yourself."

I blinked. "Wait a second. *Which* Mr. Conrad—Jinny's father, or her grandfather? And who's this Albert bloke?"

"Ah. Pardon me, Mr. Joel. There are over a dozen adult males in the immediate family whose last name is or incorporates Conrad—but by long-standing family and corporate tradition, there is only one 'Mr. Conrad' at any one time. At present that is Jenny's grandfather, Mr. Richard Conrad— Conrad of Conrad. The others are Mr. Joseph, Mr. Chang, Mr. Akwai-N'boko, and so on. Mr. Albert is Jinny's father."

"I see," I said. "Thank you." I began to understand Leo's insistence on putting Mr. before my name. I started to ask where Jinny was now, and realized the answer would probably mean nothing to me.

I paid attention to my breathing, trying to make it slower and deeper, for another twenty seconds. Then I said, "Okay, I'm ready."

"Very good, Mr. Joel."

I left the faux farmhouse, and walked through faux fields. It *smelled* convincingly like morning on Ganymede, and don't ask me to explain that. It felt inexpressibly weird to be walking through a colonial homestead, in the wrong gravity, dressed like an aristocrat, heading for a doorway of pink smoke. It was a bit of a relief to walk through the smoke and find myself in an ordinary corridor that smelled like Terra instead of Wonderland.

"I'll guide you from here, sir," Leo said. "Do you see the light at your feet?"

I glanced down, and there was a soft green light at the baseboard of the left-hand wall, pulsing on and off. It was about the size and intensity of a firefly: discreet, but impossible to miss. "Lead on," I said. It moved away.

"If you'll forgive a personal observation, sir," Leo said as I followed his blinking firefly down the corridor, "you have an excellent time sense for a human."

"Excuse me?'"

"You said, 'Okay, I'm ready,' twenty-nine minutes and forty-one seconds after I advised you that you had thirty minutes to prepare."

"Ah." I nodded. "A couple of people have told me I have a pretty accurate internal clock."

"Extremely so, sir, if this example is representative."

I shrugged. "I never burn the toast. Look, I have some thinking to do, all right?"

"Yes, sir. I'd just like to—"

"Later, Leo."

"But, sir—"

I was raised to be polite to gadgets—Dad always said it was good practice—but I was trying to get some fretting done and Leo was distracting me. "Quiet!"

He shut up, and I put my full attention on the predicament I was in. First I scanned my memory for everything I had ever heard or read about high-level etiquette, manners, or protocol. Unfortunately that only took me about two steps. Then I examined my own autobiography, looking first for things that might impress a multi-octillionaire—and when that failed, making a short list of spots that might alienate one, and going over my excuses. A step and a half, tops. As I followed the blinking green firefly around a corner, I was trying to decide whether the next priority was to imagine all the possible ways this upcoming meeting could go wrong, or to try and work out exactly how I had gotten myself into this, where I had taken my first misstep—

—when I rounded the corner, and encountered eighteen kilograms of mass coming in the other direction.

I weighed four times that much. But it caught me well above my center of gravity—square in the face—and was moving much faster, packing more kinetic energy. I believe the Terran expression is, who knows why, "ass over teakettle."

I've taken self-defense courses. I know how to fall properly, and do so as a matter of reflex in normal conditions. But not in a one-gee field. I went down *hard* on my back, and all my air left me in a single explosive syllable, and only the extreme thickness of the carpet kept me from cracking my skull. I remember feeling quite unhappy for a moment, there. Then the eighteen-kilo mass landed on my groin, and I felt much worse.

Sometime later I forced my eyes open. Closed them quickly. Reopened them cautiously. Half a meter from my nose, a little girl—

"Why don't you look where you're going?" she asked.

Make a mental note, Joel: next time you tell an AI you want quiet and it keeps talking—*listen.* "Because I'm a dolt."

"Oh." She thought about that. "I'm a Conrad."

I looked her over. She appeared to be somewhere around seven Terran years old. And adorable. "Are you all right?"

She frowned, and stuck her chin out slightly. "Yes, I am. Daddy says I don't have bones." She moved her gaze away. "But I think my skyboard's broke."

The object named lay beside us. It looked like a conventional skateboard—minus the usual wheels, motor housing,

onboard computer, and data port. Like a miniature surf-
board, in other words. I had no doubt that it could fly—when
it wasn't broken—because it had been at head height when
I'd first encountered it. But I could not guess how.

"I'm sorry." I'd have to replace it. There went my scholarship, probably. "Uh, what's your name?"

"I'm Evelyn."

"Hello, Evelyn. That was my mother's name, too. I'm—"

"You're Joel, of course. I'm not a *baby*."

"Certainly not! Not by a good ten kilos."

She giggled—then frowned. "Am I hurting you?"

"Only when I breathe."

She was off me and up on her feet at once. "Jinny is my
favorite cousin. I think she's rickety all through. Don't you?"

"Yes. I think I do, anyway." I sat up. When that didn't
kill me, I got to my feet and examined my costume for
damage.

"Are you going to marry her?"

I opened my mouth and closed it again, twice. "We're still
discussing that," I managed finally.

"Do you love her?"

"Evelyn, I'm afraid we'll have to finish this conversation
another time. I'm late for an appointment with your—"
What would the relationship be? "For a very important appointment. Please excuse me."

She grinned. "Never mind. I saw you blush."

I did it some more. This was Jinny's cousin, all right. "I
really mustn't be late."

She waved a hand majestically. "Don't matter about it.
Just tell Grandfather Rich I made you late."

I realized my flashing-firefly guide was beginning to
move off down the corridor: hinting. "It was wonderful to
meet you," I said hastily. "Sorry I broke your board. I'll get a
new one to you as soon as I can."

She giggled. "You're silly."

I followed her pointing finger. A new skyboard was just
arriving, gliding along the corridor at knee height. It was as
featureless as the other, not so much as an antenna showing.

Suddenly I saw that the firefly had nearly reached a corner. In another few seconds it would be around the bend. "Great. I'll see you around."

"It's okay, Joel. Gran'ther Rich will think you're rickety-tickety. You'll see."

I know a compliment when I hear one. I bowed—and did not quite sprint away. I found the firefly around the corner, waiting for me, but pulsing faster to indicate impatience. I breezed right past it at double time, made it scramble to catch up and pass me again, and felt the tiny satisfaction that comes to an idiot who has successfully insulted a piece of software. I slowed to walking pace—and it kept on going at double time. I ended up reaching my destination slightly out of breath, and not quite dripping sweat.

I planned to pause outside the door for at least two or three deep breaths. But the infernal thing opened as soon as I reached it. I allowed myself one breath, mostly because I had to, and entered.

BUT IT WAS only Rennick's office.

He did *not* say, "You're late," even by facial expression. But in the time it took me to walk three steps into the room, he had risen from his workstation, come all the way round it, and reached my side, without seeming to hurry. "Good morning, Joel," he said pleasantly. He took my elbow, turned me, and we were back out in the corridor and walking again—not as fast as I had arrived, but not slowly either. "I trust you slept well."

"Yes, thank you, Alex. And yourself?"

"There are things I must tell you, and we no longer have time for the standard set speech. As you know, there is only one Mr. Conrad in this house, and that is what he is called in his presence or out of it. But when one directly addresses him, he prefers, strongly, to be called simply Conrad. Thus, you might hear someone say, for instance, 'Mr. Conrad approves of this—isn't that so, Conrad?' Am I clear?"

"No honorific to his face. Not even 'sir'?"

"Not even 'sir.' 'Yes, Conrad.' 'No, Conrad.' "

I nodded. "Got it. Thanks. Do I call Mr. Albert 'Albert' to his face, too?"

"Not unless he invites you to. Which is unlikely. Until then he is Mr. Albert."

We came to a checkpoint. Five large men, four of them heavily armed and the deadliest one sitting at a workstation. Rennick didn't even slow down, and nobody killed him, so I didn't slow down either.

"Mr. Conrad does not shake hands. Mr. Conrad does not care for humor. Mr. Conrad is not interrupted."

Right turn. Another checkpoint. Another five armed men, but not large this time. Gurkhas. Their knives were sheathed. Rennick came to a halt and stood still, but ignored them. I did likewise. I could almost feel myself being scanned and sniffed and candled by invisible machinery.

"When Mr. Conrad says 'Thank you,' he means 'good-bye.' The correct response is *not* 'You're welcome,' but 'Yes, Conrad.' You say it on your way to the door."

"Got it." A Gurkha produced something I'd only seen in cop or spy stories, and gave it to Rennick: an identifier. He held it up to his eyes like binoculars for a moment, then poked his right index finger into a socket on the side, and removed it. Almost at once there was a soft chiming sound, and a blue light on top of the device flashed three times. Rennick passed the device to me.

Fighting an impulse to grin like an imbecile, I lifted it to my own eyes and looked into the lenses. Nothing but a white field. I lowered it, hesitated a second, and stuck my finger in the slot. I expected to be poked for a blood sample, but what I got was even more disconcerting, a sensation as if someone were sucking gently on that fingertip. Whether it was taking skin scrapings or sampling my fingernail I couldn't say. In any event it decided it approved of my DNA and my retinas, and awarded me the same chime and flash Rennick had received.

The Gurkha's forearms and hands relaxed slightly, and his cousins relaxed too, slightly. He accepted the identifier back from me, saluted to both me and Rennick, held it, and stepped smartly backward out of our way. Rennick was off again at once, with me at his heels.

I wondered if anyone else in the Inner System was as paranoid as these people. Or, now that I came to think of it, had better reason to be.

The pause had been almost enough to let me get my breath back. "Anything else?"

"Yes. A piece of personal advice. There's only one way to say this. Don't bullshit. If Mr. Conrad asks you a question and you don't know the answer, there is only one acceptable response—'I don't know, Conrad.' Try and bluff, and he'll smell it."

We came to a large door that looked like a polished slab of real wood. It lacked the customary ID scanner, but at about the same location it had an antique fitting I guessed at once must be the fabled doorknob: a flattened toroid like a brass onion, sticking out from the door on a short horizontal stalk. I wasn't quite quick enough to catch the procedure Rennick used to operate it. It was hard to follow: some sort of small probe, a quick torquing motion, and a small *clack* sound. Cued by the sound, I was not too surprised when the door swung inward away from us instead of dilating: it actually *was* a polished slab of real wood, a good fifteen centimeters thick. I followed him through the doorway, and had to step out of the way so he could swing it shut behind us. I was sure we had reached the Holy of Holies, at last.

Wrong again.

It certainly *looked* very like what I had been expecting to see: the serious working office of a major CEO or senior politician, tastefully decorated and lavishly equipped. It had every imaginable sort of monitor screen, display, input device, peripheral or other gadget, but the utilitarian effect was softened by a carefully chaotic profusion of exotic and lovely plant life. Dominating the room was a huge piece of furniture as obsolete as the doorknob, for some reason called a desk even though it had no graphic interface or surface icons—not even a trash can. It was basically an elaborate table intended to provide a stable flat work surface plus storage drawers. In films, such a desk is usually covered with items: a primitive telephone, a keypad and monitor, family flat photos, styli, and so on. This one was as austerely, majestically bare as I would have expected from a man of great power.

Two things immediately spoiled the picture, though. First, the absence of any men in the room. And then, the presence of a woman behind the desk. Her apparent age was five years higher than my own, and the fake was very impressive, but there were at least seventy years of skepticism in those eyes and the set of her mouth.

"Morning, Dorothy," Rennick said. "This is Joel Johnston. Joel, Dorothy Robb."

"Good morning, Alex," she greeted him. "Relax: you're early. And good morning to you, too, Mr. Johnston." She offered me her hand. Her voice was wonderfully husky, like a great jazz singer near the end of her career; I wondered if she sang.

In my social circle, my move would now have been to shake her hand firmly and release. I had no idea what was done at this altitude—even if I'd had a clue what our relative status was. Deep breath. What would Dad do? "Good morning, Ms. Robb," I said, did my second-best bow, and kissed her hand.

She removed it quickly and said, "Dorothy!" sharply, but I knew she was not offended because almost at once she softened it by adding, " 'Ms. Robb' sounds too much like—"

I nodded. "A Victor Hugo novel. In that case, I'm Joel."

Those cynical eyes opened a bit wider. "You read!"

"My parents infected me before I knew any better. There was no bedtime, as long as I was reading a book."

"What splendid parents."

Suddenly I felt myself blush. My multitrack mind was still playing with our pun, and it had suddenly realized that the full title of the book we were discussing would have been *Lay Ms. Robb*. Her sharp eyes caught me blushing, and twinkled. I realized I'd made no response to her compliment, and was too flustered to formulate one.

She saved me. "Do you know the story of the American farm wife who wrote a letter to Victor Hugo, Joel?"

"No, I don't," I said gratefully.

"She wrote, 'Dear Vic—' " I couldn't help smiling; her accent and deadpan delivery were good. " 'We shore liked that book you wrote there, Less Miserables' " —I began to grin broadly, and Rennick did, too— " 'but we wanted to ask you one thing we cain't figger out: which one o' them characters was Les?' " I broke up, turned to Rennick, and saw that he was chuckling, too—and had absolutely no idea why. Oops. Oh, well—no reason his education should include period French literature. No reason anyone's should, really.

"What a glorious story," I said to Dorothy. "Is it apocryphal?"

"Oh, I hope so. Imagine the poor man trying to compose a response."

I decided to take the bull by the horns. "May I ask your job title, Dorothy?"

She snorted. "Professional bureaucratic-gibberish composers have wept with frustration over that one. There doesn't seem to be an adequate descriptive that any of them liked. For accounting purposes we finally settled on Enabler, which they simply hate."

"Like a personal secretary, sort of?"

She did not smile. "Mr. Conrad has *seven* personal secretaries. One executive secretary, two research secretaries, a social secretary, a scheduling secretary, a record-keeping secretary, and a personal private secretary. Plus assorted personal executive assistants and chiefs of staff and first facilitators and chief counselors and senior advisors and legal counsels and a personal physiotherapist and several personal physicians and psychiatrists—a clinic, really—plus an incredibly complex impossibly sprawling extended personal family. And then of course there is the empire itself, with its hundreds of CEOs, comptrollers, and so on. And finally there are the various executives, and executive, legislative, and judicial branches, of a great many governments. I am one of two people through whom he accesses all those peo-

ple. And vice versa. I have the 6:00 A.M. to 6:00 P.M. shift—
or 1:00 P.M. to 1:00 A.M. Greenwich."

I blinked. "And you have time to tell me Victor Hugo
jokes?"

"No. That's why I enjoyed it so much. You looked like you
needed relaxing."

"I still do! How much time do I have?"

"None," she said. A previously unsuspected door occurred
behind her. "Good luck, Joel."

Rennick stepped forward and entered. I didn't. The powers of motion and speech had deserted me.

"You'll be fine," she murmured. "The suit looks terrific
on you."

When you're too scared to move, there's a simple fix. I'm
not saying *easy*—but simple. Just lean forward. That's all
you need to do. Keep it up long enough and you'll fall on
your face—but your body won't let you. It will automatically
put a foot out . . . and now you're moving forward. Repeat as
needed. Remember to alternate feet.

Before I knew it I was passing through the doorway, lurch-
ing only slightly.

4

**To understand the heart and mind of a person,
look not at what he has already achieved, but
what he aspires to.**

> —Kahlil Gibran

The room was not small, but smaller than I had expected,
and further surprised me by being furnished more like a
den or a study than an office. At the far end of the room
was a conversational grouping of four chairs. Rennick was
just reaching the leftmost of the two that faced away from
me. The two facing toward me were already occupied. In

each sat a man who appeared to be approximately Rennick's age. The fourth chair, its back to me, was obviously the hot seat.

My feet wanted to stop in their tracks again. But I managed to keep leaning forward. As I headed for the death chair, I invoked my very sharpest self-criticism. *You have not thought this through.*

Myself replied with some asperity, *And how the* hell *was I supposed to do that, chum? Using what data?*

Social customs on Ganymede are considerably simpler and more direct than those on Earth: a frontier society is just too *busy* for indirection, innuendo, and ceremony. Nevertheless, I had, under Jinny's tutelage, gradually managed to soak up enough Terran manners to get by, in the sorts of social situations in which I found myself. It had been some time since I'd heard anyone mutter, "Hayseed!" under their breath after a conversation with me.

But college life had not prepared me for this. I was in a milieu where I knew I had no faintest idea what constituted correct behavior—and I was already saddled with some complex and difficult social problems that I had about a dozen steps to solve, for the toughest audience on the planet.

When in doubt, I decided, fall back on analogy. Okay . . . royalty always takes precedence, that gets you started. Which one next? And how . . . ?

I'd expected those twelve steps would seem to take forever. They turned out to be just long enough.

Part of what threw me was the apparent ages. Both men I was here to meet seemed to be middle-aged, somewhere between thirty and sixty. Neither visibly deferred to the other by body language or chair placement. Both were dressed equally well, which was very well. Both carried themselves with authority and confidence, and had "the look of eagles"—a constant hyperalertness I had seen before only in certain very good bodyguards like the Gurkhas out in the hallway, and in a Zen priest I met once.

So which one was Jinny's dad . . . and which one merely owned half the inner Solar System?

When I reached the decision point, I put down my money,

made my bet, and quit worrying. The rest of the necessary choices seemed to have been made while I was busy.

I stopped in front of the man to my right, bowed *almost* as deeply as I would have for the Secretary General or for Jinny, and said, "Good morning, Conrad. I am Joel Johnston. Thank you for taking me into your cubic. Your home is most gracious. Pardon me a moment, please."

Without waiting for a response I turned on my heel and gave Rennick my warmest smile. "It was very kind of you to escort me here, Alex. I'm sure with Leo's help I'll find my way back to my quarters."

His own smile congealed slightly at the edges, and he opened his mouth as if to reply.

"Thank you," I said pointedly.

After an instant's hesitation, spent in reappraisal of me, he did a little indescribable thing with his mouth that was a rueful salute, and nodded. He said, "You're welcome," on his way to the door.

Again without pausing, I turned to the second man, bowed almost as deeply as I had to the first, and said, "Mr. Albert, I am Joel Johnston of Lermer City, Ganymede. My parents were Ben and Evelyn Johnston of that city. I am a recent graduate of Fermi Junior College. I love your daughter Jinnia—more than I can say!—and she loves me. I'm declaring now my intention to ask you for her hand as soon as I can. I will supply Dorothy Robb with what is necessary to allow you to inspect my background and records."

I was done. I had shot my bolt—nothing to do now but wait and see just how badly I'd screwed things up. The door whispered shut behind Rennick, and sealed me in here in the lions' den.

The man last addressed stared up at me, absolutely expressionless, yet with an attention that was almost a physical force, as if any slightest muscle twitch on my face might tell him something crucial. He stared for so long I began to suspect that I had botched the whole thing, guessed wrong—that he was not Mr. Albert, but the Lord God Conrad himself. I wished I could sneak a glance at the other man for a clue, but did not dare take my gaze away from his.

"Well and boldly spoken," he said at last. "My daughter has made an interesting choice, Mr. Johnston. Good luck to you."

It wasn't until I exhaled that I realized I'd been holding my breath. Those were the last words he said to me.

"How did you know which of us was which?" the other man asked. "You can't have seen a picture of me. There are none."

For a split second I thought about claiming to have had the foresight to google up a picture of my fiancée's father, last night. Rennick's advice came back to me. *Don't bullshit.* "I did *not* know, Conrad. I was forced to guess."

He nodded. "On what basis?"

I didn't have a clue. But my mouth did. It opened, and out came, "Jinny's cheeks."

"What did you say?"

Why, yes. I could see what my mouth meant, now that I looked. "Jinny's cheekbones, s—Conrad. Cheekbones and ears. They're distinctive. Mr. Albert has them, too."

He mimed the word "ah," without actually emitting sound. Mr. Albert was poker-faced.

I was beginning to understand why there were no pictures of Conrad of Conrad. There's an expression actors use: "He can't wear the clothes." Meaning that actor, however talented he may be, just isn't right for that part. No one would have cast this man as Conrad.

Not that he was in any way unimpressive, quite the contrary. He just didn't look nearly heartless or soulless or ruthless enough to fit my preconceptions of the head of a multiplanet empire. He looked . . . learned, and wise, and kind. He would have been excellent casting for, say, a brilliant college professor. In some warm, fuzzy subject, like ecology, or sociobiology, or poetry, or even theology. His students would all love him, and write him letters years later to tell him he'd changed their lives. But he would never make department chairman because he wasn't willing to kill for it.

I knew this impression had to be utterly false. This was Conrad of Conrad. But he did not bear the kind of face that would inspire the countless armies of remorseless sharks in suits who constituted the Conrad empire. He had the kind of face that would reassure their mothers. He was more effective as a Man of Mystery, never seen.

"Have a seat, Joel," Conrad said.

It was a superbly comfortable chair, and became more so the longer I sat in it. This wasn't going so badly . . .

"I am informed that my granddaughter Jinnia Anne has revealed her true identity to you, and you have accepted her proposal of matrimony—"

I opened my mouth but no sound came out.

He went on quickly, as one who is determined to get through his little speech however banal it may be. "I commend you heartily on your good fortune, Jinny on her good sense, and both of you on your good taste; I wish you both every happiness; I am confident you will prove a welcome and valuable addition to our great family; we will now define the terms and conditions under which that may occur—"

I opened my mouth even farther. Even less sound came out.

His eyes narrowed very slightly. The department chairman reluctantly suspected me of plagiarizing my thesis. "—unless you would feel more comfortable represented by counsel?"

I had to reject the slander. "No!" I managed to say, and got nearly halfway through my follow-up monosyllable, "I—," before he steamrollered ahead.

"No, of course not. Excellent. I'm sure Jinny has made her family situation clear to you, explained all the ramifications, brought you up to speed." She damn well had not! "Preliminary genetic analysis is satisfactory, as expected given your heritage." Apparently my consent had been assumed. "I might add that I consider such analysis a mere pro forma check on my granddaughter's intuition and judgment: you were in the moment she said you are. But I am pleased with her choice. I met your father, you know. Many years ago, when he came Earthside to receive his prize."

"Then you met me," I blurted out.

"Eh?"

"I never left his side, that trip."

"Ah." He did the math, worked out how old I would have been. "Oh!" He started slightly at a memory. "Uh . . ."

The only vowel he had not tried in front of an "h" yet was "i"—and perhaps "y." What was his problem?

Then all of a sudden I remembered, too.

"Ih!" I gasped. "I *bit* you."

I'd never seen anyone try to unfrown, before. "Yes." He gave up and surrendered to the frown. "You did." Then without warning he smiled, so broadly it was as if another man had burst out laughing. "Good for you!" It made him look much younger, and it took me an instant to work out the sad reason why: his smile wrinkles were almost entirely nonexistent. I tried to remember why I had felt he needed biting, back then, but failed. All I could recall was the fuss after I had done it. *Everyone* had been upset . . . except Dad. He had apologized for me—once—and then stopped hearing conversation about the matter.

"And good for Jinny, too," he went on. "I'm more convinced than ever that she's found just the man we need. And just when we need him, too."

" 'We'?"

We frowned at each other for a few seconds.

"I don't understand your question," he said. "Unless you are speaking French."

"I guess," I said slowly, "I had the idea marriage involved the *needs* of just two people, and the *interests* of the rest of their families. So far, I've been thinking exclusively of Jinny's needs and mine. If you need me for something, it has not yet been explained to me, and I have not yet agreed."

His jaw did not drop. But his lower lip went slack, and his eyes unfocused slightly for a moment. Then he shook his head. "I know you are not stupid; I've seen your genes. I know you are not ignorant; I've seen your transcripts. It has to be . . . a rather *staggering* naïveté."

I didn't know what to say to that.

"Joel, do you honestly believe your marriage is going to be a normal, mundane union? Do you think its purpose is simply to provide the two of you with agreeable companionship and licensed sexual relief? Can you really imagine that your life together will be anything like what you were picturing as recently as yesterday morning?"

Well, no. But neither could I imagine what it *would* be like. The furthest I had gotten in my thinking so far was trying to encompass the preposterous notion that I could stop balancing my checkbook, now: that I would never again be short of money, no matter how much I developed a wish for. "What will it be like?"

"You kids will marry and continue in school under the name Johnston, but your legal name will be Conrad. Your training has been planned for you by experts familiar with your background and capabilities—at least ten years, and as a minimum you'll take degrees in engineering, law, business administration, one of the practical sciences, and a language. I suggest Portuguese, but of course that's up to you. It won't all be academic fun and games, of course: you'll need field experience in the company, as many areas of it as you can handle. Plus additional special coaching in social skills, and in politics, both governmental and corporate, and—"

"But you're sure you won't mind if I go for Swahili instead of Portuguese?"

"Anything but French."

I gave up on sarcasm. He honestly didn't know what it was. "You're talking about grooming me for a top executive position in the Conrad empire. What makes you think—" I stopped because he was shaking his head.

"Not *a* top position," he said.

I felt the blood start to drain from my head. "Are you trying to tell me—"

"Listen to me, Joel." He leaned forward slightly, and his chair adjusted at once. "It is conceivable that one day you might sit in this chair and give the orders. It is even likely, on the basis of what can be extrapolated from your ancestry, present abilities, and accomplishments to date. It is *certain* that one or more of your children will sit in this chair one day. I've had you *most* fully investigated, else Jinny would never have received permission to propose to you."

I felt two extremely strong and inappropriate impulses, fortunately so contradictory they canceled each other out: the urge to faint, and the urge to giggle.

"Oh, I understand," he said. "Really I do, son. Your interest in music is commendable in one of your age, a sign of a mathematical mind, and Jinny assures me your work is agreeable, not at all like this . . . well. But surely you see the time for childish things is now behind you. The *real* world is now open to you: you've been given the opportunity to become one of those men music is written *about*."

CONRAD CONTINUED SPEAKING for several more minutes, and I kept an attentive look on my face, but I'm afraid it all pretty much went in one ear and out the other from that point on. To the best of my addled recollection he was explaining my destiny to me. Telling me about challenges I would face, and things I would need to know to meet them—about looming crises and how to resolve them—about potential achievements and how best to realize them. He used the word "scarcity" several times. I think he was trying to give me a short course in how to run a commercial empire over the next hundred years or so. He went on and on about the crucial importance of making sure humanity was firmly established outside the Solar System. Something about the System, any system, being too fragile a basket for the human race to keep all its eggs in. It seemed paranoid thinking even for a Conrad.

I have no doubt there were thousands of people in the System at that time who would have given a limb, maybe even one of their own, to hear that lecture from that man. It's a real shame I missed it. But my brain was so busy trying to think six contradictory thoughts at once that it had no processing power left over for new incoming audio or video. He could have told me the exact hour and manner of my own death, and I'd have kept on looking him in the eye and nodding thoughtfully. I think Mr. Albert may have realized I wasn't tracking, but he kept silent.

Sooner or later, he would pause long enough for me to speak. I had until then to come up with some really smooth, diplomatic way to begin explaining to him how many erroneous assumptions he was making, how vast was the gulf between his picture of my future and my own. The trouble was, for the life of me I could not think of any diplomatic way to express the concept, "I'm not remotely sure I want any part of you or your family or your empire, and I'm having serious second thoughts about your granddaughter." I could think of no gentle way to ask, "Excuse me, but are my own wishes, plans, thoughts, or opinions of any interest to you at all?" There didn't seem to be a polite circumlocution for, "Who the hell do you think you are?"

Besides, I knew perfectly well who the hell he thought he was—and he was right. He was assuming my assent, not because I looked like some kind of patsy, but because nobody, weak or strong, ever said no to him. He assumed that I *wanted* to become him one day because everybody he knew did, because who would not? Jinny would never have taken up with me if I weren't sensible.

I heard a story once about a PreCollapse songwriter named Russell who'd written a song called "I'm Lost in the Woods," and because its melody sounded African, he decided he wanted a background chorus to sing the title in Zulu. But all the translators he found told him the same frustrating thing: there was no way to say "I'm lost in the woods" in Zulu. They didn't have that concept. Zulu didn't *get* lost in the woods. He had to settle for a chorus singing the Zulu for, "I am in the woods and I have gone crazy."

There was no sense even trying to tell this man, "I do not want to become infinitely rich and infinitely powerful"—it would come through as noise. When that pause in his flow of words finally came, he was going to hear whatever I said as, "I have gone crazy."

Well, if it didn't matter what he heard, then I could say whatever I liked; the only question was what I wanted to say. Ideally, something that would not make me cringe every time I remembered this day in years to come. Something that would not force me to lie when asked what I'd told the old buzzard then. Something respectful, but dignified; polite but firm.

As I worked on it, I became aware of distraction. I played back the last fifteen or twenty seconds and spotted a plausible cause: a few sentences ago, he had dropped a subtle remark that implied, without stating it explicitly, that he was sure I had figured out Jinny's real identity long ago . . . and that he applauded my good sense and good taste in continuing to play dumb for the sake of her feelings. It was annoyingly difficult to work out which of us he'd insulted worse—a distraction from the distraction.

But that wasn't even the distraction. Suddenly I realized what had *really* bothered me enough to try to demand my attention in the middle of an important conundrum—a problem far more urgent than an insult to me or a beloved I was thinking seriously of strangling.

I was on my feet. In motion. Walking toward the door.

Being walked toward the door, by Mr. Albert. His hand rested far too lightly on my shoulder to be steering me, exactly. But it did make it a little easier to keep going than to stop or turn around.

The conversation was over already. The insult I'd focused on had been part of some larger pattern of unnoticed sentences that had ended it, somehow. The pause I'd been waiting for, in which I could have my say, had simply never happened. Or had come and gone in an instant, while I was thinking of something else. It was too late, now. My choices were to keep on walking, or to make a scene. Albert had handled me as smoothly as an awards presenter getting the disoriented winner the hell offstage so they can get to the next, more important award.

I was angry at myself for having been outmaneuvered so effortlessly, for letting somebody march me around like a show dog with nothing more than a combination of body language cues, feather-gentle touch, and total confidence.

But I was also secretly grateful. I hadn't been looking forward to that pause. Now I could take as long as I liked to compose, refine, and polish my manifesto—and when it was ready, I could deliver it by e-mail, rather than face-to-face to the most powerful man on earth. Since I had done and said nothing, I had nothing to wish I could take back. Since no one was interested in my opinions, why bring them up? Especially since I had no clear idea what they were.

We reached the door, Albert said something or other, I made whatever was the appropriate response without thinking about it, and the door irised shut behind me.

RENNICK WAS NOT waiting outside. Dorothy smiled as I came through the door and gave me a thumbs-up. I gave her what I thought was my very best sunny smile in reply, and she winced. "I—" I began, and stopped.

When she saw that I had no words, she stepped in smoothly. "I enjoyed meeting you as well, Joel. Would you like Leo to guide you back to your room, or would you care to see some of the grounds, now? I don't believe you've had time for the tour, yet."

"Actually, I'd like to speak with Jinny," I said.

"I'm sorry, she's offsite at the moment. An errand for her father. She should be—"

"I'll phone her, then," I said, and lifted my wrist.

"We discourage phone calls to the outside," she said quickly. "It compromises security. She's due back before dinnertime, and I'll make sure she speaks with you the moment she's back inside the perimeter."

Right. "I see." Giving me time to calm down. "Very well, then. Thank you." It might just be a terrific idea to cool down a little before speaking to Jinny. Three or four years ought to do it.

"You're welcome. Would you like that tour of the grounds? It's quite—"

"Later, perhaps. Right now I'd like to go back to my room."

"Of course. Leo? Please guide Mr. Johnston back to his quarters."

"Yes, Dorothy." Green fireflies led me away. I followed them gratefully.

When I'd passed this way in the other direction, the corridors I'd walked through had seemed wastefully, ostentatiously large. Now they seemed cramped and claustrophobic.

There was barely room for me, let alone for the billion thoughts swarming around my head, trying to gain entry. I wished mightily that I knew what I thought, how I felt, what I wanted, but I had the idea that I would not know any of those things for certain until I screamed them at Jinny. My mind kept trying to take refuge in disbelief that any of this was really happening. The trouble was, I know my imagination just wasn't good enough to manufacture a hallucination like this.

I recognized, from the other direction, the intersection where I'd collided with little Evelyn earlier. I approached it with some caution, this time, listening carefully for someone swooping through the air on a skyboard. But of course I had no clear idea what, if anything, one sounded like. I eased up on the intersection, hooked one eye around the corner for a quick peek—

—nearly bumped noses with Evelyn.

She tried to keep a straight face, did pretty well for a few seconds, and then lost it. As soon as she did, I whooped with laughter myself. The tension release was welcome, almost too much so. I laughed a little bit harder than necessary for a little bit longer than I should have. She finished before I did.

Maybe it shook loose some brains. When I finally spoke, what I said surprised me. I expected to hear myself say something polite, banal, phony. What came out was, "Can you tell me how to get a cab around here?"

As I heard the words come out of my mouth I realized I very badly wanted to be away from here. To be back home. Alone. As quickly as possible. So I needed transportation. And I had no idea how to get any. And here before me, by happy chance, was about the only person in the entire compound, including Leo the AI, that I felt comfortable asking.

She just stared at me, unblinking.

"Transportation from here back to the Lower Mainland," I amplified.

When she stared like that she looked remarkably like an owl.

"I came here in Jinny's car, but right now she's taken it offsite, and I need to get back home as soon as p . . . you're imitating an owl, aren't you?"

"I'm sorry," she said. "Yes, I was. I'll stop."

"Thanks. As I was s—"

"I'm not really sorry. But I'll pretend, as long as I don't have to do a very good job."

"Evelyn, honey—"

The owl lit up. "You remember my name."

"Look, I really need to—"

"Most grown-ups don't."

"Evelyn, how do—"

"You can't get a cab here, silly. There's no here."

I nodded. "I figured as much. But that implies there has to be some way to get guests where they need to go, when they need to be there. Do you know what it is?"

I nearly lost her with that question. Then her ferocious frown relaxed. "I deserved that. I was the one playing dumb. Yes, Joel, I do know. I'll help you."

I sighed. "Thank you, Ev. Will it take very long?"

"Is there anything in your room you have to go back for?"

I thought about it and shook my head no.

"Follow me, then."

Three turns and perhaps a hundred meters later, she stopped, and touched a wall, and an elevator door opened up where not even a visible seam had been a moment ago. She touched the wall just beside the door, in a different way, and the wall developed a monitor and extruded a keypad—at a height convenient for a seven-year-old. She typed something on it, with only her index fingers, but at a speed that would have been remarkable even if she'd been using all ten. Finally she made a small grunt of satisfaction, and turned to me.

"You'll find a car waiting at ground level. Just state your destination; it'll find it."

"How do I—"

"When you get where you're going, just get out and say, 'Dismissed.' It homes."

Of course it did. I started for the elevator, then paused. "Ev, honey?"

"Yes, Joel?"

"Is this . . . I mean, are you going to get in trouble for this?"

She grinned. "Not unless you rat me out."

"Are you sure?"

"Guest cars aren't a secret. Anybody could have called you one."

"But won't the record show that it was you who did?"

She grinned again. "The record says Jinny did."

I nodded. "Okay, then. Thank you. I owe you one." It didn't seem adequate. I bent, took her hand in mine, lifted it to my lips, and planted one just behind the knuckles. Then I straightened up and stepped into the elevator. "So long, Ev."

Her eyes were huge. "Hot jets."

"Clear skies." The door slid closed, and I rose rapidly enough to pull gee forces, reaching the surface in no time.

The car waiting for me there was generic, but much more luxurious—to the eye, at least—than the *faux* heap Jinny had driven me there in. The feature I found most praiseworthy was an exceedingly well-stocked bar. It contained the most expensive liquids, solids, vapors, sprayers, and essences then popular for the radical adjustment of attitude, mood, and energy. Being a poor student, from a frontier world with conservative customs, I was familiar with most of them only . . . well, academically—and about their synergistic effects in multiple combination I knew nothing whatsoever. I decided to remedy this deficiency by personal experiment. I attempted to try at least one of *everything*, and for all I know may have succeeded. I never noticed the takeoff, or indeed any of the trip, and I have no recollection of arrival back at my place.

I never did get my shoes back.

5

Like the fabulous Conrad compound, my apartment was mostly underground, and did not appear on any map. But there the similarities ended.

For one thing, it was not located in the middle of a glacier somewhere, but smack in the midst of some of the most densely populated land in the U.S.N.A., the White Rock district of Greater Vancouver. For another, it was the polar opposite of opulent or luxurious, as comfortable as a coffin. Vancouver itself has a tradition of quasilegal "basement suites" dating back centuries to some World's Fair, or perhaps Olympics, but outlying suburbs like White Rock acquired theirs so recently that they're still illegal, hence unrecorded, hence unregulated, hence mostly shitholes. In sharp contrast to Conradville, it had only a single virtue to recommend it.

But right then, that virtue rated high in my scale of values: it was *mine*.

I take it back: it had one other thing going for it. The thing that had recommended it to me in the first place, back when I'd first grounded on Terra: like most caves, it was a terrific place to hole up. It had been my first refuge from the unbelievable crowding Terrans considered normal, from the appalling crime rate they considered acceptable, from my own sudden shocking physical weakness, from unexpectedly crushing homesickness and loneliness, and from my own unaccustomed social ineptitude. A womb with a view.

What I needed when I woke up, that horrible morning after, was refuge from my own thoughts and feelings. The apartment did its best, but I suspect a riot would have been insufficient distraction.

The emotion foremost in me when consciousness first reconstructed itself again was sadness, grief insupportable, but it took me a while to recall exactly what I was so sad about. Then it all came back in a rush, and I sat bolt upright in bed. My skull promptly exploded with the force of an antimatter collision—I'd obviously forgotten to take antihangover measures the night before—but the blinding white light and total agony seemed merely appropriate. I'd have howled like a dog if I'd had the strength. Instead I whimpered like a puppy.

For the last—I couldn't remember *how* many mornings, I had woken up thinking of Jinny. Yearning for Jinny. Aching for Jinny. Had woken every time from dreaming of Jinny—of us—of us together—of the distant but attainable day when she would be there in the morning, there all night, the day when I would finally possess her fully.

Possess her? Ha! My lifetime net worth would probably not suffice to lease an hour of her time.

And yet she wanted me.

And God help me, I still wanted her—as fiercely as ever. I could still have her, if I chose. So why was I so sad I wanted to fall out of bed and bang my face against the floor?

The sadness was because my dream was gone. Whatever the future might hold for me and Jinny, it would not, could not, remotely resemble anything I had ever envisioned. Conceivably it could be a better future, perhaps much better—but right now, at this remove, mostly what it was, was unimaginable.

Unless it was nothing at all. I could imagine that easily enough. I just didn't want to. Like life before I met Jinny—minus hope.

Let's not be hasty, Joel. I couldn't rent an hour of her time . . . but I could have *all* of her hours, if I wanted, without paying a single credit. What *would* it cost me, though? Let's see. All my plans for my, our, future, for a start. The identity and goals and place in the world I had picked for myself. The rustic notion that the husband should be the one who supported the family, which I had already admitted to myself months ago was archaic nonsense anywhere but a frontier society like Ganymede. It hadn't been customary for the majority of the human race for well over a century now.

And let's not forget one other little cost that Conrad had been quite upfront about: most of my waking hours for the rest of my days, which would be spent working very long and hard on things for which I had little interest, training, or talent. With the very best of medical care assuring that I'd be in harness as long as possible. I would have to assume and bear a yoke of almost inconceivable responsibility—responsibility to literally billions of people, all with their own loves and dreams and plans for their futures.

And even if I washed out personally, my children would be groomed and fitted and trained for that same responsibility from birth. All of them. In my vague eighteen-year-old imaginings of the children I might have one day, I had always pictured myself advising them to pursue whatever really interested them, to follow their hearts, the way my father had with me. That would no longer be an option if they were Conrads.

I'm making my hungover maunderings seem far more coherent and organized and cogent than they really were. At the very same time that all the thoughts I've just described were going through my head, for instance, I was also simultaneously asking myself over and over again just what, exactly, was so horrible about becoming one of the wealthiest and most powerful people in human history, if that was what it took to win the most beautiful woman in the Solar System?

Well, for a start, myself kept answering, you haven't *earned* it. What good is a prize, any prize, if you don't deserve it, if you haven't done the work? Face it, Joel: you don't even have the vaguest idea what the work *is*.

To which my ongoing rebuttal was: Oh, give me a break, self. Do you think even Conrad of Conrad truly *earned* that much power and money? Do you think *anyone* could? Do you honestly believe any conceivable human being, however talented and however hardworking, could possibly *deserve* that much compensation, *merit* that much authority? The most anyone can do is *have* it. Old man Conrad happened to have been born from the right womb at the right time, and must have behaved thereafter more intelligently than any of his rivals, that was all. That was as close as he came to deserving what he had: it had been handed to him, and he had not fumbled it. Now it—or at least a piece of it—was being handed to me—or at least to my—

—children. Mine and Jinny's—

How could she do *this to me?*

DISTRACTION. DISTRACTION. CHANGE the ch—ah, that was it. I found the remote—thank you, Mr. Tesla—turned on the tube, and selected passive entertainment, genre search.

First, drama: on some unimaginably distant colony planet—because there were two moons in the sky, one of them ringed—a beautiful woman with red hair was crying as if her heart were broken. No, thank you; *change* channel—

Comedy, next: a young man my age—we did make great natural comedic victims, didn't we?—had done something incredibly stupid, and a roomful of people and Martians were laughing openly at his humiliation. Next, please—

Erotica. I was utterly disinterested, and noticed that my right arm was extremely weary. Apparently that car's drug supply had included libido enhancers. Next—

Sports. Free-fall soccer semifinals, O'Neill versus the Belt, winner to face Circum-Terra in the fall. As it came on, the mob outside the globe roared: a forward as long and lean as a Ganymedean had just frozen, fumbled his chance, blown an easy shot by hesitating. Zoom in for extreme close-up of his anguished features, his obvious shame. Next—

News, Systemwide: Luna Free State was saying very rude things about Ganymede's trade policy, and Terra was making no comment; while nobody had actually used the words "trade war" yet, everyone was thinking them, louder than they had last week. And here I was, trapped at the bottom of the gravity well. Next—

News, Global: The outfitting and provisioning of the latest colony ship, RSS *Charles Sheffield*, was nearly complete. It was expected to leave orbit in a few days, and a few days after that, assuming its drive lit without incident, its complement of some five hundred souls should go bye-bye in a big hurry. Hopeably to a star called Immega 714—known also, for reasons I could not imagine, as "Peekaboo." Only the day before yesterday, I had considered most of them to be idiots, a company of misfits, malcontents, romantics, failures, crackpot visionaries, runaways, transportees, and other defective personalities. Now I found myself fiercely envying them. Just a couple more days, and nothing the Conrad dynasty or any individual Conrad could possibly do would ever

again affect them in the slightest. What dominated my future
and my children's future was shortly to become as irrelevant
to them as the Roman Empire. Sigh. Next—

Local news. Housing riots again. This time the demon-
strators had somehow overwhelmed or outsmarted both
proctors and private security, and penetrated to the very
heart of Vancouver's most upscale neighborhood, the tony
intersection of Main and Hastings. Standard anticrowd
measures could not be taken for fear of excessive damage
to private property.

I switched to the fiction channel, scanned my favorites index for a story I wanted to reread, something really good and
solid and dependable—and long, at least a trilogy. As I did,
random sentences from old favorite books kept running
through my head. You don't turn down a promotion . . . if
someone puts money in your hand, close your fingers and
keep your mouth shut . . . let this cup pass from me . . . he
played the hand he was dealt . . . opporknockity tunes but
once, and you'd better be in tune with it. . . .

Forget fiction. I was way too scattered to read. Even fo-
cusing on titles was beyond me. I didn't bother with any of
the music channels: I just knew that whatever I got would be
heartbreaking. I shut the screen altogether and flung the remote across the room.

God damn it, how could she do *this to me?*

How COULD SHE lie to me that way, hide the truth from me
for so long, tell so many lies to me, play me for a fool? My
innocent, loving maiden turned out to be a slumming aristocrat, Harun al-Rashid's granddaughter in clever disguise,
casing the marketplace for a strapping young peasant lad
with acceptable features and good teeth, to serve as stud
back at the palace . . . smiling fondly inside at his earnest
naïveté and childish dreams. . . .

Again, rebuttal wrote itself. Joel, don't be a nincompoop.
How could she not *have done this to you?* How would you
have handled her problem differently, in her place? Placed
an ad on the Web? "Princess seeks hybrid vigor. Salary ef-

fectively infinite. Auditions daily at noon; bring résumé, genotype, and headshot."

Me: Well, no, but—

Myself: But what? Once you did catch her eye, once she did somehow, for some glorious reason, cut you out of the herd and let you sniff each other, what was she supposed to do? Tell you who she really was on the first date? Come, now.

Me: But she could have! It wouldn't have—

Myself: Oh, please. In the first place you're full of shit, and in the second place even if you're not, even if you really happen to be the kind of unique and special human being who isn't remotely fazed by small things like unimaginable wealth and power . . . *how the hell was she supposed to know that on a first date?* Or a twentieth?

Me: She kept the damn masquerade up a lot longer than twenty dates! She strung me along for—

Myself: She maintained her cover until about thirty seconds after you stated for the first time, unequivocally and with sincerity in your voice, that you wanted to marry her as soon as you were able.

Me: . . .

Myself: You tell me: can you think of any other way at all that a girl in her position could *know*, for certain, whether she's loved for her self or for her pelf? A girl needs to know these things, pal.

I: He's right, you know.

Me: Yes, but—

Myself: Wait, I'm not done. Can you think of any other way at all that a guy in *your* position could know, for certain, that he genuinely loves a girl who's worth gigacredits? Isn't that a good thing for the guy to know before he marries her?

I: You'll never have any doubts about your own motives, now.

Myself: And neither will she.

Imaginary friend, kibitzing: And neither will anybody else. Everyone will know the story: face it, it's too good not to tell.

Me: Spiffing. Everyone I ever meet will be thinking, how

smart can he be, to have been so profoundly fooled for so long.

Myself: If they know the story, *they'll know Jinny.* They'll understand.

Me: Okay, good point. Only ... only ... it's just ... it's ...

DAMN IT OUT to the Oort Cloud and back, I understood why she had to do what she did—but *how could she do that to me?*

DISTRACTION. DISTRACTION.

I found that I was on my feet, dressed, and pacing around my tiny apartment, with no memory of having willed any of these things. This suggested to me that the distraction should take the form of a depressant rather than a stimulant.

The bar in my home was a pathetic joke compared to even the field model in Conrad's guest taxi—I was a starving student, who couldn't afford to indulge, and usually didn't mind—but its sole useful content happened to be a large, unopened bottle of an ancient Greek alcoholic beverage called Metaxa, a species of brandy, given to me by a friend with family on Ikaros. I pulled the cork, decided to dispense with a glass, took a big incautious gulp. It smelled and tasted the way I have always imagined gasoline must have smelled and tasted—especially if the gasoline were on fire at the time. By the time I realized my error and tried to scream, my vocal cords were crisped. My tongue cooked through as if microwaved. Tears spilled like lava from my boiling eyes.

When I could see again, I located my arm, followed it to my hand. The bottle was still in it. I transferred my consciousness, became the bottle, managed to locate my former mouth, and made my way back there. But in attempting to make the jump back to my own brain again, in order to appreciate the full benefit of that second swallow, I got lost somehow. I thrashed around the noosphere for a while, looking for me, but eventually I decided the hell with it and just embraced the darkness. Darkness was a very good thing to embrace. You could count on it staying what it was.

* * *

AFTER THAT COMES a series of disconnected fragmentary memories, of events so unlikely and actions so unlike me I'm honestly not sure whether they were real, hallucinations, or some combination thereof.

I'm quite prepared to believe, for instance, that at one point I raced up the Granville Street Slidewalk, scattering pedestrians like duckpins, while screaming, "I am Prorad of Prorad! Absolutely nothing that happens to you is my fault!" But can it be remotely possible that I really was, as memory insists, holding hands with a monkey at the time? Where did the monkey come from? Where did he go?

Similarly, it's not impossible that I challenged half a dozen White Hat boys to personal combat for laughing at me in Chinatown. The Granville Slidewalk leads in that direction, and I was in a suicidal mood. But how I could have survived . . . whatever ensued . . . unscathed, I can neither recall nor imagine. I had no weapon, no combat skills, and Ganymedean muscles. (I never understood, by the way, why Chinatown was still called that, considering that it had been well over a century since the population of Greater Vancouver was less than sixty percent Chinese by ethnicity. I don't know; maybe ghettoization becomes funny after it stops happening. Or perhaps it was more of a "Never forget!" thing.)

And if I *was* in Chinatown, on foot—I had no money for cabs or other public transport—how could I have found myself, an eyeblink later, all the way across town at Spanish Banks beach, watching the vast boat city moored there, Little Kong, gleam in the sunlight, and boil and bustle with the indomitable industry of the doomed? As far as I could see, they were selling seawater to each other out there—but they did it with all their might, each dreaming of cornering the market one day. When a few Vietnamese came ashore, I reeled over and tried to apologize to them, for not having the guts to become a Conrad, and thus solve the politico-economic conditions that trapped them there. But the language barrier intervened—they spoke no Basic, I spoke no

Vietnamese—and somehow I ended up buying an unlabeled sprayer of something even more diabolical than Metaxa from them, instead. Maybe they did understand what I was trying to say, after all.

I remember the first rush of it, whatever it was—it was memorable, even to a man in my condition—and after that I have only one other brief scrap of memory that seems even remotely likely to be real.

I became aware that I was chilly. This rekindled enough awareness for me to notice that I was on the west side of Stanley Park—halfway up a *tall* tree. (How did I get to the Park from Spanish Banks on foot? Persuade someone to drive me? Stow away on a bus? Teleport? No idea.)

It seems clear in retrospect that my intention must have been to commit suicide. Ganymedeans do not climb tall trees in Terran gravity for any other reason I can think of. Amazing I got as far as halfway up; I had never climbed a tree in my life. Apparently I had become distracted by the magnificent view, staring across the Georgia Strait at distant Vancouver Island, just visible low on the horizon, and beyond that the Juan de Fuca Strait and the Pacific Ocean and ultimately Vladivostok, I suppose.

I should not have been chilly—I don't wear stupid clothes—but I'd obviously forgotten to recharge them. It made sense that my face would be the chilliest part of me . . . but why was the coolness there *moving*, running down toward my neck? I had just worked out that it was tears, sheets of them, when my phone went off. I knew who it was, but checked the display anyway, just on the off chance that it was a major university offering me a full scholarship and bursaries.

It was Jinny, of course.

I turned up the volume to hear the message she was recording. "—been trying to give you room, give you time to get ov—uh, to adjust to the situation. I *know* I've given you a lot to deal with. I understand why you ran away. But I can't wait anymore, I'm going out of my mind. Pick up, Joel, we have to talk. *Please* pick up. I probably won't be able to call you again, and if you try and call me back, it won't . . . oh,

God damn it, I love you, Joel. I really do. You know that. Just give me—"

I plucked the earbeads out of my ears, held them at arm's length. Jinny's voice became a faint cricket sound. That seemed a distinct improvement. If a little was good, then—I threw the earbeads so hard, they cleared the sea wall below and plunked into the Georgia Strait. Yes, that was the ticket: no more cricket.

" 'Ran away'?" I muttered. "*I'll* show you run away, lady. Watch me."

How did I get back down from that tree without breaking anything? I reject memory, which says I was assisted by a team of swans, but have no better explanation to offer.

There are, as I said, a few more shards of memory after that, but I don't think any of them represent real experiences. I don't think, for instance, that it's possible to *do* that with even an *extremely* cooperative goat. Certainly not without paying in advance.

AND THEN, WITH the shocking suddenness of running full tilt into an unseen wall, I was instantly a hundred percent cold sober, and an ugly man with lemon breath was staring into my eyes from no more than ten or twenty centimeters away, so fixedly and intently that I sensed he was grading them, by some unknown criteria.

I couldn't stop him, so I decided to grade *his* eyes. At first they seemed the eyes of a man so tired he was on the verge of a temper tantrum. But on second look I could see that he was always that angry, and the fatigue merely blew his cover. On the third look, I learned something new. Until then I had believed that anger is *always* fear in disguise. My father had told me so once, in memorable circumstances, and I'd never seen a counterexample. But now I could see that at least some of this man's anger derived not from fear, but from shame. In some way he had failed himself irredeemably—so irredeemably that there was no longer anything left to fear. His face tried to say that was *my* fault, especially his mouth—but his eyes knew damn well it wasn't.

"Am I finally addressing a sentient being?" he asked.

Early sixties. Ruddy face. Strong lemon breath. Sour lemon. "I doubt it," I said. "But I'm probably close enough to run for Parliament, at least."

He grunted and moved away. As his face receded I tried to follow it and fell off my chair, thereby learning that I had been sitting in a chair. Where this chair, *mein Herr*? There, *mon cher*. Well, I swear.

He let me make my own way back up into the chair, leaning into the force of his contempt as if it were a strong wind. It took me a while. Before I had time to congratulate myself, he said, "I'm Dr. Rivera. Do you know where you are?"

I rubbed a sore spot on my face. "On Terra, obviously. Barbaric gravity."

He didn't have the energy to be impatient. "Where on Terra, specifically?"

"In these pants," I said, and giggled.

"After what I gave you, you should be straight by now," he said. "I conclude you must be a natural horse's ass."

"Nonsense! I've had to work hard at it."

Humor was wasted on him. Or being wasted was not humorous to him. One of those. "You are in Tampa, Florida."

I giggled again. "Home of the tampon. Is this your pad?"

"You are at the Tampa Spaceport."

"You don't want to Tampa with a spaceport. Your complexion could end up even Florider." I cracked myself up with that one. But as I laughed, rusty wheels finally began to turn slowly in my head.

Tampa? Why the hell would I go to Tampa? Even if I had found some sort of pressing reason to visit a spaceport, Albuquerque was a hell of a lot closer to Vancouver than Tampa was—

"Do you know why you are—"

What did Tampa have that Albuquerque didn't? Nothing. In fact, these days Tampa was almost completely closed to normal commercial traffic, due to—something. I forgot.

"I said, do you even remember what you—"

What made Tampa different from any other spaceport in this hemisphere?

"Forget it," he said suddenly. "You're not up to this."

"The hell I'm not," I said automatically. Whatever he was talking about, who the hell was he to be talking about it?

His contempt reached a crescendo. "Young man, I doubt you'd be up to it even if your bloodstream were completely clean. It's a big decision. Too big for you. Try again another time. You probably won't be any smarter, but you will at least be older."

Wait a minute, now—there *was* one thing you could do at Tampa that you couldn't do at any other spaceport in this hemisphere, right at this time—

"I'm old enough to make up my own mind, Dr. Rivera," I snapped.

—wait a minute—

He blinked. "See here, son—you are indeed, as you point out, legally old enough to make up your mind as neat and tight and tidy as your bed used to be made up when you lived with your mother. But *you have not done so yet*. Half your blankets are on the floor, the sheets are a tangled wreck. Go sleep it off, come back in a day or two, and we'll talk. In my professional judgment, you're not ready to go to Immega 714."

My jaw fell. On my first attempt, I had very nearly gotten stoned enough to fall right out of the Solar System.

WHEN THE SHOCK wore off, I found I was more than half tempted to go through with it. Sign onto the *Sheffield*, become a Gentleman Adventurer, and head for the stars. Partly just to spite that sourpuss with the sour lemon breath, for telling me I couldn't. But mostly because it suited my mood. Star travel would certainly be a way out of the trap I'd put myself in, the trap Jinny had led me into—

—one that involved gnawing off both my own legs. No thanks. I told Lemon-Breath Rivera I *would* be back in a day or two, but we both knew I was fronting. I found myself on the street, blinking against the Tampa sunshine, sweating in the Tampa heat.

I considered various options for getting home again, balancing speed against expense with the miserliness of a student on a short budget. Then I thought to consult my credit balance, and my options shrank to one. If that. In choosing my route to Tampa, I had apparently assumed it was okay to burn bridges, and had chosen a semiballistic. Fast, comfortable—and *very* expensive, what with the price of hydrogen. I was just short of totally tapped out.

I consulted an atlas, and calculated that with a little luck, the high-speed public slidewalks ought to get me back to Vancouver in no more than seventeen hours or so. If I could just avoid getting hungry or thirsty or bored for that long, I'd end up back in my tiny basement apartment, free to gorge on whatever I had left in the pantry and all the water I wanted, while enjoying any book or film I already owned. Then I would have to start praying that my scholarship came through before the next rent payment was due. This was a bad time to go into debt; interest rates were approaching body temperature.

I made a mental note: *never* go on a bender without taping a fifty-credit bill to the sole of your foot.

I found slidewalk access without too much trouble, transferred my way up to the 320 kph strip in due course, found a seat without difficulty, and hunkered down for the trip. It took me all of half an hour to go from terminal nausea to ravening hunger. Did you know that you smell at least partially with your mouth? Holding my nose didn't help *nearly* enough in suppressing food smells. I had to keep resisting a temptation to suck on my own hand. I was already drawing enough unwanted attention as it was: it turned out that I *looked* like someone on a bender. Why wouldn't I?

After a lonely half hour I spent watching countryside whip past too fast to really see, someone sat down near me. That cheered me up until I realized the reason for his tolerance: he was well into a bender of his own, and might not have noticed if I'd been on fire. Ignoring public privacy laws, he was listening to music on speaker rather than his earbeads. I started to object—and got sucker-punched by the song that was emanating from his wrist.

It's the reason we came from the mud, don't you know
'cause we wanted to climb to the stars

Instantly, I was back in the ballroom of the Hotel Vancouver, in Jinny's arms, dancing with her at our prom. The last happy moment I could recall. Maybe the last one I was ever going to have. I know that sounds melodramatic, but that's because you're not eighteen anymore. I didn't burst into tears—quite. But it was a near thing.

> *Ask anyone which way is God, and you know*
> *he will probably point to the stars . . .*

Not everyone, I thought. Some of us would point to a glacier somewhere in northern British Columbia.

All at once I understood the real reason I had chosen not to hop a starship after all. I wasn't *done* yet. I couldn't even think about *thinking about* leaving for Immega 714 as long as my situation was still unresolved. Not until I'd done everything I could to try and fix it. I was still alive. Jinny was still alive.

Well, there was no time like the present. Automatically, I started to look round for a 'fresher, to fix my appearance—then decided it could wait. Let Jinny see the state she'd reduced me to, first. All I wanted from her right now was a phone code, anyway. *Then* I'd get cleaned up. She and I would have our own conversation, after this upcoming one was done. I punched her code from memory—my own, I mean, not pod storage—and then the call went through, and—

I flipped my wrist over to make the screen go away and shouted *"Coventry!"* loud enough to startle my zoned neighbour into muting his music.

Why was I so surprised? *Ask me which way is God*, I thought, *and I'll point to my phone*.

I turned my wrist back over, and Conrad of Conrad frowned up at me.

I HAD *WANTED* to talk to him, planned to talk to him, with great firmness and determination. In a few minutes, once I'd gotten his code from Jinny and prepared my lines. Now I was off balance. Great start.

He began speaking nearly at once. I could see his lips

move. But I was now forcibly reminded that I had thrown my earbeads into the Georgia Strait, last night. I could only point at my ears and shake my head, feeling like an idiot, even further off balance.

He glanced way offscreen at someone to his right, lifted an eyebrow, and my phone put itself on speaker. I'd have thought of it myself in a second. I could feel my cheeks burning.

"I said, I understand your problem, Joel."

I hoped to call myself a man one day. It simply did not matter if I was unprepared, or my hair was uncombed, or my pants were on. Showtime! "I'm very glad to hear that, Conrad." There now—I'd remembered in time not to call him "sir."

"You have grave doubts that you'll measure up." I tried to respond, and he kept talking right over me until I stopped. "Any sane man in your position would. You have no life experience to reassure you yet. Or to reassure me, for that matter. Women's intuition has historically been a chancy method of selecting winners—else Troy would still stand. But your genes and grades are excellent, for what that's worth. And you have off-planet experience, which broadens a man. Maybe you are what we need. I think you are. In any case you are going to be given a chance. One moment, Joel."

His gaze shifted up and to his left slightly, and he began a conversation with someone in a corner of his screen. The audio cut off, and the image of his mouth fuzzed so that his lips could not be read. Very slick.

I used the pause to get hold of myself, control my breath, and figure out what to say to cure his misconceptions. I even had a second or two to appreciate the surreality of having a phone conversation on a public slidewalk with one of the wealthiest living humans. Then I waited to seize control of the conversation the moment his eyes returned to mine.

Waste of time; once again he simply ignored the fact that I was speaking. "If you do measure up, you will become a Conrad, with all that implies. If you don't—well, you and your children will be Johnstons, but considerably better off than you would otherwise be. One of the pleasant things about this dynasty is that we can be liberal in pensioning off those who don't quite make it." I'd have tried to interrupt if there'd been any point. "If you turned out to have no real head for business but were tops in research, say, you might end up as Dr. Johnston, Chief of Kindelberger Research Laboratories. Or you might choose to simply lie in the sun in Cairns, and that can be arranged, too—we can afford to be generous. One moment."

Once again he spoke briefly and inaudibly with someone else, this time in his lower right-hand corner. This time when his gaze returned to me I was ready with a very loud, "Mr. Conrad, sir!"

I think he literally didn't know how to process insolence. Insufficient experience. It shut him up long enough for me to wedge four more words in edgewise. It took a surprising amount of courage to say them.

"The answer is no."

He tried to frown and raise his eyebrows in surprise at the same time. Even Conrad of Conrad *must* have heard those words before—or he'd own *everything*, instead of only about a quarter of it. But he clearly hadn't expected to hear them now, from me. "You mean you *don't want* to marry my granddaughter?"

Surprising him cheered me up. I reminded myself that I had once bitten this man. Hard, as I recalled. "Don't misunderstand me. If Jinny wants to get married right away, we'll get married. I'll swing it somehow. But I do not intend to let someone else lay out my life according to some kind of time table and tell me when to wipe my nose—no matter how well the job pays. It's not a question of measuring up. I'll do my own measuring. And I'll pay my own way. Thanks anyway, I appreciate it, I do appreciate it—but keep your free lunch, it's not for me."

He glanced up and to the right, and this time forgot to mute his audio. "Tell the Secretary of State I will be a few minutes late." I think he really did forget, because when he said those words his voice was flat and cold, and when he turned back to me it had become warm and fatherly. "I admire spirit in a young man, I really do. We can't hold this thing together with yes-men and flunkies at the top. Your answer convinces me more than anything else that little Jinnia Anne has made a wise choice. Nevertheless, I must convince *you* that we need you—and that you need training. We've got to crowd thirty years of training into the next ten—it's been proved over and over again that, despite the wonders of modern geriatrics, young men must be allowed to make top decisions before age, experience, and caution grow on them like rust or mold. We must strive for a young man's drive and an old man's knowledge. Not easy." He sighed. "And the young have all the time in the world. I wish I did. You want to sleep on it, I can see that. Looks like you could use the sleep, too." Without taking his eyes from mine, he told someone, "Joel will call me at this code tomorrow at 0900 PST."

I started to ask him what code to use to reach Jinny—but he had already broken the connection.

I TRIED REDIALING the number—and was told it was a null. I could guess it would remain one, at least for me, until tomorrow morning at nine.

I went to Jinny's apartment that night. She had moved out. No forwarding address. I caught one of her neighbors looking at me with pity. I agreed with her.

I did not call Conrad at 0900 the next morning. For the next half hour, I was braced for him to call me, or have some flunky summon me, but he did not. For the rest of the morning, I was halfway prepared for two large men to bust in my door and drag me out to a black limo, but nothing of the sort occurred.

A little after noon, there was incoming mail, a text-only message. It was a letter from Stony Brook, informing me without even a polite pretense of regret that my scholarship had been turned down. It didn't say why, but it didn't need to.

Every single plan I had made for my life lay in ruins. No degree, no career, no future, no Jinny, no family—unless I consented to serve at stud while training to run a multiplanet dynasty. My only two lifestyle choices were to be a dole bludger, or one of the wealthiest gigolos alive.

I wanted, very badly, to get so wasted that my previous bender would seem a mere preamble.

Instead, I did not so much as drink a beer or take an acetaminophen. I spent the day taking care of a number of tedious details and formalities. I ate a healthy dinner, retired early, got a good night's sleep. In the morning, I filled a backpack with the belongings and food I hadn't disposed of the day before, locked the apartment behind me for the last time, and headed for a crosstown slidewalk.

A little over seventeen hours later I persuaded Dr. Rivera (whose breath smelled like strawberries that day) that I was sober enough to apply for a slot on the waiting list for a berth on the RSS *Sheffield*. The expedition's backers had no connection whatsoever with the Conrad dynasty; my application was accepted. That very afternoon, one of the colonists who'd already been accepted managed to kill himself on one last rock-climbing trip. The next day I was informed that I had been chosen to replace him.

I was on my way to Immega 714, aka Peekaboo. Where I would live out my life on the planet called Brasil Novo.

6

There is no wealth but life.

—John Ruskin

There were other candidates, of course, some of whom had been waiting *years* longer than I had, and a great many of them had more impressive skill sets or resources than I did, as well. But such decisions are rarely made fairly. What got me the berth—late starter, dead broke, and all—was a combination of three specific unfair advantages I had over my competitors.

First, of course, was what would have been a disadvantage in just about any other enterprise, with the possible exception of prostitution: my extreme youth. I had only just become a legal adult. You want young people on a voyage expected to last nearly twenty years, ship time, and over ninety years Earth time—but not a lot of them volunteer for such a trip. If they do, and are turned down, they tend to go away and make another plan. It's not really the sort of trip young people sit around and pine for, at least not now that the first waves have gone. Not happy healthy ones, anyway.

The next important factor was sheer coincidence: the *Sheffield*'s boost rate. She would blast at a constant acceleration of exactly one-third gee—and I was from Ganymede. I'd be one of the few around who felt normal, for a change. For once, I'd be markedly better adapted, *more* effective, than those I was with. Even fewer Ganymedeans or Marsmen tended to sign up for star travel than did teenagers; they were just too busy.

But what cinched the deal was, I was from Ganymede. That is, I was one of no more than a handful of star colonists who had any practical, hands-on experience whatsoever with . . . pause for ironic drumroll . . . dirt farming!

You can't blame Earthlings for not knowing much about that: despite what they named their planet, really good dirt is getting hard to come by, there. (God knows the Prophet wasted enough of it for them, may his concept of Hell actually appear, for just long enough to accept him.) But most Terrans haven't even done any *hydroponic* farming, and the few who have are generally too rich to make good candidates for interstellar refugees. There is something to be said for scarcity. The total food-growing experience of most *Sheffield* passengers was almost indistinguishable from zero.

And I had a *ton* of it. Not theoretical experience, either. Not classroom knowledge, but the kind where bilging the course means you starve. Like most Ganymedeans, and many colonials in or on other worlds, I had spent a portion of my childhood turning earth, hauling manure, outguessing weather, making crops—performing some of the most ancient labor there is, using tools so primitive by Terrestrial standards that most of my fellow colonists probably could not have identified them without help. That's what we were all so *busy* at, up there, if you've been wondering: turning rock into rutabagas, because they tasted better, and were also more nutritious.

Go ahead, laugh—I did. The one aspect of my background that had always been guaranteed to elicit gales of laughter from those Terrans I admitted it to ended up being the deciding factor in sending me to the stars. Pretty good joke, even for fate.

Even those three factors might not have been enough to get me aboard one of the very earliest colony ships—the *Gaia*, say—not at the last minute. For the first dozen voyages or so, crew and colonists alike were minutely scrutinized, rigorously tested, and meticulously matched according to carefully worked out social, psychological, and ergonomic principles (it says here), with hopeful alternates ready to fill a last-minute opening in any niche, long before the ship was ready to boost.

But by now, almost two dozen ships had left the Solar System—and the supply of applicants was beginning to thin out just a little.

Correction: the *cream* was beginning to thin out a little. There was still a copious supply of applicants . . . 99.99 percent of whom were eliminated by gross tests. Half the remainder then changed their minds halfway through.

Part of the problem was, hardly anybody still left *wanted* to pioneer, wanted to leave everything and everybody behind forever, and go plant beans by the sweat of their back under the miscolored light of an alien sun. It wasn't really a question of pioneer spirit being just about gone, as jeremiahs were always complaining on the wire. Even way back in history, so-called pioneer spirit was usually the result of intolerable conditions back home more than anything else.

That applied back at the very dawn of star travel. Volunteers to leave the Prophet's Paradise were not hard to come by. But the Solar System was a fairly tolerable habitat for most people about now, particularly Terrans and O'Neillers. There was still plenty of frontier to go around, too, for those who hated crowds and regulations. The Asteroid Belt seemed unlikely to fill up anytime soon. To want to leave Sol altogether, forever, you almost had to be a born misfit, or a perpetual tourist, or as brave and curious as a bodhisattva. Most of the last category had signed up already and left in the first or second wave.

I've omitted two other historically significant categories of pioneer. Fortunately, things had not yet reached the point where colony planners willingly accepted members of the first category: perpetual fuckups. But this *would* be the third ship so far to carry transportees—prisoners, guaranteed by their various sentencing jurisdictions to be "nonviolent," "suitably skilled," "highly motivated" "volunteers." But there would be just over two dozen of them, five percent of the colony's total population, and the majority would be political prisoners rather than predators. Neither of the previous transportee experiments had sent back reports of any problems so far.

One other thing I've speculated about. I said that the Immega 714 colony's underwriters were not allied with the Conrads. In fact, they were instead associated with the Kangs and the da Costas, both houses that were hereditary enemies of the Conrads. The RSS *Sheffield*'s designers, the prestigious firm of Ray, Guy and Douglas, belonged to neither house—but were all notorious defectors from the giant Conrad subsidiary Starship Enterprises MDA.

I knew nothing of the history between the three houses, and still don't—but sometimes I wonder whether a deep enough background check on me mightn't have turned up the information that the Conrad family had put the Black Spot on me . . . and why. Are relationships between financial empires really petty enough that some Chinese or Brazilian exec way beyond his Peter Principle point might have upchecked my application purely to spite Richard Conrad?

I don't know. Do you?

I EXPECTED SOMETHING like a vocational/educational boot camp on the ground—several rigorous weeks at least of cramming, training, testing, observation, evaluation, and ultimately final placement in my proper place on the great ship's table of organization.

I didn't even get orientation indoctrination. They called me at a little after 7:00 A.M. Pacific Standard Time in White Rock—near the end of business hours in Brussels, where the decision had been made—to tell me I'd been selected to take passage on the *Sheffield*. By nine that night, Pacific time, I was aboard her.

WHERE IT WAS 6:00 A.M. local ship's time, since the *Sheffield* was using the same Central European Time that Brussels did, for reasons left as an exercise for the reader who likes easy lifting.

I emerged from the airlock braced, I thought, for a barrage of new sensory data and impressions, expecting the unexpected insofar as that phrase has any meaning. Which is not much: I was definitely sideswiped by the smell.

It's possible to cut your nose out of your breathing circuit completely, and I did at once. But that aroma was just pungent enough to taste with the tongue, and there's no bypass for *that*, short of tracheotomy. I'd have stopped in my tracks . . . if I had not been so busy bracing my brain for new impressions that I'd neglected to have the more useful portion of my body maintain a hold on the airlock door. Having thus committed myself, I kept on sailing forward, with the stately inevitable grace of a runaway hospital bed on ice, until I crashed into a naked bald man.

I'm a colonial. We maintain some conservative (public) attitudes about sexuality, by contemporary System standards, but at the same time, being on the frontier we tend to be somewhat more practical and matter-of-fact than most Earthlings are about nudity. It was the bald part that startled me.

Thanks to the unnamed ladies who did us all the favor of tearing the Prophet into little bloody gobbets and bits of bone, it is finally once again permissible to do biological research, so happily all baldness is voluntary today, and is not a popular choice. And extremes of body weight are becoming so rare, one body looks much like another from a distance nowadays—so why would a man who spent time nude choose to shave off his only visual identifier? Was he antisocial? Or just self-effacing?

Neither. "I know exactly what you're thinking," he said, and managed to brake us to a halt without sending either of us drifting. His speaking voice was just audible, despite our proximity.

I became aware that I was holding him in something very like a lover's four-limbed embrace, and forced myself not to flinch. I was the stranger here, he was my host. But I hoped our sexual orientations matched. "So?"

He let go of me, again without setting me adrift. His expression was no clue at all. "You're thinking, if it smells like this after only a few months of occupancy, what is it going to smell like in twenty years?"

I had to admit I had been on the way to formulating that very thought when I'd crashed. "Right in one."

"And the answer is, in *far* less than twenty years you will be prepared to swear, truthfully, that this ship has no smell at all, other than local cooking and your wife's perfume." Once again, his voice was just barely as loud as it needed to be.

I wasn't convinced. But I didn't need to be. "What *is* it I'm smelling, exactly?"

"Us," he said simply.

I tentatively half opened a nostril, and frowned. "I know what people smell like, what a ship smells like, and there's more than that here."

"You know what Ganymedeans smell like, and Terrans in a limited portion of a third of its northern hemisphere. This isn't just *everybody*, it's everybody all *together*. And more *of* 'em than you've ever been shut in with before. Terrans from all over that varied planet, Loonies, O'Neillers, Martians, Ganymedeans, Belters—all at the same time, in combination. Fewer than two dozen times in history have all those smells been mingled, in large amounts—and the other ones have left the Solar System already."

"Oh."

"No one group's smell is intrinsically better or worse than

any others', and you might very well find the personal body odor of an individual from just about any racial, political, or social group aboard perfectly agreeable to you. But put them *all* together, in one place, and ancient instinct makes you uneasy. Think of it as one of the last remaining traces of our physical predisposition to xenophobia and racism. Like the appendix."

I had never seen anybody real talk for so long without even momentarily developing a facial expression. "I hope you're right," I said politely.

"Also, the two decks immediately above this one are both agricultural decks. We're sort of in the bilge of Noah's Ark here."

"I apologize for crashing into you."

He shook his head—slowly, the way one does in free fall. "All you did was fail to realize you would need someone to catch you, and that was so close to inevitable that I was waiting there specifically to catch you. Shuttles are always overpressured: *everyone* comes sailing in the door. Apology respectfully returned unopened."

I shook my own head even slower, to underline the point I was about to make. "You don't understand. I was *born* in free fall. I could at least have docked more gracefully."

He nodded, even more slowly. Was that a twinkle in his eye? Or a tic? "Ah," he said. "In that case, you *are* a dimwit. And an oaf. But you can't help being either one; so apology is still unnecessary. Come with me, please."

And as I gaped, he turned over, grabbed a rung on the wall with one hand, and jaunted off down the corridor, at a pace suitable for dimwits and oafs.

In my embarrassment, I nearly mortified myself completely by bleating out "Wait!" like some fool groundhog. To say "wait" to someone who has just jaunted away from you in zero gee is basically as sensible as saying it to someone who just stepped off a roof: barring unreasonable effort, they're *gone*. Barely in time, I managed to end the "W—" with "—hat about my luggage?"

"You'll never see it again," he called back without turning

around, just loud enough to be understood, and continued to drift away.

I realized to my dismay he had left me stationary. That's not supposed to be possible in free fall, and I suppose technically I must have had *some* sort of vector, but I could see it wasn't going to close the half-meter gap between me and the corridor wall anytime soon. I had no thrusters, or even wings.

It turns out you *can* swim in air, if it's thick enough. But not well at *all*, and definitely not without looking like a dimwit and an oaf. By the time I got one hand on a rung, he had receded so far there was great temptation to complete my disgraceful display by flinging myself after him too hard, the classic newbie mistake. Instead I carefully set a measured pace, just faster than his own, and settled back to—

He stuck out his arm as if signaling a turn, grabbed a rung—*zip*—made an abrupt turn in the direction I was falling right at the moment, and disappeared.

When there's nothing else you can do, breathe slower. There's no way it can hurt, and it might help. Long before I reached that rung which I had failed to spot as larger than the rest and therefore a corner rung, I had calmed down enough to find at least a few small items to place in the This-Might-Not-Be-So-Bad column.

If it was possible to swim in air *at all*, then the air pressure in this dump was considerably better than that in the low-budget liners and the one military vessel I'd previously traveled aboard. Which explained why smells were more pungent than I'd expected . . . but also promised that the food was going to *taste* as good as it did on Terra. Presuming, that is, that it started out that tasty.

If you've never experienced anything other than Terran normal pressure, I may need to explain that. Most Terrans don't seem to realize more than half of what they think of as their sense of taste is actually their sense of smell. This confusion becomes clear the first time you eat something you like in lower pressure. Federation military standard pressure is just barely good enough to appreciate superb coffee.

Aboard an economy liner everything pretty much tastes like varying consistencies of warm cardboard or tinted water, and you can chew Red Savina habañeros. (Half a million Scoville units.) Economy passage on a luxury liner, I'm told, gets you *warm* spiced cardboard and *flavored* water. I had tolerated both ends of that spectrum, without too much difficulty.

—for the length of an Outer to Inner System hop, most conveniently measured in weeks! Twenty years was going to be a decidedly different matter. It was nice to know I would not spend my first weeks on Brasil Novo weeping with joy at the rediscovery of garlic—of any spice subtler than Scotch bonnet peppers. (A mere third of a million Scovilles, tops.)

Very nice, really, I conceded to myself as I jaunted along that I was in rocky emotional shape, and in need of consolation. And my father had once told me nothing consoles humans like gratifying our appetites. And a good half of my own total appetites were of no further use to me—I was done with women, for good and for all time. Food, music, and good books had damn well better be enough to fill in the hours, because there were going to be roughly 175,000 of them to fill.

There, that was another good one for the Not-So-Bad side of the ledger: thicker air means better sound. And more wind! The music here would be good. Well, as good as the musicians, anyway.

The corner rung was approaching—on my left, now, since I had rolled over while in trajectory. I put some care and effort into my pivot turn, did a *lovely* job, and immediately crashed into the naked man again, this time from behind, and upside down. If you can't work out where that placed my nose, good. And never mind.

Of *course* he had stopped and waited for me to catch up. Far enough away for me to stop in time, too—if I had happened to round that corner at a more prudent speed, while paying attention to where I was going.

"Excuse me," I said. It came out somewhat muffled, and nasal, with a small echo.

"I do," he said, and jaunted away again, leaving me drifting ever so slightly after him in his wake this time.

Fortunately I was near a wall this time. I blinked, wrinkled my nose, and jaunted after him. Again I matched speeds, and this time we were still within conversation distance, sort of. "I'm Joel Johnston," I called.

He precessed to face me without disturbing his trajectory. "I'm surprised to hear that," he replied softly.

"Huh?"

"I'm surprised to hear that," he repeated, perhaps a decibel and a half louder.

I'm surprised *I* hear it, pal. "I meant, why is that?"

"The First Officer told me to meet a Joel Johnston at the aft airlock."

And you did. "And you did meet Joel Johnston."

"And at the aft airlock, too," he agreed. "That's why I'm surprised."

Should I ask why? No clue on his bland face. "What did you expect?"

"This is the *Sheffield*," he said. "Naturally I expected to meet a Joan Johnson at the midships lock. I only came here first so I wouldn't confuse you by being on time. Naturally I ended up confusing us both—so symmetry is restored." I was pretty sure that was a twinkle in his eyes. But it could have been a detaching retina. Or lunacy. "I'm pleased to meet you, Joel. I'm George R Marsden."

We were starting to pass other people in the corridor, a few at least. All of *them* had clothes on. All of them ignored us, busy with their own affairs, or possibly their own business. "Glad to know you, George."

He didn't wince or frown, exactly, but the twinkle in his eyes guttered. "I prefer George R."

File for later. "Of course, George R. May I ask what you do?"

Again, poker-face delivery. "I am one of the ship's six Relativists."

I'd reached boggle point. I couldn't stop myself from blurting, *"Pisam ti u krvotok!"* Well, it should have been safe enough. And his expression still did not . . . well, come to exist. But somehow I knew I'd poo'ed the screwch. "Let me guess, George R: you're part Croatian."

He nodded. "I have the honor to be descended from the family of Nikola Tesla's mother."

I was weary of apologizing, and even wearier of needing to. "No offense. My mother was part Croat, too. It's usually a safe language to swear in. There can't be enough of us left to keep a newsgroup alive."

"I understand, and realize you did not mean the expression literally, but merely as an ejaculation of surprise." His eyes twinkled up again. It wasn't quite a facial expression, but it did hint which one he might have worn if he'd gone in for them. "Ironically, it is in fact literally correct. By the end of this journey, we will all end up pissing in one another's bloodstreams: the system depends on it."

I couldn't help laughing.

And at last his face came alive: he laughed. It was a pretty good laugh, too, clearly the with-you rather than at-you kind. "Oh, good," he said. "For a minute I was afraid you'd left your sense of humor in your luggage."

"Just my dignity."

"You'll fit right in," he assured me. "Don't worry: both dignity and luggage will catch up with you again, from time to time."

I wish to record that this time when he made a turn, I was paying attention, and turned with him as crisply and elegantly as if we'd drilled in this.

(I did *not* realize we had been traveling until then in a direction that would later come to be called "up," and were now moving horizontally again, on a deck much closer to the ship's nose than the one we'd started from.)

What I wanted to ask, of course, was, "Why is one of the six most important people aboard this tub herding newbies from the airlock to their cubic?" But it didn't seem polite. And I couldn't think of anything lesser I wanted to ask, just now. I mean, this guy was one of the six most impor—

"I know just what you're thinking," he said.

I didn't actually hear the last word, because a door *chuff*ed open in the corridor behind us just then and drowned him out. But I knew what it was. I was destined to spend the next nineteen years being his straight man. "Okay, why are you, then?"

"Because this is the *Sheffield.*"

"Of course." No, *what* is the name of the man on *second* base.

"What would have constituted weirdness would've been if they'd sent, for instance, one of your cubicmates, who actually *knew* where the damn place—wait, now, this looks right, something must be wrong—no, this *is* it. Let me catch you." He grabbed a rung just this side of a door (hatch, Joel, think hatch) with one hand and braked himself to a halt, while letting me use his other hand to brake myself. Somehow I ended up stationary in front of the hatch, with him beside it to my right.

The hatch bore the stenciled label "RUP-0010-E." Below that was a sign hand-painted in some ancient font, with rather good calligraphy. It read:

The 10th Circle: a band of dopes, all we who enter here.

George R released my hand. He was smiling again. "Doubtless this will be a disaster for you, since you came to it quickly. Just try to remember at all times the Prime Law of the *Sheffield.*"

I don't know plays third base. "I am keen to know it, George R."

"No refunds."

"Ah."

He was drifting away before I knew he had eyes to go. "Satisfaction guaranteed, or you're screwed. Good"—and I'm pretty sure the last four syllables as he was passing out of earshot were—"bye, Joel Johnston."

But he might have said, "bye, Joan Johnson."

I found myself grinning after him. His sense of humor was drier than fossil bone in vacuum. And it's hard not to like a man whose only facial expression is a gentle smile.

Ah, that wonderful moment just before you meet new bunkmates. Like the moment just after you step off a roof, and just before you open your eyes and look down to see how many floors away the ground is.

Deep breath. Best smile. I palmed the door. After George R's buildup, I half expected it to shock me unconscious and call for the Proctors. But it accepted me as a resident rather than merely someone unknown seeking to annoy one, and opened to me.

As it slid open, a faint cloud of pale smoke emerged and intersected with my face. Tobacco. I smiled, mildly pleased. I'm not a nicotinic myself, but I've always enjoyed having a smoker cubicmate. It's hard not to like that scent, especially in thick air.

It's going to be a while before the biological sciences really get back on their feet, but safe tobacco was one of their very first new fruits after more than a century of enforced barrenness. The Prophet repressed the weed so savagely that it became a mark of defiance, then a symbol of rebellion, and finally a way to identify other members of the Cabal. Now he's ashes, and cigarettes no longer produce them. As my father once said, the weed outlasted the Creed.

I could see the nicotinic was the only one present in the cubic at the moment, drifting near the center. It seemed an awfully small space for four people. Then contradictory clues resolved, and my perspective shifted. The room was fine. It was just that he was awfully large for a four-person cubic. Much better. I could always kill him.

I'd have to sneak up behind him with a pretty big chainsaw, though, and take him down a limb at a time. He was enormous. Between his mass and the copious white beard he looked like a Viking chieftain, or perhaps Santa Claus's big brother. The latter impression was strengthened by the eyeglasses I could see he wore. People who do that are usually writers or visual artists of some kind: most normal people with astigmatism are willing to risk surgery with a failure rate of about one percent. At worst you need eye transplants—what's the big deal? He wore classic jeans and a baggy blouse with elbow-length sleeves.

As he rotated lazily the front of him came into better view and I saw that he was typing on air, and a hologram glow unreadable at this angle was keeping station with his face. A writer then, I surmised. He kept rotating until he should have seen me, but didn't, and kept typing furiously. Definitely a writer. I hoped he was a poet. If you threaten one with death, and mean it, they always stop. Then he rotated to where I could see his hologram from the back, and my heart sank. It was way too far away to read, even if it had not been backward—but even from here I could see it was properly formatted text, with consistent margins, nothing centered, and words arranged in paragraphs that began with indents. It was about as bad as it could be: he was a novelist.

I think I made a small moaning sound. His eyes refocused past the holo and locked on to me, and the holo vanished. His hands drifted at waist level, but somehow less like they were poised over an invisible keypad, and more like they were poised over the controls of an invisible weapon.

"Johnson," he called.

I shook my head. "Johnston," I corrected.

He shook *his* head. "No," he insisted. "Johnson."

"I'm pretty sure," I said.

"I'm positive," he said.

I closed my eyes and opened them again. "One last time: *who*'s on first, *what*'s on second," I said.

He frowned thunderously. "I don't understand you."

"My point exactly. Let's start this routine over from the top, and see if we can identify just where gangrene set in. Ready? *Straight man:* Say, who's that handsome bastard floating outside the doorway? *Talent:* Joel Johnston, junior agronomist. Honest, I really am."

His brow and hands relaxed. "You got a corrupted copy. My script reads differently. *Dipshit:* Say, whose work am I interrupting? *Talent:* Herb Johnson, the writer. Dishonest, but I really am."

Light dawned. We had been talking at cross-purposes. "Glad to know you. Which one am I, again?"

"The other one. You coming in? I'm losing smoke."

I was starting to enter when the choice was taken from me. Three men arrived behind me, all talking loud and fast, and I found myself swept into the room before them. I grabbed the nearest handhold, which turned out to be what would be an overhead light once we were under acceleration.

The loudest voice was holding forth on English history, I'm pretty sure, though I don't know which period. "—that not many people realize is that the dukes of hazzard used up nearly three hundred dodge chargers."

"So it wasn't a total loss, then," one of his companions replied.

"Right. And who is this before me?"

"Johnston," I said.

He shook his head. "Close. Johnson. And who are you?"

Herb and I exchanged a glance. "My name is Joel Johnston."

"He's the new guy we heard about," Herb said.

"Ah," said the third arrival. "John's *ton*. You are him, plus T."

"Actually," Herb said, "he's me, minus coffee." He turned to me. "It's going to be a long twenty years, isn't it? They've got *me* doing it."

"Welcome to Rup-Tooey, Joel," the second newcomer to speak said to me. "Home of the Lost Boys. I'm Pat Williamson, one of your new roommates."

We did the free-fall equivalent of shaking hands: approach, squeeze both hands briefly, release. "Hi, Pat. Why do you call it Rup-Tooey?"

The history expert snorted. "Because he's a phlegm-ing idiot."

"You saw it on the hatch," Pat said. "Residential, Unclassified Personnel, cubic 0010-E. RUP-0010-E . . . Rup-Tooey."

"Ah." I could think of nothing to add.

"That's your bunk over there. You'll have to tell me all about yourself."

"I'm sure there'll be plenty of time to talk," I said politely.

"No, I mean you'll really have to tell me all about yourself."

"Professor Pat is ship's historian," the third arrival explained. "Thinks this makes him biographer. I tell him is dangerous: he should let sleeping bags lie. But he is encouragable. Glad to please you, Joel. Well come on the board of *Sheffield.*" He pronounced it like "shuffled." "Am Balvovatz, of Luna. Am miner."

"He looks like an adult," the loud expert on ducal matters said. "They age fast in Luna."

"Give to me a fracture." Balvovatz glared at him, and turned back to me. "Balvovatz *mines.* In *mine.* You got rock, give you ore. You understand?" I managed a nod. "So when *Shuffled* reach Immega 714, am big shoot. Till then, like teats on male person: no more use than historian or writer. That is why slum here in UP dump with you bowl budgers."

"Dole bludgers," Williamson corrected gently.

I had to admire his restraint. And his optimism in even trying.

"I think I see," I said. "A pattern begins to emerge. How about you?" I asked the loud expert. "What's your line? Horse whispering? Weatherman?"

It is difficult to smirk without being offensive, but he managed it somehow. "I'm a Relativist," he said. "My name's Solomon Short."

My mouth slammed shut. I had just met my second wizard, in my first half hour aboard. And this one I had actually heard of. Maybe you have, too. That arrest record.

He was smirking at *himself,* that was why. "Yeah. You remember the headline they all used. *Short grounded.* They loved that one. I keep meaning to bisect a baby; they'd all die of biblical ecstasy. *Solomon subdivides tot.* Unfortunately I haven't been able to locate a donor. Was your father—?"

"Yes."

He nodded and stopped smirking. "Well chosen, sir. May I ask your own line of interest?"

It was diplomatically asked. Most people said, "Are you a physicist like your father?" and thought themselves tactful because they hadn't said "great physicist." So instead of giving my standard deflective response ("I'm involved in pneumatic generation of sequences of higher order vibratory harmonics designed to induce auditory maximization of local endorphin production"), I just told him, "I'm a composer and musician."

He smiled—no smirk component at all, this time. "This voyage has just become distinctly less intolerable. And what is your axe?"

"Saxophone."

Now he *beamed*. It made him look like a cherub who you do not yet know has just lifted your wallet. "Which one?"

"Well, since they didn't count against my mass allowance, I brought the standard four. Soprano, tenor, alto, and baritone."

He shivered with joy. "I often wish I could manage to make myself believe in a god, but hardly ever so that I can *thank* him for something. Welcome aboard, Maestro."

"You haven't even heard me play, yet."

He nodded. "And the agony is delicious. I'll leave you to sett—oh, my word! I don't see them!"

"What?"

"Tell me you didn't entrust your instruments to your luggage?"

"I didn't have any oth—"

"Don't panic yet!" he cried, sprang for the door so fast it barely had time to iris out of his way, and used both hands to swing himself out into the direction of traffic. "There may still be time," his voice said as it dopplered away.

A hand closed on my shoulder. The bone held. "Do not worry, friend Joel," Balvovatz said. "A snitch in time saves mine." He let go before I would have had to scream, whacked me on that shoulder blade, and drifted away again. Somehow I retained my grip on the overhead light, but it took me a moment to stabilize again.

"He's right," Herb assured me. "It takes time to wreck luggage, and they always save the best stuff for last."

"And they're all afraid of Sol," Pat put in.

"They should be," Herb said. "They're staying behind—so he doesn't need them alive."

"This is your bunk over here, Joel," Pat told me. "Right

above my own. Unless you care to discuss the matter with pistols?"

"Knives better," Balvovatz said.

"Fine with me," I said. Once we were under way it would be the upper bunk on the right. "I've had a preference for the upper ever since I figured out that farts are heavier than air."

He grinned evilly. (I don't care what my spell-checker says, of course there's such a word. "In an evil manner"—okay?) "Not mine."

I carefully jaunted, in a direction soon to be known as "down," over to my bed, and docked with it. I'm not sure why, since I had no luggage or other belongings to secure. I guess just to symbolize taking ownership. It didn't wait to find out. The moment I grabbed it and started using it to brake my arriving mass, one of the two (*two?*) folding angle-braces intended to support it under acceleration tore right out of the plasteel bulkhead. All three bolts—and two of the bolts on the other support. The bed immediately rotated around the remaining bolt, about sixty degrees clockwise, and jammed to a halt against the top of the folded-up lower bunk. This left me dangling from the other end of it like a tyro, trying desperately to clutch bed as well as bedclothes and avoid the indignity of being thrown altogether. I never even noticed banging my face against the wall.

The shriek of frictionally stressed plasteel, and my scrabbling-rat noises, gave way to an omnipresent rather glutinous sound, which was like silence, but different. As I stabilized myself, I realized it was the sound of men not laughing.

I turned to face the room and made, very loudly, the sound of a man not murdering anyone, yet.

Pat Williamson pointed to a spot just "below" me. I glanced down, and in a moment realized that his own bed was *not* folded up against the bulkhead. It was duct-taped to it. His had torn out of the wall, too. I could see the bolt holes. They were *not* empty. Each contained a little shiny-ended bolt stump. All six had snapped off clean. I looked, and all five of my failed bolts were the same. I looked back to Pat, and raised my eyebrows inquisitively.

He spread his hands, palm up. He wanted to explain, but couldn't do it louder than he was not laughing at me.

Balvovatz took it. "Well come into *Shuffled*, Joel. Do not worry. Is warrantee. Air leaks out, just say so. Kang sends more from Terra."

Maybe my expression made Herb stop wanting to laugh. "There's still time," he said softly. "You can still jump ship and go back down to Terra, if you're one of those fussbudgets who expects everything to *work*. It's not too late to be sensible."

I closed my eyes. All I could see was Terra . . . with Jinny's face. "Yes it is," I said. "Where's the duct tape?"

I LATER LEARNED the bunk-support bolts had been specified by a Kang Cartel engineer, and supplied by a da Costa Associates subsidiary. Both halves of the financial Siamese-twin behemoth that was underwriting this little interstellar venture. The desk that wouldn't interface properly with my PDC or phone despite nominal system compatibility for the next two days was the other way round: da Costa design, Kang manufacturing. And the blame for the complex cluster of systems failures that combined to keep all my luggage *except* my four saxophones (Sol Short rescued them, somehow) from catching up to me for another two weeks was, I was eventually able to establish, divided up roughly evenly between the two houses.

Fortunately nudity was not taboo aboard the *Sheffield*. It was not commonplace either—but nobody got upset if I sat around the laundry room naked while waiting for my only set of clothing to dry, each day, or went to and from the 'fresher without a robe. (There were ship-issue jumpsuits and robes I could have had. I preferred skin. They were, visibly, the plasteel bolts of the clothing world.)

I did end up with a lot of time to reflect that most of the Conrad empire products I had ever purchased had worked pretty reliably. And I retained just enough sanity to realize this was probably an omen of some kind, perhaps even an unfavorable one.

But I had told Herb the truth. It was way too late to change my mind. The center of my personal Solar System had turned out to be a dangerously variable star. It was imperative to break free of her pull, while I still could, and go somewhere else, far far away.

7

> I only know we loved in vain—
> I only feel—Farewell!—Farewell!
>
> —Lord Byron

Jinny phoned two days later, about eight hours before we left.

Theoretically she should not have been able to. I'd contributed my phone to the ship's recycler on arrival, and gotten a new one—under a false name, using nonexistent credit, and paying a premium for a *super*-unlisted code. That account would vanish like a bubble when the first bill went unpaid, of course. But by then I expected I would no longer need one. I only needed it now to say good-bye to a few friends and acquaintances, and to dispose of my few remaining assets on Ganymede.

I *think* that might just have been good enough to foil, or at least slow, a Federation agent hunting me. Against a Conrad, it was a gesture. As I slipped in my earbead, I reflected that she could probably have called me five minutes after I'd activated the phone. Her first words practically admitted as much.

"Damn it, Joel, I admire your stubbornness. I really do. You've held out to the last possible second, I give you that. But we are *out of time now*. Stop this foolishness and come home, this fucking minute!"

I'd known this call would come. It wasn't surprise, even at

the word I had never heard her use, that kept me from answering her for several seconds. It was just her face. There on the inside of my wrist, thumbnail-sized, poor quality 2-D image. I had never seen her so clearly or so vividly.

She had never looked more beautiful. I wanted to eat my whole forearm. Her image cut off at her waist, but I could see the rest of her almost as clearly in my mind's eye. What blurred it a bit was that she was wearing an outfit considerably more expensive than anything I had ever seen her in. That realization restored the power of speech to me.

"I can't, Jinny. It's too late. We were out of time yesterday. The last boat has—"

"You idiot, I can be there to get you in two hours! How long do you need to pack your four saxo—"

"Bring me where, did you say?"

"—phones and your one spare—what?"

"Where exactly is this home you speak of? Certainly not your apartment. Some mansion in Nepal accessible only by copter? A secret village at the bottom of the Marianas Trench? A stealthed palace at L-1 or—no, why would you care about saving fuel—somewhere in space, then? Or perhaps a few kilometers below the apparent surface of Jupiter, there floats a—"

She overrode me by yelling, *"I deserve that!"* I was so surprised I stopped talking. "And I ask you to believe that I have already administered it to myself, and to trust that I will continue to do so, okay? You can kick me all you like, I agree I have it coming—but you won't be able to if I don't come get you and bring you back home, and even my window is closing!"

I shook my head wearily. "I meant what I said. Where is 'home' for us? No place we've ever been. No place I've ever been. I don't think we even mean the same things by the word—or have any clear idea what the discrepancies are, either one of us."

"Joel, I didn't have any choice, why can't you see that? I *couldn't* tell you, not until—"

"I know that."

"You do? Then—"

"Jinny, we've never really met."

"We *can*. We *will* meet, and we'll love each other—we already know how—and the money won't make any damn difference, none at all."

I had to grab something with my left hand just then to keep myself from colliding with a bed; I'd been drifting free since her incoming call had caused me to lose my handhold on my own desk. I guess from her perspective it looked like I was turning away. "Joel, I love you!" she cried.

I started to regain eye contact . . . and paused. I found myself looking around my room. My cruddy little dump of a room, just a bit worse than what I'd have expected as a freshman at university, possessed of few and feeble amenities, shared with three other smelly hairy creatures. In a place where nearly everyplace smelled faintly like feet, and *all* the water tasted like a school hallway water fountain, and the food aspired to be two-star, and you always saw the same people. The *Sheffield* would in fact be remarkably like another nineteen years of our courtship as we had known it until recently. Freshman year of university, forever. The only thing the big tin can had to recommend it, really, was that it was going to leap the Big Deep—

I yanked the phone back up to my eyes. "Jinny, come with me!"

Shocked silence. On both sides. I recovered first.

"Right now. Without a suitcase. Without a pot. If the money really doesn't matter, walk away—come homestead with me on the other end of the rainbow. I know you don't know how, any more than I know about your world—but I'll teach you. Trust me: it's a *lot* easier to grow potatoes than empires. It's more satisfying to get in a good crop than to play with billions of people's lives and fortunes. It leaves you time to make babies, and to pay attention to them, and to occasionally notice each other past the babies and make more of them. For God's sake, Jinny, you remember the song. Let's die on the way to the stars! Together . . ."

I knew exactly how stupid and romantic and naïve my words were. I had never intended to speak them—aloud.

They left my mouth with the force and honesty of vomit, but with the same despair as well. Without a particle of hope.

That was only born when a full second had gone by and she still had not answered yet. At birth, it was tinier than a lepton's shadow at noon. It took less than another second to grow into something large enough to choke on. I was beginning to worry by the time she broke the silence.

But the problem solved itself, when my heartbeat ceased. "God damn you, Joel, you gave me every reason to believe you were an adult. With a pair of balls, and at least half a brain. You *cannot* be this cowardly and stupid and prideful, I won't tolerate it. I've invested too much time in you! I'm coming up there, and I'm—Joel? Joel!"

My arms had gone limp with cessation of pulse, of course: she was looking at my left hip. Purely from reflex politeness I pulled my wrist back up. So then I had to say something, and thus began breathing again.

"Jinny, listen to me. Please. I honestly don't know if I have what it takes to be a Conrad, I admit that. But I don't know if *anybody* does, so I'm not at all afraid to find out. What I do know is, it's not something I *want* to be. I guess it seems self-evident to you that any rational man would. So you won't want an irrational husband." She tried to interrupt, and for once I overrode her. "If you think even your gran'ther has enough proctors and bailiffs to delay the launch of a Kang/da Costa Cartel starship by five minutes so you can arrest a junior apprentice farmer for breach of promise, you're being irrational yourself. Now, listen to this last part, and don't interrupt until I'm done, and then you can call me any dirty names you like until they light the candle in eight hours and reception goes to hell for a while. Okay?"

"Go ahead."

She was deploying her ultimate weapon and we both knew it: her voice was trembling on the edge of tears, and they were absolutely genuine.

My own voice tightened. "Jinny—Jinny Hamilton—you were my first love. You may be the last. You certainly are the last I will have in this Solar System. For what it's worth, I forgive you for not telling me who—what—you really were. I understand, I really do: you had no choice, no other way to play it. I am sorry, genuinely sorry, that you wasted your investment. Maybe *nobody* is as sorry as I am. I'm pretty certain I'm in the top five, anyway. All I can tell you is that the prospectus you were offered was complete and accurate in every particular. I answered every question I was asked. Honestly." I took a deep breath. "My own investments haven't done too well lately, either. Thanks for teaching me to dance, and listening to me play my music. Really. Good luck in your future investments. Maybe I'll see you in a couple of hundred years, and we can swap notes." Anything else to say? Yes—but all of it angry. Delete it. It was way too late for anger to serve any purpose worth the indignity. "Your turn."

The pause this time was probably as long as the earlier one, but with no hope in it, it went by faster.

"Good luck, Joel. I really am sorry." She let go on the last word, cried so hard the screen image became a sideways close-up of her scrunched-up left eye.

Somehow I held on myself. "I know, honey. Me, too. Really."

"Good-bye."

The phone was dead.

For some reason I was not. So I went looking for strong drink, and did the best I could. By the time we left the Solar System I was far from feeling no pain—I was probably in maximum emotional pain, and in considerable physical discomfort from being loaded in free fall—but I was momentarily too stupid to mind either. Terra sure looked pretty, shimmering there in the simulated window, and slow shrinking didn't spoil the effect at all. In fact, the smaller she got, the prettier she looked.

The same seemed to hold true for Mama Sol. She was prettiest just before I passed out, as a single pixel of pure white in a sea of ink.

WE DID NOT really achieve enough initial velocity for the sun to show detectable shrinkage, that first day: that last view was an effect of my vision graying out. A matter/anti-matter torch is not something you want to start up quickly and max the throttle—certainly not in the vicinity of an inhabited planet! We left High Orbit under conventional fusion drive, albeit a hellacious big one. Even in my stupor, it seemed noisy.

Unsurprisingly, the menu of recreational drugs obtainable on board was considerably shorter and tamer than what I'd had available to me back in Vancouver. A man who wished to stupefy himself pretty much had to rely on alcohol and/or marijuana. They did the job, in combination.

But once you used your month's ration of either one it was *gone*, so the binge burned itself out faster than it might have if I'd had more powerful tools. By the time I had binged, crashed, died, revived, and been restored to feeble continued interest in events outside my own skull and thorax and indigestive system, the Captain had just throttled the fusion plant back from a space drive to a mere power plant, and things got much quieter again for a while. The sun looked just perceptibly smaller in disk size, there in my simulated window . . . and considerably dimmer than normal, even though all the other stars now seemed *brighter* than usual. I thought of trying to locate Ganymede by eye, to bid farewell to my birth planet, but it was already way too late; she was in opposition.

Within an hour, the Old Man had gotten the antimatter torch lit, and some noise and other vibration did resume, but by no means as much, or as loud. Or as unpleasant. Less like an ongoing earthquake, more like a waterfall, or rapids in a stream.

Then the sun's dwindling could be detected, if you had the patience to watch long enough.

I did. For far longer than made any sense I can explain. There could be no Key West sunset, no final Last of the Light. I knew that even by the end of my journey I would not have traveled so far that Sol's light could not still reach me. It would be old light, that was all.

And still I watched, until Herb came and dragged me off for dinner. I felt so weary, it was a noticeable strain to be

back in normal gravity again, for the first time in so many
months. Free fall is as addictively comfortable as the womb.

THREE KINDS OF gentleman adventurers participated in the
Sheffield's voyage. The real gents, senior partners, invested
very large amounts of money, and remained behind at Sol
System to see how it all worked out. Just below them were
the limited partners, who put in considerably less money, but
tossed their personal bodies and futures into the pot as well.
At the bottom rung were the provisional partners, whose entire stake was their head, hands, and health.

Chumps like me.

My father died thinking he had provided well for me, because he had. But such provisions don't always last. By the
time my orphan's allowance had run out at eighteeen, market
shifts (as always, unexpected) had all but wiped out the
value of the stock Dad had left me; I'd had to sell nearly
everything to finance that last semester at Fermi. After that,
I'd been pinning all my hopes on the scholarship that Conrad had blocked.

Now my only remaining assets were nominal: some
shares in one of the very earliest starships—which had vanished in the Big Deep years ago. They were worth so little
I'd instructed my guardian not to bother selling them; the in-
come would scarcely have covered the assorted charges and
taxes. They weren't worthless, quite: there was always the
infinitesimal chance that the *New Frontiers* might be found
and rescued one day. But no missing starship had ever been
heard from again. Only once had they even been able to establish just what had gone wrong.

So I took my meals with most of the others, in Stark Hall,
one of the ship's three mess halls, designed to accommodate
up to a third of us at any one time with good solid unspec-
tacular food, drink, and ancillaries, without charge. But for
those who had the money and inclination, there were also alternatives. Such as the Horn of Plenty, the *Sheffield*'s equivalent of an upscale nightclub, with four-star food and more
expensive amusement options, open all three shifts.

I had not expected to ever set foot in the place, unless a

live waiter's job should open up, but it was there that Herb insisted on dragging me for my last dinner in the Solar System.

I did try to resist. I had known several novelists, but none with even as much money as I had. "Herb, I don't know about you, but I can't afford this. There's an old PreCollapse blues song that goes, 'If money did my talkin'/I couldn't breathe a sigh—' and that's . . ."

And my voice trailed off, because the next lines of the song suddenly loomed up out of memory and clotheslined me: "But my baby's love is one thing/even money can't buy/Ain't that fine?"

Herb said, "This meal is on me. You have almost nothing in your system but poisons and toxins. The food you take on to absorb it all should be of the highest quality."

"I don't know if I'll be able to pay you back."

"I know: you probably won't, and I'll get to hold it over you forever. Cheap dominance. Come on, it's right up ahead."

I stopped us at the door and tried to thank him, but he brushed it away. "Sheer self-interest. I have to live with you."

They seemed to know him inside. As we were conducted to our booth, I had that weird feeling you get entering a place that's a little out of your reach, the irrational sensation that everyone is looking at you and can tell you're out of place, which is caused by everyone looking at you and knowing you're out of place. Herb had a way of walking as though *they* were out of place, but he was a broad-minded man. Jinny had had it, too. . . .

A dance performance was in progress on a cleared area of the floor, something classic-modern, I think, though I have trouble keeping the distinctions straight. I don't think ballet is ever done in silence. Serious dance, at any rate, not mating dance, and apparently very well done, by three energetic people a little older than me. They finished to thunderous applause as we crossed the room, and sprinted backstage.

I did notice a bandstand, an interesting one, just beyond the dancers' Marley floor. It was powered down at the moment, unoccupied, but it looked nicely equipped. The keyboard system was built into a very good replica of a

PreCollapse grand piano; it looked as though the player could produce "real," mechanically produced acoustic sound with the thing if he chose. The drum kit too could have produced reasonable accompaniment for most purposes even powered down. The stringed instrument cases I saw were all obviously for either acoustic or hybrids. I mentioned that to Herb as we were seated.

"You watch," he said, "pre-electric music is going to become very popular in this ship over the next twenty years. We all know deep down we're going to a place where we may not have power to spare for luxuries for some time to come. Subconsciously we're preparing. Brunch menus, coffee and orange juice for two, please."

I hadn't noticed the waitress approach until he spoke, and she was gone by the time I turned around. Yet I later learned she was human. "Brunch?" I asked, checking the time.

"In a restaurant that never closes, in a ship with three shifts, it's always brunchtime. Or dinnertime. Or midnight snacktime, or tea. You need serious food that doesn't challenge digestion; ergo, brunch."

The food was indeed wonderful. It penetrated my depression, forced me to concede to myself that I did have some interest in continued life, even if I had no idea why. I was continually conscious of a sensation of having gnawed off one of my feet to escape a trap, a pit-of-the-stomach feeling that wouldn't go away. But for some reason it didn't interfere with my appetite much, or even my mood.

Herb, I was very gratified to learn, was the kind of man who did not chatter over his food. Save for a handful of conversational politenesses, he used his mouth for intake only. It gave me permission to do the same. We already knew we were going to be friends. And there was going to be plenty of time to use up our conversation stores.

When he did speak, it was with a friend's directness. "So," he said, setting down his fork, "have you decided whether you're going to cut your throat or not? Inquiring minds want to know."

"No."

He relaxed slightly. "Yes, you have. You're not."

"I really hate it when somebody tells me what I'm thinking. Or are you a telepath?"

"As a matter of fact, yes, but not the way you mean. A real one."

I snorted. "Right. *Your* mind isn't fast enough."

In fiction, a telepath can read minds. A real telepath is just a glorified radio, with a single receiver. But *really* glorified—way faster than any radio. Our time rate and the System's were already diverging very slightly, under the constraints of Einsteinian physics, and would get steadily worse for the next twenty years. Every day, radio and laser signals took just a tiny bit longer to cross the widening gulf between us, and by the time we reached our destination it would take them the greater part of a century. But telepathy, for reasons nobody understands, takes place *instantaneously*, across any distance yet measured. That single perverse exception to the laws of the universe, and the fact that the gene for it is dominant, make a star-traveling civilization just barely possible. Our ship, like all of them, carried several people capable of telepathic rapport with a partner back in the System, usually, but not always, their identical twin. With luck, their children would be able to maintain the link.

Herb was looking at me strangely.

At first, the way his jaw was squared off, and his eyes seemed to have receded deeper into their sockets, and his shoulders were slightly raised, all combined to tell me he was *angry*. That was odd. Then a second later I saw I had misread the signals completely: he was *amused,* trying his best not to laugh in my face. At something I had done in the last few moments, apparently. Or said . . .

He saw me start to catch on, and let the laugh out.

"Are you *kidding* me?"

"Did you really think I was accepted into this company because I'm a *writer*? You figure a fledgling colony, fighting to stay alive and establish a foothold, has a lot of use for fiction?"

"You never mentio—"

"You never asked."

"Who——?"

"My sister Li," he said. "In Oregon. The one on Terra. Two hours a day, we handle message traffic between Kang/da Costa HQ and the colony, and we're available free-lance for private communications."

"I never noticed you doing that!"

"How would you? I stare into space, and then start typing like crazy. It must look exactly like I'm writing a story. Sometimes I am, if what I'm supposed to type annoys me enough."

"Holy shit." I was so busy rearranging my presumptions and misconceptions in my head, I forgot I had not yet expressed an opinion. "I can't believe it."

"Believe it. I'm a telepath. A communicator."

His voice cued me. A lot of people are weirded out by telepaths. A few people call them the kind of names that cause a proctor to show up. He was waiting to learn whether or not his new friend and roommate for the next two decades was one of those people.

Quickly I said, "No, I mean I can't believe there's some poor girl back in the System who looks just like you."

His shoulders dropped. "Back to our argument—I was winning. How can you stay a bachelor? Have you no appreciation for fine womanhood? No sense of obligation—"

My mind took a left. Talking about Jinny and the Conrads had reminded me of something, a small burr under my saddle. An unfulfilled obligation behind me. "As a matter of fact, I do. Both. So much so that I'm going to presume on our friendship and ask you for a favor."

"What friendship?"

"I know, but it's all I've got. I want to send a private message back to Terra."

He frowned. "Phone still works. So does mail."

"No, I mean *private*. I need to thank a young lady for defying her grandfather to help me out of a tight spot, and I don't want to risk getting her in trouble."

His frown deepened. "Just tell me one thing. Is this young lady rich and beautiful?"

"That's two things. And yes to both."

"Maybe there's hope for you yet. Okay, this once, I'll do it. You want visual, or just voice?"

"Voice is fine."

He shook his head. "Hopeless. Name?"

"Evelyn Conrad."

"How do you want to route it to her?"

"Through an intermediary I think I can trust. Can your sister put a really serious privacy shield on a message?"

"Yes," was all he said.

"Okay. Ask her to get it to a Dorothy Robb, two b's."

"Address?"

"Ms. Robb is the Chief Enabler for Conrad of Conrad."

Herb came as close as I would ever see him come to betraying surprise. His nostrils flared just perceptibly for a moment, as if he had begun to doubt his deodorant. His eyes did a funny little thing where for just an instant they tried to widen and narrow at the same time. There was maybe a quarter-second hitch in the soundtrack, and then he said, "I take it back. There *is* no hope for you."

I spread my hands. "When did I claim there was?"

"You know a Conrad. Well enough that she defied . . . oh. Kindly tell me her granddad is not—"

I nodded. "Conrad."

"Of course. She defied Conrad of Conrad for you. And you're *here*."

"Herb, she's seven years old."

He smiled broadly. It had taken him about ten seconds to gear up and start *enjoying* this. "To be thoroughly sure. Say no more. Unless you want to live."

So I told him the whole damned story.

I'D ALWAYS KNOWN I would, *some* day. It was going to be a long voyage. But not in the first year. I probably couldn't have told it yet to anyone who didn't listen as well as he did. He didn't mind if I needed a couple of minutes of silence to get a sentence completed.

When I was finished, he took a couple himself. Then he said softly, "Amigo, you're the first person I've talked to in this bucket of rust so far that actually has a sensible reason to be here. All right, you want little Evelyn to know you're grateful for getting you out of there, but without tipping the Old Man, have I got it?"

"Something like, 'I enjoyed the last moments of our relationship even more than the first,' maybe. Do you really think you can get that to her privately? Now that you know who she is?"

He closed his eyes, then opened them again. "Li says yes. She knows a way. You don't need to know what it is. It's covered."

"Thanks, Herb."

He lit up one of his cigarettes. "Well, at least the cord is cut clean. With Jinny, I mean. Seldom in history have any humans gotten to have a breakup as final as the one you've had. By the time we get to 23 Skiddoo in twenty years, she'll be . . . 108 years old, if she was honest about her age."

We were making a jump of about eighty-five light-years—at such a hair-raising fraction of c that the trip would seem to us to take twenty years, total. But back in the normal universe, clocks run faster, thanks to Dr. Einstein's Paradox. To an observer at, say, Tombaugh Station around Pluto, our voyage would appear to take roughly ninety and one-half Standard years.

"Of course, with *her* money, she'll probably still look twenty, by then," Herb added. "But you'll know better."

"I don't want her old," I said bleakly. "I don't want her to suffer. I want her to be here with me."

"Happy to be your mate, even if you both starve on alien soil. Was she really that dumb?"

"Obviously not."

"You'll love again. I'm sorry to be the one to tell you."

I grimaced. "Not soon."

He shook his head. "It doesn't have to be too soon. You have twenty years to decide what you want in a wife. But don't put it off too long, either. The supply is limited, and you don't look like a man who'd be happy as a celibate."

"Don't be so sure," I muttered darkly.

"Look, you have decisions to make. Some short-term, some long-term. If you plan to spend the next twenty years licking your wounds, and letting those decisions make themselves for you, you're going to be a tough friend to have. I suggest you get started working on them."

"Decisions like what?"

He leaned back in his chair. "What do you want to *do*?"

A PERFECTLY SIMPLE, sensible question: the logical first step in making any plan.

He might just as well have whacked me in the forehead with a plank.

I did not really see a burst of bright white light, and then find myself on the ground beside my horse, godstruck. The earth did not literally tremble and roar at my feet. My heart probably did not actually pause, and I have it on good authority that time did not, at any time, in fact come to a stop. But Herb's perfectly obvious question hit me with that kind of impact. He and the room went away while I tried to cope with it.

Surely, I thought, I have an answer for him. But I could not find one. I rewound mental tape and realized with shock that I had not asked myself that question once since the night of my graduation from Fermi.

Throughout all the terrible days since, I had been focused intently and exclusively on what I did *not* want to do.

Well, *that* had been silly of me, hadn't it? Now that I was finally and forever safe from the terrible danger of becoming one of the richest humans alive, married to the girl of my dreams, perhaps it was time to give some quantum of thought to what I might find preferable. If anything.

Great blathering mother of morons, what was I going to *do* with the next twenty years? Or the twenty after that, if it came to it?

HERB WAS SAYING something. Why did I know that? Oh. He had touched my hand to get my attention. I rewound my ears. "—don't have to come up with an answer right this minute," he had said.

I wasn't absolutely sure I agreed—but just then I heard my name called. It was Solomon Short, in a larger nearby

booth with three companions. He waved emphatically to us
to come and join them. I looked to Herb for help, and he
shrugged, so we got up and went over to the other booth.
Sol's companions slid over to make room for us, while he
made introductions.

As I'd guessed, his friends were all Relativists like him. I
had now met five of the six people on whom our whole voyage depended. Nearest me was Tenzin Hideo Itokawa, a tiny
man whom I learned later was a Zen Buddhist monk; then, I
got only that he had twinkling eyes and seemed to lack vocal
cords. Between him and Sol was a hearty and voluptuous
woman named London McBee, who turned out to be married to George R Marsden, the Relativist I'd literally bumped
into in my first seconds aboard. She and Sol volleyed with
words, vying to outpun each other. But the most striking of
the three was clearly the man on the other side of the table,
Peter Kindred, and for the life of me I could not decide why.

There was something electric and sheepish about him,
that's the best I can say it—he gave off the disconcerting
sensation that at any moment he was likely to switch from
talking to quacking like a duck, or barking like a dog—that
at any given time there was utterly no way of telling *what* he
might take it into his head to do—and that at the same time,
he was just a little embarrassed by it. It was more than just
mad eyes, though he surely had those. His name seemed
ironically chosen; he had "Loose Cannon" written all over
him. Sol and London both seemed to find him delightful.

I was overawed. Most of the ship's power, literally, was
seated at that table. I'm used to famous people, even great
people. This was different. In a pinch, the *Sheffield* could
have gotten by without her captain—but her Relativists were
essential. These men and woman spent their days reaching
into the cosmic vacuum with their naked organic brains, and
persuaded it to yield up its inconceivable energy in a measured fashion.

I realize that description has about as much meaning as
saying that a nuclear fission plant works because the gods
breathe upon its mojo in such a way as to cause it to be far
out. One of my hopes, as I sat down, was to perhaps solicit a

better explanation from one or more of the Relativists I was privileged to talk to. But I got off to a bad start.

Things went fine at first. Sol introduced his companions to us. Then he introduced Herb to them, giving them a two-sentence thumbnail bio. Then he introduced me—and that's where it went sour. His second sentence for me began, inevitably, with, "His father was the ___"

But by the second word, Peter Kindred had gone berserk. He kicked his chair over backward with his butt, leaped backward over it, landed several feet away in combat crouch, making finger gestures to ward off evil.

At me.

I opened my mouth—

"SHUT UP!" he screamed.

I blinked.

"Not a word! AIYEEE!" He averted his gaze. *"No facial expressions!"*

I looked at Herb, then Sol, then everybody else, without finding anything I could use. I decided I needed to leave, started to rise.

He screamed, hopped back a pace, and snatched a plate from someone's table, holding it like a cream pie in an ancient comedy. "Back!" he shrieked. "You lunatic! Are you crazy? What the fuck are you trying to *do* to me?"

I shrugged. I had to: it was all he had left me.

It was the last straw. He shut his eyes, made a strangling sound, turned, and left the room at high speed. Taking the plate with him, despite loud protest from its owner.

"Don't mind Peter," Sol said imperturbably.

"He's terrified of Centipede's Dilemma," said London.

"Ahhh," I said. "Of course."

"He's rude," Herb said.

"No, no," I said. "I think I actually get it." And after I explained my thinking, they agreed that I did.

WITHOUT ITS RELATIVISTS, no starship can operate its primary drive, open the Ikimono Portal into the dark energy universe. Not without becoming a Gamma Ray Burst in short order, anyway.

That monstrous engine of mass creation had not been invoked, yet, and could not be until we'd gotten a little farther away from Sol—but without it and its kind, most star travel would have been impossible, and the rest would have awaited the development of suspended animation to accomplish. And thanks to the Prophet's distaste for fiddling with God's allegedly clear intentions, safe suspended animation still seems to lie as far in the future as it did centuries ago.

Thanks to Relativists, though, mankind finally had a drive that could really take it to the stars, within normal human life span. The only problem was that, countless generations of folklore to the contrary, the relativistic engine really was the first engine ever invented that literally required the constant attention of a human operator to function: the Relativist. Somehow, an organic brain was able—*some* organic brains were able—to ensure that every time Doc Schrödinger opened his box, what came out was a live cat. Even if none had been in there to start with.

The last I'd heard, the entire Solar System held something less than two hundred humans—out of dozens of billions!—who had the necessary combination of talents, skills, attitudes, and education to perform that task reliably. More than half of them, I had read, wanted to do something else. The rest probably commanded a higher salary than Jinny's father.

When the mathematician/poet and Soto Zen Buddhist priest Hoitsu Ikimono Roshi (whose name means "life," "living creatures," "farm products," or "uncooked food") discovered the first practical star drive in 2237—or perhaps was merely the first such discoverer to survive—he thereby created the profession called "Relativist." The best definition ever offered to the layman of what a Relativist does is (naturally) the Roshi's: he said they meditate on and with the engine, in order to make it happy enough to function.

He held back the part about how they dissuade the star drive from becoming a star . . . until humankind had invested heavily in star travel, both economically and emotionally. Fortunately that did not take long: the Roshi's only significant character flaw was reluctance to keep a joke to himself. (A great pity: it finally killed him . . . a joke he must have loved.)

Technically one could argue that Relativists should be called relativistic engineers. Without them, no engine; *res ipse loquitur*. But as it happens, the term "engineer" is already in use—by people who find the very kind of science that relativism requires to be witchcraft, spooky science, mumbo jumbo, perhaps even hocus-pocus. To them, it stops *just* short of being that most despised of all modes of thinking: a religion. The very first word in its technical description ruins all hope of conversation, sets engineers' teeth on edge, and makes all the hairs bristle at the backs of their necks.

Quantum ramjet.

The quantum ramjet relies on the well-established theory of quantum fluctuations in the energy of the vacuum. These occur throughout the universe on extremely small scales of time and distance. Over times on the order of 10^{-15} second and lengths of about 10^{-55} centimeter, masses as high as 10^{-5} grams and energies as large as 10^{-6} ergs pop in and out of existence interminably. Conventional physics supports this picture, but it is an entirely different matter to make *use* of vacuum quantum fluctuations to propel a starship. A quantum ramjet, first proposed by H. David Froning (an engineer!) back before the Collapse, would work by "ingesting" the energy of the quantum fluctuations and converting it to propulsive energy. If the quantum starship could tap only a very tiny fraction of the theoretically available mass/energy of the vacuum, it could accelerate rapidly to relativistic velocities. But until Ikimono Roshi tried visualizing something in his mind, as he sat zazen in his ship in the Belt one day, and found himself half a light-year from home before he could stop doing it, no one had a clue how this might be accomplished. It almost certainly never occurred to anyone before then that human attention might be a necessary condition for the phenomenon. It was fortunate indeed that Hoitsu Ikimono *was* a Roshi—a Zen master, for whom sustained attention was a given—or he might never have made his way back to Sol to spread the news.

The philosophical implications of the quantum ramjet alone are startling. If, as the inflationary theory of cosmology mandates, the universe evolved from a quantum fluctuation that somehow grew to its present enormous scale, the same thing might occur as a matter of course in the heart of the quantum ramjet. Does each quantum ramjet create and destroy countless universes as it travels our cosmos, and are their crews as gods to the countless beings in the universes that support their flight?

The engineers have already left the room to vomit. And I can't really say I blame them. But who knows? You, maybe?

To an engineer, it's simple. If you can explain what you're doing in numbers, and prove them, it's science. If you can't, it isn't. End of story. There is much to recommend this view: it is essentially what keeps the black heart of the Prophet rotting in his stained coffin where it belongs. And any Relativist will happily admit she does not know how she does what she does. Nobody does. It's not at all certain, in fact, that anybody ever will.

One thing is generally agreed, however: the man who had so far come *closest* to providing an explanation—who had at least provided some useful mathematical tools for approaching the problem, and pointed out a promising theoretical path through what had been an impenetrable thicket—was a Nobel prize-winning physicist from Ganymede named Ben Johnston.

My late father.

No wonder Kindred was terrified of me. Kindred did not *want* even the slightest morsel of understanding of the process by which he made himself one of the wealthiest individuals alive to creep into his mind. The thing that most Relativists fear the most is *burnout*: utter annihilation of personality. Not Kindred. He might even have yearned for it a little. As London had said, he was terrified of the Centipede's Dilemma. Once the centipede got to pondering just how he managed all those legs, he couldn't do it anymore. Kindred feared that if he understood what he did, he might stop being able to pull it off. For all he knew, my father might have told me some significant datum before he died, shared some crucial insight that I might be stupid enough to blurt out, whether I understood it myself or not. The risk was tiny, but to him the stakes were *everything*. So he averted his eyes and fled.

An engineer would call that raw superstition, primitive bullshit, childish magical thinking. But nobody cares what an engineer thinks about this topic, until he can make a big can full of people move at close to lightspeed without carrying any fuel for its primary drive. So of course they're working on it, and good luck to them.

But I can't think of any engineers I'd have been as excited to talk with over postprandial coffee as the three Relativists who remained at the table.

NEARLY AT ONCE, and without warning, I found myself skateboarding right off a conversational precipice.

One minute I was enjoying the ride; the next, I looked down and saw, kilometers below, the rock-strewn base of the cliff I had just left behind me.

Why it took me by surprise, I cannot tell you. I admit it: in retrospect, I look dumb. How smart would I have had to be to guess that one of the very first polite questions to be directed at me would be:

"And what do you do, Joel?"

Now, *where* did I put that parachute?

It happened to be London who asked. The correct honest answer was: *it sheets the bit out of me*. I hadn't even had time—during my walk here from my room—to draw up a master list of my options, arranged by category, much less zero in on anything. What I did these days was mostly get loaded, and mourn my lost love. It seemed to be all I had been doing, for quite a while now.

I kind of did not want to tell three of the most interesting people on the ship that I was that big a fool. But I had no other answer to give them.

Technically I could have said, "I'm a farmer," without perjuring myself. I had contracted, as part of the price of my ticket, to spend twenty-one hours a week working down on the *Sheffield*'s Agricultural Decks, sharing my putatively valuable experience and expertise in hydroponic farming. Somehow I didn't feel like going with that answer, either.

I am no longer sure, but I think I had decided on an enigmatic smile as my best response, when Sol answered for me. "You're going to love it. Joel plays the sax."

"And composes," Herb amended for me.

I opened my mouth—

"How wonderful," said Hideo the little monk.

I closed my mouth—

"Saxophone? Oh, I *do* love it," London said. "Are you any good, Joel?"

That one, at least, I had numerous stock answers for on tap. I tossed out the first one that came up. "I *think* so. Being tone deaf, I've never been sure."

"Sol?"

Sol shrugged. "I haven't heard him play yet."

"Herb?"

Herb shrugged, too. "Hasn't played a note in my hearing yet either. Stingy bastard."

"Nonetheless I am prepared to bet cash he's very good," Sol said.

"On what basis?" Hideo asked.

"I've examined his instrument closely. It is the saxophone of a man who loves it dearly, and is loved in return."

I stared at him. "You can *tell* that?"

He just nodded.

"Well, we simply have to hear you, then," London said. "Solomon, do you think the management would have any objection if we were to send for Joel's instrument and ask him to play for us, here? Failing that, we could adjourn to my cabin."

I took advantage of the discussion that ensued to think, hard and fast. I was on the edge of being committed, to something I had not chosen. Lately.

Playing sax and composing music *had been* what I did, once. They had been just about all I did, aside from thinking about Jinny. They and she had together constituted what I was, what I wanted, what I was for. Together. It had been a long time since I had thought of a future as a composer without Jinny as part of the picture.

Maybe when all the dust settled, and all the fallout faded to endurable levels again, I would still—or again—want to be a composer/ musician. I had to admit, in fact, that it was highly likely. What the hell else was I qualified for? What else did I love nearly so much? (Don't answer that one.)

But I had not *made* that decision yet. That had been the old plan, for a universe that had Jinny in it.

And more than just that, I suddenly realized with dizzy shock—it had been a plan for a universe that had the entire existing musical establishment of the Solar System as part of the given. All the other musicians, critics, and composers, all the vast potential audience, all the sources of funding, all the supporting institutions. In a society of many billions, composer is an honorable and even sometimes honored occupation. With a target audience that huge, one need not reach all that many of them to earn a living, and respect. Now that I was going to be living, forever, in a society of five hundred people and their offspring, everything needed to be rethought.

Another not inconsiderable point: I had hired on this tub as a farmer's helper. The Colonial Council might decide to hold me to it, feeling that the colony needed shit shoveled more than it needed sax played, and until I could afford to put up enough credits for at least one Basic Share, they had as much say over my time as I did. The prudent man would divide his time between the hydroponic farm, and whatever would bring in the highest possible return in the shortest time—which did not describe sax playing in any known universe. Not even the currently most popular kinds of sax music . . . which were decidedly not what I wanted to compose.

If I did not speak up right now, these folks were going to accept me as a composer/musician. That would be awkward down the line if I ended up concluding that my life was best spent as something else altogether.

What else? I hadn't admitted it to myself until now, but what I had always been *second* most interested in, after music, was history, particularly PreCollapse history. Terrific. If anything, history was even less use than serious music, to a frontier society. If, after a long day in the fields, my hypothetical descendants had any curiosity at all about the planet the Old Farts were always nattering about, they would be more than satisfied with the copious data we already had aboard, and any new historical fact I could ever learn would already be over ninety years old back on Earth, already chewed to death. The Libra colony would one day be interested in its own history—presuming it survived—but not until at least two generations after we landed, which itself was decades away.

Okay, Joel, don't think about what else, now. But start backtracking, *right* now . . . right up to the point where you'd have to commit to some other track. Otherwise you may spend the next twenty years being thought of as the composer who couldn't cut it.

"Sol and Herb spoke a little hastily without realizing it," I heard myself saying. "Music is what I *have* done. I'm not certain it's what I will do now, aboard the *Sheffield*. Or when we hit dirt at Brasil Novo either, for that matter. I'm still giving that thought."

"What other areas interest you?" Itokawa asked.

"Well, I've always wanted to try space piracy," I said.

"A step up from musician," Sol agreed drily.

"Or perhaps dowsing."

London whooped with laughter, a bracing sound. "Yes, I imagine aboard a ship would be a good place to learn how to locate water. You could check your answers without having to dig all those pesky holes."

I smiled back at her. I wanted to banter with her, but also wanted this part of the conversation over as soon as possible. I had given just enough comic answers to hint that a serious one would not be forthcoming.

"You will find your path," Itokawa said. He sounded a lot more certain than I felt.

"With luck," I agreed. "Speaking of things we weren't speaking of—"

But I didn't have to manufacture a subject change, because one presented itself just then: my axe. The decision to send for it had apparently been made while I was deep in thought. Nothing for it but to play now.

But first they all had to ooh and ah, of course.

I had brought four saxophones with me, actually: soprano, tenor, alto, and baritone. (Musical instruments did not count against personal weight allowance.) But someone, almost surely Sol, had sent for my personal favorite, the one I considered my primary axe: Anna, a genuine Silver Sonic—a PreCollapse Yanigasawa B-9930 baritone, solid silver with a gold-plated hand-engraved bell and keys. The Selmer is more famous—but how often is the most famous really the best? Anna is a thing of beauty even to a layman, so elegant and precise you'd think she'd been finished by a jeweler . . . and a special joy to play for those who can handle her. Featherlight keys, lightning-fast response, tone-boosted resonator pads . . . never mind, I see you yawning. Let it stand that three people who spent their working days contemplating the infinite beauty that underlies the universe thought her special enough to admire extravagantly.

Even before they'd heard a note.

The baritone sax has never been a terribly popular instrument with musicians, because it is, physically, such a screaming bitch to play. It's huge and ungainly and requires you to move an immense volume of air. But some of the greats—Gerry Mulligan, James Carter—understood that it is worth the effort. Baritone sax is probably the most powerful resonant wind instrument there is, the Paul Robeson of horns, and no other is so immediately impressive to the layman.

(A purist would note there are actually two deeper saxes, the bass and contrabass, just as there are two higher than soprano, the sopranino and soprillo, and some even recognize one lower than contrabass called the tubax—but you're unlikely ever to hear any of them.)

While I wetted up my reed, I tried to decide what to play for them. Naturally, I wanted to play them one of my own compositions. And I was reasonably sure all three were sophisticated enough to appreciate it, if only mathematically—

very sure, in Sol's case. But what if they were sophisticated enough to *hate* it? Also, I was far less sure of everyone else in the place, and perfectly well aware that some of my work can strike a civilian as dry and complex. To pick the most polite words Jinny had used.

Okay, wrong time and place for an original Johnston. Something immediately accessible, but not crap. I reached into the air, and pulled down a tune Charlie Haden wrote to his wife Ruth called "First Song." It was the opening number of the last set Stan Getz ever played, and it always tears me up. You'd think a tenor piece wouldn't sound right on a baritone, but that one does. It snuck up on me; before long I had forgotten anyone else was listening, and played my heart out.

I hadn't played a note in weeks, hadn't even thought of it. My fingers were stiff, my embouchure weak, my wind less than optimal. I *killed* them, that's all. You can tell when it's working. I was playing smarter than I actually am, and could tell.

For the first three or four minutes, I was imagining accompaniment. Kenny Barron, who backed Getz by himself on that long-ago night in Copenhagen. Piano as crisp as snapping sticks.

And then suddenly the piano was really there.

I nearly clammed the phrase I was playing, and spun toward the bandstand. It was empty.

Wherever the keyboard player was, he was really good. *Really* good. I quartered the room without finding him, then eighthed it with no better luck. There were several side rooms and alcoves in which he might be lurking—or he could have been anywhere on the ship, listening in and tapping into the house sound system to play along. I decided to worry about it later, and put my attention back on Anna.

That piano was just the floor I'd needed to set my feet properly. We talked, briefly, and then he set me loose to wander. Before I knew it I had disappeared down the mouthpiece. When Getz played the song that night, he was saying good-bye to his life. I used it now to say good-bye to mine. God knew what new life I would build for myself, but the old one was over for good and for all, as unreachable as a moment ago, or the second before the Big Bang. Out of the bell of my Anna I blew my scholarship, and the mentor who would appear someday to nurture and teach me, and my master's, and my debut at the legendary Milkweg II in Amsterdam, and my discovery by the contemporary serious music establishment, and System-wide recognition, and the respect of an entire generation of my peers . . . I blew away my courtship with Jinny, and our marriage, and our wedding night, and our first nest, and our first child, and all our children, and their childhoods and adolescences and adulthoods, and their children, and all the golden years she and I would have spent loving and cherishing them all . . . I blew away both my dead parents, whose widely separated graves I would never see again . . . I blew away Ganymede my home, lost to me for so long and now lost for good, and all those who still lived on her . . . and not incidentally I blew away a quantum of wealth and power that perhaps could have been expressed as a fraction of all there was using only a single digit in the denominator.

I didn't get it all out—didn't come close—but I made a start.

I actually didn't hear the applause; Herb told me about it later.

I left the Horn of Plenty that night minus about a million kilos I'd been carrying on my shoulders . . . and with a steady gig, two nights a week, Tuesdays and Fridays, for a scandalous sum, tips, and all I could eat. Plus the private phone codes of three Relativists. Four, since London and George R lived together.

On the down side, I also left without finding out who had been playing that piano. Nobody seemed to know. The sound source had apparently been the house MIDI system—but the originating keyboard might have been in a sealed booth somewhere in the Horn, or up in the Control Room, for all anyone could tell me. All I could positively rule out was a player back in the Solar System . . . because our communication had unquestionably been conducted in real-time, without any lag at all. So I didn't worry about it. I had twenty years to find him. He could hide, but he couldn't run.

On our way back to our room, I tried to thank Herb, to explain just how much he'd unwittingly done for me, but he brushed it away. "I think everybody made out on that deal," he said. When I pushed it, though, he allowed me to promise to bring home a doggy bag on Tuesday and Friday nights. And perhaps a doggy bulb of good Scotch.

After half an hour at his desk, Herb gave me a data cube and suggested I play it privately. I did so at once, so I could stop thinking about it.

It was little Evelyn Conrad, back in the Solar System. Audio and video, stereo both ways. She told me gravely that I was very welcome. She said she was very cross with her gran'ther for making me go away. She said she was going to marry me one day, just the same. She told me not to marry anyone else without checking with her, first. She gave me a "private" mail address, but warned me it was not totally secure. And she closed with a solemn Bon Voyage and a blown kiss. By that point I was grinning and crying at the same time. I popped out the cube, stretched out on my bunk, and slept like a stone for thirteen hours. And when I woke, rude things and implausible suggestions had been written all over my face and hands with a laundry marker. I guess I snore.

8

The squeaking of the pump sounds as necessary as the music of the spheres.
—Henry David Thoreau

The first thing I did when I woke next morning was to sit down at my desk and summon a list of Positions Available.

There were a *lot* more than I expected. It had apparently occurred to the expedition's planners that not only could nearly all the actual useful work of preparing to start this colony be safely put off until the last few years of the voyage . . . it probably would be anyway, humans being human. Therefore, it would be good to keep them all occupied doing some damn thing or other for the first eighteen or so years. *Lots* of helpful suggestions had been provided. The full list of jobs the Colonial Authority was willing to pay someone to do took well over three hours just to scroll down through at normal reading speed.

But basically most of them broke down into categories you could skim in less than half an hour, if you were a fast reader. Here's a typical screen's worth, which was sent in response to my query by an astronomer named Matty Jaymes:

- —Refining knowledge of the location and plasma properties of the heliopause between the solar wind and the interstellar medium, on the way out of town—and then the same for the heliopause of Immega 714 when we got there.
- —Again as we were leaving, helping refine our comet map of the Oort Cloud, detecting comet nuclei with radar.
- —Once we were good and gone, measuring, in situ, the density, charge, mass, species, velocity, and temperature characteristics of interstellar plasma and gas.
- —Continuous measurement of the orthagonal components of the galactic magnetic field.
- —Continuous monitoring of the interstellar medium for molecular species. Determination of mass, composition, size distribution, and frequency of interstellar grains. Performance of interstellar erosion experiments with various models of shield configurations.
- —Using the long baseline formed by the starship and Solar System to carry out high-resolution astronomical measurements with optical and radio interferometry. Performing astrometric measurements of nearby stars, extrasolar planet detection, extrasolar planet imaging, and atmospheric spectroscopy. Using the same long-baseline techniques for astrophysical measurements, for

example, to image radio galaxies, quasars, and neutron stars.

(It had long been hoped that with multiple starships under way at the same time, the capability of this long baseline interferometry could be vastly enhanced by combining their observations of distant sources. It didn't seem to be working out well: the problem in this kind of interstellar interferometry was how to agree on common time-tagging of data from probes moving in different directions at significant fractions of the speed of light.)

- —Observation of low energy cosmic rays, normally excluded from the Solar System.
- —Attempting detection of gravity waves from astrophysical processes such as supernovae or neutron stars, by tracking anomalies in the Doppler effect of our signals.
- —Refinement of the dark matter map of the Galaxy . . .

. . . and so on. Mind you, all these are from the list of jobs Dr. Jaymes figured he could train just about any chimp aboard to do satisfactorily. But before he sent me those, he sent another, shorter list of jobs for especially smart people, with specific qualifications, which I won't even bother to excerpt, because I didn't understand it.

He *appeared* to be saying that he wanted to make an extremely intensive examination of the sun—*our* sun—okay, our *former* sun—of Sol, all right?—even as we were leaving it behind us forever at high speed. Why, I couldn't imagine. You'd think if there was an adequately studied star in the universe, it would be Sol. Studied even from vessels receding at fractions of c, if that made some sort of difference. And information about that particular star was going to be of purely academic interest to anyone we would ever meet again. But Dr. Jaymes certainly sounded terribly concerned about it. When I told him I lacked the qualifications for his first list of jobs, he allowed his disappointment to show even through mail; whereas when I politely declined his second list, too, he didn't seem to care one way or the other.

Now, I don't know about you, but if I had been forced to pick one of those I just listed as my shipboard occupation, I think the option I'd have selected instead would have been euthanasia. Like any literate citizen, I love to read what astronomers have to say after years of patient data collection and astute analysis . . . but the actual gathering of the data was not my idea of a way to spend the next twenty years.

When I came right down to it, not much was.

It was that growing realization, about five or ten scrollings down the list, which caused me to stop and approach it from the other direction. Instead of wading through the Big List of Jobs, the sensible way to do this was to make a Small List of Jobs I would be willing to endure for twenty years, if I had to, and then see if by chance any of them were on the Big List.

By dinnertime I had settled on the following:

- —Teach the saxophone. Or composition. Or music history. Or history.

    But did I in fact have any pedagogic skills? Forget the skills: did I have the *talent*? The indefinable intangible something that would make strangers find learning from me preferable to learning by themselves? How the hell did I know?

- —Conduct. Assuming an orchestra of some kind could be assembled out of five hundred people, and made good enough to be listened to by the rest.

    Again: Did I possess whatever variant offshoot of charisma it was that would make musicians find watching me more helpful than listening to their own internal metronome?

- —Act. An orchestra might prove to be beyond the resources at hand, but surely a theater company or trideo studio would form sooner or later.

    Let's just keep assuming the unanswerable question, "But did I have a particle of talent for that endeavor?" from here on.

- —Direct, for either live or canned drama.

- —Write, either live, canned, or prose fiction. Or nonfiction if necessary; I'd been given to understand that it did not pay a writer to be too fussy. Just possibly journalism, if it turned out that a town of five hundred souls produced enough gossip to need writing down. Herb could give me pointers.

  And finally, of course:

- —*Play* the furshlugginer saxophone. There were other venues aboard offering dining or entertainment or dancing. If I could line up enough different sorts of gigs, in different musical genres, then between that and private parties it might just be possible to make a whole entire livelihood out of my single favorite activity, pushing air out the end of a pipe.

That, God damn it, was finally something I did know I had the talent for. The crucial question however was: Did anybody care? Or rather, did enough people care that I would be able to live on my tips?

I looked back over my list gloomily, and detected a pattern. All the occupations that interested me shared two characteristics: they all might just manage to sustain me during the two decades of the voyage . . . and they would all become nearly worthless when we reached Immega 714. Pioneers don't have a lot of time or energy for art, either making it or consuming it. It was unlikely that anybody would be willing to feed me just because I made a pretty noise, or made up stories, or pretended to be someone more interesting.

But what did it matter? Doubtless I would end up scratching so hard to feed myself and get warm and dry that most of those things would lose their appeal for me, too.

I brooded about it for the rest of the evening without useful result. I was about to collapse my keypad for the night when I noticed that I had incoming mail. That was odd. Practically everyone I knew lived in my room. Surely my Relativist acquaintances were all too busy for chat. Then I saw the header title, "Where are you?" and felt my pulse begin to rise as I leaped to the conclusion that it was from Jinny.

But no. Instead, it was from the Zog. My job search was over, at least for a while. Reality had caught up to me.

I wrote back that I would report at the start of shift next morning, at 0900. Then I went directly to bed and immediately to sleep, determined to be at his office no later than 0800.

I HAD FORMALLY reported to the Zog back on the morning of my second day aboard the *Sheffield*—but found now that I had almost no memory of the event, or the man. Indeed, I had very little recall of anything that had happened that day, or for that matter any of those last days we'd spent in Terran orbit. This was not surprising, for two reasons.

First, it turns out to be oddly difficult to make a human brain remember events that occurred in free fall: the sleeping brain, which does the filing, insists on treating such experiences as dreams. The phenomenon wears off after a few weeks of zero gee, but we hadn't hung around in orbit that long.

And second, I had spent that whole period in a mental-emotional state approaching fugue—the sort of zombie numbness one must maintain during the process of sawing off the trapped limb. The Zog must have taken one look at me and realized I would be useless until we left the Oort Cloud.

With that symbolic cutting-of-the-cord, and the colossal bender with which I had marked it, and finally my musical catharsis with silver Anna at the Horn of Plenty, I had finally snapped out of my funk, rebooted my brain—just that day, really.

And several decks away, a man who had seen my vacant face exactly once, for less than a minute, had sniffed the air that morning and somehow sensed that I had finally germinated, and was ready to plant. That's the Zog for you.

Kamal Zogby was a Marsman who made you think of Martians. He didn't have three legs—as far as I know—but he was unreasonably tall and thin, even for a Marsman, and bowlegged, and slow moving unless he was in a blurring hurry, and he had an almost Martian distaste for sitting down or any posture but bolt upright. Also he was as taciturn as a Martian, with a similar sort of gravitas, and sometimes could be almost as hard to read. And like a Martian, the Zog never needed to look anything up.

But no Martian ever had a nose like that great ice-axe Lebanese honker of his—or many humans, for that matter. Nor did Martians have teeth anywhere near that big and white and frequently displayed. And he was unlike any Martian ever hatched in two important ways that made it possible to work for him. He genuinely cared about everybody he ever met, found them interesting. And he had a strong and subtle sense of humor.

He was not a botanist, or an agronomist, or a plant physiologist, or a hydroponicist, or an anythingist, really—not on paper, anyway. He had no degrees at all. He was just the Straw Boss.

Back on Mars, literally dirt poor, he had once kept a whole dometown in food, water, and air for twenty years after a catastrophic ecocollapse nearly wiped them out. They said if a thing could be grown, under any circumstances, he could grow it hydroponically. He could grow *lemon trees* hydroponically, or succulents, or even fungi.

And in theory we might even have managed to survive a hypothetical total failure of the hydroponic farm—because with part of his time the Zog also oversaw an experimental two-hectare half-meter-deep dirt farm that took up an entire deck, just above the Hydroponics Deck. It attempted to mimic the conditions we expected to find on our new home-to-be, Brasil Novo, second planet of Immega 714. The hope was that by the time we got there, we would know as much about how to dirt farm there as we knew about hydroponics now. And meanwhile, if something ever went horribly wrong down on the Hydroponics Deck, two hectares of land were just barely enough to feed five hundred people. In theory.

Finding the Zog's office, down on the Voyage Farm Deck, was easy. Gaining access was even easier, even though I had arrived well before the beginning of shift as planned. There was no execassist or persec or even door sentinel program to run interference for him. There was no *door*. Just an open doorway beneath a sign that read "Straw Boss." Unfortunately, there was no Zog on the other side of it either. Or anyone else; the office was empty. I waited expectantly for his desk to tell me where he was, or at least when he would arrive, but it didn't. So I told my own doppleganger to consult the ship system and locate him. After a noticeable hesitation, the ship politely declined to cooperate: the Zog was delisted. If he had a schedule on file it was not public. The ship declined to make an appointment in his name. It advised me to either take my chances and wait, or leave a message for him and go do something else.

I didn't much like either alternative. Especially after looking around the office: my strong impression was that he dropped by there once or twice a week at best. So I decided to hunt around for him.

The choices were a) this, the hydroponic Voyage Farm Deck, or b) the dirt-based Destination Farm Deck immediately above it. The choice kind of made itself.

The hydroponic farm operation was as intricately choreographed, complexly layered, and densely packed as any terrestrial jungle, with trays of assorted growing things stacked up to four high in places on frail-looking frames, and a bewildering variety of different lighting, watering, drainage and airflow systems, each tailored to a different variety of crops. The longest uninterrupted sight line on that deck was about three meters—and the lighting was so weird, with LEDs, metal halides, and sodium bulbs of assorted colors and intensities competing and clashing in odd ways at different places that you wouldn't have wanted to see much farther than a few meters in any direction anyway. The air circulation was so intense, in order to carry away the heat from all those lights, that there was a constant wash of white noise muffling all other sounds.

The farm immediately overhead, on the other hand, was basically a huge heap of somewhat modified dirt, above

which a few seedlings, sprouts, and shoots should just be
starting to become visible. If the Zog was on that deck, I
could probably pick him out by eye very quickly. It was definitely the place to start looking. And I had a hunch it was
where I would find him: where green things grew up out of
soil you could plunge your hands into.

It wasn't quite that easy, in fact. But close. The Destination Farm was designed to be as close as possible to one
enormous deck, with *long* sight lines in nearly all directions.
But it was also designed to be kept at destination-normal
conditions. That meant, among other things—at least at the
moment—air that was half again as rich in oxygen, slightly
denser, a *lot* more humid, and a bit warmer than ship-normal
(Terran Sealevel Standard). All of which meant, among
other things, *weather*—specifically, fog. It was controlled
somewhat by air circulation, but less than it could have been,
obviously by intent. Apparently we were all going to spend
our golden years on a planet that was prone to low-lying fogs
and mists for at least part of the year. Brasil Novo would be
a kind of Jungle World, a steamy hothouse of a place.

(It began to dawn on me that there was a *lot* I did not know
about our destination planet—my new home-to-be. I had
more or less presumed that if a whole lot of people were
willing to go there, forever, it must be a nice place. It might,
I thought, be well to delve into that just a little deeper.)

Another problem facing me was that since this was the
deck with the most open space and the most experimental
food, this was the deck where the majority of the livestock
was quartered and processed. Not to put too fine a point on
it, the fog *stank*, and rude noises seemed to come distantly
from all directions, as if some mad ventriloquist had descended to fart jokes.

And finally, it was blinkin' dark in there. Brasil Novo had
a day just a hair *over* twenty-four Terran Standard hours
long—thirty-six minutes longer. Therefore so did this deck,
which meant that its day and ours diverged. And had been
diverging since whenever the Zog had started its clock. It
was the beginning of the morning shift everywhere else in

the *Sheffield*, but here it appeared to be at least an hour before dawn.

Despite all these handicaps I found the Zog within a minute or two of my arrival. I had heard him laugh once before, and heard him now from a few hundred meters away. That got me started in the right direction, and luck took me the rest of the way. If that's the word I want: he was at the goat quarters, one of the riper of the animal enclaves. Goats just are not happy unless you give them some equivalent of a cave or shed to hide in at night, even though there's nothing to hide *from* . . . and then it concentrates the smell wonderfully. Maybe that's what they like about it.

Admittedly they are worth a bit of smell. A goat eats ten percent as much as a cow, but produces twenty-five percent as much milk. And many, among them me, say it tastes better than cow's milk. It's also easier to digest.

"Ah, Joel." He looked up from a hoof he was trimming and gave me a slow once-over, beginning and ending at my eyes. He had done that the first time we'd met, too. I wondered why I didn't find it offensive. When he was done, he smiled with his whole face. "I'm very glad to see you're in better spirits."

"Director Zogby, I want—"

"Zog, please."

"Zog, I appreciate your understanding and patience, this last week. I needed to work some things out, and I have."

"I can see that. You're ready to come to work."

"Yes, sir."

"This is Kathy—she's a Marsman like me, new to farming."

Intent on my new boss, I had almost completely tuned out the companion holding the goat for him. She was about my age, slim, fit, and extremely uncomfortable holding a goat. We exchanged polite noises.

"Kathy, Joel's from Ganymede. He has a lot of farming experience, dirt and hydro both. You'll be his assistant." She nodded, too busy to keep eye contact.

I took a deep breath. I was not looking forward to this next bit, but there was no sense putting it off any longer. "Uh, Zog, perhaps I should correct one small mis—oh, shit."

The sentence aborted in that odd way because I had just seen what she was about to do. There was no time for me to say anything to stop her—and it wouldn't have helped anyway, because there was nothing she could do about it. She couldn't have gotten a hand free without being kicked. There was just time for me to drop to my knees, cup one hand behind her head, place my other index finger just below her nose, and press hard. She let out a yelp and tried to shake free, but I wouldn't let her until I was sure the job was done. Then I released her at once and backed away.

"I'm very sorry, Kathy," I said. "I had to do that."

She was staring at me as if I'd grown fangs. *"Why?"*

"It's the only sure way I know to stop someone from sneezing."

"What?"

"Excuse me just a minute, Kathy," Zog interrupted. "Joel, what was it you were just about to say?"

"Oh. Uh . . ."

"You were going to correct something?"

"Why shouldn't I sneeze if I want to?"

"You *really* don't want to sneeze in a goat shed," I told her. "Look, Zog, I—"

"Why the hell not?"

"Kathy, please, he'll explain in a minute. Go on, Joel. Correct what?"

"No, wait a minute, Zog," she insisted. "That *hurt*."

"I know," I said, "and I'm really very sorry."

"No, you're not."

I started to argue, and stopped. "You're right. I kind of feel like you had it coming, for not knowing what you're doing. And now I'm also a little annoyed at you for presuming that *I* don't. If you'd—"

"Joel," Zog cut in firmly, "I understand that you'd rather have that conversation. First, though, we're going to have the one where you tell me just what misunderstanding on my part needs to be corrected. Kathy, pipe down and let her go."

She sighed in exasperation and released her hold on the

goat, which sprang up and trotted to the far end of the small shed, limping slightly on its half-trimmed hoof. I turned to meet the Zog's eyes. Irritation was in them, but compassion as well. "Well, look, what you have to understand—"

Kathy sneezed.

I think it was at least half deliberate, a gesture of defiance. Her hands were now free; she could have done as I'd just shown her. Instead she sneezed. And not just a ladylike little *choof*, either, but a breathquake that might have snuffed out a blowtorch.

Unfortunately, a human sneeze apparently sounds very much like the word for *"Run for your life!"* in Goat.

So we all got very busy there for a while.

WHEN THINGS SETTLED down a bit, I poked my head up and found that I was in the corner of the shed farthest from the exit. The original exit. I had begun to congratulate myself on my good instincts when I realized there were now several brand-new exits, one of them less than a meter from my head. A goat hoof can be a weapon of terrifying power, and a partially trimmed goat hoof could only be worse.

Then I discovered Kathy, underneath me. Maybe my instincts were okay after all.

I rolled off her, intending to ask if she was all right. Instead I let out a squeal and kept on rolling. Killer monkeys—

But, no. Within a revolution or two I had seen that what was dangling from the ceiling was not the huge ape my brain had first decided it was seeing, but someone with considerably better instincts than mine. Only by luck had Kathy and I managed not to be in the path of a fleeing goat—but *none* of them had been running *up*. Zog let go of the rafter and dropped back to the floor. He landed just beside Kathy, and lifted her to her feet with one big hand. "Are you all right?" he asked, and she ran a quick inventory and assured him she was.

"I'm sorry if I squashed you," I said, getting to my own feet.

She shook her head. "No problem. You know how to use your elbows."

I found myself blushing.

And her blushing back. "Besides," she went on quickly, "if I'd only listened to what you were trying to tell me—"

"No harm done," Zog said. "Except to the shed." He glanced around at the damage and sighed. "It was guaranteed goat-proof."

"I'll bring it back to the store," she said.

He shook his head. "Traveling at relativistic speeds voids the warrantee."

"Figures."

"I'll go round them up," I said.

"We all will," Zog said.

"That's okay," I said. "I'm the new guy. And I really should have taken the time to explain to Kathy why—"

"We all will," Zog insisted. "Once we patch this shed together well enough to hold them again."

And of course he was right. Catching a goat is just barely possible for three people working together; I doubt any two of us could have caught even one. The hairy little bastards led us a merry chase. A goat can leap pretty well even in terrestrial gravity; in one-third gee they begin to seem more like large birds than mammals. Large smart birds, with offensive armament.

By the time we were done, I was thoroughly exhausted, and quite understood why many cultures have used goats to represent Satan. I left the shed and flopped down not far from the entrance, with my back against an intact section of wall. Zog took a seat beside me—with noticeably less effort, even though he had nearly twenty years on me—and Kathy dropped into a tailor's seat facing us. The three of us sat in silence for a while, Kathy and I because we were getting our breath back, and Zog because he had nothing to say.

Finally Kathy frowned, shifted position slightly, reached beneath her, and removed something. She held it out on her palm to examine it. A slightly squashed goat berry. I managed to choke off the giggle and to slap on my poker face, but it took me a few seconds, and I was sure she'd heard me at it. She looked up, our eyes met, I waited to see if she would flare up at me—

It so happens that the average goat turd is just the size, shape, and color of the data beads used to hold video or audio programming. When she took it between thumb and forefinger, and pretended to be trying to insert it into the docking slot on her wrist CPU, it wasn't what you could call a hilarious jest. But it was excuse enough for a tension-releasing blurt of laughter from both of us.

"That music sounds like shit," Zog said, and we laughed harder.

After a while we went back inside, and Zog had Kathy and me finish hooving that goat together, and pass out treats to all of them, to calm them down and by way of apology for our carelessness. Then we left, and Zog said, "Joel, I believe you were about to correct a small misunderstanding on my part about your background."

Ah yes. "Well . . ." His eyes met mine, and I heard myself say, "Not a misunderstanding. I lied, Zog. Not about dirt farming—but pretty much everything I put down about my experience in hydroponics is pure goat berries. I'll come in real handy in twenty years, when we all start doing this kind of farming on a large scale, at our new home. But right now, you're going to need short words and long patience."

He just nodded. "Why did you lie?"

"It was the only way I had to get a berth aboard the *Sheffield*. And I *really* wanted one."

I'd been sweating this moment for days now. He nodded again, and that was the end of it. "We'll begin your education in hydroponics tomorrow. For now follow me," he said, and took us on a grand tour of that deck.

It really was a wonder, a Garden of Eden such as no planet had ever seen, designed and constructed so that the local light intensity of any given square meter of that vast area could be varied from zero to noon in Baghdad, with equivalent control of humidity, airflow, O_2 and CO_2 content, and some other factors I forget. Those crops that were able to thrive on a twenty-four-hour light cycle (or other variant) could do so, without disturbing the slumber of the ones nearby who liked things the old-fashioned way. Those that were reasonably happy in the different conditions that obtained on our destination planet were already enjoying them, and all the rest would, hopeably, be successfully reconditioned to enjoy them over the course of the next two decades.

The goats notwithstanding, the staple meat aboard the *Sheffield* besides chickens was not chevon but rabbit—low fat, a milder taste than chevon, and easier to cook. (You couldn't subsist on rabbit alone—not enough vitamins A or C—but we weren't trying to.) They're less fussy eaters themselves, too, happy to live on alfalfa with a pinch of salt, which both upper and lower farms produced in plenty. Each doe and her litter took up about a square meter of living space—but a stackable square meter—and about twelve times that in alfalfa; the yield works out to about 150 kilos of boneless meat per hectare per day.

What was left of the rabbits was fed, along with each day's dining-hall waste, to chickens. They too insist on a dark stinky home, like goats. But it's safe to enter it even with a head cold, and the reward is four or more eggs per colonist per week, plus fried chicken.

And finally there was fish—the last stop on the tour. Mars-bred fish, as productive as the rabbits in terms of protein, and less trouble to care for. As we were strolling there from the chicken run, Zog told us that one of the very few stabs at genetic manipulation the Prophets had ever approved was an attempt to breed a chicken that would reliably lay an egg a day—the Holy Ones *liked* eggs. "The Church's breeders were successful, technically," Zog said, "but unfortunately the resulting chicken was literally too dumb to eat. If you want to take that as a metaphor for the True Church's whole approach to science, you're pretty astute in my opinion."

"God," Kathy said, "what a shitstain in history."

"Middle Ages were worse," Zog said.

"Maybe—but *we could have had immortality by now!* We could have beaten cancer by now. We might have had telepathy by now." She sounded angry.

"We have telepathy," Zog said mildly.

"Sure, terrific. But only in identical twins, and fewer than four percent of them—*and* we don't have the faintest idea how they do it, or why they can and the rest of us can't."

"True. There remain mysteries to be solved."

"It's infuriating."

She really seemed upset. I decided to distract her with a diversionary anecdote. "Let me tell you both my very favorite mystery," I said. "You reminded me of it just a second ago, Zog, and it's related to what you're talking about, Kathy. Kind of, anyway."

She didn't answer. "Go ahead, Joel," the Zog said.

"I ran across this in a book. Just before the Hiatus, natal medicine got so good that they were sometimes able to save babies born *so* prematurely that they had not yet even developed the sucking reflex. And now that the Prophets are all finally holding services in Hell, we can do that again: rescue babies that are, in the Zog's colorful phrase, too dumb to eat."

"How?" Kathy asked. "Force-feed the poor things?"

The Zog shook his head. "They'd *never* learn, then."

"No, they train them to suck," I said.

Kathy frowned. "*How?* If something is too dumb to figure out that eating is pleasant, what the hell do you *reward* it with?"

I smiled. "Music."

Her face smoothed over. "Oh, I love it."

"Rhythm?" Zog asked.

"You'd think so, but no," I said. "Melody. The little buggers will work hardest to bring about repetition of a favorite scrap of melody. *That's* how hardwired love of music is, in the human brain. It *predates survival instinct*."

"It doesn't seem reasonable," Zog said. "How would a brain evolve so?"

I spread my hands. "Ask God. I just work here. All I know is, it's my very favorite mystery."

"You like music, too?" she asked. "I like it a lot."

"What kinds?"

The question seemed to puzzle her, but she gave it a try. "Audible."

She liked everything? It seemed to me, in my sophistication, that people who liked everything must understand hardly anything. I was eighteen, all right?

"For the past hour I've been thinking this place could use a banjo player," I said.

"There are two listed," she said, "and one other who isn't. They're all pretty good."

"How do you know that?" I asked.

She shrugged. "I did a data search for musicians, way back on Terra, and listened to all their audition recordings. I also asked the ship to alert me anytime someone makes live music, and let me listen in if they haven't put privacy seal on it. I discovered at least half a dozen unregistered musicians that way. In fact, the best musician I've heard aboard so far was unlisted. He came aboard at the last possible minute, so they waived his audition."

I opened my mouth, closed it again.

"What's his instrument?" the Zog asked her.

"Saxophone. I sat in with him, remote, for a few numbers. I wanted to introduce myself afterward, but by the time I got the system to give up his phone code, somebody he was sitting with put a heavy privacy shield on the whole table."

"Have you tried him since?"

My kindly wristband produced the chip-chirp indicating a watch alarm. Today's shift was over. Saved by the chip. "Zog," I said, "I really hate to act like a clock-watcher on the first day I've bothered to show up, but I really do need to—"

"There are things we need to talk about," he interrupted.

"I know. Uh . . . I could meet you somewhere in a couple of hours. Your office?" I shifted my weight from foot to foot as if I badly needed to pee.

"Go. Our AIs will work something out."

"Thanks Zog nice to meet you Kathy see you both tomorrow."

I fled.

9

One can travel this world and see nothing.
To achieve understanding it is necessary
not to see many things,
but to look hard at what you do see.

—Giorgio Morandi

I don't get it," Herb said, squinting at images on his wristband's monitor. "This girl is clearly much better-looking than you are, even with the baldness, string warts, and that glass eye. You raved about her piano playing—and you say she appears able to endure your own instrumental atrocities, so it's certain she has a forgiving nature. Did she google up bad?"

"I haven't tried yet. I mean, I haven't tried. I'm not interested, I keep telling you."

"Age, height, mass, marital status, economic status, state of health, attractiveness, talent, all apparently compatible within reason. And you can forget *all* those factors, and remember just the three important things."

I rolled my eyes. "Go ahead."

"She is a female mammal, she has a pulse, and she thinks you're the best musician in the colony."

I grimaced in exasperation. "Didn't you hear me? I'm . . . not . . . interested. I told you: I *took* that class. I'm done with women."

He put his own exasperation into a sigh instead of a grimace. "Joel, twenty years is a long, long time. And it's going to seem even longer, with an attitude like that."

"She and I have nothing in common. Didn't I tell you what her greatest dream for mankind is? Telepathy, for Murphy's sake!"

"Something wrong with telepathy?" he asked mildly.

I blushed. "Aw, you know what I mean. She's talking

about the kind where nobody has any secrets and yet we all love each other. Fantasy."

Herb had successfully passed two other Secret Messages back to little Evelyn Conrad for me so far. Her replies always cheered me up. But they always came back via conventional electronic mail rather than telepathic courier; for some reason she was willing to accept information from a telepath but not give information to one. I was a little afraid she might be overestimating the security of whatever mail route she used. So I kept my own messages to her to a minimum, for fear of getting her in trouble with her elders.

Thinking about telepathy gave me an idea. "Hell's bells, Herb, why don't *you* take a run at Kathy?"

He looked at me strangely. "Really?"

"Well, you're obviously interested in her. And she doesn't find telepathy weird."

"You wouldn't mind?"

I closed my eyes, counted to five, opened them again. "Why would I mind? Haven't you been listening? I'm through with romance, I'm through with love, I'm through with counting the stars above."

"You're really serious about that, then."

I rolled my eyes upward and asked the ceiling to bear witness to the tribulations I had to endure here below. "Yes, for the love of—is that you or me?"

He brought his wrist to his ear. "You. Go ahead."

I tapped my own wrist. "Yes?"

The face on the screen was unfamiliar to me, as his first words confirmed. "Mr. Johnston, we haven't met yet. My name is Paul Hattori. I am the colony's banker. Forgive me for disturbing your privacy, but there is a matter we should discuss at your earliest convenience. A matter of some importance."

I thought for a second. The day was young—hell, it was still before noon. But my morning had been overfull of stimulating inputs. I was tired, and confused, and wanted only to put my feet up and try to get some thinking done about everything that had happened that morning. "How about tomorrow?" I temporized.

He hesitated. "I will of course follow your wishes. But I have information you really should have as soon as possible."

What could he possibly be on about? Was this some sort of pitch for investment advice or banking services? He had access to my financial records—record—surely he must know I was a dry hole. "Can you give me some idea what it's about?"

He was smiling, but there was something odd about the smile, something I couldn't put my finger on. It wasn't phony, exactly. Just odd. "I can, but if you will forgive me, I would greatly prefer to tell you in person."

I met Herb's eyes, raised an eyebrow. He shrugged. "Are you sure you don't want Communicator Johnson? Same address, he's my roommate."

"No, it's you I need to speak with, Mr. Johnston." He gave an address only one deck below the officers and crew. He was a VIP.

"All right, I'll be there in half an hour. But I still think you have the wrong bloke."

"Who was that?" Herb asked.

"Never mind," I said. "It can't be important."

I started to change to better clothes—and changed my mind. Why should I dress up for this joker? I wasn't the one who'd asked for this meeting. Showing up was courtesy enough; putting on formal tights and collar would be obsequious. I had no reason to impress the man . . . because I had absolutely nothing to impress him *with*. He had nothing I wanted. Pausing only to empty my bladder and comb my hair, I left dressed just as I was: like a man who had recently been in a goat shed when somebody sneezed.

I took my time on the way, too. So I had time to develop a dark suspicion as to what he might want to talk to me for, which quickly built itself into an ugly and plausible theory.

Hattori was a banker. Bankers know all about very large sums of money. Did I know anyone who was connected in some way with very large sums of money? Had I not, indeed, recently roundly pissed off some people of that description? If they took a notion to have some sort of heavy weight dropped on my scrotum in retaliation, might not a banker be their chosen instrument?

It was hard to sustain alarm. As far as I knew, I really was bulletproof, from a financial point of view: I had nothing to steal, no credit to ruin. If the Conrads wanted vengeance, they would just have to have me beaten or killed like civilized people.

Nonetheless by the time I reached Hattori's cabin I was paranoid enough to be feeling just a bit belligerent. I was going to stop just outside his door and take a few deep breaths to calm down, but the door recognized me and opened before I had the chance.

I had expected his quarters to be impressive. They exceeded my expectations. They were tasteful, supremely comfortable despite a Zen simplicity, luxurious without ostentation. A Hawaiian slack-key guitar played at background level—Cyril Pahinui, I think. I was given an understanding chair, and offered a beverage impressive enough to denote respect, which I accepted.

Banker Hattori was a pleasant-looking cobber. I'd have guessed his ancestry at a combination of something like Hawaiian or Japanese and Scottish or German. He was short by Ganymedean standards, a little short even by Terran reckoning, but well proportioned and clearly in excellent physical shape. Back on Terra, he might have sailed, climbed mountains, run marathons, flown an ultralight. Now that those joys were lost to him for the next twenty years, he probably played a competitive but noncontact sport, and worked out. But he was not hard to take the way some jocks can be, did not challenge.

In person, his smile was as subtly *off* as it had been over the phone. The surprisingly few seconds he wasted on polite ritual and pleasantry gave me just enough time to figure out what was odd about it. He was clearly a man who smiled a lot, in his off hours—the placement and depth of the smile wrinkles at his mouth and eyes told you that—but he was unaccustomed to smiling like that *at work*.

In retrospect, it's actually pretty impressive that he didn't drag it out longer than he did, surround it with even more of a big drumroll buildup. I couldn't have blamed him if he had. He must indeed not have gotten to impart news of that particular sort very often.

But he was a professional, and also I think a reasonably kindly man, so he merely teased me with it until I wanted to throttle him.

"You have made no financial investment in this colony so far, Joel," he began. We were Joel and Paul by then. "Looking over your records, I see that your motives in joining us were personal and emotional rather than economic. I would like to explain, briefly, why I think that was a mistake, and then—"

"Paul, excuse me for interrupting, but your pump is sucking air. I have no capital at all."

He held up his hands. "Please—indulge me for just a moment. Think of it as a hypothetical. I did say 'briefly.'"

He really did have a nice smile. Odd or not. "You have the floor."

"I say I am the ship's banker, and that is one of the things I do. I am also our colony's chief financial adviser, and act as its representative."

I nodded, impressed. "Quite a job. It can't be easy, arranging to borrow such stupendous sums, let alone handling them wisely."

"Let me give you an imaginary hypothetical conversation between me and a Terran banker, shortly before we left the Solar System."

He proceeded to act it out, using different hokey but clever cartoon voices:

"Banker: Greetings, gentleman merchant adventurer, hereafter known as GMA. I assume you're here to ask about a loan, and I'm sorry to say money is very tight just now—

"GMA: I have some lubricant with me.

"Banker: Excuse me?

"GMA: I can help solve tight money. I am here to discuss a loan, as you suggest. But I don't want to borrow. I want to lend *you* money.

"Banker: Really? Well, now. That would certainly be agreeable, in principle. What sort of terms and conditions did you have in mind?

"GMA: Here is a check, representing gold dollars in Zurich.

"Banker: How m—oh my, a great many.

"GMA: A very great many.

"Banker: I . . . see. And you want to give it to us.

"GMA: I want you to invest it for me at compound interest. A rate of eleven percent a year would be acceptable.

"Banker: That is a very high rate of interest!

"GMA: Not if I undertake not to touch the money for twenty years . . .

"Banker: Ah. I begin to see. But what's in it for me—besides the usual fees? How does this loosen tight money?

"GMA: You have the full use of that money for twenty years, and keep all the profits. All you have to do is invest soundly enough so the capital sum remains intact . . . a trick venture capitalists like yourself are rather good at.

"Banker: Well, thank you. But I don't see what's in it for *you*. For the same twenty years, you're depriving yourself of that same money, receiving no payments.

"GMA (smiling broadly): Yes, but you see, I intend to age more slowly than you. . . ."

He smiled.

"I get it—I think," I told Paul. "It really is a clever swindle."

"It's not a swindle," he said.

"It has to be. People are earning large sums of money for either sitting and waiting, or else for traveling expensively. *Somebody* has to be getting swindled for it. TANSTAAFL."

"That principle doesn't apply here. In this one case, there *is* such a thing as a free lunch. Wealth is being created by *time*. Nobody's being swindled because nobody's *losing* anything."

I must have looked stubborn.

"The key phrase was, 'You will have the use of that money for twenty years.' Suppose the moment we get to Immega 714 we do an instant one-eighty, slingshot around it and hotfoot it right back to Sol at the same speed. It took us twenty years to get there, twenty years to come back; we arrive at Terra forty years older than we started. But what we find when we debark—"

I started to see it. "Finagle on fire!"

"—is a Terra more than one hundred and sixty years older than when we left it."

"With a hundred and twenty years of free interest!" The beauty of it washed over me.

"Not free," he said. "We had to get our butts up to a large fraction of c, and keep them there for forty years. But real cheap. Are you ready for more of the special blend?"

"Oh, that really is lovely, Paul," I said as he poured generous refills for both of us. "You're absolutely right: for the first time, I genuinely regret not having been able to kick any money into the pot myself."

"Well, theoretically, of course, a person could choose to buy in even now—or for that matter, at any point in the trip, although the degree of participation would naturally go down some as the voyage gets longer."

I grinned, and a faint tingling of the lips told me the special blend was beginning to hit me. "With what I make turning shit and piss back into food, plus what I hope in my wildest dreams to earn in tips playing at the Horn of Plenty, by the time we reach Peekaboo I can confidently expect to see profits in the low five figures."

That mysterious smile had never quite left him, even when he was playing Banker and GMA. It was still there, and now his eyes were twinkling, too. "Joel, let me tell you about another starship, a long time ago. One of the unlucky ones. There was bad sickness aboard, one you didn't get over. Both their telepaths died in the first wave, so the only reports were by radio and laser. Some of their Relativists died, and then it was reported that all the others were infected, and the quantum ramjet was being shut down. That cut the power for the radio and lasers, and the ship passed from human history."

This was sounding oddly familiar. Hard to pin down the memory, though: when I closed my eyes to try, the room began to rotate around me. Counterclockwise. "Heard about a ship like that, once." No, clockwise. "Lost in the stars, forever."

"Only, not," Paul said. "They were very lucky. Their first bit of luck was that their plague, whatever it was, burned itself out completely with seventy-five percent of them still alive. They were able to keep the antimatter engine alive, stroke of luck number two, which gave them enough power to survive, and run all the machinery. Including the data-banks they'd brought along with them, the total accumulated knowledge and wisdom of the human race at that time."

"Very important," I agreed. "Keep them from going crazy with boredom and despair."

"Way more important than that, because of their third bit of luck."

I knew he was toying with me somehow, but it didn't feel unpleasant, so I played along. "And what was that, Mr. Inter-locker . . . Mr. Inneroculator . . . what was that, Mr. Hattori?"

"One of the Relativists had conceived and bore twins on the voyage. The children lived."

"Really? Oh. *Oh.* I think I get it! When they—"

"When they grew old enough, they studied everything they could find on their mother's profession. One day when they felt they were ready, they somehow relit the quantum ramjet—and resumed the voyage."

"That *is* amazing! What a story. Oh, they must have flipped back at Terra when they started getting radio mes-sages from a ghost ship! How long did . . . wait a minute . . . oh, hell, I can't do math when I'm *sober.*" (The gene for my father's kind of mathematical talent is, fairly self-evidently, recessive.)

"Nonetheless, your intuition izh correct—excuse me, is correct." Nice to know he was feeling it, too. "If the happy news came by radio, we would not be receiving it for several years yet. That's the fourth bit of luck. One of the twins in-herited some of her father's talent, as well—and Dad had been a Communicator. She scared the witch—the wits—out of her uncle back in Luna, the first time she made contact. He thought he was being haunted: his late brother had never mentioned any offspring."

I shook my head, which stayed on. "Incredible! I have to tell my friend Herb that story—he's a writer, *and* a Commu-nicator, he'll make a meal of it. A dozen movies will be made about it just in the next year, and at least one miniseries. Thanks for telling me, for, thanks for, why the hell did you *tell* me that, Paul? I mean, it's a great story, but what has it got to do with what we were talking about, swindling money out of time? What's the connection?"

That omnipresent smile suddenly blossomed into a full-blown grin that lit up his whole face, and his eyes beamed happiness. "The name of the prodigal starship, Joel."

All the pieces finally fell into place, and I knew exactly what he was going to say next. Unfortunately it cost me the power of speech, so he said it anyway.

"It's the *New Frontiers*."

I suppose a similar effect could have been achieved by turning every other atom in my brain to antimatter.

"Your father meant for you to be a rich man, Joel," Hattori's voice said from the far side of the cosmos. "Now you are. All shares have been reactivated, and you have a *lot* of them. Should you choose to, you could become one of the *Sheffield*'s biggest investors . . ."

I began to laugh. Then I laughed some more, after which I kept on laughing, and finally realized I was not going to be able to stop anytime soon. I was on the floor by then, in fetal position, Hattori fussing futilely over me, and I discovered that I could convert the laughing to crying for minutes at a time, which was a change at least.

All I kept thinking was that I had abandoned everything there was, left everyone I knew, burned every bridge ever built, and literally fled the Solar System on a one-way trip, to escape the dread danger of becoming rich. . . .

Some days, you just can't lose a buck.

I HAD TO do some fast talking to get out of Hattori's office without being reported as emotionally unstable and sent for therapy. I'd freaked him out a little with my outburst of hilarity. And I had to edit what I said on the fly, too: if I had tried to convince him I'd been betrothed to a granddaughter of Conrad of Conrad, he'd have been *certain* to send for a counselor. Especially once I told him I'd broken the engagement.

But after hearing a version of my recent history that dialed Jinny back to "a girl from a very wealthy family," he finally agreed that hysterical laughter was an appropriate response to the way things had turned out, and stopped physically recoiling from me. He even had the grace to postpone picking my pocket, urging me to take my time, and come back for further discussion of my participation in the colonial partnership when I'd had a chance to, as he put it, "encompass everything."

I thanked him and left, with every intention of finding Herb and asking him to be my designated keeper while I got hammered. If he was not interested, Balvovatz or Pat would do. And if none of them were available—well, I had survived a solo bender in Vancouver, a very tough town. I could probably handle the *Sheffield*.

But halfway back to my room I remembered that I had already *done* so. More than once. For most of my first week aboard, actually. Nobody had reported me because—well, a *lot* of us had spent some portion of that first week drinking or smoking or snorting more heavily than usual. But if I were to start back up again after only a day of sobriety, eyebrows would be raised, and sooner or later someone would mention my name to the Healers. I was damned if I wanted to waste hours explaining myself and my decisions to some well-meaning headcandler, who might take it into his head to start messing with my brain chemistry. Ganymedeans didn't hold much with that sort of thing.

So I did the sensible thing instead, and didn't get hammered.

That was a pity, because then I had no excuse at all for the fistfight. Or my miserable performance in it.

THE WAY I remember it, I plodded back to my room in a fog, like a cow on its way back to the barn, so confused by my own thoughts that I could barely lift my feet. And then I raised a weary arm and palmed my door open, and there were these two guys.

You know how sometimes you'll meet a stranger, and it's as if a closed caption appears at the bottom of the screen, summing them up in a word or two for those who just tuned

in? "Professional victim," or "Could bore the balls off a buffalo," or "Wants money," or the like? My first sight of these
two went freeze-frame for a second, and below each of them
I clearly saw the subtitle "Perpetrator." Only after the action
restarted did I notice their armbands, and realize I was meeting my first transportees.

They were big guys, too. Bigger than me, anyway. They
didn't look sophisticated enough to be political prisoners or
incorrigible monoreligionists. The one sitting on Pat's bunk
had the arms, shoulders, and thighs of one who lifts weights
regularly and faithfully while he's in jail, but has been out
for some time now. He had short black hair just beginning to
thin and a short sanitary sideless black beard, of the type
called a "doorknocker." He had a glass of some dark fluid
cupped in his right hand, and took a quick pull from it when
he saw me—but he didn't drop his eyes.

His partner, sprawled on Balvovatz's desk chair, looked
more as if he tended to win his fights by knowing more dirty
tricks than the other guy. He had the body of a high school
sports star . . . who had been expelled before graduation, and
had expended as little effort as possible ever since. Instead of
pumping iron when in jail, he just hung out near his friend.
He wore his dirty blond hair in an arcane style that involved
grease, and hinted that it came from a motorcycle or copter
engine. There is no name for his beard type, nor is it likely
any will be needed. Sweeping scimitar sideburns failed to
reach *quite* as far as his mustachios . . . which did not descend *quite* far enough to reach the goatlike goatee. The net
effect was of a satyr too dumb or drunk to realize his gay
barber is making fun of him. He was as unguardedly furtive
as his friend was poker-faced. That caused me to notice that
Balvovatz's desk monitor was darkened, not switched off.

"Oh, hi," he said, too heartily. "You're back."

The one on Pat's bunk said, "We're real sorry to barge in
like this, okay?"

"Yeah, but everything's totally cool," Weird Beard said.
"Nothing to freak out about."

"How did you two get in here?" I asked the dark one sitting on the bunk.

He shrugged, being careful not to spill his drink. "Everybody's got things they're good at," he said reasonably.

I nodded. "And this is okay with me because . . ."

The other one said, "Because this is one of those fuckin' situations where, you know, like it says upfront, viewer discretion is the better part of value."

His friend stared at him, took a deep breath, let it out, and turned back to me. "We have a proposal for you. A business opportunity. Joint venture. Low risk, high return. But yeah, Richie's right, it's definitely what you'd call a little gray-market."

Well, I thought to myself, you happen to catch me at a moment when I have a few gigabucks I need to invest somewhere. "How gray?"

"Just barely beige," Richie said. "And only right at the end. Up until then it's mostly red, and some green. Tell him, Jules."

"Richie, will you take it easy? Joel—can I call you Joel?—it's real simple. You work down on the Farm Decks, right?"

I agreed that this was sometimes so.

"Dirt or High Japonics?" Richie asked.

I looked at Jules. Jules looked at me and his face said, *What am I supposed to do?*

"Both," I said.

"So you like to make stuff grow," Jules suggested.

"Like you said, everybody's got something they're good at."

"And you know your way around down there. Like, where things are, what parts get looked at all the time, what parts don't get looked at so often."

Light was beginning to dawn. "Why?"

"We got some stuff we'd like to grow."

"Without bothering the Zog with a lot of fuckin' paperwork and formalities," Richie put in.

"And we figure a smart guy like you could work that out."

I closed my eyes. The world spun as if I were drunk. But the moment I opened them again, it *slammed* to a halt. "What sort of plant are we talking about?"

"Just flowers," Jules said.

"Herbs," Richie amplified, pronouncing it like my roommate's name. "From the country."

"'Erbs," Jules corrected, glaring at him.

"Well, sure, *now*," Richie said, annoyed. "But *originally* they grew it in the country."

Jules and I exchanged another glance, and he took a deep pull on his drink, wiping his mouth with his wrist. *YOU wanna try it?*

"Richie," I said gently, "*which* Herb, exactly?" I pronounced it like my roommate's name, and Jules nodded. *That's the way to deal with him.*

Richie frowned. "Look, if you're gonna get all technical on me—just because I haven't got my grade eleven, you—"

I turned back to Jules. "Why don't you tell me which flower you mean?"

He looked me in the eye. "Poppy flower, okay?"

I took in a deep breath, and then when I was done, I found more room in my chest somewhere and took in a lot more breath. "Get the hell out of my room before I call a proctor," I said, loudly enough to use up a lot of it, and began exhaling the rest.

Jules didn't move, or even wince. But Richie came up out of Bal's chair like a boxer out of his corner, yelling something of his own—

—and then a whole lot of things happened too fast to grasp—

—and then a proctor with somebody's blood on his tunic blouse was holding me gently but firmly by the upper arm, a really nice guy from the smile on him, and offering me a mood elevator. That sounded like a great idea; it was only after I let him put it under my tongue that I realized the elevator's cables had been cut, by my anemones. It got exciting then for a few years, but fortunately the basement, when we reached it, turned out to be made out of marshmallow, and I decided it was safe to take a nap after all.

Not really.

* * *

I WALKED CORRIDORS for a million years. The same ones, for all I know. I didn't mind. I wasn't tired. I wasn't even bored. Funny things kept happening as I walked. Silly-funny. A cat danced with a fire extinguisher. Doors grew phallic knobs, then dilated and swallowed them. The floor was furry beneath my bare feet, then grassy, then hard and cold as ice. A section of pale yellow wall started to melt like frozen urine from the heat of my passage—nothing odd there, but it ran *up* instead of down. *Less* than zero gee whiz. It started to collect overhead, but I ignored it and walked on. Goats sang harmony—in Rabbit rather than Goat, a ludicrous choice. A bubble began to keep station on me, ahead and to my left, and inside it grew a holo, a lifesize headshot. It was Jinny—hundreds of years older. She smelled like fields of barley, light as flax. Her face was in ruins, beyond the power of even power to save. Her hair was still widely red, but often misunderstood. Her eyes were hazel, stoned, rolling. Then Ganymede devalued the debit, the economy went bad, and her bubble burst. Well, at least the goats finally got their butts out of their heads and started singing in Goat. I began to encounter members of a race of Easter Island statues, huge mouths gaping like Art Deco urinals, making fluttery sounds like pigeons as I went by.

Then one short one blocked my path, and turned into my roommate Pat. "Joel?" he asked me. I waited with interest to hear the answer, but it didn't come. He asked if I could hear him, and after considering it, I said, "Sometimes." A pigeon fluttered, and Pat said loudly, "Just a moment, please, Proctor," and then softly, "Take this." A piece of notepad paper, folded three times. He folded my fingers around it, used them to tuck it into my breast pocket. "A time will come for you to speak," he said, very quietly, but with an unmistakable urgency that reached me in my fog. "When that time comes, say exactly what is on that piece of paper, and nothing else. You hear me, Joel? Say it back to me."

I nodded. "When it's time to talk, say what's on the paper, just that."

He nodded back. "Okay," he said loudly, and was dissolved by the sudden strong tide that swept me forward. I remembered that I should have told him about his bunk being destroyed. Instead I tried to interest the goats in a strained pun about a farmer who cared for seven or eight goats, even though he never cared for chevon or ate goats. It shut them up, at least. I trudged on in comfortable silence until I came upon my mother. I knew her at once, and was delighted to learn what she looked like, how she moved, how she smelled. It was only when I saw the concern in her troubled eyes that I began to realize how much trouble I must be in. That made me dizzy, and I told her so. She said I could sit down, so I did, and by the time I realized she'd meant I should sit in some chair somewhere nearby it was way too late. My tailbone hit the floor with a crash, angering the floor so much it reared up and smacked me on the back of the head. It burst, like Jinny's bubble had earlier, disintegrating me just as effectively.

10

> No, no, you're not thinking: you're just being logical.
>
> —Niels Bohr

I was wide awake and clearheaded. I was in an absolutely anonymous cubic, a generic plasteel box of air, about the size of a small studio. Its only features were doors at opposite ends, generic chairs, and a monitor. I was seated on one of the chairs, facing one of the doors, the monitor on the wall to my right. Seated facing me was Solomon Short. Behind him was another man I did not know, who sat facing the monitor and seemed absorbed in it. My tailbone hurt, quite a bit, and so did the back of my head, but I did not mind much.

"Do you accept me as your Advocate, Joel?" Sol asked me. I blinked. "Sure."

"I understand Pat has given you your lines."

I remembered what he must mean, and patted my pocket; the folded note was still there. "Yes."

He nodded, and gestured to the monitor. "Stick to the script. Now pay attention to that."

The screen showed a room larger than this one. At its far left, three people sat behind a long table on a short shallow stage. On the right three smaller tables faced the stage, with people seated at them, one at either end and two at the center table. They were the only ones I recognized: Richie and Jules. "Is this real-time?"

"Yes."

Oh, fine: they got to tell their side first.

"Closest to us on the left," Sol said, "is Coordinator Merril Grossman, representing the colony. Beyond her is Magistrate Eleanor Will, and after her is Lieutenant Frank Bruce, Third Officer, representing the crew. With me?"

"So far."

"Good man. Nearest to us on the right of the screen is Prosecutor Arthur Dooley, representing the Covenant. Look him over carefully. I believe you've met the next two, transportees Butch and Sundance. Beyond them is their own Advocate, Counselor Randy Lahey." He spoke over his shoulder. "Sound please, Tiger?"

The man addressed, a Japanese of great grace and dignity, lifted a remote control he hadn't been holding a second ago, and turned up the volume on the scene we were watching.

Coordinator Grossman was speaking. ". . . chance to rebut or amend afterward before this recording is formally entered into evidence. Do you both understand?"

"Sure," Richie said sullenly. "If it's bullshit, we can tell you after, I got it. Only I'll tell you right now, it's bullshit."

His partner Jules threw him a glare. "We understand, Your Honor." I noticed that his right hand, under the table, visible to the camera but not to the panel onstage, held a half-full drink.

Dr. Will, a striking slender brunette with skeptical eyes, spoke up in the formal tones of one reciting ritual for the record. "The *Sheffield*'s AI began this recording when one of you spoke one of its trigger phrases, 'gray market.' Under the terms of the Covenant, the recording was brought to official human attention only upon the observed commission of a breach of peace which occurs several seconds in. It is that breach with which I am primarily concerned today."

I was delighted. If there was an audiovisual record of what had occurred, I had nothing to worry about—and Jules was going to need whatever he had in that glass he was always holding. I could remember everything that had happened, very clearly. Well, clearly. Clearly enough. The broad outlines at least.

Let's see now. Richie and Jules had confessed that they were trying to recruit me into a conspiracy to traffic in heroin, or morphine, or possibly opium. Any of the three was an offense not merely detainable but serious enough to get one sent to Coventry . . . in jurisdictions where one existed. On a starship, for all I knew it was a spacing offense. Naturally I had been angry and afraid. I had asked them to leave my cubic, and had been ignored. When I tried to urge Jules toward the door with a hand on his shoulder, Richie had abruptly attacked me. Releasing a lot of my own pent-up frustration, I had admittedly overresponded a bit, knocked him all the way across the room—back onto my own bed, destroying it. Then Jules had sucker-punched me from behind, and we'd all ended up entangled on the deck, where I'd managed to keep them both restrained until the proctors arrived.

Yep—that was everything. I realized it was a bit unusual for someone of my size, mass, and background to make such easy work of huge bruisers like those two, so I was glad to know a visual record existed to back up my account.

"*Sheffield,* please begin playback."

"Yes, Magistrate," the ship said.

I settled back to watch myself in action.

. . . "*gray-market,*" Jules's recorded voice said.

"*How gray?*" I heard myself ask after a pause that now seemed to me incriminatingly long.

"*Just barely beige,*" Richie answered. "*It only gets black for a day or so right at the end. Up until then it's mostly gray, and some green. Tell him, Jules—*"

That's odd, I thought. Poppies aren't black at any part of

their life cycle. Or gray, or beige. I'd grown them for the Lermer City Hospital, back on Ganymede. They're extremely colorful flowers, which ultimately yield a white or pale yellow seed pod that oozes a white sap. How could a drug dealer know less about his product than I did? Or was Richie simply talking through his ass?

I glanced at Sol when Richie's "High Japonics" line came, expecting to share at least a grin if not a chuckle. I was sure it would delight him. He didn't crack a smile.

Solomon Short failing to find humor in a situation was so out of character, I was still puzzling over it when I suddenly realized the crux of the whole matter was approaching, and resumed paying close attention. Here came the sentence that would exculpate me. My heroic battle scene would not be far behind.

Richie's voice blathered something about his grade ten. My own voice asked Jules, *"Why don't you tell me which flower you mean?"*

Here it came—

"Happy hour," Jules said.

My jaw fell. I was so shocked, I stopped paying attention to the events unfolding onscreen. Someone had to have altered the recording!

"Sol—" I cried.

"Shush," he said loudly and firmly. "Reserve your questions and observations."

"But damn it, he said—"

"Pipe down, I said!"

Damn it to hell, he'd said *poppy flower*, not *happy hour*.

Developed in one of the L-5s—all of them publicly disavowed blame and all of them privately claimed credit—Happy hour was a flower whose leaves contained a mildly entheogenic alkaloid just slightly stronger than marijuana in effect, and no more habituating. It was about the opposite end of the spectrum from opium poppies. It just barely qualified as a restricted drug on Terra, and there were jurisdictions—among them Ganymede—where its use was legal. I had no idea what the *Sheffield*'s policy on it might be.

There were shouts and other loud noises from onscreen, but I was oblivious, aghast at this unexpected turn of events, trying to reconcile the impossible. The only rational explanation was that someone, somewhere, somehow, had been able to corrupt the *Sheffield*'s AI. If so, I was about as screwed as screwed could be. I began to panic. "Sol, you have to listen to me!"

"I know," he agreed, eyes on the screen. "Isn't it terrible?"

"But I—"

"Don't call *me* Butt-Eye," he said, and used the remote to raise the volume enough to drown me out.

It wasn't easy. The fistfight playback had finished while I was distracted, and the sole audio output now was the soft voice of the magistrate. But Sol mashed down on that volume-up button, and only backed it off when I resumed paying attention to the screen.

And found Dr. Will in mid-lecture, a more-in-sorrow-than-in-contempt tone in her voice. "—even mention your ridiculous attempts to claim your names were actually Corey Trevor and Jay Rock."

"I told you, it was a fuckin' reflex—" Richie said off-camera.

"However," she went on determinedly, "this court does take notice of your special request regarding language, and reluctantly agrees with your argument that for you to defend yourself adequately you must be allowed to use your own natural idiom. To require you to use my vocabulary would be a distraction roughly equivalent to you asking me to speak to you freely and eloquently . . . without ever using any words that contain the letter 't.' I rule that you—*only* you—may use profanity in my court."

"Wow. Thanks, Your Magistrate, that's really fuckin' awesome."

"Richie," Jules began.

"Well, it is," Richie said. "Okay, so you saw it. That dick got all pissy for no reason, and started talking about proctors and shit. Well, I'm already on probation, like you pointed out before, and who's a proctor gonna listen to, me or some citizen? So I got mad and told him he was being an asshole, 'cause he was. And what does he do? He punches me in the face!"

No. That wasn't possible. *Surely* I hadn't—

Dr. Will said, "At that point, a proctor would have seen your face and his knuckles and believed you. Why didn't you call one?"

"Well, I would've got *around* to it," he said defensively. "I was kind of fuckin' busy just then."

"Busy whacking him," Jules muttered.

"I was trying to, like, knock his punches aside," Richie insisted. "So I kept missing. Big fuckin' deal. What am I, a boxer? Anyway, Your Wordship, my point is, after that the whole thing kind of got out of hand and nothing that happened was really anybody's fault, and the stuff that *was* somebody's fault wasn't really, so much, because all of us were full of shit, so what I say is, why don't we let water under the bridge lay where Jesus flang it, and just forget the whole thing? That's fair."

Jules said, "I hate to admit it, but he's right, Your Honor. It's a wash. No harm, no foul."

Dr. Will sat breathing through her nose for a while, looking at the pair of them. Finally she said, "Here is my judgment. You will both apologize to Mr. Johnston for invading his privacy, disturbing his harmony, and ruining his furniture. You will repair the damage yourselves. For the next month you will each be confined to your quarters whenever you are not either working or eating." She closed a folder that lay before her.

Richie couldn't believe his luck. "That's *it?*"

She cleared her throat meaningfully, and his grin vanished. "I would be considerably harsher," she assured him. "But the *Sheffield*'s Senior Healer, Dr. Lewis, has advised me that she considers moderate recreational use of happy hour acceptable on this voyage, and the Captain concurs. Neither of you knew that when you approached Mr. Johnston—but it was a fact all the same. You have narrowly escaped serious sanctions. Consider yourselves lucky that camera's microphone did not malfunction."

"We do. Thank you, Your Honor," Jules said at once. "Let's go, Rich."

They both got up and left the frame, and a few seconds later, the door I was facing dilated, and they both came out together, accompanied by Lahey, their potbellied Advocate. They were striving hugely, and without much success, to suppress grins big enough to frighten a hired killer or even a real estate agent. When they saw me, their grins did not falter, just became more wolflike somehow. "Hey, Farmer Brown," Richie called. "Knock knock."

I was so confused and demoralized I played along. "Who's there?"

"A fucked-in-the-head dipshit with manure on his shoes who goes around punching people 'cause he doesn't know his ass from his elmo," he said triumphantly.

I opened my mouth . . . but if there is a comeback to that remark, I still don't know what it is.

"Good luck in there, arsehole," Jules said, and took a sip of his ever-present drink. "Come on, Rich, let's go." They both walked boldly through us, making us step out of their way, and left through the door behind us.

"You have your lines?" Solomon asked again.

I started, and patted my breast pocket. "Damn. I should have studied them—"

"Too late now," he said. "Let's go."

I soon found myself in a surprisingly comfortable chair, facing The Three Bears.

To the left sat Coordinator Grossman. She wasn't *that* big, physically. But she was a little bigger than the human average in all dimensions—and more important she was one of those larger-than-life people who can dominate any room she cares to. Right now she was just observing, but she was doing even that with gusto, with appreciation, hoping I would prove entertaining.

Directly ahead of me was Middle Size Bear, Magistrate Will, average height and mass. On the monitor outside her eyes had seemed skeptical. Now they were more . . . *knowing*. Mothers always know what you're thinking, I've been told. Until you reach a certain age, anyway. Apparently I hadn't reached it. I was glad there was a third bear because it gave me a reason to pull my eyes away from hers—

—and then was sorry I had. Littlest Bear, Lieutenant Bruce, was really more of a bantam rooster. Most small men learn to deal with it, but if they get picked on enough, early enough, sometimes they never do get over it. He was permanently pissed off at everyone. And me he was *allowed* to be pissed at. I tried not to look, and failed, and sure enough, his feet did not quite reach the floor, even with the lifts he was wearing. And he caught me looking.

"Good afternoon, Joel," Dr. Will said.

I turned back to her and opened my mouth, and only then realized that every molecule of moisture in my oral tract had gone someplace else. I made a faint croaking sound. Solomon said, "Good afternoon, Doctor," and gestured to someone outside my peripheral vision,

"You speak for Citizen Johnston, Dr. Short?" Lieutenant Bruce asked, surprised.

"Yes, Third Officer."

A bottle of water was put before me. Once again, I was glad—but only momentarily. The instant the first sip touched my lips, I suddenly knew exactly where all that missing moisture had gone to, where all the moisture in my body had gone to.

Use of his honorific had pleased Lieutenant Bruce. "Do you mind if I ask why, Dr. Short?"

"He plays the saxophone, sir."

This response clearly baffled Bruce. He wanted to find it contemptible—but even he couldn't be contemptuous of a Relativist.

Dr. Will cut in, and *again* it was one of those glad-but-only-for-a-second deals, because with her first words, I realized she was speaking in courtroom tones. "Joel, we're here to adjudicate the events that occurred in your quarters earlier this afternoon. First we will establish what facts we can. You will have an opportunity to explain, interpret, argue, or rebut, afterward, but please reserve your comments if any until we've finished examining the record. The *Sheffield*'s AI began saving this recording when one of you spoke one of its trigger phrases, 'gray market.' Under the terms of the Covenant, the recording was brought to official human attention only upon the observed commission of a breach of harmony which occurs several seconds in—"

Oh, shit, here we go, I thought. Okay, okay: when it gets to the crucial point in the playback, they'll all hear how *close* it sounded like "poppy flower." They'll see how it was an honest mistake.

The playback began on the monitor before me, with a peripheral echo over on Prosecutor Dooley's table.

And of course they'll agree that if somebody *had been* trying to peddle poppy products in a small society like this one, they should have been spaced. Anybody might take a poke at guys like that, before getting control of their emotions.

Reluctantly I admitted to myself that onscreen, they did not look particularly like villains. They looked like idiots— somehow still optimistic enough to think they might put one over on The Man despite a consistent record of failure. Worse, they were clearly harmless idiots, not nearly as menacing as I remembered them.

Richie said his High Japonics line again, and Sol brayed with laughter, even though he'd heard it already, outside in the anteroom.

Then the recording reached the point at which I'd heard "poppy flower," and what Jules said onscreen now sounded nothing at all like "poppy flower," it was clearly and unambiguously "happy hour," and nothing else.

And then *nothing* that followed was as I remembered it. I watched in growing dismay at what resembled nothing so much as a performance by an ancient comedy team called The Three Stooges.

I did not land a single punch. Nobody did. I was the only one who even tried very hard.

The me onscreen cussed Richie and Jules out, and told them to get out of his room or he'd call a proctor. Richie jumped up indignantly, shouting, "Hey, fuck that, I'm on probation, okay!" He put a hand on my shoulder—to turn me around to face him, so he could argue more effectively; it was quite clear he wasn't attempting a sucker punch. And I tried to spin on my heel and punch his face in. And tripped over my own feet and missed by a kilometer and fell heavily into him, staggering him a little. And behind me, Jules tried to step forward and pull me back by the collar, except the place he planned to put his foot turned out to be full of my tangled ankles, so *he* tripped and fell into *me*. That tipped Richie the rest of the way over backward, and we all crashed onto Pat's bunk together, tearing it right out of the wall and dropping us to the deck. Richie and I both got the breath knocked completely out of us, but Jules was able to rise far enough to reach a musclebound arm up and grab hold of my bunk, which promptly also tore out of the wall and whacked him hard enough on the head to knock him cold. It drove his head forward and down, so it slid off the *front* of his head, and landed edge-on on the middle of Richie's contorted face, smoothing it out completely, at just about the same instant that Jules's kneecaps impacted both of my kidneys. Then it fell over onto the back of *my* head, and Jules's face landed on it. And then we all were very quiet and still . . .

"Do you wish to see the recording again, Joel?" Dr. Will asked.

My mouth had once again become dry as a balance sheet. I shook my head no, reached for my water, and allowed myself the tiniest possible sip.

"Is there anything you wish to say on behalf of the colony, Prosecutor Dooley?"

"No, Doctor. I believe what we've seen twice now speaks for itself."

"It certainly does," Bruce muttered sotto voce.

"Joel, if there is anything you would like to say, now is the time."

Oh. Oh. I was ready for this one. Thank you, Pat! I fumbled at my pocket, took out my lines, tried to unfold the paper under the table unobtrusively, so it wouldn't be totally obvious I was using a crib sheet.

And when I had it open, the damned thing was blank.

I looked at Sol. Sol looked back at me. I looked down at that piece of paper. Then I looked back up at the judge and shook my head no.

She merely nodded, but her mouth changed slightly in a way that gave me the impression my response pleased her for some reason. "Anything to add, Advocate Short?"

"Yes, Doctor," Sol said. He tapped a few keys on the table's terminal. "You will all find my representation before you. It speaks to certain facts and circumstances which I hope you will agree are mitigational in this matter."

As all three looked down at their screens and began to read, I looked at ours, but it was blank. I looked at Sol. Sol looked back at me. I faced forward and waited.

"I see," Magistrate Will said after a few moments. "Thank you, Advocate."

Coordinator Grossman was next to finish reading; she sat back, turned her head five degrees to the right, and studied me, frowning slightly.

When Bruce spoke, there was something odd about his voice. "You appear to have been under a great deal of stress lately, Colonist." It took me a moment to identify the subtle change in his tone. He was addressing me with respect. It confused me so much, the interval into which I could have inserted a response passed before I could think of one.

Dr. Will polled her companions by eye. There was some brief silent communication I didn't get. "Very well," she said then, and fixed me with an eagle's remorseless gaze. "Citizen Joel Johnston, physical violence aboard this ship is intolerable. You have damaged fellow citizens and colony property without cause. Examination suggests that you may have done so because of situational emotional imbalance, and possibly perceptual error, rather than from an unhealthy belief that you are entitled to correct the moral lapses of your fellow citizens with assault. Therefore, this matter will be held in abeyance indefinitely. You will not be required to accept remedial neurochemistry at this time. You are released in your own recognizance, on the conditions that, first, you enter treatment immediately, and satisfy all requirements of your chosen Healer to the best of your ability, and second, you either make peace with Transportees Bent and Rafuse, or mutually file a standard hundred-meter restraining order. In addition you are fined their medical expenses, and the cost of materials for repairing the physical damage to your quarters."

"Do you understand all that, Joel?" Grossman asked. Her voice was deep, raspy, kindly. "Settle the score, bury the hatchet, do as your Healer tells you, this all goes away and you get to keep on being who you are right now. Otherwise your brain chemistry gets readjusted until you're fit to live with people. It's our only choice, I'm afraid: we have no Coventry aboard."

I stood there listening to the blood in my ears until Bruce said, "Is there anything you wish to say for the record, Citizen Johnston?"

I looked at Sol. Sol looked back at me. I looked down at my crib sheet, and it was still blank. I looked up at the panel, and found that there was enough moisture in my mouth to permit speech, and that decided me.

I said, "Thank you," to Magistrate Will, and "Very much," to Coordinator Grossman, and "All of you," to Third Officer Bruce.

All three gave the same inclined nod of polite acknowledgment. All three stood up. So did Sol. So did Prosecutor Dooley. So, finally, did I.

"Hot jets, Citizen," Dr. Will said formally.

"C-clear skies," I responded automatically, but she had already spun on her heel and left, followed by her fellow panelists.

I turned to Sol, and found him beaming at me. "Some people are *really* hard to drag to a shrink," he said. Then his expression changed slightly. "Whoa, now. Okay. Let's sit down and have a nice drink of water. That's better. Now a nice deep breath. Hold it for a moment. That's it. Let it out. Wait. Deep breath again. Hold. Release. Hold. You've got it. A little longer each time." The breathing thing was very hard to do, but soon it did start to clear my head a little. My heart was pumping a klick a sec. I felt like I was on the Upper Farm Deck: the temperature seemed to have shot up five degrees. I was pouring with fresh sweat from head to toe.

"Idiot," Sol said, shaking his head. "*Before*, you sweat."

"I don't know why I hadn't figured it out for myself, but I hadn't," I said. "I'm usually *much* quicker on the uptake, but it never occurred to me I was in danger of being put on neuromeds until she said I wasn't anymore. It's kind of a phobia of mine, having my personality altered by someone else. You probably think Ganymedeans are backward primitives in that regard, but—"

"It is precisely because I share your unconventional horror that I chose to act as your Advocate."

"Sol—"

"Don't thank me until you hear my fee. I want a new composition. It has to be at least fifteen minutes long. It can have anything you want in it as long as there's a lot of sax, baritone. Theme, style, tempo, key—all up to you. And it has to have my name in the title. You have until we reach our destination."

I looked at his goofy kindly smile for a long moment. "Sold," I said finally. "Thank you, Solomon."

"Don't forget to thank Pat for writing your speech. You delivered it eloquently. I might almost say movingly."

"I won't. Which one of you put the other up to this?"

He was gone like the Cheshire Cat, leaving behind only a ghost of his dopey grin.

11

Life is painful;
Suffering is optional.

—Sylvia Boorstein

My Healer said, "Will you excuse me for just one moment, Joel?

"Of course, Dr. Louis," I said, and she put her full at-

tention on her screen for a few moments, keying in an occasional input. To pass the time I examined her office, a fairly
large cubic, soothingly furnished, gimmicked so that no
matter which way you looked, the light was never directly in
your eyes.

Suddenly I burst out laughing. A small outburst, easily
suppressed, but audible. She looked up and met my eyes
again and smiled faintly. "You got it, did you?"

"Just now," I agreed.

Behind her, a midsize image hung framed on the wall, a
rather striking photo of a large lizard, of a breed that had
adapted better than anyone had expected to Martian conditions and was now considered a minor pest there. I had noticed it when I'd come in, but it had taken until now for my
memory to yield up the odd name of that odd creature: Gila
monster. It was a visual pun. She was the Healer monster.

"That's about how long we've been around," she said.

"Healers?"

"Meddlers. Busybodies. Pains in the ass. Healing is
merely one of the few remaining socially acceptable excuses
for poking one's nose into another Citizen's affairs. Excuse
me again for just one moment."

She went back to her screen, and this time I decided to pass
my time by studying her more closely instead of the room.

She was perhaps twice my own age or a bit more, I
guessed, of average height and weight, and looked healthy,
fit, and content with her life. In another context I'd have
called her attractive for her age. She wore her brown hair
short, so nothing obscured any part of her face. In its various
contours and configurings I found evidences suggesting decency, kindness, patience, considerable humor . . . and beneath all these a strength, or perhaps simply a determination,
so awesome even in repose I had the crazy idea that if she
were ever to go out the airlock, get a good grip on the frame,
and plant her feet on the vacuum, the *Sheffield* would slowly
come to a halt. Her clothing, however, was slightly more casual and comfortable than many would have deemed appropriate for our situation, indicating that the strength was not
the kind rooted in iron stupid discipline.

I glanced around again. A pair of flat images on the side of a bookcase caught my attention, precisely because they seemed so pointless. Each photo had been cut out of a magazine or other hard copy and put there with pins. The one on top was of a donkey, or burro. Below it was a medium shot of a golfer lining up a putt. And just below them both was a line cut from some advertisement: *"For those who know the difference!"* If there was a point to the arrangement, it eluded me.

"Thanks for your patience."

"No problem, Dr. Louis."

"Call me Amy, please. Joel, I think there are four questions you urgently need to consider."

"That many?" I said sourly.

"I don't think you've thought through any of them yet." Perhaps my least favorite criticism; I swallowed a comeback. "And you must. They're all very important."

"Somehow, Amy, I have an idea you're going to tell me what they are soon."

She shook her head. "Not if you're going to get cranky right at the jump, just because I said you have some thinking to do. If you like, we can spend this whole session dicking around. But we're going to get to it eventually. Suit yourself."

I think if she had looked back down at her screen, I would have gotten up and left, then. But she didn't. She just kept looking me in the eye, waiting, not offended by my antics, just waiting patiently until I decided to move on instead.

"Hell of a thing to say to a man, that he doesn't think things through," I grumbled. But it was clearly a backing-down grumble.

She nodded sympathetically. "It is an embarrassing thing to be caught at. But, Joel, face it: you're *caught*. Your presence here is not voluntary, remember? Ergo, you have screwed up *big-time*. The embarrassment is one of the smallest things you're going to have to deal with."

She paused, visibly giving me a few seconds to see if I was going to jump salty again.

Well, God damn it, Joel, is she right or isn't she? Can you face facts, or not?

"The majority of clients I deal with have been driven into this room by their own egos. You have not, for once, so I don't want to waste as much time dealing with yours. Can we simply assume goodwill on both sides, and start with the basic agreement that you need help, and that I may have some?"

The stars themselves knew I needed help. And I knew she had some. I'd known that before I'd gotten from her door to the chair I sat in.

"I guess . . ." I began.

And a stuck switch somewhere in my brain went *spung*, and I burst out laughing—a hold-your-belly-and-fold-over guffaw.

She was not offended in the least, just surprised. And interested. I wanted to explain but was laughing too hard. But she was in no hurry. Finally I got enough air to hoot, "I do! . . . I do! . . . Honest!" which only further confused her until I was able to get one arm free and point to the clip art pictures on the side of her bookcase that had puzzled me earlier. "I do know!" At once she began to laugh, too.

I *do* know the difference. Between my ass, and a hole in the ground. "Sometimes, anyway—"

She had a great braying loon hoot of a laugh, and knew it, and was not at all self-conscious about it. So we had us a good one. By the time it was done, I was pretty sure I trusted her. It's humorless people who frighten me, because I can't begin to understand them.

At last I said, "I'm sorry, Amy. Please tell me the four questions you think I need to address first."

She nodded. "Who. What. Where. Why."

I blinked. "Not 'when'?"

She shook her head. "The answer to that is always 'now.' "

I took a deep breath. "In that case, let's do it."

"First, 'who.' That's almost always a good place to start. Who are you? Not, who did you plan to be, or who are you expected to be, or even, what would you like to be. Who are you? Who the hell is this Joel Johnston, when he's at home? I don't think you know. And I'm certain I don't. It would be a useful thing to know, don't you think?"

I was past sarcasm or irony. "Yes, Amy, it would." My
voice was hoarse. From the laughing.

"Next, 'what.' What led you to this place? To this ship,
this twenty-year voyage to the back of beyond? What led
you to abandon literally every single thing you've ever
known except the concept of associating with other humans?
Why did you leave the world, leave the rest of the race, leave
the Solar System, for good? This is probably the question
you think you know the most about, and I'm pretty sure
you're wrong. Or only part right."

It was a broken heart! Wasn't it?

Wait. Had I expected heartbreak to be *permanent*? Did I
really intend to die a virgin? If my Jinny was not to be with
me, nor I with her, how was it any better if she was eighty-
five light-years farther away?

"The third question, 'where,' might actually be your best
place to start. Where are you going? I mean that not rhetori-
cally, but literally."

I didn't understand. "Literally? That's easy. To Peekaboo
Two. Brasil Novo, if you want to be formal. The second
planet of Immega Seven-Something."

"Tell me about it."

"Huh?"

"Tell me about the planet. When it was discovered. Its
physical parameters. Its atmosphere. Its geography, and ge-
ology. Climate. Seasons. Flora. Fauna. Most intelligent-
seeming organism identified. Most dangerous-looking
predator identified. Intended location of our First Landing
site." She paused expectantly.

"Uh . . . it's real hot and damp, for . . . for extended periods, and there's a whole lot of oxygen," I said, and realized
with dismay that I had shot my bolt.

"You're going to spend twenty years getting there, and
you'll stay there the rest of your life. I would spend some of
the twenty years studying just what you've gotten yourself
into."

All at once I felt immortally stupid. She was absolutely,
shockingly right. Not thought this through? Hell, I hadn't

started thinking. Look before you leap, my father had often said. I hadn't even looked *after* I'd leapt. After weeks on board a starship, my principal curiosity about my destination so far had consisted of wondering what to wear to work on the Upper Ag Deck. I had just sort of assumed there'd be a planet of some sort at the end of this, and what of it?

Could a broken heart cause brain damage? On this scale?

"Finally, why. Once you know the destination, the question becomes, why are you going there? Why go anywhere, for that matter? For what reason? What will you do there? Above all, why will it *matter*? Here, take these. Basket over there."

I accepted the box of tissues she offered out of politeness, and was startled to discover that my face was soaking wet and I really did need to blow my nose. The wastebasket had been placed so that it was a hard shot to miss. I hit it six times running before I was done. By then I was seeing little black spots overlaying everything.

"So that's it?" I said, my voice quavering. "That's everything? Shit, I thought I had a problem."

"You do," she said simply. "And that is a *lot* to chew on. So much that twenty years might not be enough time. And I promise you it will be painful. And you may fail completely. Would you like the *bad* news, now?"

I giggled. "Sure."

"You have no fucking choice."

"Tell me there's good news." I tried to parody desperation, but did too good a job.

She smiled. "You have the best Healer on the ship. I will give you some good tools, and yell encouragement, and take your crap, and share your breakthroughs, and tell you when your exciting new profound insights are horseshit."

"Tools?"

"Techniques. Disciplines. Attitudes. Drugs. In addition, I will listen to anything you want to tell me, and give advice if I happen to have any."

"That sounds good," I said. "When do I start?"

"Now."

"Okay. *How* do I start?"

"First, you have to stop."

"Stop what?"

"Everything."

"Huh? I mean, 'Crave pardon?' "

"To grow, you must learn about yourself. To learn, you must listen to yourself. To listen, you must first learn the hardest trick of all: to shut the hell up."

I was so startled, I did. And then realized it would have been a not-unclever reply, if I'd done it intentionally. So I tried to pretend I had, and made an elaborate show of obligingly cocking my ear to listen to some imaginary sound, and then tried to pantomime hearing some transcendent insight. She just kept looking at me with no expression, and suddenly I had a sense of seeing myself from the outside, watching myself mug and fidget. And *finally* began to get a sense of what she was driving at. I let my face go as blank as hers, took a deep breath, and tried my best to listen. To myself . . . to her . . . to whatever. After a few seconds I closed my eyes to help myself concentrate.

I don't hear a damn thing/wait/is that the air circulator?/it's gone now/this is silly/really silly/stupid kid's game/hide and go fuck yourself/wait, now/a hum/a note at the very upper limit of audibility, somewhere right around 20,000 cycles per second/no, two of them/dysharmonic/I never diss harmonic/what's wrong with dat harmonic?/ God, I'm sleepy/hey, why can't I hear my own pulse?/I wonder if—

"There's a certain interior monologue that never stops, isn't there?"

Her voice startled me, enough that I opened my eyes. "Yes. Yes, there is."

"Try and make it stop."

"Stop thinking? Completely? Hell, that's one of my best tricks."

"Go ahead."

About five minutes later, I admitted defeat.

"Whose is the voice you hear?"

"My own."

"To whom does it speak?"

"To . . . to me."

"Why?"

It was a good question. How could it be so important to tell myself things I already knew that I couldn't seem to stop, even for a second? I had always prided myself on controlling my own mind . . . but it now seemed I only had limited control of what it thought *about*. But I could not make it stop.

"I don't know," I admitted. "It must be terribly, terribly important, because I can't make it stop even as long as I can make myself stop breathing. It's like my heartbeat—if it ever pauses, even for a few seconds, I'll die. But that can't be true: I've stopped thinking altogether a lot of times. Drunk . . . stoned . . . sedated . . . anesthetized for surgery . . ." I trailed off, realizing I wasn't sure whether I'd stopped thinking at those times, or just stopped recording the thoughts. "Maybe not. I don't know."

"You don't need to be afraid of it, I promise."

"Are you *sure*?"

"Your record says you're a musician and composer, but is vague about what kinds of music you're interested in. Do you know the classics? The Beatles?"

"Sure."

"Turn off your mind. Relax, and float downstream. It is not dying. That advice was ancient back then."

I shrugged. "Okay. How?"

"People have been trying to make their minds stop for thousands of years. It's called meditation. There are some useful tricks that have been passed down. Come here and I'll show you some."

She got up and moved to an area with no furniture. I could tell she was a Loonie by the way she handled herself in a third of a gee, but it wasn't so much awkward as unpracticed. She had the necessary strength to handle twice her normal weight, and would get more graceful at it with time, like perfecting an accent. I got up and followed her. She was just placing on the floor two objects like giant black cloth hamburgers. Pillows, it seemed: as I watched, she dropped effortlessly into a cross-legged seat on one of them, seeming to melt slowly like the Wicked Witch of the West despite the double gravity. She gestured at the other. "Sit down, Joel."

I did so far more clumsily, despite being in my native gravity. Pillow? It was just barely a cushion—made of soft cloth, but filled with something unyielding, as soft-but-firm-underneath as a . . .

"It's called a zafu," she said. "Don't sit square on it, but a little forward on it, almost falling off the edge, and put your legs like so." She demonstrated.

I dug in my heels. "Hold on a minute. Is this some kind of religious thing? Buddhism or something?"

She smiled. "Atheist?"

"Agnostic."

"Fear not. Buddhists are only one of many groups of humans who have found this a useful posture for meditation. So have Hindus, Taoists, TM'ers, and a dozen other groups. And in any case, Buddhism isn't a religion, strictly speaking."

"It isn't?"

"No god, or gods, or goddesses—except in a couple of the more obscure sects. No heaven or hell in the theological sense. No patriarch or matriarch, no Prophet or Pope. They don't go in for holy wars, or heresy hunts."

"Really?"

"Buddhists believe the Buddha himself was simply a man, who woke up one day. As far as I understand it, anyway. I know hardly anything at all about Buddhism. If you're interested, you can talk to Tenzin Itokawa, the Relativist. He is a Zen priest, of the Rinzai school. Right now, forget Buddhism. Forget religion. Just put your legs like this and trust me, okay?"

I tried. "Show me again."

She unpretzeled, and then pretzeled again slowly. I tried to copy it. This time I came closer.

"Other way round. This one over that one. There—that's it. Now work your knees around a little until they're comfortable."

Suddenly I seemed to just snap into place. "Like that?"

"That's it. Good. Okay, now. Spine straight. Stack those

vertebrae. Hands together, palms up, left hand on top, with the thumb tips touching. Settle your skull on those stacked vertebrae. You've got it."

It did indeed feel like a position I could hold for a while in relative comfort. "Now what?"

"Don't just do something: sit there."

I mentally shrugged and did so. Or rather tried to stop doing anything. As before I tried to stop thinking, too—with no better success. But I did become aware that I was starting to relax. My thoughts didn't exactly slow down . . . but they became less intense, somehow.

After a few minutes of silence, she said, "Now we do a breathing exercise so childishly simple it can't possibly have any effect."

"Sounds good."

"There really is nothing to it. In your head, count to four, at intervals of about four seconds, or a little longer." I did as she asked. "Okay. Now, you inhale for a count of four . . . then hold your breath for a count of four . . . then exhale for four . . . then hold for four. In, hold, out, hold. Repeat, and keep repeating. Try it."

I played along. A full cycle, then another, then another. After half a dozen or so, I found the rhythm, and settled into it. Easy as pie. Considerably easier than pi. Stop that, Joel.

"Good. Now with each cycle, slow it down just a skosh. Not much, and when it seems to be too much, let it come back up again, until you find your slowest natural speed. As soon as you're sure you've found it, stop counting and just breathe."

It wasn't hard. It was mindless, was what it was. Silly, and pointless, and . . .

. . . and I could feel my shoulders settling. Feel my facial muscles relaxing. Feel my pulse slowing, and deepening, and steadying. *Hear* my pulse, playing bass under the alternating E-A E-A organ chords of my breath. As I became aware of it, I had the idea I could hear it slowly changing from electric bass guitar to acoustic standup bass, quieter but more resonant.

I let myself sink into it. I closed my eyes, and paradoxically as I did I became more aware of the room, of my position in it, of its position in the *Sheffield*—and as I followed the thought to its logical next stopping place, it was as if the ground fell away beneath me without warning. Have you ever been so stoned or drunk that you suddenly fancied you could actually *perceive* the vast slow spinning of whatever planet you live on? Not just as something known intellectually but as something felt in the gut? Ever find yourself clutching the ground, to keep from falling off? Well, something like that happened to me then. For the very first time, I suddenly *got* where I was.

I was in an incredibly, pathetically flimsy bubble of moist air, hurtling through interstellar space at a speed so intrinsically terrifying that its friction with *nothingness* was enough to require powerful and clever shielding, propelled by a force no man really understood, so powerful it could have wrecked my star if invoked too near it. With a would-be village of other misfits and refugees I was plummeting through the universe so fast Time itself couldn't keep up—living by Dr. Einstein's Clock, while behind me the rest of the human race continued to age as God or random chance had intended. In these hair-raising conditions I would, if I was very lucky, spend approximately the next fifth of my life racing toward a destination I had not given a second's serious consideration, a place where, if I was incredibly lucky, it would prove possible to raise turnips and keep hogs, and the monsters wouldn't be able to kill me.

All this in a microsecond—then in the time it took me to open my eyes the feeling popped like a bubble and I was back in my body again, was just a guy sitting in a room doing nothing at all. It happened and then was over so impossibly fast that I was still relaxed: there hadn't even been time for my heartbeat or breathing to increase. But when I did get my eyes open the first thing they saw was Dr. Amy's eyes looking straight into them, and I knew at once that she knew what had happened to me. She'd been expecting it to happen. No, that was wrong. She had known it might happen, and had hoped it would. My whole head vibrated for a few seconds, like a hummingbird in denial. "Whoa!" I croaked.

"See, Joel? You sat still and quieted down . . . and you noticed where you are. Sit still longer and you'll start to notice where you're going. Sit still long enough and you may figure out why you're going there. You could end up with some clues to just who the hell is doing all that."

"And that would be a good thing?"

"*Yes,*" she said, raising her voice two notches higher in volume for the single word. "Stop looking dubious. When you peel back enough layers of your own bullshit to finally get a good glimpse of yourself, you are going to find you respect yourself a good deal more than you expected to."

I said nothing.

"I promise that, Joel. The journey you need to take isn't going to be easy . . . but you're going to like the destination. Certainly a lot better than where you are now. Now lie to me."

"Beg pardon?"

"Tell me you believe me."

I tried unsuccessfully to suppress my grin. "I believe you believe it."

She nodded. "Close enough. That's enough for one session. Here's your homework. First, I want you to spend an hour a day sitting zazen—that's what you just did—and I'd like you to do it in a Sim Room."

"I was thinking of a spot on the Upper Ag Deck."

"Later. Starting out, use the Sim. Accept the simulations it offers you for the first two weeks, the ones I'll program for you. After that you can override if you want, using your judgment. After three or four weeks we'll slowly bring you back out into the real world again. The Ag Deck might be a great place to start."

I thought up some objections, and decided to hell with them. If she wasn't smarter than I was, this was all a terrible mistake. "Okay. That was 'first.' What's next?"

"I want you to get in shape. You're healthy enough, but you're quite out of condition for your age. Do what the Gym tells you."

It was easier to think up objections this time, and they

were better objections. The one I wanted to admit to was, "Where do I find the hours?"

"Shave them from either your farmwork or your music. Whichever is less important to you personally."

It is annoyingly hard to object to a reasonable proposal. She was right. I *was* out of shape. "Okay. Meditate, work out. What else?"

"Study your destination. Learn everything you can about it. The star, first—where Immega 714 lies in the sky, why it took so long to discover, how it's different from Sol. Then the planet: What kind of world is Brasil Novo, how is it like and unlike Ganymede, what's living there already, what kind of place is it going to be for a kid to grow up in?"

To that I had no objections. "Done. Meditate, exercise, look out the windshield—anything else?"

She nodded. "Yes. I want you to start dating. Joel? *Joel!*"

"You go too damned far," I said on my way to the door. It would not iris open fast enough to suit me, so I tried to hurry it with my hands and it jammed in its tracks, not quite all the way open. I had to stop in my own tracks, my exit spoiled by an absurd social dilemma. I could not walk away and leave her with a broken door like some kind of barbarian, but I had no idea how to repair it. I stood there, unwilling to turn around until I had some idea how to cope with the situation. I'm pretty sure in another second or two I'd have remembered that I was a rich man, now. But before I could think of it, behind me she said drily, "My door is always open."

It is very hard to remain annoyed at someone who has just made you burst out laughing. I gave up and turned around and she was laughing, too. She had a great whoop of a laugh. We got into one of those things where each time you're just about to get it under control, the other cracks up again. It always ends eventually with you smiling at each other, breathing like runners after the marathon.

"Okay," she said finally. "If you can laugh like that, you can take a few weeks before you start dating again. Go do your homework."

I nodded and gestured at the door. "I've got this."

She nodded and put her attention back down on her screen, as she'd been doing when I'd first seen her.

I GUESS THAT was really the day I finally joined the colony, became a Brasiliano Novo—or at least, decided to try. I had already been utterly committed, physically, since the *Sheffield* had left orbit, but it was only after I left Dr. Amy Louis's office that afternoon that I finally started to become *emotionally* committed to anything but numbness. Until then, I had been not only drifting, but paying no attention where I was drifting. Reefs or deeps, rough seas or doldrums, all had been the same to me. But from then on, I was at least back on the Bridge, trying to work out my position and best course, trying the rudder, learning how the sails handled, testing the diesels, scanning the horizon for clues to the weather ahead.

I don't mean to suggest it happened in an hour. It took weeks to happen, months, years. But that's the hour when it began happening.

12

There is no easy way from the earth to the stars.

—Seneca

The first thing I did about it was not move out.

Everyone seemed to assume that now that I was stinking rich, I would of course move out of the prematurely decaying hovel I had been sharing with three hapless losers, leave Dear Old Rup-Tooey behind me in the dust, and settle into vastly more lavish solo quarters several decks higher, and with all the privacy, comfort, and (most prestigious of all) roominess that could be desired by a healthy young nouveau millionaire whose Healer had advised him to start dating.

But I had lived alone before. I had *always* lived alone before. Until I'd been accepted into the Tenth Circle, I'd had no idea how much that sucked. I remembered it well. I had no particular reason to suppose money would make it all that much better.

Also, I kept remembering that I might very well have been spaced as a danger to the *Sheffield* by now, if it had not been for my bunkies Pat and Herb. And for Solomon Short, who was one of the six wealthiest people aboard, and had chosen to be my friend when all I had to my name was a good sax.

Besides, as Mark Twain says, two moves equals one fire. I'd already moved once recently.

So I stayed where I was. But I reached out to another friend, as wealthy as Sol and considerably more practical, and sought his counsel. And George R smiled, and pointed me toward the best mechanics, engineers, artisans, electricians, cyberpeople, *and* plumbers aboard, and snipped some bureaucratic red tape to get me permission to clear out storage cubics immediately next door on either side and cut through some walls. When all the busy beavers had gone away again and the dust had settled, RUP-0010-E was the most solid, reliable, comfortable, luxuriously appointed, and technologically advanced living space on that deck—and its 'fresher was probably the best in the *Sheffield*, so unreasonably large that all four of us could have used it at once, with a guest apiece. And so advanced in terms of hedonic technology that we all suddenly found ourselves very popular fellows in shipboard society: people wanted to be invited over for long enough to need to use the 'fresher. It didn't work well because we were usually in there ourselves.

Pat got all the data-chasing and pattern-spotting software his heart desired, and enough processing power to provide practical, real-time access to any historical datum on board. Or behind us in the Solar System, although that was already becoming more and more out-of-date as Einstein effect started to mount up. But historians aren't in a hurry.

Herb received the power to seal off his quadrant of the room at will with two mirror walls that would not pass light or sound in either direction, within which he could not-write in privacy.

So did Balvovatz, but I doubt he got much writing done, because he never activated his field if he was alone in there, and never stopped smiling when he came out. He told me years later, weeping drunk, that it was the first place he had ever lived that a woman who did not love him desperately would come to. I laughed so hard he stopped weeping and began laughing just about the time I quit laughing and started to cry.

For myself, I settled for two major infrastructure improvements. First, a robot that made French Press style coffee from fresh-ground recently roasted beans on demand and adulterated it to my taste; it claimed to be fully automatic, but actually you had to push a little button. And second, a bunk that was as comfortable as any in the *Sheffield* . . . and on top of which I, my roommates, *and* Richie and Jules could all have piled at once and done jumping jacks without making it creak, much less rip free of the bulkhead. Nothing in that room was breakable by the time I was done with it.

So much for change in my *physical* environment.

On my way to the Sim Room for my first session, I wondered what sort of exotic locale Dr. Amy had programmed for me to meditate in. The *Sheffield*'s Sim gear was less *perfectly* convincing than what I'd experienced at the Conrad enclave back in British Columbia . . . but not by much. It was one of the few areas Kang/da Costa had splurged on. I guess I expected something grandiose and imposing and sacred—the Eiheiji monastery in Japan, or Jaipur Lake Palace in India, or Vatican City before the Prophet's Angels got ahold of it. Or possibly some secular but stunning scenic vista: Vancouver Harbor, or Rio de Janeiro in *old* Brasil, or looking east from Olympus Mons on Mars, or Titan seen from the Rings, or my own favorite, Jupiter from Ganymede, at night, through an aurora. Nor would I have been surprised by a simple flood of sheer kaleidoscopic imagery, like a screensaver display, or the fireworks you can sometimes see behind your closed eyelids.

I got a blank white wall. About half a meter from my nose.

I've since learned that several schools of Buddhism do that, too: meditate facing a blank wall. It makes a certain amount of sense. Minimal visual distraction, maximal visual canvas for any visualization imagery you may find useful— and a constant, ongoing, gentle reminder that you are doing something not-ordinary, that you are now removed from the conventional world where sensible people do not sit staring at blank walls.

An equal number of Buddhists find this appalling, and instead sit with the blank wall *behind* them, facing another one across the room . . . and any co-practitioners in the way. What distinguishes Buddhism from any other faith I've studied—from most human beings, really—is that the people who face the wall and the people who face away from it have never fought a war over it. They're never going to agree . . . but they feel no need to. Buddha himself is supposed to have said, "People with opinions just go around bothering each other."

I thought both sides were crazy myself, when I first started, and Dr. Amy too for assigning me that program. My second day I mutinied, and reset the Sim for a Ganymede vista, as close as it could come to my own pasture at night. But at the end of the hour, I realized I had wasted the whole thing thinking. And worse, feeling, which was even less helpful. Nostalgia hurt too much. I tried it her way the rest of the week.

I spent nearly every minute of that first week more than half convinced I was wasting my time, waiting for something to happen and then uncertain whether or not anything had. But at the end of the week, I found that I was looking forward to it. Imagine that you've been carrying twenty kilos of sand in a backpack without knowing it, all the days of your life. Then one day somebody shows you how to take it off for a moment. It was that much of a relief, I learned, to be able to set down now and then, for whole minutes at a time, the ongoing burden of thought, to briefly silence the constant chatter of my mind compulsively reassuring itself that I was still alive. For periods measurable in whole long seconds, I could sometimes become transparent to my own feelings and emotions. Occasionally there would be what I can only call moments of clarity, when I seemed able to see without distortion and accept without fear. After a week of staring at that silly blank white wall, I was sorry when the time came to change it.

Until I saw the new Sim.

It was a series of paintings, or rather two series, acrylic on canvas, by a PreCollapse artist named Alex Grey, who lived and worked on Terra, in New York, in the twentieth and twenty-first centuries. You sat zazen for a while, and then you started up the image slideshow and looked at the paintings, and at programmable intervals they changed. That doesn't sound very dramatic—but I'm talking about the kind of art that ought to be served with a whisk broom, so the customer can brush the sawdust off his shirt when he gets back up. Grey made timeless art that probably would have spoken to a Neanderthal. Indeed, many parts of his vision were at least that old.

All the twenty-one paintings in Grey's Sacred Mirrors series are at least man-tall. First in the sequence is a pale gray human silhouette, facing you, arms slightly apart from its sides, palms outspread, almost as if to say, "Here I am."

Second painting: the background goes to black, and the silhouette is filled by an extremely realistic skeleton, man-tall and detailed. Third painting: the same skeleton is overlaid by an incredibly detailed and accurate rendering of all the nerves in the human body; the complete electrical wiring system for the skeleton, brain at the top, and nothing else. The golden nerves seem to leap off the canvas, rendered with the same sort of gilt that medieval manuscripts used to be illuminated with. Fourth painting: the nerves vanish, replaced by the circulatory system, rendered in blue, heart in the center of the breast—and for the first time the body is recognizably male, with testicles. The fifth painting details the complete lymphatic system—but this body is female. Successive paintings detail male viscera, then a female musculatory system complete with fetus in a cutaway womb. And finally the body grows flesh, becomes a naked Caucasian woman, facing you calmly. The next painting morphs her into a naked Caucasian man; the next an African woman; then an African man; then an Asian woman, and finally an Asian man.

Each of these figures, from the skeleton on up, has been depicted with such exquisite realism that the next painting has more impact than it might have alone. It shows the psychic energy system. The flesh has melted away, leaving bones and organs and nerves and veins and staring eyeballs . . . but all are shot through now with gleaming shimmering crackling filaments of energy, and the six chakras of so many mythologies are visible at brain, throat, heart, navel, abdomen, and groin, glowing with power like white coals, and the entire body is enveloped by a translucent pale blue aura made up of infinitely tiny threads of energy, and it is quite clear that all of it—body, chakras, and aura—is physically connected to the rest of the universe, exchanging energy with it. The next painting takes that even further: the flesh and meat and bone melt away, leaving a human-shaped form composed almost totally of the strings and threads of energy that generate it, extending outward to meet the cosmos at head and feet, wrapped in a great bubble of unimaginable power. And in the next painting, even the vague body shape is gone, leaving only a boiling torrent of loops and circles and lattices of universal fire that Sol later told me was remarkably like the mental picture he had going through his head when he was doing his job.

There were more paintings in the series, but most were top-heavy with denominational religious iconography, so I usually chose to fast-forward through them. Such imagery was perfectly fine back in those days, indeed laudable . . . but now of course feels faintly indecent, a reference to a bloody period in history we would all prefer to erase, if it were not that the horrid lessons learned in it must never ever be forgotten. Those images have all joined the swastika:

symbols of spirituality perverted, than which there is no greater evil.

After that came a different series of thirty paintings, which Grey called "Progress of the Soul." Each depicted one or more of his strange, skinless, fleshless glowing people, connected by powerful invisible energies to the world around them, carrying out a variety of utterly basic human activities. A man with bowed head, praying, a halo of golden energy pouring from his head. A man and woman side by side, staring rapt at the heavens together, information flowing in *both* directions. A man and woman kissing in close embrace—surely the most intimate embrace ever rendered, since you can pick out every sinew, nerve, or capillary in their bodies, *see* the normally invisible pulsing energy they create being passed back and forth, heterodyning, lighting the world. The same couple, copulating—an almost nuclear explosion of energy indescribable in words. Then the same couple standing, he reaching around from behind her to touch the hugely swollen belly inside which their child can be seen; that particular painting is framed on either side by an ontogeny sequence of ten images, one for each month, starting with sperm meeting egg, and ending with a full-term fetus. Then one I found it easy to stare at forever, called "Promise," in which the expecting lovers face one another, and promise each other what they will do for this child they're making together. On the ground between them is a two-year-old . . . holding a skull.

There are quite a lot more in the series, but I'm going to stop describing them now, because the next one in sequence, "Birth," is simply so powerful that I've never been able to endure looking at it for more than a few seconds; then my eyeballs start to cook and I have to look away.

But near the end of the series is one often considered Grey's masterpiece, called "Theologue." It depicts a man doing exactly what I was doing the first time I saw it: sitting zazen, legs folded beneath, hands placed on his lap in the mudra position, head slightly bowed, meditating. A translucent golden round halo surrounds his head, and a transparent blue egg-shaped halo surrounds his whole body. He is seated at least a foot off the ground, on a kind of net made of interwoven strands of energy running in three directions, bright white and so intense flames lick up from them in the vicinity of the seated man, but do not come close enough to burn him. Behind him, through the grid, gray mountains can be seen to recede forever. All six of his chakras shine with universal fire. It is clear that he is engaged in theologue: in a dialogue with God. Who is himself.

Maybe I've conveyed nothing at all to you. If so, just take it from me that a few weeks' exposure to those paintings helped me heal—physically, mentally, psychically, spiritually. Grey himself said one of the specific purposes of his work was to make people healthier. He had seen a study which showed that people who had just seen a frightening, disturbing 2-D movie called *The Exorcist* left the theater with their immune systems weakened, more vulnerable to disease. He decided if art could do that, it could damn well do the opposite, too, and should—so he devoted his life to learning how to create images that left the viewer healthier. I could not begin to describe how he does it, even if I understood it. Just take it from me that if you are ever mindblown or heartsick, what you want to do is look up the works of Alex Grey, in the best reproduction you can find, and let them work on you.

Then for two weeks, I reset the Sim to place me on an imaginary satellite orbiting low over Brasil Novo's equator, at a speed that kept the primary, Peekaboo, always behind me. I forgave the simulated satellite for impossibly having local gravity, since sitting zazen in orbit would have been impossible without it. And finally, I moved out of the Sim Room altogether, and set up my personal traveling zendo in the second of the two good spots I had mentally marked on the Upper Ag Deck.

As Dr. Amy had decreed, in addition to sitting, every day also had sweating.

For the first several weeks I chose swimming as my primary exercise, because it develops every one of the useful muscles and none of the others. That meant long trips to the upper decks, just below the Bridge Deck. The *Sheffield* kept its swimming water as far forward as possible, to act as some additional protection against the constant shower of deadliness from dead ahead—the bitter complaints of the very tiny, very nearly nonexistent bits of the universe we were enraging to white heat by hitting them at a large fraction of c. (Our drinking water was stored at the opposite end of the ship, against the day when we would flip over and begin decelerating for the last half of the voyage.)

The Pool area turned out to be a lively, buzzing social center, one of the primary places where the people aboard *Sheffield*, colonists, crew and transportees alike, went to meet each other for sociosexual reasons—practical when you think about it, since everyone there would be naked sooner or later. While I still was not ready to follow Dr. Amy's advice, I did notice that I worked harder at my swimming than I would have exercised if I had been alone.

While swimming there I got talking with Tiger Kotani, the kindly man I'd met briefly in the antechamber before my examination by Magistrate Will. He turned out to be a soft-voiced dignified astrophysicist from Terra. He persuaded me that simple fitness was not enough, and talked me into signing up for a self-defense class he taught.

Nowadays, of course, most citizens reliably expect to live out their lives without ever being involved in a violent altercation. People looked at me a little funny because I had been. I agreed that it had been a shameful event I should have been prudent enough to avoid. But I also found myself thinking that I was on my way to a frontier world, where people often acted in primitive ways, and where native fauna often acted in murderous and unpredictable ones. If, Heaven forbid, violence should ever come my way again, it seemed to me that it might be very nice to *win* the fight this time.

By the time Tiger-Shihan was through with me, I had reason to be confident that I might at least survive. He did not teach me to be a killing machine. But he did teach me to be pretty damn unkillable, and to sharply discourage attempts. I believe he himself could have massacred the entire ship's

complement, proctors and all . . . *if* we'd attacked him first.
All his technique was defensive.

He was also kind enough to teach me a few utterly nonviolent evasive techniques, which became necessary when I
learned that some girls who take self-defense classes are the
kind of girls who find a man who has been in a violent con-
frontation with other men interesting. Thanks to Tiger's
footwork advice, I was able to keep them all at arm's
length . . . but sometimes I worked harder in the corridor
outside the locker rooms than I did in the dojo.

The one female I was always happy to see was little Evelyn, so many trillions of kilometers behind me, whenever
one of her rare brief letters came in. She always found some
way to make me smile. I tried my best to return the favor.

One day another student of Tiger's named Matty Jaymes,
a pleasant-faced man in his forties who showed a lot of
quick in class, happened to come past as I was explaining to
a persistent brunette that I couldn't join her for coffee because I had to study: my Healer had told me to learn everything I could about our destination. This was the truth; I
simply omitted to mention that I had already been ducking
the task for over a month, and fully intended to keep ducking
it that night. Matty stopped short, managed to accept the
date I had just evaded without awkwardness for any of us,
then placed a tractor beam on me somehow and took me in
tow. He wanted to discuss music history, about which it soon
developed he knew about as much as I did myself.

But he was no musician. By the time we got back to his
quarters I knew he was an astronomer, like Tiger, and when
I saw that he shared the space with no one, I twigged that he
must be *the* ship's astronomer. The same one who had originally tried to interest me in his intensive study of Sol, back
when I'd made my abortive stab at a job hunt.

If I'd met Matty—he flatly forbade me to call him Dr.
Jaymes—in person back then, instead of by e-mail, he
would definitely have met my definition of interesting. I
haven't met a lot of men with genius-level minds whom
women found irresistible—but at least a dozen of them

called warm greetings to him during the few minutes we were in transit.

He certainly saved me a lot of time, once I got him off music history and onto his own field. Except for Claire Immega herself, there may not have been a better expert on Peekaboo and Brasil Novo anywhere in the Galaxy—because it had been to Matty that the report of Immega's successor Anabel had been addressed, a fact he mentioned as if it were of no significance. If you don't count the telepathic communicator who passed on the message, and probably had no idea of its importance, Matty had been literally the first person in the Solar System to know that Immega had discovered gamma Boötes was *not*, as thought, an A7 III star—a giant—but a binary star, whose companion was a G2 very like Sol. Her robot probes had found a very promising planet orbiting the new G2 star—news that had rocked four different planetary stock exchanges when it became public, and had ended up causing the construction and commissioning of the RSS *Sheffield*.

It didn't seem to impress him much. Matty spent the entire trip to his room explaining to me the problem with his Sol study, and I think he believed I understood what he was saying, even though I did *not* try to fake it. He simply was so focused and so excited, he failed to notice my incomprehension, which would have been incomprehensible to him. All I gleaned was that his research was really frustrating to him, because for some reason he absolutely hated the data he was getting.

He had happened to catch a perfect solar eclipse by Terra as we were leaving the Solar System, a major stroke of luck—I understood that much. And something about the displacement of a few stars *behind* the sun was very very slightly wrong, and somehow that was very very bad. It indicated something about the "J2 component of angular momentum" was bollixed.

But when I tried to find out just what that meant, and why it bothered him so badly, he changed the subject back to the star he was supposed to be telling me about: the one at the *other* end of our trajectory, Immega 714, AKA Peekaboo.

"In all the catalogs, gamma Boötes or HR5435 is commonly listed simply as 'gamma Boo,'" he explained cheerily. "So when Claire Immega of the 44 Boötes colony sent back word that gamma Boo was not a single star but a binary, with a G2 companion, the formal name of the G2 became Immega 714 in her honor—but it took about fifteen seconds for the System's media to name it Peekaboo. And when she added that its second planet looked *extremely* promising in terms of habitability, naturally that became Peekaboo Two. The name was just annoying enough to stick in a lot of minds, and the da Costa consortium became interested right away."

But of course, you don't start outfitting a starship on the basis of promises, however extreme. It wasn't until Immega's robot probes confirmed the good news that da Costa formed its partnership with Kang and began seriously planning our expedition. That took a while. Long enough that Immega herself did not live to learn just how spectacular her find had been.

Picture the geometry. 44 Boo, a variable star (eclipsing binary), lies a little more than forty-one light-years from Sol System. From there it's another forty-three and change to the newly discovered Immega 714. The first colonists to settle on 44 Boo's fourth satellite were a bit too busy surviving to stargaze a whole lot, but eventually two of them combined to produce Claire Immega. She became an astronomer, and soon discovered Peekaboo and Peekaboo Two. She was twenty-five before she had amassed sufficient clout to browbeat her fellow colonists into letting her divert what must have been scarce resources for ultrahighspeed probes. Even though these very tiny but very intelligent robots managed a very high fraction of c on their journey, it naturally had to take them *well* over forty-three years to make the trip, and then another forty-three years for their reports to make it back to 44 Boo at lightspeed.

From there, of course, the colonists' telepaths were able to pass the data back to their siblings back at Sol System in zero time. But Claire Immega was over thirty years dead by then. So she never knew, at least not for sure, that the new planet she had given mankind was one of the best it had yet found within its reach.

"G type stars like gamma Boo are damned scarce within eighty light-years or so of Sol," Matty told me, "and G2s that happen to have planets of the right mass orbiting within the zone that will permit liquid water to exist are less common than buttons on a snake. By now nearly all the really promising ones already have colonies either in place, or on the way there. And so far, nobody else has drawn the kind of jackpot Immega did."

"It's really that good?"

"Well, if you had your heart set on skiing, or ice fishing, I'm afraid you're screwed. If you like bone-breaker gravity, you'll hate the place. If you adore hostile environments, harsh conditions, scarcity, and surly natives, you'll be bored silly. But if you can steel yourself to a world where your feet never hurt, food and energy are cheap, and everybody goes naked most of the time . . ."

13

That is happiness: to be dissolved into
something complete, and great.

—Willa Cather

As soon as we got back to his luxury digs, he started bringing up Brasil Novo stats for me. Normally I'd rather read figures in printout than onscreen . . . but what he used for a monitor was an entire wall, bigger than any two walls in my place. So I sank back into an armchair so comfortable I kept murmuring thanks to it, sipped Matty's excellent Scotch, and learned.

Brasil Novo is roughly the same size as Mars, but thanks to a smaller iron core, it is twelve percent less dense, giving it a surface gravity of .33 gee rather than Mars's .38 gee. It lies more than 1.1 AU from its star—but Immega 714 is slightly brighter than Sol, so it seems normally bright in the sky for a sun, despite being ten percent farther away.

Here is how the planet stacks up beside Terra:

	Brasil N	Terra	BN/Terra
Mass (10^{24}kg)	0.5648	5.9736	0.095
Volume (10^{10}km^3)	16.318	108.321	0.151
Volumetric Radius (km)	3390	6371	0.532
Mean Density (kg/m^3)	3461	5515	0.628
Surface Gravity (m/s^2)	3.26	9.8	0.333
Escape Velocity (km/s)	4.43	11.19	0.396
Distance from Primary (ΛU)	1.1	1	1.1

And here, for perspective, is a set of similar comparisons between Terra and another reasonably well-known planet of comparable gravity:

	Mars	Terra	Mars/Terra
Mass (10^{24} kg)	0.64185	5.9736	0.107
Volume (10^{10} km^3)	16.318	108.321	0.151
Volumetric Radius (km)	3390	6371	0.532
Mean Density (kg/m^3)	3933	5515	0.713
Surface Gravity (m/s^2)	3.71	9.8	0.379
Escape Velocity (km/s)	5.03	11.19	0.450
Distance from Primary	1.38–1.66	1	1.52

Brasil Novo comes complete with two moons, quite similar to those of Mars. For that reason, and for emotional/political reasons less susceptible to analysis, it had been rather illogically decided to name them, too, Phobos and Deimos.

"What difference does it make?" Matty asked when I raised the issue. "Nobody's likely to confuse them in conversation with the ones we left eighty-five light-years behind. And very soon after arrival, everyone is going to become sharply aware that those two moons will have radically different *effects* than their namesakes, at least."

Always happy to play straightman to a speaker who truly enjoys his subject. "Why's that?"

"Because of something Mars lacks that Bravo has in great plenty."

It took me a second to recognize "Bravo" as an Anglicized contraction of Brasil Novo. It was the first time I'd heard the shorthand, but it would by no means be the last. Within a year, even the two dozen or so real Brazilianos aboard would be using it. "What's that?" I repeated.

He blinked at me. "Water. Teratons of water. The original Phobos and Deimos have tidal effects, but there's not enough surface water on Mars to make them visible. Bravo is going to have *very* complicated tides, and I suspect its version of a king tide will be an *emperor* tide."

I thought about it. "So, moist air, then."

"It better be."

The only reason it didn't get tedious saying "Why is that?" to this man was that he always answered, and the answer was usually interesting. So I said it again.

"We expect, or at least hope, to live there. So we'll probably want to breathe a lot. You have probably noticed that we are not carrying along with us in this bucket five hundred and fifty Mars-type low-pressure masks, plus several thousands more for replacements and the next several generations of offspring, nor are we spending any time drilling in them or trying to become acclimatized to them. If not, you've surely noticed that you don't wear one when you're working on the Upper Ag Deck."

He paused, and did not say, "Think it through."

Let's see. Atmosphere breathable without assistance. But even less gravity than Mars or home. So to get Terra-standard pressure, there are only two possibilities: the atmosphere must be thicker, or it must be much higher in oxygen.

Okay, take Terra. Its surface gets that much pressure from lying under a troposphere about twelve kilometers high. Brasil Novo's lower atmosphere would need to stand an unreasonable thirty-six klicks tall to yield that much pressure. So . . .

"The place is a tinderbox!" I exclaimed.

He shrugged carelessly. "The drier parts of it, yes. The air is a little over thirty percent oxygen. Here, take a look at this." He gestured shamanically with his hand, working some virtual remote control only he could see, and the wall display changed to:

ATMOSPHERIC COMPOSITION

Gas	Bravo	Terra
Oxygen	30%	21%
Nitrogen	60%	78%
Water	4–8%	0–4%
CO_2	0.10%	0.04%
Other	1%	1%

"Clearly it's going to be a warm, moist planet, by human standards. A jungle world, very much like the Amazon Basin of Old Brasil back on Terra, I imagine. Its fauna seem to be fantastically better at photosynthesis than ours. But your guess is correct: that thirty percent oxygen is going to make for severe fire danger. I suspect that if an expedition to one of the drier regions were to be struck by lightning, the lucky ones would be those killed outright on the spot. I doubt the rest could outrun the flames."

There are times when I'm happier to have a vivid imagination than I am other times.

"But there will be no shortage of damp places. Bravo has almost as much salt water cover as Terra—a bit more than half its total surface, compared to Terra's seventy percent. What you get basically is three major continents, more or less evenly spaced around the globe, each supporting a large dense jungle, with a major river flowing out of each, as in the Terran Amazon or Congo. There are also several large continental islands analogous to Australia, and if you'll pardon the technical terminology, umpty gazillion smaller islands, ranging in size from humungous to teeny-weeny."

"Okay, got it. The farther from the seashore, the more fire danger . . . but there's a *lot* of seashore."

He nodded. "The planet's axial tilt is only fifteen degrees, as compared to Terra's twenty-three point four five degrees. So there will be distinct seasons . . . but less pronounced than on Earth. No freezing winters. No polar ice caps."

That was good. I hate wearing stanfields—as long underwear is called in Canada, for reasons probably lost to history and certainly unknown to me. A world without snowdrifts was just fine with Joel. And no polar ice meant more of the total surface available to live on; more places to put usable seashore.

"And the day/night cycle—"

That one I could address. "—is nearly identical to Mars. Twenty-four hours, thirty-something minutes. Uh, thirty-seven."

"Of course, that must be what the Zog has you using on the Upper Deck. Well, the farming is probably going to be even better on Bravo than it is in Zogland."

"Really?"

He caused images to slideshow on his wall, some still, some moving—and all striking. "As you can see, the place is tectonically quite active. Volcanic mountain ranges. Good thing; it keeps the atmosphere replenished. So volcanic ash fertilizes the land—and the mountains present useful minerals and metals which we reach by blasting a little bit sideways instead of digging way down and hauling it back up. But from a peasant's point of view, the best part is going to be the weather: probably the most stable climate humans have yet encountered."

Well, I hadn't said it in several minutes now. "Why is that, Matty?"

"Consider the geography." He smiled. "Or bravography, if you will."

"*I* won't, but you go ahead."

"Thank you. Look at those three major continents. All more or less equatorial. Roughly evenly spaced. Each of them will have a bravographically anchored transportation zone, where jungle trees pump a regular fountain of water into the atmosphere. Ergo, climate patterns will be anchored, too, with weather infinitely more stable and reliable than anyplace in the Solar System."

I understood what he meant when I saw the planet in 3-D projection. Terra is continually plagued by nerve-racking El Niño events because the committee that designed it (it had to be a committee) inexplicably omitted to place a large jungle in the middle of the Pacific Ocean, to anchor that evaporation zone. Bravo lacked this defect. "And that stable weather forecast will be . . . gray skies, lots of clouds? Rain in the morning giving way to rain in the afternoon, followed by a high probability of rain all night?"

"In general, yes, around the equator. With more temperate zones to north and south. But the three big continents themselves will be fairly temperate, and covered with boreal forest."

"A lot of our oldest myths will still work."

He nodded happily. "And some others will become for us historical curiosities, requiring footnotes. On Terra, there tend to be large deserts to the north and south of all the jungle areas, including the Sahara, Kalahari, Gobi, Patagonian, and Sonoran deserts. But Bravo does not seem to have real deserts, probably thanks to its more favorable climate distribution."

"Okay by me," I said. "I never met a desert I liked much."

"Oh, I have!" he said emphatically. "I'll miss them. Splendid places to do astronomy. But by surrendering them, I'll get to see something unique in their place. I've *seen* a desert. I've lived in a few. But so far, as far as I know, *nobody* has yet seen a Hungry Ghost with his own personal eyeballs, much less spent time in one." He sounded gleeful at the prospect.

"A Hungry Ghost?"

"A firestorm the size of a state or province."

The name sort of explained itself to an extent. One-third gee, and a teeming stable biosphere—the land would be lush with life. The trees must grow to fantastic heights, and sprawl across the sky in the competition for sunlight. But the air they spread through was nearly a third oxygen, fifty percent more than a sensible planet needed . . . which they themselves were replenishing! Let things get dried out in the stable weather, let the ground cover vegetation and tree droppings crisp up nicely into tinder and kindling, let one of the inevitable sparks occur in a very bad place . . .

"Tesla's eyebrows, Matty! It must be all the circles of Hell."

"Worse, I think." The bastard was still gleeful. "I'm not saying those were fun, but they all *stayed put*. Once you reported to your Circle and took your assigned spot in the lake of burning pitch, you pretty much knew your address and postal code for the next quadrillion eternities. But Bravo has more sunlight and higher temperatures than Earth, so—"

"—so it's going to have *serious* winds."

"Sometimes. And sometimes hurricanes. Primarily in tropical ocean regions. But also in high elevation land plateaus . . . where forests tend to dry out."

"Oh, that's not good!" Now I fully understood the aptness of the name he'd picked. I had all too vivid a mental picture of a firestorm, the size of Central British Columbia, say . . . that lurched and lunged randomly across the landscape at hurricane speeds, gulping biomass like a drunken sailor on a spree, spewing flames to altitudes previously reached in human experience only by mushroom clouds and weather balloons. Hungry Ghost indeed! Like the Hungry Ghosts I had encountered in my quick surface reading of Tibetan Buddhist mythology: spirits consumed with lust for things that never satisfied, hunger that could not be eased, thirst that nothing could quench. Damned souls condemned to yearn forever, and destroy all they touched, knowing it was pointless. I wondered if a Hungry Ghost typically had an eye, like a hurricane, and how long you'd have to live if you ever found yourself in one. Would it be even theoretically possible to move quickly and correctly enough to *stay* in such an eye, until the Ghost's terrible Hunger burned itself out?

"But that's only going to worry certifiably insane explorer types like me, who go looking for danger," he said with a chuckle. "Farmers who pick their homestead site intelligently, on the other hand, are probably going to be very happy people in Saudade."

Incongruous image of pigs on the Ag Deck. "Sow what?"

"That will be the name chosen for the first town we'll settle. You heard it here first."

"How can you be so sure, this far in advance?"

"Because that's what I strongly feel it should be, and nobody aboard with a contrary opinion is a bigger bully than me."

"It would be impolite to argue with my host. Say the name again, and tell me what it means."

"*Saudade*. 'Sow,' like a female hog. 'Da,' like the Russian for 'probably not.' 'Day,' light come an' me wan' go home."

"You can't possibly know that song."

"Neither can you, son. And if you do, you ought to know the word '*saudade*.' It's a Portuguese word, and the heart of the Portuguese music called *fado*. You could say it is as important a word to fado as 'soul' is to blues, or 'cool' is to jazz. And as difficult to define."

It came back. "I know that word. I've seen it written, anyway, I just had no idea it was pronounced like that. It means . . . well, sort of . . ."

"The best I've heard it rendered into Basic so far," Matty said, "is 'the presence of absence.'"

"The thing you know because it isn't there."

He nodded. "Which, when you think about it, is a pretty fair description of what powers this ship."

"Do you understand the relativistic engine, Matt?"

He smiled. "You flatter me. That's my point: there is some reason to believe there's literally nothing there."

I shrugged. "Big deal. Is nothing sacred?"

He winced politely. "I asked George R once, what do you guys actually *do* down there in the Hole? He looked around, leaned close, lowered his voice, and told me the secret. They strap toast onto a cat's back and toss it in the air."

And he waited. I *knew* there had to be a gag, and if I didn't guess what it was, he would win the exchange I had begun by essaying a pun. Well, it served me right. "But how do dat make de ship go, Mr. Interlocutor," I asked ritually, conceding defeat.

"They butter the toast, you see."

Light belatedly dawned. "Ah. Of course. The toast *must* fall butter side down—"

"—but the cat *must* land on its feet." He spread his hands: QED. "Hence the array spins forever, generating power."

It was a good gag; I grinned in surrender. "It's so simple once someone explains it."

He accepted my sword by saying, "To answer your question seriously, I confess the word that best describes my understanding of relativism is probably saudade."

"The mystery of the ages," I said, thinking to agree.

"No," he said with a sudden seriousness that took me by surprise. "*That* it is not. Not even the mystery of *this* age."

"Uh . . . I'll bite. What *is* the mystery of the ages, this one included?" I said, trying for lightness.

He kept frowning, and had stopped meeting my eyes. "Fermi's Paradox."

It took a second. "Oh. 'Where is everybody?' you mean."

He made a single nod. "Nobody even talks about it anymore. We know that life can come to exist in the universe, because it did, once that we know of. We know life can evolve sufficient intelligence to leave its star, because we've done it. It is, granted, conceivable that this might occur only once every twelve billion years or more." He made a face as if he'd bitten into a lemon. "But as for me, I find the creation myth in Genesis considerably more plausible."

"Didn't someone settle this back before the Dark Age?" I asked. "Webb? Wrote a book listing forty-nine possible solutions to Fermi's Paradox—and demolished them one by one, leaving only the fiftieth solution, namely: we're alone?"

He looked as if he'd chased his lemon with milk. "Webb was an idiot. His analysis presumed that if other life did exist, it could not be more intelligent than him. It was the characteristic flaw of the entire PreCollapse millennium: the assumption of vastly more knowledge than they actually possessed." He closed his eyes and rubbed them. "Over and over like a recurring flu they developed the imbecile idea that they understood nearly everything, in all but the finest details. They had no slightest idea what lightning was, how it worked. They had absolutely no clue how moisture got farther than about ten meters up a tree—the highest that capillary action can push it. Fifty years after the splitting of the atom, they accidentally noticed for the first time that hurricanes emit gamma rays. There were quite a few large, significant phenomena they could 'explain,' often elegantly . . . over and over again . . . and had to, because the explanations kept falling apart at the first hard-data-push. Things like the Tunguska Event, gamma ray bursts, why an airplane wing generated lift, what ninety percent of our DNA was doing there . . . yet they were solemnly convinced they basically understood the universe, except for some details out in the tenth decimal place.

"They somehow managed to persuade themselves that computer models constitute *data*. That very complicated guesses become facts. They made themselves believe they had the power to accurately model, not merely something as inconceivably complex as, say, a single zygote . . . but a national economy, a weather system, a planetary ecosphere, a multiplanet society—even a universe. They made solemn pronouncements about conditions a trillionth of a second after the Big Bang, on the basis of computer models, which they had produced with computers not even bright enough to talk, let alone understand speech. They were unlike all the generations before theirs in several ways, but chiefly in that they had no faintest *clue* how ignorant they were. Previous ages had usually had a pretty good handle on that."

"Things got worse in that direction soon."

"Sure. Scientists were claiming godlike knowledge, and couldn't deliver. It got to where even the average citizen could sense they were bluffing. They could go on for literally days on what happened in the first five minutes of creation, without ever saying a single thing that *meant* anything, did anybody any good. They wouldn't even *discuss* what happened when you died, let alone how random chance produced life. No wonder the citizens decided to go back to a different kind of omniscience, that came with omnipotence *and* omnibenevolence thrown in at no extra charge. Twentieth-century science *handed* the world over to Nehemiah Scudder, on a plate. No wonder some people preferred 'intelligent design' to evolution. At least it put intelligence somewhere in the mix. Unfortunately, not much."

I was getting a little dizzy. "I think I lost you around that last curve, Matty. What's your answer to the mystery? If intelligent life has arisen more than once, in this corner of the cosmos, where *is* everybody?"

He drew in a long slow breath, and held it for long enough to make me think of the breathing routine I still used at the start of meditation. I kept on thinking of it as he exhaled, and his frown melted away and his face smoothed over and his body language relaxed. He fiddled with his remote, and said, "Authorities differ, but for my money, probably the closest thing to intelligent life we'll find on Bravo is the spit-tooth sloth," and the wall showed what I hoped was an enlarged image of the ugliest creature I had ever seen. "Admittedly it is difficult to assess intelligence based on observations made from orbit. Once a probe is fairly sure a given life-form is not a serious threat to man, it moves on to other things that might be. But the sloth's competition is not impressive."

It seemed clear he was changing the subject, and he had been so helpful and generous with his time, that was fine with me; his reasons were none of my business. We moved on to an interesting discussion of exotic fauna like hoop snakes, snippers, blimps, and the truly disgusting rocket slugs, which dodge predators by expelling feces so violently they shoot into the air and glide great distances. A whole pod of such frightened slugs, Matty said, can apparently fill the air with a ghastly green mist. . . .

Later on, though, after I'd read up on spit-tooth sloths, I became less certain he'd been changing the subject. A sloth sits high in one of those preposterously tall trees, waiting with infinite patience until something preyish-looking happens to wander by below. Then she (once the males are done with their fertilizing, their only remaining function is as hibernation food) spits out a poison tooth, with high velocity and great accuracy. It drops the prey for so long she has time to slowly descend, retrieve it, and bring it back up the tree to consume at her leisure.

In other words, they conceal themselves perfectly, take no risks at all, and attack without warning or mercy.

I would recall that later in the voyage.

IT ALL STARTED to come together at some point. The meditation improved my disposition and outlook, without which no beneficial change is possible. The physical exercise began to pay off next. When you're in better shape, you think better. When you're thinking better, meditation produces more useful insights. As I came to understand Bravo better, my work on the Ag Decks became both more effective and more meaningful to me, and before long I started to acquire something I hadn't even realized I'd been lacking: a feeling of worth, of making a contribution, having something tangible to offer. I actually did have a knack for it, too, I learned—for sensing just how the new conditions would alter plant requirements and capabilities, and figuring out ways to compensate. The Zog told me once, after I managed to bring a fungal disease under control without quite knowing how myself, that I thought like a Bravonian vegetable. I don't know if I've ever been more flattered.

In time, it became possible to dimly imagine a future life on Brasil Novo, an endurable and maybe even pleasant one in which I might have both purpose and value.

Two moons in the sky. Similar to Callisto, Europa, and Io back home on Ganymede. I liked that. One moon wasn't enough to keep a sky interesting, in my biased opinion.

There would also be the giant A7 star in the sky, too. Immega 713, as it had been renamed, in preference to some horror like alpha gamma Boo. (Which Solomon of course liked, saying it would make a great name for a fraternity.) According to Matty, since it lay one hundred AU away, it had only four percent of the brightness Sol had from Terra—but that made it a hundred thousand times brighter than Luna. It might only get really dark at night when there was

heavy overcast, or when the A7 was on the other side of
Peekaboo. I liked that, too.

The music I composed became better, stronger, deeper.
The music I played finally started to approach what I'd always heard in my mind's ear; I had better wind, a clearer
head, and a much clearer idea of who it was playing. Not
only did my reputation begin to spread throughout the ship, I
began to feel more and more as if it was deserved.

As I said, after a certain point it all began to heterodyne. I
felt better, so I did better, which made me feel even better,
which . . . So that first year of star travel would probably
have been an extremely happy and satisfying one for me, on
balance.

If I had not taken *all* of Dr. Amy's advice, and resumed
dating six months into it.

I DON'T SUPPOSE it will stun you to learn that Kathy was the
first girl I asked for a date. It certainly didn't surprise anybody I knew in the slightest. I'm given to understand that
people I'd never met or heard of on the far side of the
Sheffield knew it was going to happen weeks before it did.
God knows Kathy was not surprised to be asked, and had the
kindness to accept before I'd quite finished getting the words
out, which cut my interval of agonized suspense down to just
the hundred million years it took me to not quite get the
words out.

And why should any of us have been surprised? We were
such a perfect couple on paper that even if we'd disliked each
other's body odor, which we didn't, we'd have *had* to at least
give it a try. Musically we shared a bond, a level of communication, that many married couples never do achieve, and others do at the cost of great struggle. Even tone deaf people in
the audience could sense it, and responded to it. She was very
good, in the same way that I was, and we brought out each
other's best. We helped each other say important things we
could not express alone, and how far can that be from love?

Loving Zog's Farms was another profound connection,
one that went back in time almost as far as music. Plunging

hands into soil together is very close to thrusting them into one another. And of course both of us were simultaneously fertile and ripe, a paradox whose metaphorical impossibility accurately reflects the turmoil of that condition. Afterward you look back on it and call it golden. At the time it is hell on rusty wheels.

Part of the problem was precisely that we were so *self-evidently* perfect for each other—a cliché looking for the spot marked X. Enough so to have made us both self-conscious from the very start, enough to make each of us want to dig in our heels out of sheer stubborn unwillingness to be that predictable. We'd both read and seen enough romantic fiction to know that if the writer seems to insist on throwing two characters together, it's their job to resist, for as long as they can, anyway. A silly reason not to love, I know . . . but are there any that aren't?

But in an utterly closed community that small, you can run but you can't hide, not forever. Twenty years stretched before us. Eventually you say, why not get it over with and find out? Or maybe I mean, why not find out and get it over with? One of those. And that too was predictable. Like I said, nobody was too surprised when I asked Kathy out, including her, and nobody was *too* surprised she said yes, even me. I took her to a play, the second production of the Boot and Buskin Society, and afterward we went to the Horn, ordered Irish coffees, and talked.

Five minutes into a discussion of the play we'd just seen—Simon, very well done—I interrupted myself in the middle of explaining why the lead actress's performance had been so remarkable, and launched into a ten-minute monologue of my own. Kathy listened patiently.

I told her about Jinny—first about Jinny Hamilton, and then about Jinnia Conrad of Conrad—and I worked in my father, and the little I knew of my mother, and my experiences with sudden poverty and solitude, and anything else I could think of that might help justify being a basket case. That was probably pretty predictable, too. At a conservative estimate, I was perhaps the hundred billionth asshole since

Adam to try and tell a woman, I find your company enjoyable but I am too damaged for any long-term emotional involvement, so don't place your hopes on me. They almost always listen patiently, for some reason. But I doubt if anything I said surprised her very much.

Probably the only person in the entire ship who ended up finding anything at all surprising in that entire date was me, after I finally shut up long enough for Kathy to tell me that she'd gotten engaged two weeks earlier, to two very nice people, and had I ever thought much about opting into a group or line marriage myself? Because they were looking to expand. Full bore omnisexual, of course. But no pressure.

I haven't the slightest idea what response I made. That date lasted another hour and a half—Herb and Balvovatz agreed I got back two hours after the play ended—but I cannot for the life of me recall another word either of us spoke, or anything that occurred.

14

If you don't live it, it won't come out your horn.
—Bird

Things gradually settled, as they always seem to do eventually, into a routine.

AT WHAT SEEMED the approximate speed of mold forming on a corridor wall, life aboard the RSS *Charles Sheffield* began to take on discernible shape, and then flavor, and finally texture. Five hundred people slowly got to know one another, heard (the first version of) each other's back stories and dreams, learned each other's strengths and weaknesses, discovered what we needed and what we had to give, slowly began to design and assemble, by trial and error and what few lessons history had made clear enough, a society that would use all of us and feed all of us and give us all something to be part of for twenty uninterrupted years.

Complicating the task, of course, the society was intended to become something utterly different at the *end* of that twenty years, and needed to be kept aimed in that direction at all times. For most humans, anything farther ahead than this time next year is the "far future." It can be all too easy to lose sight of a goal that far off, and we *had* to be ready when we got there. The good news was that Merril Grossman was our Coordinator. She had a keen mind, a great understanding of her job, and a way of bullying people that was so transparently an act of love everyone let her get away with it.

Six months into the voyage, she organized and chaired the *Sheffield*'s first town meeting. It had to be electronic, naturally. Any cubic large enough to have held all of us at once, even in free fall, would have been a preposterous waste of space, in a ship that never seemed to have enough. Even the Pool could barely have accommodated half of us, and only on the friendliest of terms. But a well-run ETM works *better* than a live rally in the park, and Coordinator Grossman knew how.

I mean, speeches *were* made, inevitably: we are talking about humans here. But they were kept short, and they assayed out remarkably low in bullshit content. Captain James Bean, a man who looked *exactly* like you want the captain of your starship to look, and had the reputation to back it up, got five minutes, and used three. The whole ship rocked with applause when he was done; he was well liked. Five-minute gab-slots also were awarded to Colony Governor Jaime Roberts, and to George R representing the Relativists. Another would have gone to Governor-General Lawrence Cott, representative of Kang/da Costa, but he was ill so his slot was given by his lifemate Perry Jarnell, who took six minutes. At that point his audio and video both cut out.

After that, even the most pompous speakers quickly figured out that if they hadn't gotten it said within five minutes, Merril wasn't going to let them keep trying. By the time everyone's screens went dark that night we had accomplished what I considered an astonishing amount.

Names, for one thing.

People had been arguing them for months, occasionally at a volume that drew proctors, but somehow our Coordinator cut through the confusion in a way that didn't seem to leave anyone feeling disenfranchised, and before too long we had all finally reached consensus on names for most of the places and things that would really matter to all of us when we got to Bravo.

I for one found most of the choices cheering, too—our colony seemed to be a jolly crew.

The three major continents, for example, were christened Samba, Cerveja, and Carnaval. What lay ahead we knew not, but we intended to have a good time there if we could. At the same time, once he'd explained it to everyone, Matty Jaymes's suggested name for our first settlement, Saudade, passed by a landslide, with fewer than two dozen opposed, the closest to unanimity we came that night. We all understood that our good times would always, always be seasoned with a sharp regret, a longing for all the lost loved ones and planets and habitats we had left so far behind us forever. To pretend otherwise would be foolish.

Nearly as popular a choice were the new names given to our two moons. *Nobody* had liked the unimaginative names Immega had given them, New Deimos and New Phobos. For one thing, they didn't look like their namesakes, and would not behave like them in the sky. For another, a lot of us were *from* Mars, and did not want our good times tinged with nostalgic regret every single damn time we looked at or discussed the night sky. (That was one reason the two closest alternatives to Saudade—Rio de Janeiro and Niteroi—had found so few supporters, I think.)

So I'd been expecting the grassroots effort to rename the moons. But the names chosen were a pleasant surprise, from the music of the twentieth century: Tom and Joao. The great composer Antonio Carlos Jobim, known as Tom, and his great disciple Joao Gilberto between them created samba, the lush basis of all subsequent Brazilian music . . . which

became a major influence on the work of my favorite saxophonist of that period, Stan Getz. I took that as a good omen,
and made a mental note to find out if Kathy knew his work
with Tom and Joao. (She did—and knew a guitarist who
could play Gilberto style. We killed 'em at the Horn of
Plenty all that week.)

Governor-General Cott's partner had by that point leaned
on somebody hard enough to get hooked back online, and
expressed his co-husband's strong distaste, on behalf of our
noble patrons at Kang/da Costa, for the growing tendency of
some colonists to shorten the name of our new home-to-be
from Brasil Novo to Bravo. His partner found it disrespect-
ful and Jarnell found it vulgar, if I've sorted them out correctly. He stopped short of demanding prohibition of the
name Bravo, but asked for a resolution agreeing that the
proper name was Brasil Novo. The Brazilians aboard registered strong support.

Merril sighed and asked if anyone else wanted to address
the question. A colonist named Robin Feeney spoke up,
pointing out that "bravo" was a word used to applaud a feat
of great difficulty, and a jump of eighty-five light-years certainly qualified: our successful arrival would itself be a
Bravo to Captain Bean and his excellent crew. That went
over well. The word was also, she added, one we commonly
applied to artistic effort that moved us, and as an actress and
painter, she hoped hearing it often might help to remind us
that the arts would have an important place even in a frontier
society. Someone promptly said, "Bravo!" and was widely
echoed around the ship. Merril squelched further debate, put
it to a vote, and that was the end of the Cott resolution. Many
of us would continue to say Brasil Novo, most of the time,
because let's face it, it was more elegant. But when we did it
was our choice.

More time was nearly wasted on the contentious question
of just where on exactly which continent Saudade should be
founded. It was a big planet. Almost none of us had an opinion, but the few who did were married to them. Fortunately
before it got out of hand, Merril pointed out to us that the
reason most of us had no opinion was that none of us was

entitled to one. It was not yet possible to state with certainty where the best site for a colony might be: we simply didn't know enough yet. Robot probes were good, but they weren't *that* good. We would simply have to wait until we approached the Peekaboo System and could take a closer look for ourselves.

We did more than just pick names that night. Some sensible suggestions were made. Survivor Gerald Knave, for example, proposed we establish a prize of some kind for Most Constructive Complaint of the Month. Sol Short broke in to suggest we establish some sort of penalty for the *least* constructive, but Merril ruled him out of order and made it stick.

The most popular speaker of the evening was clearly the Zog. He spoke on what it was now believed our new home would be *like*, the local conditions we expected to find, some of the flora and fauna we knew about—not in any great detail, really: just enough to give a *sense* of the place. More than a few of us were still as ill-informed as I had once been, and all were spellbound by his descriptions. He made it sound exciting, enticing, mysterious. A steamy jungle planet, shrouded in mists, teeming with life as exotic as if it had been made up to entertain a child at bedtime. His description of the hoop snakes, which bit their own tails, curled up into the shape of a wheel, and then by deforming their belly muscles were able to roll along the trails carved through the jungle by the snipper beasts, had everyone chuckling. Then his straight-faced explication of the propulsive method used by the rocket slugs caused such a shipwide convulsion of laughter Merril had a hard time restoring order. For months thereafter, the words "green mist" had the power to make us crack up. I remember thinking at the time that it was the first time the entire colony had laughed together about something, and that I hoped it wouldn't be the last.

Zog even managed—don't ask me how—to make the ever-present mortal danger of fire we would face and even the threat of Hungry Ghosts seem like only bedtime-story monsters, thrilling but not truly terrifying. I think if you took a poll, most people would agree with me that Bravo Colony's history as a real rather than merely potential entity begins with the moment Kamal Zogby began to speak that night. Before that we were a big can full of smelly strangers. When he was done we knew that we were a family, and one that was going to create an entire world from scratch together one day, in an environment strikingly like the one in which humans had first evolved back on Terra, and that it was going to be an adventure. Everything we did would be legend for ten thousand years: the first legends of our planet.

There were a couple of obligatory anticlimax speeches and announcements, and then Merril closed the meeting precisely when she had said she was going to, at 2300 *Sheffield* time.

SHIP'S TIME, THAT is. By that point in our voyage, six months out, we were already beginning to use Dr. Einstein's Clock instead of Sol. Lorentz contraction had set in, and we were aging just measurably slower than the people we had left behind.

How much slower? Not a lot—yet. At the instant when those of us in the *Sheffield* passed the six-month mark of the trip, residents of the Solar System were only about seventeen and a half hours older than we were.

But it would get steadily worse as our velocity mounted up. And constant boost mounts up *fast*.

At the one-year mark, the differential would be about seven days and seven hours.

At two years, it would be more than fifty-eight days.

By the five-year mark, the divergence of our clocks and mankind's would surge up to almost three years. We would be traveling at more than $0.938c$.

And when I had been traveling for ten years, and was twenty-eight years old, more than *forty-five years* would have elapsed on Terra. Behind me Jinny would be closing in on sixty-four.

And receding at 99.794 percent of the speed of light.

Then we would flip over and do the whole thing in reverse. And assuming we got it right, and made orbit around Brasil Novo as planned, we Peekaboobs would be twenty years older, and Solarians would be something like eighty-five years older. Jinny would be one hundred and eight, and probably wouldn't look a day over eighty.

Time has always struck me as one of the Allegedly Intelligent Designer's ideas that was never properly beta-tested before its implementation.

I know: they say it serves to keep everything from happening at once. But what would be so bad about that? You'd get to see both the Big Bang, if there really was one, and the Heat Death, if there's going to be one. Either way at either end, you'd *know*. That and everything else knowable. You'd have what Adam and Eve got cheated out of, what they *thought* they were bargaining for. Gnosis.

So would everybody. No more bullshit.

Okay, so it would lack suspense. But it wouldn't lack surprise. *Everything* would be a total surprise, always.

I have a great career ahead as a consultant in the thriving field of universe design, Sol once told me. I told him he should hire me: some experts said he and his fellow Relativists generated mini-universes like soap bubbles every working day. He said the moment he got a complaint from one of them, I was the guy he would hire to do the renovation.

I DON'T CARE what Dr. Einstein says: my own clock seemed to *speed up* as the days went by. Those first few hours after leaving orbit took forever to pass. The first few days went by at a glacial pace. Then for weeks, every minute of every day brought new information, new people, new situations, new problems, new mistakes, new things to learn and unlearn. After a few months, of course, it began to slack off. At six months, I had a fair idea of where to find most of the good stuff and how to avoid most of the bad stuff, and the days started to slide by while I wasn't paying close attention, and events began to sort of lurch forward in quanta rather than unfold in a smooth flow.

Things did move forward, though. By the end of the first year, I was on my sixth girlfriend of the voyage.

I'VE ALREADY MENTIONED the first one, twice, but you probably didn't notice her go by. Robin Feeney was the female lead in the Doc Simon play I took Kathy to see, on our first and last date—the actress whose performance I was championing just before everything went to hell. When Robin spoke up at that first Town Meeting, in support of the shorthand name Bravo, I was just out of frame beside her, holding her hand and smiling encouragingly. I'm the one who said "Bravo!" first when she was done. It got me soundly kissed about two minutes after the meeting ended.

And that, I'm sorry to admit, is very damn nearly all there is to say about that relationship. That kiss may have been the high point.

If my life were a play Robin would have had to be a pivotal character, vivid and vibrant, the source of several life-changing insights, and utterer of at least one or two lines that would come back to haunt me in the third act. It was a role she was perfectly cast for, too, one she could play the hell out of. Unfortunately she had no one to write it for her—and no skill at improv. Onstage, she was vivid and vibrant. Off-stage, she was usually thinking about how to be thought vivid and vibrant the next time she was onstage.

I sound like I'm implying that she was more self-centered than I, which is both unfair and untrue. In all honesty, Robin's principal attraction for me was that she was a female mammal with a body temperature of thirty-seven degrees who was willing to share my company in a social context. I certainly didn't think of it in those terms then, of course, but looking back on it I can see the most powerful emotion I felt throughout was probably relief at finally being able to get Dr. Amy off my case.

We couldn't even manage a meet-cute. She came up to me after a set at the Horn, to ask the name of the piece Kathy and I had just played. "Shaping the Curve," it was: a soprano-piano duet by a twenty-first-century composer named Colin MacDonald. I said if she gave me her address I would mail her MacDonald's own recording, and I did, and after a couple of days of increasingly chatty mail we finally made a date. That was all there was to it.

Herb says a relationship that begins without a good anecdote has no future. He may be right. Jinny and I met online at the campus bookstore, the first week of class. She asked if I had a battery wafer she could borrow, and I did. Yawn. And look how *that* turned out.

For our first date Robin and I picked a common choice: we shared Sim. And once there, the simulation we agreed on was again one of the most common options: background sharing. I showed her typical scenes of life on Ganymede, some of the places and activities that had once mattered to me. She walked me through comparable scenes of life in The Wheel, one of the smaller O'Neills, where she had been born. In my opinion it's also one of the goofier ones, an odd combination of mystical and uptight. They believe in the anthropic principle, and live communally and take entheogens, but nobody ever leaves a surface unpolished or an item out of place. I didn't express this opinion, and in return Robin was far too polite to tell me that Ganymede struck her as materialistic and sloppy. Our truth level never did improve much.

I did notice that she was a different person when we were in The (simulated) Wheel, one I think I maybe would have liked better. But she didn't.

If I want to, or need to, I can reach back into my mental file storage and pull out long stretches of footage representing just about all the major periods and significant people of my life—usually in ultradefinition video with supersaturated color, and full spectrum audio with enhanced treble and bass. In the drawers marked "Dad" and "Jinny" there are extended sequences in true 3-D, complete with textured smells, and sometimes even tastes. Sadly such mental files are like analog recordings rather than digital, in that they decay slightly with each playback. At the same time, paradoxically, some of the earliest memories are the most detailed and evocative.

But when I try and retrieve memorable scenes from my relationship with Robin, what I get is a series of disjointed dim still images, like old photographs, that occasionally animate for a few seconds, with snippets of soundtrack that often fail to match the action.

There don't seem to be any inconsequential relationships in drama. I guess they don't have the time. We had *plenty* of time. If we'd been a play ourselves, and unsubsidized, we'd have closed in a week. As it was we managed to keep the house lit for months by giving away comp tickets to each other and pretending not to notice the canned applause. But the reviews were never worth clipping.

The upside, of course, is that in the end we were able to disengage without doing any important damage to one another. We carried on as though we had, of course, for the drama that was in it. But we gave it up soon, and with secret relief on both sides. On mine, anyway.

About a week later, as I was wandering around in a daze thinking, *Well, that wasn't as horrible as it could have been*, I had a meet-cute with Diane Levy. She did not notice me sit down next to her at dinner, tried to turn around and grab the sugar from the table behind us, and coldcocked me with her elbow. *Or was it?* I thought, and woke to find her large liquid eyes as close as one might expect to find those of a lover. Four hours later, she was one. To my complete astonishment, I had made her a thankfully unnoticed gift of my virginity.

I lay beside her gasping for air, and grateful for the excuse. What would I say to her, now? My brain settled on something or other just as my lungs returned to active duty; I opened my eyes and opened my mouth . . . and discovered Diane was not at all interested in any of *those* organs.

A while later, floating on a rich postcoital sea of relief and pride and satisfaction and regret, I found the perfect words with which to let her down easy. I would simply explain, tell my story truthfully, help her see that I was damaged goods, too scarred by a tragic love to ever love again. If she then chose to take up the chal . . . to pursue a relationship, my conscience would be clear. (Somebody said the gray component of semen is draining brain cells. It may well be so.)

No sense dragging it out; I opened my eyes to begin her disappointment as gently as I could. And found myself alone.

FOR THE NEXT three days my calls reached only voicemail; my text messages went unanswered. The *Sheffield* resolutely refused to supply me with any useful data, not location of quarters, usual whereabouts, names of friends, or biographical information. The third time I tried to wheedle it, the ship threatened to rat me out to Dr. Amy if I asked again.

By that point I knew the truth. This was love.

The real thing—not the pathetic charade Jinny and I had mugged our way through, but the love of the ages, the true mystical union of two souls. I knew things about Diane that she didn't know herself, and she was going to explain me to myself, and I was absolutely certain that if she would only give me thirteen words I could make her see it all as clearly as I did. I had it down to thirteen words, so good I felt they'd have done the job even as flatscreen text—and I couldn't get a single one of them before her eyes.

The first night I just moaned a lot. The second, I raged and wept and made myself a stinking nuisance to my roommates. Balvovatz finally took it on himself to drink me under the table, and laid me out on my bunk. The third night, I went to the Horn, and laid a drunken monologue on Kathy that would damage our friendship for months to come. At the time, she limited her remarks to a polite hope that things would work out well for me, and a slap with so much wrist to it that a proctor was halfway to the table before I could wave him off.

Tossing in my comfortable bunk that night, I got it down to six words. I'd need eye contact, but if I could just get six lousy words in—

The next morning while I was in the 'fresher, paying in ugly coin for two nights' debauchery, Diane phoned.

"Diane! Uh . . . let me call you back—"

"Joel, dear, I appreciate your interest. I had a wonderful time with you. Perhaps I will again, one day. But it can't be soon. It's just simple math, dear."

"I don't understand. Look, can't I—"

"I have to make a big decision sometime in the next twenty years. It's going to affect my whole life. Obviously my information has to be as complete as possible. Even after I rule out seniors, mono-gays, and other permanent ineligibles, there are something over two hundred possible mates in the world. I like to keep my weekends for reading. So that means I'll work my way back around to you again in a little over forty weeks. Not even a year."

I stared at my wrist, and reminded myself that my guts had been churning *before* the phone had rung. "Are you telling me you've already—"

"Yes, dear, but I assure you I remember *you* with particular fondness."

Spasm. "One day isn't long enough to—"

"I find that by the second or third day one forms attachments, don't you? At that rate I could easily take the whole *voyage* identifying the right husband. I'd still be breaking him in when we hit dirt at Bravo. You understand, I'm sure. Or rather, I hope. If so, I'll see you in forty weeks, give or take. Unless I get lucky and lightning strikes, of course." She hung up before I could wail her name. It didn't stop me.

Let's just say the next five or ten minutes stressed that 'fresher to its design limits and beyond, and leave it at that.

So I SOUGHT a mojo.

That's a term from PreCollapse times. It means a love charm. A magic spell or fetish of some kind that I could use to make Diane see her search was over.

Naturally I sought the advice of an expert. Matty Jaymes listened sympathetically to my tale of woe, nodding in all the right places. Until I named my beloved; then his face went blank, and he sat back in his chair and shook his head. "Son, I'm afraid I am powerless to help you."

"Huh? What do you mean? Why?"

"Diane made love to *me*, once." He sighed. "I spent two hours down on the Ag Deck eating dirt, before I resumed my human shape." His left foot was tapping uncontrollably on the deck. "My advice is to be thankful you weren't two hundredth on her list, and quit trying to hog a natural resource."

FROM THERE, MY love life went downhill. Eventually I gave it up as a failed experiment and put my mind on my work.

Let's see. There was Barbara Manning, a student of Dr. Amy's—her suggestion—and then an engineer named Mariko Stupple—Tiger's suggestion—followed by a

physics student named Darren Maeder who had the superstitious notion that perhaps something of my father's innate
genius might be exuded in my sweat, or something, followed
closely by his former girlfriend when I proved a dry hole—
both of those his idea—and then, if I have the sequence correct, there were . . .

Can I stop now? This emotional striptease not only em-
barrasses me, it's boring. *Everyone*'s early love life is boring, sometimes even to the protagonists at the time. Let it
stand that eventually the awkwardness started to wear off,
and when the dust settled, I found myself a normal healthy
het-bi bachelor with somewhat less than average interest in
casual sex and even less interest in emotional commitment.

That described a lot of us in the *Sheffield*. There was no
rush in forming a partnership that had nothing much to *do*
for another couple of decades. Unless of course you decided
you wanted to arrive on Bravo with children tall enough to
be useful, which an unsurprising number of colonists did.
But a nearly equal number concluded, as I did, that a ball of
mud, even alien mud, had to be a better place to raise children than a metal can. And the last five or six years of the
voyage, when things were just starting to gear up to their
busiest, would be a poor time to be ass-deep in bored, surly,
invincibly ignorant teenagers. Such as I was now.

Sol Short once told me mankind is divided into two basic
sorts: those who find the unknown future threatening . . .
and those who find it thrilling. He says the rupture between
those two sides has been responsible for most of the blood-
shed in history. If change threatens you, you become conservative in self-defense. If it thrills you, you become liberal in
self-liberation. He says the Threateneds are frequently more
successful in the short run, because they always fight dirty.
But in the long run, they always lose, because Thrilled people learn and thus accomplish more.

I don't know. In those days, I would have to say my basic
orientation was toward the Threatened school. I had begun
life by losing a mother I never knew, except as a source of
rhythmic thumping sounds and intermittent gurgling noises

and comforting warmth. Then, when I was just old enough to get the full impact, I found out how infinitely much worse it is to lose a parent you know. My world had just begun to shake with the changes of puberty when it exploded in my face; at the moment I most needed adult guidance, my supply of parents dwindled to zero.

Then for a while *everything* had been change, and almost all of it had been unpleasant. I had not until then fully realized that I was odd, that there was anything strange about growing up with a single-parent genius. I thought *all* homes had equations scrawled with disc-marker across all the cabinets and walls, and clean laundry in the freezer, and defrosting chicken in the tool drawer. I thought everyone read a book a day and listened to hours of ancient music.

My father raised no wimps. I'd buckled down and got to work, examined my options, made a plan, made it work, started at last to acquire the confidence that I could get a handle on this life business just like everybody else—

And then I'd met Jinny.

So maybe you can understand that my instinctive tendency, in those early years of the voyage, was to tuck my chin down into my chest, hunch my shoulders, cover up with both forearms, and keep backpedaling. The temporary insanity with Diane was my last flirtation with grand passion and romance. After that I was more in the market for companionship, intellectual stimulation, perhaps a little cautious friendly sex every now and again, perhaps not.

I really did comprehend, intellectually at least, that I was engaged in one of the most profoundly thrilling endeavors in human history. How conservative can you be, if you've jumped off the edge of the Solar System? Do conservative people travel at relativistic speeds? By the end of the first year of our voyage, we were already traveling at more than a third of the speed of light—and even though there were no sensory cues at all to confirm that, we were all well aware of it, and believed it, and I think I can safely say we all found it more than a little thrilling. By the time we reached turnover in nine more years, our velocity was going to peak at a hair-frying $0.99794c$. Does a conservative man race photons?

It wasn't that I couldn't see the future was going to be thrilling. It wasn't that I was unwilling or even reluctant to be thrilled. I just had little experience with it.

THE MORES AND customs we had all been raised in, fruits of the Covenant, continued to work their unlikely magic: even in close and closed quarters, we found ways to live together without violence, to a large extent without malice, and with as much kindness as we could find within ourselves.

At the end of that first year, we celebrated with a party that would become so legendary I don't think I'll discuss it here. There are several detailed accounts available, and I disagree with every one of them on some of the details. One point on which there is agreement, however, is that there were no quarrels. No relationships broke up, no feuds were born. If anyone had a really bad time, they managed to conceal it from one of the best gossip networks in history.

I'm not saying there were no unhappy people aboard. A predictable percentage of us concluded, *much* too late, that they'd made a terrible mistake in joining the colony. A predictable few of those became merchants of gloom, prophets of doom, carriers of that most infectious of diseases, fear. And a few just became so profoundly miserable they lowered morale wherever they passed. Dr. Amy and her three colleagues had their work cut out for them.

It made me want to stop being a jerk faster, to free up her time. So I worked at it.

By the end of that first year of the voyage, I had at least a working two-part answer to the question, *Who is Joel Johnston?*

First, I was a guy who was going to sing to the stars.

I would sing with my horn and with all the other instruments of man, to a star whose very existence had been unsuspected for most of history. I would sing of human beings, since words would not do, to a star system that knew nothing of them or anything like them. I would sing of my fellow colonists, in what I hoped was a universal language, to a planet we hoped would see fit to nurture and sustain us all. And I would sing of myself—and perhaps another—to two strange new moons in the night sky, and slightly distorted constellations.

Second, I was a guy who was going to talk to strange dirt.

On the long voyage I would speak softly to alien soil, in my best approximation of its own language, asking it as politely as I could to accept Terran plants that would feed my colony. I would open negotiations with the ecosystem of Bravo, and listen intently to the responses that came back. Zog and I and all the rest of his crew would spend the years staring until our eyes watered at the probes' surface recon images of Brasil Novo's surface, trying to outguess the planet, speculating endlessly over what sorts of new predators, parasites, or other perils were most likely to exist, arguing endlessly over what we might do about them. It's difficult to plan for the unknown—all right, it's impossible—but we were going to do our level best.

It was a place to stand. Sing to new stars; speak to new dirt. Two planted legs to help keep me upright for the next couple of decades. First we love music. Then we love food. *Many* years later, we evolve high enough to love another—if we're lucky.

15

> The real miracle is not to walk on water, or on
> thin air, but to walk on the earth!
>
> —Thich Nhat Hanh

The second year of the voyage of the RSS *Sheffield* was eventful only by ship standards.

People you don't know fell in and out of love, had and did not have babies, worked and goofed off, succeeded and failed at amusing themselves and each other, did mediocre work and accomplished minor miracles and screwed up completely, were and were not happy.

Al Mulherin, said to be the best physicist aboard, and Linda Jacobs, editor of the ship newspaper *Sheffield Steel*, were the first couple to birth a child, a boy they named Coyote, and a dozen more babies had joined the colony before the year was out.

A machinist named C. Platt got careless with a torch and became our first death. He was not widely mourned. Not even his roommates knew what the C stood for.

One of the residential decks beat all the rest at soccer, and you'd be shocked to hear which one, if you cared.

Relativist Kindred had a fairly gaudy nervous breakdown and for a couple of weeks his colleagues had to cover for him, but this had been expected and planned for and caused no difficulties. It would become a roughly annual occurrence. I think most of us colonists half expected that Peter Kindred was going to Burn Out eventually, at some point along the way—but none of his fellow Relativists did. His shift was taken by Dugald Beader, the only one of the Relativists I haven't mentioned yet, because it took me months to meet him. Dugald was sort of the backward of the flamboyantly eccentric Kindred—quiet and sane and empathetic, with a diabolical dry sense of humor. It was said that he'd been involved in the design of the *Sheffield* somehow, but he didn't talk about it.

The story of the year was probably the totally unexpected marriage of the Zog and Coordinator Grossman. Nobody had a problem with the match; they were both widely admired, and when you thought about it, they were perfect for each other. It had simply never occurred to anyone aboard that either party might have *time* for a social life, let alone an active one.

He moved into her quarters, and they honeymooned by sealing the door for a week. Zog left me in charge in his absence, high praise.

So I got to be the only one in the ship to whom Machinist Platt's death mattered much.

A proctor named Hal DeMann showed up at the Bravo farm one day, pushing a body bag on a gurney. He looked like an old-time pirate or gunfighter, but had a warm, soothing voice, a good combination in his line of work. He explained that Colonist Platt—maybe that was what the C stood for—had left instructions that he wished his body to be recycled, so that he might always be a part of the colony's ecosystem. But old C had given no specifics as to just how this should be done, leaving the question up to the relevant authorities.

Who turned out to be me.

The problem itself was admittedly trivial. Solving it was not. There was certainly plenty of dirt to plant him in, and there were several places where he might even prove useful as fertilizer, and as a check on how Bravonian conditions would alter the usual processes of decomposition and fertilization.

But there was *not* enough dirt to plant him two meters deep. And we had long since learned that no fence is always foolproof. Having his corpse dug up and eaten by pigs or goats or dogs would technically have met the requirements of Platt's will, and I was tempted to, as the poet Buckley said, just "scoop some sand over his wig, and swoop the scene." I was fairly sure he wouldn't have complained, or even minded.

But I was *absolutely* sure I knew what the Zog would say if he came home from his honeymoon to find some of the leftovers being dragged across his Ag Deck by one of his pigs.

Devising a solution wasn't all that hard. Implementing it was. Kathy and I dug as deep a hole as we could, about a meter, and laid Platt in it. Then we stood on either side and covered the corpse over completely, me with broken glass and busted springs, she with curry powder and a spray bottle of lion urine. (Chemically simulated, of course. Zog had fetched a *lot* of odd things along from Sol.) Then we replaced *all* the dirt we'd dug up, leaving a mound of loose earth, but one that was unlikely to be disturbed.

The first problem I had with implementation of this simple solution should be obvious. Nowadays it takes something close to total destruction of the brain to beat the autodocs. I've told you the damage was done by a torch, and you know where the brain is generally kept: work it out. The smell alone was memorable.

My second problem was less gruesome, but bothered me for a longer time. When we were done with our shoveling, Kathy and I stood there for a few moments, catching our breath and thinking deep thoughts. And then as I was about to turn and walk away, she said, "Shouldn't we say something?" Phrased that way, it meant, "Shouldn't *you* say something?"

And of course I was in charge. And of course I should say something; it didn't seem right to just plant the man and go. But of course I had absolutely no idea what kind of words the deceased would have wanted, did not even know if he subscribed to one of the religions humane enough to be permitted under the Covenant or not. If nobody knew what his first initial stood for, there was no point posting a query about his metaphysics on the ship bulletin board. I had no all-purpose nondenominational homilies on tap; I had experienced only one death, and hadn't heard a word anyone had said at the funeral.

I stood there for a long time feeling inadequate, stymied by the question, hating Kathy for raising it. She waited. And finally I heard myself say, "Let the universe take note of this man's passing. Somebody should. He was one of the bravest adventurers our species ever produced: he died on the way to the stars." That night instead of sleeping I thought of better things I might have said, and said them in my head to a man I had never known.

The Zog told me I'd done well when he returned. He'd had a different spot in mind for the ship's cemetery, but was fine with the one I'd picked. I warmed to his praise. But it took me a while to stop resenting Kathy for asking that question.

THIRD YEAR, THIRD year . . . let me scan my diary.

The social bombshell of that year, beyond question, was the surprise wedding of Sol Short and Hideo Itokawa.

If the nuptials of the Zog and Merril the year before had startled everyone, this one stunned us all speechless. The Zogby-Grossman match had paired two strong people, both administrators, one quiet and the other loud. Sol and Hideo were two *extremely* powerful minds, both mavericks, one loud enough to dominate any cubic he entered and kind and hilarious enough to get away with it, and the other so impossibly quiet and still that the eye tended to subtract him. I hadn't even realized Buddhist priests were allowed to marry.

I don't believe anyone aboard opposed the match, once we thought about it. But to do that you had to first imagine it, and that took us a while.

I found out when Tenzin Itokawa asked me to play at the wedding. I don't remember what I said.

The wedding feast was a memorable blast, and there is nothing in the world duller than hearing the details of someone else's blast memories, unless you were at the same blast, so I won't recount any.

That was the kind of year it was. The most exciting event in it was not really worth recounting, to anyone who was not conceived that night.

YEAR FOUR WOULD probably have been downright dull if it hadn't been for the Happy Disaster.

Three months into the year, the Sim Deck went down.

And stayed down, for weeks. The *Sheffield*'s diagnostic systems furnished an explanation, and the six people aboard capable of understanding it all agreed that it sounded reasonable to them, but I never comprehended a word of it, and will not reproduce it here.

By that point, most of us were making fairly heavy use of Sim, for recreation and for emotional therapy and for a way to fight the growing monotony and claustrophobia of life in a great big can. If Dr. Amy or one of the other three Healers decided you were using it too much, they could limit your access, and by that third year they were starting to do so often enough that it became a subject of jokes, unhappy ones.

When the Sim hardware first failed, I worried for colony morale. It doesn't matter how huge it is: any space becomes confining if you absolutely can't escape it. Without the escape valve of assisted fantasy, I was afraid the ship would start to shrink on us. A few folks did panic, at first, and the general tension spiked.

It didn't help when Matty Jaymes had a public flameout. He had no regular partner, and Sim use was not monitored by the Healers like drug intake, so no one had really noticed as, over the years, Matty had quietly turned into a *hardcore* Sim addict. But when he was forced into withdrawal, he switched instantly to a hardcore drunk, and that became very ugly very fast. Dr. Amy did all she could, but even sober he was unmanageable, and finally she was forced to put him in his quarters: his door stopped opening for him. It was only the second time in her career that she'd ever suspended anyone's Covenant rights, and it devastated her. And upset the rest of us. Until then he had been much liked and highly respected; his collapse left everybody on edge.

But then word went around there would be an unscheduled ETM, and when we all logged in, it was Dr. Amy leading the Town Meeting. That was surprising in itself, but what she proceeded to do was probably the last thing any of us would ever have expected.

She yelled at us.

She didn't say a whole lot. She never used profanity, obscenity, or blasphemy. But what she did say was as memorable as an unexpected enema.

"If you cannot function without sucking on a holographic fantasy teat that does all your imagining for you every day of your life, what good will you be to Colônia Brasil Novo?

"It usually takes a *life-and-death crisis* to show you what you're made of, and what your neighbors are made of. Thank whatever powers you believe in that all it will cost *you* is a few weeks without your favorite soap operas.

"The overwhelming majority of your primitive ignorant ancestors managed to get through their lives without 3D-5S Simulation somehow. It must be possible, don't you think?

Children in an empty playroom can amuse themselves, for Covenant's sake.

"Some say anyone who goes to the stars is a loser, running away from reality. I have never believed that of anyone aboard this ship. I'd rather not start."

Those were some of the highlights.

I guess she summed it up in her literal last word, and in the force of the exasperation with which she delivered it:

"Cope."

And do you know, later on when the dust settled, it turned out the Sim systems failure had been a *good* thing, after all— maybe even one of the luckiest things that had happened to us so far. Forced to amuse and inspire ourselves, we rose to the challenge. Social groupings of all kinds sprang up throughout the colony. Get enough people talking long enough and sooner or later someone will say something interesting or useful. Happy meetings occurred. Good conversations got held. With more time to read, we spent more thought on what might be good to read, and began to learn things. Creativity that begins with off-hours amusement soon accidentally spills over into work, and into social interaction. Weddings and less formal partnerships of all kinds spiked to record levels. The theater group acquired competition, and rose to the challenge. The ship's daycare program finally got serious—none too soon. Shipwide drug intake went *down*.

And when the system finally came back up, Sim use never did reach its previous level again, let alone exceed it.

Indeed, toward the end of the year I developed a funny suspicion about how well it had all turned out, and queried the *Sheffield* as to whether any previous starships might ever have suffered Sim failure, and discovered an overall benefit. I was absolutely certain it was physically and emotionally impossible for an untrue word to pass the lips of Dr. Amy, but for all I knew any or all of her three colleagues could have conspired to hoodwink us all for our own good. But if that was the case the ship's AI was in on the gag: it told me only nine previous ships had even carried 5S Sim gear, and none had ever experienced more than momentary failures, save for the one that had blown up.

Clever con or sheer luck—either way it was damned good luck. The colony was emotionally healthier than it had ever been as it entered its fifth year of star travel, gaining confidence in its own ability to cope. That proved useful when disaster struck.

WHAT GOES ON in the Power Room of a relativistic starship like the *Sheffield*?

Maybe God knows, if She exists. The Relativists themselves aren't at all sure.

I remember I was sitting at a table at the Horn once with Herb and all five off-duty Relativists, everyone but Kindred—I can't recall what led them all to be awake at once—and Herb asked what it was like.

I'd never have had the hairs to ask, myself, and there was a silence that lasted nearly ten seconds. Then Dugald Beader shifted his pipe in his mouth and said, "It's like staring at a random-visuals screensaver until you can predict what it's going to do in the next second."

George R said, "It's like playing jai alai with fifty different opponents at once, in zero gravity, blindfolded."

London, her head on his shoulder, said, "It's like being inside a spherical mirror, in free fall, and remembering at all times where the door is."

Sol grinned. "It's like running full tilt across a tightrope in spike heels with your eyes closed while cooking an omelette with a blowtorch," he said, and turned to his husband. "Your turn, Spice. 'It's like . . .' "

". . . not being . . ." Hideo said.

"Aw, come on," Sol said. "I declare that answer void."

Hideo blinked at him, and then nodded. "Very well. It is for me like an archery exercise, in which you must first hit the bull's-eye, then hit that arrow, then hit *that* arrow, and the next, continuing until you can retrieve all your arrows with a single tug, without taking a step forward." He turned to the rest of us. "The secret," he confided, eyes twinkling, "is to aim."

Sol hooted with laughter and hugged him. "Much better."

Dugald took another crack at it. "Sometimes I think of it as looking for a hayseed in a giant needle stack."

"Oh, Duggie, that's *good*," George R said, wincing as he mimed rummaging through needles.

His wife said, "To me it's always seemed very much like hearing a very complex unfamiliar four-part harmony in the distance, and trying to instantly, intuitively improvise fifth, sixth, and seventh harmonies."

That one boggled my own mind. Most people have trouble intuiting the *third* harmony.

Nobody else came up with anything better that night. But I later learned someone had asked Peter Kindred, and he'd offered two of his own, "It's like looking at a Rorschach blot until it means *everything*," and, "It's like repairing nothingness."

None of which tells me anything.

Despite years of friendship with five Relativists, and close friendship with Sol, George R, and London, I don't know what it looks like inside the Power Room, or even the antechamber; nobody does who hasn't been inside one. The convention that has become established in film and other forms of fiction is to portray Relativists sitting before banks of instruments with lots of blinking lights, intently studying gauges and readouts, constantly making fine adjustments with levers, dials, wheels, or mice that invariably cause beeping sounds. But no such layout has ever been certified authentic, and as far as I or anyone really knows, it is equally likely that what they do in there is simply sit in meditation in a bare white cubic . . . a meter off the floor, held aloft by sheer spiritual purity. I have no idea what takes place in a Power Room, and I particularly have never been able to conceptualize what it is like in there at the moment of transition, when one's shift ends and another's begins—how that handoff is accomplished.

I am not one of those fools who believe Relativists guard their guild secrets to protect their monopoly. None of the ones I knew had an avaricious bone in their bodies. Avarice would appear incompatible with the mindset that produces a

Relativist, or that a Relativist produces—a rare case of fortune bringing immense wealth to people fundamentally indifferent to it. But I have no idea why it is that they *do* discourage specific questions about their daily activities. I simply know it is their right if they choose, and they do. It is purely my own intuition that they do so to *protect* the rest of us from the knowledge, for some reason.

It may equally well be that they simply literally *can't* explain what they do—that you and I have no referents for the information, nothing in our experience that any words we know could evoke. Maybe I'm like a cat trying to understand exactly how the fish get into those little cans, or a man trying to understand women: unequipped.

For all I know, something happened in that room, every day, all day, that was simply beyond ordinary human understanding. That's the way I lean, anyway.

The one thing I'm absolutely certain of is that my last chance to ask any of the Relativists I know about such matters is gone for good. I waited too long.

ANYBODY WHO WAS aboard can tell you where they were and what they were doing when it happened.

Any society has such events, benchmarks in its shared history. Usually they involve great tragedy. It may be the untimely death of some universally beloved public figure, or a natural disaster of uncommon magnitude; in the old days it was most often a war, and sometimes a plague.

But in those times, war and plague were expected dangers, and survivable ones. I doubt there have been many humans in history who've known anything like the instant ice-cold horror that comes to every passenger aboard a relativistic starship when they suddenly find themselves in free fall.

Where *I* was that day was on Bravo Ag Deck, goofing off behind the goatshed, chewing the fat with Sol Short, while the two colonists I'd drawn as my unskilled labor that shift, John Barnstead and Adewale Akbage, listened and tried not to look awed. We were passing around a flask of wine Zog had made from the Brasilian flower Muira Puama (*Pty-*

chopetalum Olacoides), which was making a very happy adjustment to Brasil Novo conditions.

I can even remember what we were talking about. At the gentle urging of Dr. Amy, and with Sol as intermediary, I had long since buried the hatchet with transportees Richie and Jules, going so far as to comp them for a night at the Horn so they could hear me play. It made a difference, Richie came backstage after to stare at the floor and say he "apollenized," and Jules put one arm around me and hugged me, and from then on whenever we encountered each other in the corridors, they were both loudly friendly.

So I had begun a small but precious collection of Richie-isms, and loved to compare specimens with Sol, who appreciated them as much as I did. That day, I recall, I had shared with him, "Don't kill the goose that laid the deviled egg," and, "You can't sell a fuckin' book by looking undercover." John threw one in, then: he'd heard someone ask the pair why they were constantly together, and Richie had said, "Two heads are better than none."

And Sol had just gifted us all with the gem "Atojiso," as in, "I knew that would happen. I hate to say atojiso, Jules, but I fuckin' atojiso," and we were roaring with appreciation, when all at once the ceiling came down to join us, and the floor fell away.

SUDDEN UNEXPECTED WEIGHTLESSNESS can only mean drive failure, and this is never good news.

But if you're on a starship, it probably means you're dead. You and everyone in your world.

It is just barely possible to restart a quantum ramjet at velocities higher than $0.5c$. But time is critical—and luck even more so.

It had been done. Twice before in history, in each case by a Relativist said to be particularly adept. Successfully, I mean. There had been two spectacular failures—by colleagues generally agreed to have been equally good. That was why the *Sheffield* needed a minimum of four Relativists—six hours was the longest one could reliably sustain the necessary concentration—and why it carried six.

We'd have carried more, if Kang/da Costa had been able to hire more.

If the quantum ramjet was *not* restarted, and damn quickly, the *Sheffield* would literally never get anywhere. There would be plenty of power for life support—and nowhere near enough to slow all those megatons of mass appreciably. We would drift for all time through the void at more than nine-tenths of the speed of light, forever unable to decelerate to any more reasonable speed, incapable of making any port.

John and Adewale and I were none of us spacemen. We panicked. The blood did not drain from our heads because there was no gravity; but we didn't become as ruddy as we should have. We'd all been in free fall long enough to learn some basics, but none of us had free-fall instincts or reflexes. All we had was enough intelligence to understand how much trouble we were in.

The goats didn't even have that—they knew only two gradations of terror: none and total. They simply happened to be right for once. The goat shed exploded, and jagged pieces of its walls became lethal Frisbees, followed by a second wave of hay, hooves, and horns.

Miraculously, none of us was hurt by any of these. It was Solomon Short who broke my collarbone, using it to launch himself toward the stairwell, and who dislocated Adewale's shoulder using him to leapfrog, and busted John's nose when he couldn't get out of the way fast enough. I figure I'm responsible for my concussion; I could probably have ducked that goat, if I hadn't been watching Sol dwindle in the distance. But how can you look away from somebody crying like that?

To be honest, I don't think I'd have been much help to him even if I hadn't gotten my skull kicked. I was already thinking in terms of coping with my own responsibilities: my livestock, my farm—both my farms! Everywhere, things would be going to hell, delicate hydraulic systems pumping dry, containers spilling over, lattices coming apart, koi trying to swim in damp air—

So it was John, not even particularly a friend of Sol's, who thought of it first, and did it in time, and so ended up accomplishing far more good than I would that day. The instant he had drifted within reach of something substantial enough to change his vector—a light fixture in the ceiling, still on, still hot—he used it to launch himself after Sol. He stayed close to the ceiling, and used every surface feature he passed to add speed, so he had soon built up nearly as good a head of steam as Sol had.

At about that point I heard the right rear quadrant of my skull make the sound "KLOP!" and decided to take a little nap, so I missed John's triumph.

Sol had sensibly ignored the lift, beelined for the emergency stair-shaft/drop-chute, and flung himself down it like a hungry ferret going down a hole. It was the mental picture of him in that ship-length tunnel, reaching ever higher velocity with the help of the handholds that were usually rungs under gravity, that had galvanized John. He was far less free-fall savvy than Sol, but massed more, so he arrived at about the same speed. He knew there was no way he'd make the turn. But he never even attempted to decelerate, just sailed into the chute, slammed against its far wall, and accepted the damage. *"FLIP! FLIP!"* he was screaming as he came through the doorway, and after he crashed and got his breath back, he resumed screaming it at the top of his lungs down that long Freudian shaft. *"FLIP, SOL! FOR CHRISSAKE, FLIP!"*

Would I have understood what he was saying, if I'd heard it? Interesting and pointless question. Adewale said later he did hear it, and didn't get it—as far as he could see, *everyone* around there had flipped.

Halfway down that stair-shaft—any and all gods be thanked, once they've been cleared of any involvement in the original catastrophe—Solomon Short heard John Barnstead's scream. He was then in a kind of frenzy, or fugue state, as fixated as a heat-seeking warhead. But John had selected a word from the tactical menu used by warheads. It was a legal command, and as Sol received it he instantly saw the sense of it and obeyed. By a process that has never been properly described because everyone who's spent time in free fall knows it, and nobody who hasn't can ever understand it, Sol tumble-flipped his body end over end, and continued his plunge feet first.

John's mental process had gone more or less like so: If Sol is the first Relativist to reach the Power Room, we're all screwed. By the time *he* can get there from this far away, the ramjet will probably have been off too long to restart safely. So we must pray that another of his colleagues beats him there.

But if so, what of Sol, in the stair-shaft?

Sure enough, the *Sheffield* was later able to tell me that it was less than a second after Sol stablilized in his new position that weight suddenly returned—followed a split second later by the siren blast that was supposed to give ten seconds' warning before any vector change. At once he began slapping at passing rungs to kill velocity, and looking below for his landing site. In the end, he landed with nothing worse than a sprained ankle, which became severely sprained after he ran on it.

By the time he landed, that was important. Crucial, even. Because by then George R was dead, and London was . . . was permanently out of action.

The *Sheffield* was down two Relativists, now . . . and that left us exactly enough to keep the quantum ramjet running twenty-four hours a day. There was going to be no acceptable excuse to miss a shift . . . for the next fifteen years.

WHAT HAPPENED IN the Power Room that day?

There's a lengthy report on file, which I am assured is accurate and complete; you're welcome to look it up. It's full of what look like words, arranged in sequences that seem to be sentences, and the one I come closest to understanding seems to say that the Zero Point became briefly numerable, and George R was unable to deny it. Maybe that conveys something to you; it's noise to me.

Months later, at various times, I heard Dugald Beader say that George R had "stopped surrendering," and heard a massively drunken Kindred assert that his colleague had "lost his focus." How those two things could describe the same event, I cannot imagine.

Here's what little I do understand.

First of all, George R was not supposed to be on duty that shift. Hideo was. That was why Sol lost it. But at the last minute, one of Hideo's Zen students had come to him with a spiritual crisis, and he'd asked to be replaced.

This was no big deal. By that point in the voyage, all of the Relativists had missed a shift or two; it was part of what spares were for. Hideo had probably missed fewer than anyone else but Kindred—and had extracurricular responsibilities the others lacked. If anyone was entitled to blow off a shift, it was him.

The person he was supposed to succeed was George R. When his request showed up on George R's board, George R should have messaged backup, confirmed availability, then let Hideo know he was off the hook—a total of three keystrokes. He did only the third.

Who can say what was in his mind? Of the Relativists aboard, Sol was the loudest, and Peter Kindred the most egotistical, but George R was far and away the most sheerly *confident*. There was no leader, but he was senior among equals. The backup he should have called was London. She was asleep just then, in their quarters. Perhaps he just wanted to do something nice for his wife. Maybe it was a gesture of apology to get him out of some marital doghouse. It may simply have been easier for a man as confident as him to push one key than three.

He certainly was not the first Relativist ever to work a double shift. But I think it's safe to say he was the last.

Fatigue? Monotony? Bad judgment? Bad luck? None of them ever said, and none of us ever had the balls to ask.

Something Horrible happened in there, that's all.

Whatever it was took something like thirty seconds to finish burning his brains out, and matters should have ended there. It is certain that he did not at any time trigger an alarm or send out a message of any kind. The ramjet should have failed, and then whoever won the race to the Power Room should have yanked his smoking body out of the way and, hopeably, restarted it.

I do not know how London got there before he finished dying. She knew exactly how dangerous it was to try and go in there, just then, and never hesitated. Whether she believed she could save him or simply didn't care to outlive him is not for me or anyone to say. If it was a mistake in judgment she paid dearly enough for it—with her eyesight, most of her hearing, and about eighty-five IQ points.

A rain of shit can take time to stop. It was doubtless lucky for all of us that Hideo was the next to reach the Power Room. Of all of them he most had the kind of iron discipline and diamond calm it must take to toss the smoldering bodies of two friends out in the corridor for others to deal with, forget them, and try to restart a quantum ramjet. I honestly think any of them could have done it, but I'm glad it was Hideo who got the job.

But when he emerged, and had been thanked in turn by Captain Bean, Governor Roberts, Governor-General Cott, and Coordinator Grossman, Sol and Dr. Amy had to take him aside and tell him that the student he'd blown off his original shift to counsel had pieced events together, and committed suicide from guilt.

A poor reward for heroism.

16

During this period, Tesla spoke out vehemently against the new theories of Albert Einstein, insisting that energy is not contained in matter, but in the space between the particles of an atom.

—Tesla, Master of Lightning
PBS-TV documentary, Dec. 12, 2000

The next few weeks were dark.

    Disaster on that scale can demoralize a community— or draw it together. The crucial factor seems to be, how fast does the fear ease?

It was touch and go. Dr. Amy and her three other Healers had their work cut out for them. Coordinator Grossman and the Zog, Governor Roberts, Governor-General Cott and his partner, Chief Engineer Cunningham, even Captain Bean himself, all made a point of wandering around the ship with cheerful optimistic expressions fixed on their faces. It did help, a little. But only a little.

How do you tell someone falling through the universe at nearly the speed of a photon there's nothing to worry about? When the most valued, pampered members of the ship's company can die and worse than die, who is safe? I don't think any of us had really expected any dying to begin until we got to Bravo. Now all our lives and plans and hopes depended on four particular people remaining not only alive but healthy enough to work for every day of the next fifteen years.

And that was the heart of our darkness: theirs.

THANKS FOR COMING in ahead of schedule, Joel," said Dr. Amy.

"No problem," I said, settling into my chair. "To tell you the truth, though, things haven't been too bad lately."

"I'm glad to hear that," she said.

"I mean, I know you must have your hands full—"

"That's what I want to talk to you about, this time."

"Crave pardon?"

"I'm going to be more blunt and candid with you than I have been with the rest of the colony, Joel."

Yikes. "Okay."

"This ship is in trouble."

I nodded. "I know."

"The morale crisis is not responding to anything we can do. I think you know why."

I nodded again. "The Relativists. The rest of us . . . colonists, administrators like you, crew . . . none of us can begin to heal until they do." All four stalked the corridors like golems, now, and were given as wide a berth by all they passed. All four had politely declined to speak to a Healer, as was their right. They didn't even seem to crave each other's company. They spoke as little as possible at shift change, and less at any other time.

Her turn to nod. "They do their duty. They keep the engine running. But that's the absolute limit of their strength right now. They're the heart of the ship. And they're heartsick."

"I have to say I can't blame them a bit," I said. "One of the best of them died, another wasn't as lucky—and it could happen to any one of the rest at any time. It can't be easy healing if every day you have to spend six straight hours utterly devoid of all emotions . . . in the presence of the force you most fear and hate. I'm amazed they can function at all."

"Nobody blames them, Joel."

"No—but nobody has the hairs to tell them to suck it up, and let you Healers help them."

Her shoulders relaxed. "Exactly. You do understand."

"Well, that much. What you can *do* about it, I have no idea. A year ago, I'd have said, have Matty Jaymes talk to all of them."

She nodded. "They all used to respect him a lot."

"He used to deserve it."

Matty had long since been restored to the Covenant. But the man who'd emerged from his room was not the Matty Jaymes anyone remembered. He was pale, dwindled, and taciturn, and he did not want to talk to anybody. Something had changed him, and no one had any idea what.

She grimaced ruefully. "Suppose you were in my chair. Where would you *start*?"

"That's easy," I said. "With Sol. He's the linchpin, now that George R is gone. Until you turn him around, you'll never . . ." I trailed off as I realized where this had to be going.

"I agree," she said.

I held up both hands, shook my head, and shut my eyes briefly, refusing delivery with all the body language at my disposal. "No way. Don't look at me."

"Joel—"

"I *tried* already. Twice, okay? Both conversations together totaled a single word, and I didn't say it."

"Tell me about it."

"The first time I saw him after . . . afterward, I walked up to him, and we stood about a meter apart for a few moments, and after a while I opened my mouth, and he shook his head no, and I closed my mouth, and he went away."

"And the second time?"

"Two days ago. I waited outside his room, where his door couldn't see me. I had a zinger prepared. A brutal, stinging line that would shock him into paying attention to me. Use anger to invoke his fighting spirit. Healing 101. The door opened, he came out and saw me, and this time I didn't even *get* to open my mouth. 'Don't,' he said. Just that."

"How did he say it?" She was leaning forward slightly.

"Way back at the dawn of video, there was a short time when animation was so expensive, they made cartoons in which little ever moved but the characters' mouths, which were real human lips superimposed on 2-D drawings. He looked just like that."

She winced.

"So I just nodded, like, 'Okay, I won't.' And he gave one little gesture of a nod, like somewhere between 'Thank you,' and 'Fuck off, now.' So I fucked off."

She was wearing her most empathic expression. "And now if you try a third time, without some kind of direct invitation from him, you'll lose him as a friend. I see that."

"You're good."

"How horrible for you. Okay, never mind. Thanks, Joel. I should have known you would already have tried your best. I apologize."

She stood up. We were done. I got up, too, and we gave each other the Japanese style bow that was our half-ironic custom. But I did not turn and head for the door.

"What was it you were going to suggest?"

She waved it away. "No, never mind. Thanks. Probably wouldn't have worked anyway."

"If this is reverse psychology—"

She smiled. "No. It was just an idea."

"So just tell it."

"I read a line somewhere in an old book once, to the effect that when you're really depressed, the only person you'd be glad to see coming is somebody who wants to pay an old debt."

"I don't follow."

"You've never paid Sol for his services as your advocate, four years ago. You promised him an original composition of at least fifteen minutes, on the baritone sax, with his name in the title."

She was right. I had certainly meant to do it. I'd even made a start on it, once. But what with one damn thing after another, it had fallen between the cracks, and eventually been silted over. I told myself I would have recalled my promise eventually.

"I was thinking maybe you could offer to do it now, ask him for direction, use that to get him talking. But you're right: if you raised the subject now, he'd tell you where to put your saxophone. Don't worry. I've got a few other approaches I can try. Thanks for sharing your insights with me."

I left. But when I got back to Rup-Tooey, I stayed only long enough to grab my Yanigasawa B-9930, and then headed for my studio. Now that I was a rich man, I was renting a soundproofed cubic on the lower of the two VIP decks, so I wouldn't have to inflict my saxes on my roommates. When I got there, I had enough forethought to phone both the Zog, and Jill and Walter at the Horn of Plenty, and beg off my upcoming shifts at both jobs. Then I sealed the door and shut off phone and mail.

Three days later I switched the phone back on, called Dr. Amy, and outlined what I had. It was she who figured out how to try and put it to use.

COMING OFF SHIFT, Solomon Short craved only oblivion. If he could manage to sleep twelve hours—and he could, easily—that left only six to fill. Same amount of time spent in and out of the Hole, each day. When he entered his quarters and found the sitting room full of people, he simply backed out again before the door could shut behind him.

At least he tried to. It didn't work. He encountered someone coming in the other direction, found himself back in the sitting room, heard the door dilate behind both of them.

He didn't bother to turn and find out who it was, didn't even bother to take note of exactly which assholes were cluttering up his parlor with this moronic Intervention attempt. Like a soldier removing the muzzle cap from his assault weapon and jacking one into the chamber, he slowly opened his mouth and took in air—

A face was suddenly decimeters from his own. An angry, brutal, stupid face. Its mouth was already open, and had already taken in lots of air.

"Shut the fuck up," Richie bellowed at him.

His own mouth slammed shut.

"Sit down there."

Sol sat.

Richie sat down to his right. The man behind him—Jules—took a seat at his left, and shifted his drink to his left hand. Proctor DeMann stepped across the doorway and dropped into parade rest, then softened it by taking one hand from behind him and stroking his gunfighter mustache, in the manner of one who wishes he still smoked a pipe.

And before Solomon could get himself planted, let alone prepare his first withering wisecrack, I began to play.

AT FIRST, HE was so pissed off he didn't hear a thing I was playing.

That was okay. I'd expected that. I kept on playing.

He tried to stop me by talking over me.

That was okay. *Nobody* can talk over a baritone saxophone. Not my silver Anna. Not even Solomon Short. I kept on playing.

With elaborately insulting body language, he stuck a finger in each ear, screwed his eyes shut, and stuck out his tongue.

That was okay. The sound struck him with renewed force again at the same instant muscle-bound arms were flung across him from each side, pinning him in place—so he opened his eyes just in time to watch his own fingers jammed up his nose. They released him at once. Richie leaned into his field of vision, shook his head no very slowly, and sat back. I kept on playing.

He tried making faces at people, clearly hoping to escalate to mime. He tried everyone in the room.

That was okay. Nobody would play along. I kept playing.

Finally he fell back on his last line of defense, and met my eyes, wearing an expression that said, *I don't care if you are the reincarnation of the Yardbird himself playing me a previously unknown Beiderbecke masterpiece, you aren't getting in as deep as the layer of moisture on the surface of my eyeballs, motherfucker.* Most musicians have seen that look, and it is indeed demoralizing, and Sol did it better than most.

But that was okay, too, because by the time he had it fully in place and the mortar had set, it was already starting to show tiny cracks. Because I kept on playing. And kept on playing.

It took longer to penetrate than it would have in his normal mindset. But eventually, even in his depression he couldn't help but notice that I had been playing for something like a minute and a half by now.

Without stopping to breathe.

Even once.

A fellow amateur historian of music, he caught on to what I was doing faster than most would have. And in spite of himself, he started to grow interested. . . .

The technique known as "circular breathing" is in fact nothing of the sort. But it looks like it to a civilian.

If you're doing it right. This is vastly easier said than done.

I hold with the school of thought that says modern music (as they were now calling it, *again*) copied it from the Aborigines of the continent Australia, on Terra. So it could be as much as 47,000 years old—a little under a thousand *generations*. The Australian didgeridoo is an immensely powerful but intrinsically limited instrument; like haiku, it finds enormous beauty within severe constraints. Denied the endless variety offered by pitch, however, it finally began to lack the bandwidth to carry concepts as sophisticated as those that some didgeridoo players wished to express. There were only so many things, and combinations of things, you could do before you ran out of air and had to start a new phrase.

So they abolished breathing.

Obviously they did nothing of the sort. What they did was improve it. All the necessary parts were right there: all they had to do was train and exercise them. Not to say that was easy.

What I actually do when I "circularly breathe" is to use my cheeks as a storage bellows. It's a four-step process, that begins during exhalation:

1. As I start to run low on air, I puff my cheeks as far as possible, a configuration called a Dizzy for more than one reason.

2. I slowly contract my cheek muscles, using the air trapped in my cheeks to keep the sound coming out the other end of the pipe—while simultaneously inhaling through my nose. Very like learning to wear a Mars-mask, and no harder.

3. If I've timed it right, my cheek-bellows empty out at the same time my lungs fill up. My soft palate closes, and once again it's my lungs pushing air out the horn.

4. My cheeks return to normal embouchure, until my air starts to run low again. Repeat from 1. above.

During all this time, of course, my fingers are busy doing even more difficult things to turn all that air into pleasant sounds. They say that anybody can learn to do it . . . with enough beatings.

Anyone who's studied the saxophone has heard about circular breathing, and most of us have attempted it, and a few have persisted long enough to get it—six months of daily practice, minimum—and then played around with it a little.

Hardly anyone keeps it up, once they've proved to themselves that they can do it. There's little point: the number of compositions in the database that call for it can pretty much be counted on the fingers of one foot. The last composer of merit to mess with it much was probably MacDonald, just before the Prophet took *everyone's* breath away for a century and a half; his "Thaumaturgy" is definitive.

I'd developed an interest in it about a year before the Disaster—for much the same reason the Aborigines had. After many long slow years in one place, I was beginning to find my own limitations unbearably confining. First I'd fooled around with playing more than one horn at once. But like everyone who tries that, I'd found that everything you can do along those lines that isn't just a gimmick was done a long time ago, by Rahsaan Roland Kirk and Sun Ra.

So I'd switched to circular breathing. It took me about three weeks just to be able to do it *with nothing in my mouth*, then three weeks more with a straw making bubbles in a cup of water. After six months, I could produce recognizable melodies on sax, and six months after that, I was just beginning to get to the point where I might have been willing to let another human hear me do it . . . when Hell broke loose in the Hole, and the roof fell in on us all. I hadn't played much music of any kind for a while after that. Nobody much wanted to hear any.

But after my conversation with Dr. Amy, I had worked continuously for seventy-two hours, getting by on catnaps and helmet rations. I had to. I already knew I was going to be half cheating Sol as it was: I did not have time to actually *compose* a fifteen-minute-long work, and was going to have to improvise something that had his name in the title. But by the Covenant, the man had asked for whatever it was to be played on Anna, and that was what he was going to get! He was the first person aboard to touch her, had brought her to me with his own hands, that first week.

Up until those last three days, all my circular breathing had been done on my *alto* sax—on which I could barely get through the nine-and-a-half-minute "Thaumaturgy."

It is *much* harder to do on a baritone—even a cherry like my silver Anna. Simple physics. A bigger volume of air has to be moved farther. There's a finite limit to how big you can make your cheeks. The lower notes in particular require breathing *very fast*, and that's hard to hide.

(Counterintuitively, it is also harder to do circular breathing on a tenor, and perhaps hardest on a soprano, because of the increased lip pressure required. This is not a paradox: the universe just hates musicians. Envy, I think.)

I'd finally found a way to fake it, but I don't think I can describe it. What it *feels* like I do is to use my sinus cavities as auxiliary bellows, somehow isolating them from the nasal-inhalation pipeline, but Dr. Amy assured me that's just not possible. I asked how I *was* doing it, then, and she said she'd need to saw my head in half while I was doing it to tell me; would I care to book an appointment?

So I HAD his attention, finally.

Sol was knowledgeable enough to recognize circular breathing, and he was sophisticated enough about the physics of wind instruments to realize how insanely hard it must be to do it on a baritone, and he loved Anna's voice as much as I did, and its sheer power in such a small enclosed cubic was enormous, and I was playing my heart out. I simply overwhelmed his indifference shields, denied him the power of denial, forced him to listen to what I was playing.

I was playing phrases that *did not end*.

We call them phrases because there's only so long they can be. Some go so far as to say that the pauses between the notes are the most important parts of the music. Sooner or later even the most complex phrase dies—to be phoenix-reborn a moment later, in the next phrase. This happens even with instruments not constrained by breath or any other limitation. Most music unconsciously echoes the generational nature of human creation, death at either end of every life, an instant of silence before and after each new melody.

I played melodies and themes and motifs that did not end, but flowed endlessly, one into the next without pause, without rest, without hesitation.

At first I underlined that, by playing what first seemed to be conventional sequences, building naturally toward inevitable ending places—that always took an unexpected left turn just before they got there, and turned out to have actually been lead-ins to some *different* familiar series.

Once I saw in his eyes that he got it, I abandoned all convention and just played.

I forgot everything I knew about composition, reattained what Zen people call beginner's mind, acquired once again the mighty power of ignorance. I shut down most of my brain, except for the part way back by the stem that knows how to make a saxophone work, and gave control of it over directly to my heart. I learned what I was going to play at the same instant Sol and the others did: as it emerged.

If what I played had had lyrics, they would have had to be "Fuck Death," repeated in every human tongue ever spoken.

I blew phrases that *refused* to end. A structure that climbed as stubbornly and relentlessly and defiantly as the one at Babel rose up from the bell of my horn. I stated a theme that had no resolution and sought none, and proved that it needed none. George R was woven in and out of it—a face whose only expression was a smile. So was London— the London we had known, whose laugh required a baritone sax to do it justice. So were both my parents. Machinist C. Platt made an appearance.

Einstein said, "People like us, who believe in physics, know that the distinction between past, present, and future is only a stubbornly persistent illusion."

I dispelled it.

I did not take my eyes away from those of Solomon Short once. Until I saw, in his eyes, that I had won. That I had penetrated deep enough. I had *forced* him to see that he could feel, and not die of it. It was like watching a man in agony as the morphine hits.

Have you ever had a serious fever? The misery seems not only to last forever, but to have lasted forever—and then it goes on like that for days. But there comes a point when some kind of knot inside suddenly lets go—at the base of the throat, it feels like—and something starts to ease, or melt, or release. It's a little like drifting off to sleep, only it leaves you more conscious. At first you can't believe it, and then for a time you're tearful with gratitude, and about ten minutes later you're demanding food and the remote control.

I held on until the tearful-with-gratitude stage. I've mentioned my unusually accurate time sense. I knew when I'd been playing for fifteen minutes. At sixteen, I yanked the mouthpiece from my lips, chopping off short in the midst of an ascending arpeggio. It took me a ridiculous number of seconds to remember how to take in air by mouth.

Sol didn't notice. His eyes stayed closed. At the unexpected cessation of sound he first froze, then slumped slightly.

When I had enough control back, I said formally, "The name of that piece is 'Sol Keeps Shining.'"

Nobody said a word or moved a muscle. Except me, getting my breath all the way back and unkinking my neck.

For maybe thirty seconds he moved nothing but his nostrils and chest, so long that I was beginning to wonder if he had entered meditation.

He sat up straight then, and opened his eyes, and looked into mine, and said, "Okay."

Anna and I bowed.

He turned to meet Dr. Amy's gaze. "All right," he told her. "I will."

She nodded. "I know, Solomon."

He addressed the room. "Thank you. You are all good people." He turned back to me. "Except you. You haven't even left us the option of saying 'I'm breathless,' you hammy bastard."

"I could throttle you," I offered.

"Well, you're probably not the only one who's had that idea lately," he admitted.

"I've *never* been the only one with that idea," I assured him, and noticed I was leaking tears. It didn't seem to be a problem.

The old Solomon Short lopsided grin lit the room. "Look—"

"Yes," I said. "We *will* excuse you. Love to Hideo."

He nodded, and stood up. He bent slightly, looked up to me for permission, and kissed Anna on her upper lip. Then he straightened, and without asking my opinion kissed me firmly and wickedly on the mouth. Hal opened the door for him, and he left at once.

I started feeling better immediately. It took him four days to finish bringing the other three Relativists around—Peter Kindred took the longest—but the outcome was never in doubt from the moment when he told Dr. Amy, "Okay."

WORD GOT AROUND.

The next morning, at the Horn, I looked up from my breakfast to find a complete stranger a meter away, seeking to be noticed but looking sheepish. He wanted to know if he could have a copy of "Sol Keeps Shining."I hadn't thought about it, but found I didn't need to. "You've come to the wrong window, cousin," I told him. "That piece and that recording both belong to Solomon Short. It was a work-for-hire, performed in his private cubic, and I've waived moral rights. I don't even have a copy myself."

He thanked me and went away, and later that day, my mailbox began to overflow with copies of "Sol Keeps Shining," at least half sent by people I'd never met. Over the next few days, I started hearing it played all over the ship.

Later that day, Dr. Amy came down to Rup-Tooey to hug me. She pretended not to see my tears.

Strangers stopped to bow to me in the corridors. The sets I played at the Horn became full houses, of people who had come to listen. In a musician's ultimate wet dream, I was literally *commanded* by my community to formally release an album of my work, so that I could sign copies of it for them.

One of Kathy's husbands, Paul Barr, recorded and mixed it. My backup was her, a bass player named Carol Gregg, Garret Amis on guitar, and a utility infielder named Doc Kuggs filling in on this and that. Richie and Jules handled the mechanics of burning, packaging, and marketing, robbing me no more than an honest ten percent. I called it *On the Road to the Stars,* and included a reinterpretation of that tune.

Shortly after that Herb came up to me, grinning like a Viking after the plunder but before the rape, to inform me that a VIP of the Apple empire back on Terra wanted to know who represented me. Badly enough to pay a fortune for telepathy rather than wait 2.85 years for an answer by laser. I got Paul Hattori to represent me, and three months later my album reached number seven in the Inner System chart, and number three in the Outer. It would have time to win one major critics' award, as well.

I couldn't help but wonder what Jinny thought of it. But not hard, or for long. I was busy. Come to find out, a saxophone hero in a small town has absolutely no trouble getting all the dates he wants, on whatever terms suit him. Who knew?

After a few brief holy-shit experiments, I think I did pretty well resisting the temptation to be a jerk and abuse it. I kept remembering that I was always going to live in a small glass-walled town with all these people. Leaving town or planet and reinventing myself was no longer an option.

But I did have me some fun, I did. Herb actually stopped clucking over me.

Immense wealth, creative validation, System-wide fame without any downside, personal popularity, emotional support, great sex—if I'd had any idea how much fun it would turn out to be, I'd have leaped off a cliff *years* earlier.

IT ONLY UNDERLINED things when word reached us that the long-threatened trade war had finally broken out between Ganymede and Luna, and I discovered that I did not give the least particle of a damn.

Some of the more panicky newsnitwits back there were shrilly predicting that the conflict would not only metastasize and become Systemic, but would finally trigger the "inevitable" return of armed violence to human affairs, and destroy the Covenant. Of course they'd been saying similar things as long as I could remember, and for every one of the nearly two hundred years since the last recorded shooting war. But even when I ran it through as a hypothetical—no behavior is beyond human beings—I was mildly surprised to find how little it worried me.

Was I really that self-centered and callous? Screw you, Jack, I'm all right? I *knew* people back there. Nice people, who would feel great pain if someone shot them, and feel worse pain if they shot someone. Didn't I care about them?

Sure. Theoretically. But I think we can only really worry about things that, deep down, we believe we could *do* something about, if we tried. I could no more affect the Solar System than I could events in Sparta, or the Land of Oz. My friends on Ganymede were going to have to look out for themselves. So were my friends on Terra, and in Luna.

I did arrange for a few musicians I knew to get their demos listened to at Apple. But I knew as I did it that it was a message in a bottle, and would probably be my last contact with the Solar System. And unless any of them could afford to spring for telepathy, it was going to be something like five years at a minimum before I could possibly hear any results. They would crawl after us at the speed of light, and we were moving at well over ninety-five percent of that ourselves by now.

Psychologically, I was already becoming a Brasil Novan.

And I wasn't the only one. As we entered our sixth year, most of us had experienced similar changes. Hits at the ship's System News website registered a steady decline, without reference to the juiciness of the headlines or sexual attractiveness of those depicted. Mail traffic to sternward showed a similar trend curve.

Terra, Luna, the O'Neills, Mars, Ganymede, the Belt—all of them had become The Old Country. To our children, some of them now three years old, they weren't even going to be that. When they grew up they'd have trouble keeping them all straight. "I forget, Dad—was surfing invented on Mars, or Luna? I can never remember which one of you had to live inside of." All but a handful of their own children would possess such information for only one week of their lives, right before final exam week, and then discard it forever with no ill effect.

We not only started to realize that, we started to be okay with it.

We began in subtle ways to function less like a collection of random refugees in a temporary shelter, and more like a community.

There was a fairly long period in its history when Canada was a collection of isolated outposts, its citizens separated by vast gulfs of uninhabitable space and incompatible regional interests, even different languages. Yet they found it possible to maintain a solid, workable sense of national identity based on little more than unusual pleasantness and a shared loathing of their national airline's coffee.

In the *Sheffield*, it was green mist jokes and shared loathing of rabbit meat in all forms. And, eventually, all things rabbity. Any joke that ended with a bunny covered in green mist was a surefire laugh.

Nations have been founded on worse.

I don't suppose many of us really despised rabbit as much as we affected to. But it is a virtually fatless meat, pretty boring no matter how you cook it, even in a ship with good air pressure. And rabbits lend themselves to jokes. Few of us like a coward.

And there were ancillary benefits at which one did not *have* to turn up one's nose, for a change: if you rejected rabbit meat, you either ate syntho—unsatisfying—or you were a vegetarian until the livestock got decanted at Bravo. And while vegetarians fart twice as much as carnivores, *the farts smell ten percent as bad,* or less. There was a noticeable net improvement in . . . ambience, shipwide.

Things were actually starting to look pretty good, just before everything blew up.

Well, very damn near everything.

17

My opinions as to the future of Mankind are
hedged in by this statement: I think it is
necessary for the human race to establish
colonies off this planet.

—Admiral Caleb Saunders,
interview, Butler, MO, USA, Terra
July 7, 1987 ("Anson MacDonald Day")

Y ou know the date. Everyone does. Everyone always will.
If we're lucky.

Everyone everywhere has their own story. For me, this is the way the world ended. Not with a whim, but with a banker.

PAUL HATTORI WAS a closet soap fiend. We had dozens of them aboard, I had been surprised to discover. But I guess Paul felt an addiction that silly was beneath his dignity as colony banker. I only knew about it because I spent more time than anyone else in Herb's company.

The phenomenon was perfectly predictable, when you thought about it; I simply never had until I encountered it.

Imagine you are a devoted fan—a much politer term than "addict"—of a daily soap opera. One of the real classics, let's say. *Corry*, or *The Sands of Mars*. And you happen to be on a starship, boosting at a steady one-third gee.

After an arbitrary time . . . let's pick 6.41 years. After six years and 150 days of such acceleration, you are traveling at 0.976 *c*. Naturally you are impressed.

But you're also frustrated. Because while it's been six years and change for you, *thirteen* years have elapsed back in the System. A full six years and 215 days of *Corry* episodes—representing more than the total time you've been traveling—exist, are in the can, and have been seen by billions of people. But you are going to have to wait *forever* to find out what has happened to all your favorite imaginary friends. You're outracing the news.

Unless you know a telepath you can go lean on. He's your one and only source of series cheat sheets.

Paul arrived at Rup-Tooey that afternoon just as Herb was saying good-bye to navigator Mort Alexander and roboticist Guy Atari, who were collaborating on a book and had sought his professional counsel. It had boiled down to "don't," but they left undiscouraged. Paul got there in time to hear Herb's final words of advice: "If you really don't mind doing twice the work for half the money, we should all get together for poker sometime."

"Weren't you a bit hard on them?" Paul asked as the door

dilated behind them. He took a seat near Herb's desk and facing my bed, where I sprawled in lazy comfort reading a biography of Johnny Hodges. We nodded to each other, and I collapsed the display and sat up; I had come to like Paul.

Herb said, "Anyone who can possibly be discouraged from writing should be." He shuddered slightly. "Besides, the idea of sharing a keypad freaks me out. I'd rather share a toothbrush."

"I feel the same about my saxophones," I said.

"I feel the same way about money," Paul said, deadpan.

"Philistine," I said.

Herb frowned. "Please—let's not corrupt the language. It's pronounced, 'Fill a stein,' and I agree, it's the least he can do."

Paul sighed theatrically, got up, and went to the fridge, one of several improvements I'd had made to the room. "You, Joel?"

"Sure," I said. "I presume you're here for your fix."

"Can you squeeze me in today, Herb? It's been a month."

Herb's telepathic time had always been pretty heavily booked, and got more so as the voyage went on, and the amount of information that only he and his colleagues Stephanie Gaskin and Gene Rubbicco could supply increased. By now it was a distinct nuisance for Herb to fit things as frivolous as soap opera synopses into his traffic load. But as a nicotinic he did empathize with addiction. And Paul was the recipient of something like a quarter of his usual, official daily traffic. "Yes—but only because I've just thought of a pun so hideous I've basically lost the will to live."

Paul brought each of us an opened container of beer, and sat down with one of his own. (There *were* real glass steins aboard—packed deep in the hold, so we'd still have them when we reached Bravo.) "Okay, I'm seated, and I have beer. Go ahead." He flinched anticipatorily.

"You spend half your working day staring at the stock situation, concerned about corn futures. Then you come here and pester me so you can get caught up on stock situations and corny futures."

I groaned. Paul's nostrils flared. "If you're calling *Corry* corny, ya dozey pillock, I'm glad I pissed in that beer."

"I was referring to the ethanol served at the Rover's Return, wanker."

Paul relaxed. "Ah well, ethanol sterilizes anything."

I said, "If that were true, the human race would have died out a long time ago."

"And there'd never have been a second generation of Irishmen," Herb agreed.

Weird, now, remembering that was the last thing I said that morning. Reality can get away with things you'd never buy in fiction.

"I really appreciate it, Herb," Paul said. "How late should I come by, tonight?"

Herb checked the time. "Stick around; you can take it with you. I was just about to log on. I always put private stuff first, so if anyone runs out of time, it ain't me."

"Are you sure?" Paul said. "I wouldn't want to . . . intrude."

"You *can't*."

"Well, 'distract,' then. Extra work—"

"Got your keypad on you?"

"Sure." He took it from his belt and opened it.

"Give it here," Herb said. "I'll type the data into it, then just toss it to you and keep going on my own. No extra mousing required."

"Okay. Thanks." He opened the display, accessed his mail account, collapsed the display again, and tossed the keypad to Herb.

Herb set it on his desk without bothering to reopen the display. He reconfigured his chair for maximum long-term comfort, and placed his beer where he could reach it with his weaker typing hand.

"You're sure my being here won't . . . I don't know, disturb your concentration?"

I snickered.

"Not if you set yourself on fire," Herb assured him. "Be alert: this keypad is just going to suddenly come flying in your general direction, and I can't predict vector."

"This is really nice of you."

"Remember that when I'm on my knees, begging you for a loan," Herb said. "See you later, gentlemen."

He found home row on Paul's keypad, closed his eyes, and went away. An indescribable series of expressions passed across his face in only a few seconds, ending in a wry grin. He began typing so rapidly, it was as if the inefficient QWERTY layout were the only thing keeping him from typing too fast for the electrons to keep up, and jamming the machine.

We watched him together for maybe half a minute.

"God, look at his face," Paul whispered then. "Transcendence. I'd give anything for his gift." That was the last thing *he* said. I swear.

I was going to tell him that he didn't need to whisper, that he could sing it at the top of his lungs while I accompanied him on tenor. But just then we both saw Herb's face change. Saw the transcendence start to drain out of it.

First he frowned. Then he stopped typing, became still. He started to inhale. His jaw dropped, slowly and steadily. His eyebrows lurched upward, in stages. Surprise. Amazement. Astonishment. The rising brows dragged open his eyes, and they widened in more rapid stages. Alarm. Dismay. Fear. Panic. Terror. Horror. Disbelief. Awe.

It took a total of maybe ten seconds. Maybe less. I will never forget a picosecond of it.

Paul and I knew something was terribly wrong. The color had drained from his face, veins writhed on his forehead like cooking pasta, cords of muscle stood out on his neck. My only wild hypothesis was that he was having a stroke. By now his gaping mouth had sucked a huge volume of air into his lungs. I was afraid it might never leave.

And then was horrified when it did. It may have been the worst sound that ever left a human throat. And he had very big lungs.

The devil himself would take pity on a man who screamed like that. Perhaps he did: the room's microphones all blew out after only a second or two, and that scrambled the video feed as well. You've seen and heard the surviving footage, and you know how indelibly soul-searing those couple of seconds are. It went on for a good fifteen seconds. I heard the whole thing, live, four meters away in an enclosed cubic, and it did not deafen me *near* as much as I wished it would.

It started out as a scream of pain, very quickly escalated to mindless agony, stayed there for what seemed like a million years, mutated into despair, and then in its final seconds added in powerful undertones of unimaginable heartbreak, unendurable regret, insupportable grief.

I had absolutely no idea what had happened. I just knew it was the worst thing ever.

And it was.

WE WEREN'T THE only ones to hear a scream like that, either. Not even the only ones aboard.

BY THE TIME it dawned on me that Paul could help me carry Herb, I'd left him way too far behind. "Call Dr. Amy," I brayed, and lurched on.

From Rup-Tooey to the elevator—nearly the ship's radius. Black spots. Upward five decks, at the speed of capillary action. Ears pounding. From the elevator to the Infirmary, only about half a radius, but with a complicated route. Bad design. Red spots, now. Got lost and had to backtrack. Made mental note: sob the moment you can spare the air. Spotted big red "ER" and red cross ahead, just as vision began to dither out. Kept going, confident door would get out of my way.

I presume it did, but something hard just beyond it did not. I felt the impact, realized I had lost my horizon somewhere, let go of Herb, bawled, "Take him!" and waited with mild interest to learn whether I would injure my face or the back of my head.

The answer was both, but I did not find out for some time. It was the back of my head that hit first, and it hit hard enough to bounce. That was unfortunate, because just then Herb landed on my face. They say my skull made a much louder sound the second time.

I want to be clear: the problem was not shortage of autodocs—the *Sheffield* stocked two hundred, which someone had calculated should last five hundred people until they could build their own. It wasn't even a shortage of autodocs warmed up and ready to use. Four casualties at one time didn't even begin to strain the resources Dr. Amy had in place. And while many parts of the *Sheffield*'s infrastructure were underspecified or even shoddy, she had made damned sure medicine was not one of them: those were 'docs fit for the Prophet's generals.

It was nobody's fault. It was confusion, that's all. Everyone in that room was probably as saturated with excess adrenalin as I was or more, and most of them had more than a single emergency to deal with at once. Only one of them knew me well enough to even be in a position to infer how *far* I had probably just run as fast as I could, carrying a man who outweighed me by more than thirty-five kilos. And not only was she the busiest person in the room, she already knew, as almost no one else did, what had happened to cause all this. It is remarkable that she was able to function at all, and she dealt more than competently with the three acute patients she knew about.

Nobody noticed for a while that I had died, that's all.

OBVIOUSLY, SOMEBODY DID catch on before I passed the critical threshold. And those really were top of the line 'docs. I was never in any real danger. But Herb and his colleagues had already been discharged by the time mine decided to decant me.

I woke as the lid unsealed, opened my eyes to see Solomon Short seated a few meters from my 'doc, looking at me. His face was distant, unreadable. As he saw that I was awake, his eyes hardened. He got up and came to my bedside. He looked so solemn I was about to tease him, when I suddenly noticed his lower lip trembling.

He leaned close, looked me in the eye, and said, without a trace of humor, "If you die one more time, I will be very angry with you. Do you understand?"

"How's Herb? I *died*?"

He straightened and nodded. "A little bit, yeah."

"Wow. How's—"

"He's all right physically."

An LCD lit yellow next to me, on a panel inside the 'doc. "And otherwise?"

"Dr. Louis is the best there is."

As I thought about what that statement said, and what it didn't say, the yellow light turned amber. I knew that wasn't good, and started doing my quartered-breathing trick. By the first exhalation, the light had dropped back to yellow. "Li died, didn't she? His twin? While they were in rapport." The light went out.

"Everybody did," Sol said. "Almost." He turned away and began pacing slowly around the room.

I assumed he spoke metaphorically: all of us aboard shared Herb's pain. His voice was as odd as his words.

"Covenant, how horrible for him!" Involuntarily imagining what it must have been like for him, to share his twin sister's death, turned my panel light yellow again. I focused on my breathing, tried to force the image from my mind, but the light stayed on. "What did she die of?"

He hesitated a moment, his back to me. "Let's talk about it later."

"That bad?"

"Worse." He resumed his pacing.

It was beginning to dawn on me that Solomon Short had spoken seven sentences in a row to me without saying a single funny thing. "Sol, what's wrong? Is Herb brain dead? Did somebody else aboard die?"

"No one on this ship has died, physically or mentally," he said.

"Okay, what is it then? Why are you acting so weird?"

"Let's talk about it later," he said dully.

"Why? Look at me."

"You're not ready."

I sat up on that one, yellow light or no yellow light. "I'd like a second opinion on that," I said. "Come to think of it, where the hell *is* Dr. Amy, anyway? Why isn't she here?"

"She is," he said, and pointed.

I followed his finger. Dr. Amy was in the autodoc next to mine.

I had never before seen anyone in a 'doc with any sort

of facial expression whatsoever. Hers looked as if it weren't working, as if she were in serious pain in there. That was silly, and a glance at the monitors confirmed it, but still—

"Prophet's *dick*, Solomon, what's wrong? What is going on? I want to know *now*." Yellow became amber.

For the first time he smiled—and I was very sorry. It was a ghastly parody. "Of course you do," he said softly.

He came back to my bedside, and to my astonishment and alarm, reached into the 'doc and took both my hands in his, captured both my eyes with his. "This will sound crazy. Because it *is*. I swear to you it's true."

"Okay."

"Sol is gone."

WAS HE TELLING me that he had gone insane? Or that he was an alien who had taken over my friend's body? Did it make a difference? Had *he* put Dr. Amy in that autodoc?

All that went through my mind in the second that it took him to see my incomprehension in my eyes, and to realize that for the first time in his life he had failed to notice an obvious pun.

"Not me," he said. "My namesake. The star."

He wasn't helping. "What the *fuck* are you—"

"Joel, Sol has exploded. It's gone. The whole System is gone. What isn't annihilated is sterilized."

I must have gaped at him. "Don't be silly. The sun can't explode! Gs don't go nova. They don't have the materials. It simply isn't—"

"I know," he interrupted. "I know that."

"But—then—I—what are you saying? Did a, did a black hole, or a neutron star, or a, a, some extrasolar—but that's *silly*! It would have been detected, we'd have known about it *long* before it got to . . ." I trailed off, confounded.

"I'm telling you Sol exploded. I know it can't happen. It did anyway."

"What?"

"I'm telling you everyone we left behind us is dead. Clear out to the Oort Cloud by now. All that's left in the universe of the human race is nineteen colonies. Excuse me, twenty; I was forgetting the *New Frontiers*."

By now the literal meaning of his words, at least, had reached me. "You're serious. You *can't* be serious. *The sun blew up?*"

He could shrug with just his face. "The one we used to use, yeah."

"Bullshit. How—how can that possibly be? It has to be the most studied star in the universe! How could they conceivably fail to notice an instability so—" I was distracted by a pulsing in my peripheral vision, took my eyes from his, and saw that my panel light was now bright ruby red, and blinking.

Sol said, "I see only two possibilities. First, it could be there is some fundamental and monumental mistake in our understanding of stellar processes. A true scientist *never* says, 'That cannot have happened.' The most he can say is, 'This is the first instance of that I have observed, and I cannot account for it.'" He let go of my hands, and spread his. "Maybe G2s *do* explode sometimes. This one did."

"Sol, we've been looking closely at the stars for half a fucking millennium—"

He nodded. "And it is perfectly possible that G2s explode at a rate of one a millennium or less. That may turn out to be the clue that leads to an explanation one day."

"What does Matty say?"

He pointed farther down the row of autodoc capsules. "He's over there. Sedated."

"Prophet!"

"He said he's been half expecting it for six years. Something about observations he made as we were leaving the System, that nobody would have believed without backup, and nobody else was in a position to repeat."

"That's what's been chewing his guts?"

"It'd chew mine."

My mind rejected Matty's problem. I could tell it was going to take a lot of time to imagine what it must have been like to have known about this, for years, and been unable to do anything about it. I was busy now. "You said two possibilities. What's the other one?"

His face became as perfectly expressionless as Dr. Amy's should have been. Except the eyes, they looked as haunted as hers. "Just before Hal disarmed him and put him out, the last thing Matty was screaming was, 'The paradox is fucking resolved, Enrico! I told you so!' "

"What?"

His meaning slowly percolated in.

Enrico Fermi asked, *Where is everybody?*

If intelligent life can arise once, it must arise more than once. There must be other star-going civilizations, lots of them. Where are they all?

Answer: maybe laying up in the tall bushes. Behind cover, wearing camo gear and face paint. Slowly and methodically quartering the battlefield through sniperscopes. Looking for game big enough to be tasty, but stupid enough to step out on the plain and start yelling, "Yoo hoo! Anybody out there?" Every millennium or so, one gets lucky.

I rejected the question, as I had Matty's torment. The *emotional* impact was just beginning to arrive, then. To start arriving.

It started to sink in that everyone I knew who wasn't aboard this ship was dead. Irretrievably, beyond any resuscitation, even if anyone were left to resuscitate them. *Everybody*, from Terra to Pluto. Everyone from the Secretary General of the System down to whoever ranked lowest in Coventry—hell, down to the last *virus*. Dead and already cremated. Tens of billions of human beings. Martians. Venerian dragons. All animals of all planets, cooked. All birds, baked in a pie. All fish, fried. Uncountable lower life-forms gone extinct ahead of schedule.

Lucky humanity. The cockroach did not outlive it after all. We had none aboard.

I started to ask how we even knew what had happened, when death must have arrived out of the sky before any possible warning could be given or received. But before I got the question completed, I knew the answer.

Two of the System halves of the *Sheffield*'s three telepath pairs had, for obvious reasons, been well paid to locate themselves equidistantly around Terra. One of them, Herb's sister, must have chanced to be on the nightside of Terra. Perhaps with several minutes of useless warning, before the wave of superheated steam arrived at well below lightspeed—

I glanced down. There were three lights on the panel, now, all ruby red, all flashing.

And the third System twin, I recalled, had lived at the north pole of Ganymede, which could easily have been in the blast shadow of Jupiter. I found myself trying to picture what Jupiter must have looked like from behind as she was being destroyed by her bigger sister. The nature of the cataclysm must have been as unmistakable as it was inconceivable.

And the precise relative timing of the two telepathic reports would have nailed it down.

At *that* point it started to sink in that everyone I *cared about* who was not aboard this ship was dead. Friends, relatives, teachers, colleagues, acquaintances, people I'd always intended to look up one day—

The ruby lights were slightly out of synch. The rhythmic interplay was very interesting. It gave me an idea. I wished I had a sax with me. I looked up at Solomon, with the vague intention of asking him to fetch me one, and the moment I saw his face, the final punch arrived. The others had all been solid, bare-knuckled lefts, but this was the big right hand, square in the heart.

Jinny was dead.

Not "dead to me." Not hypothetically dead, at some future time. Dead.

The moment I'd stepped aboard a relativistic starship without her, I had known and accepted that I would now probably outlive Jinny by many years. When I arrived at Brasil Novo, still just on the sunny side of forty, ninety years would have elapsed on Terra, and Jinny would be—

Absurdly, my brain actually did the math.

—ash, seventy-nine years cold—

If she had taken me up on my offer—my plea—and come aboard with me, to homestead in the stars . . . she'd have lived.

I discovered that Solomon was holding my head against his chest. I hadn't even noticed him approach. I pulled back, found his eyes, and smiled broadly.

Doing Richie, I said, "I hate to say atojiso, Jinny, but I fuckin' atojiso."

But I couldn't hear a word I was saying. Some asshole was playing a tenor too loud. Probably Philip Glass's first piece: the same note endlessly repeated. *Beep! Beep! Beep! Beep! Beep!* I didn't *give* a fucking fly how many measures he waited before he varied it, and I tried to ask Sol to durn it town. But Sol's eyes were widening. Kept widening until they covered his whole face and met around the back. Pupils turned yellow, became big yolks, and not very funny ones, either. Felt him laying me back down in the autodoc. Splendid old James Raymond song. *"Lay me down in the river, and wash my self away. Break me down like sand from a stone. Maybe I'll be whole again one day."* Lay me down . . .

The lid of the autocoffin closed over me, and washed my self away.

18

We need to have as many baskets for our eggs as possible. Even if we don't manage to ruin this planet ourselves, natural disasters or changes—or even changes in our star—could make it impossible to live on this planet.

—Philosopher Anson MacDonald,
radio interview, Butler, MO, USA, Terra,
July 7, 1987 ("Anson MacDonald Day")

When I did emerge from the Infirmary, nothing had changed, and everything was different.

I HAD ONCE read a book, a whole book, about what it was like to be in New York City during the week following the 2001 terrorist attack. So none of the things I saw surprised

me. I'd just never expected to see them with my own eyes.
Not everywhere I looked.

I suppose by definition there had never been a more emotionally traumatized bunch of people in history before. We
were the first sons and daughters of Terra, grandchildren of
Sol, who had ever *literally* lost everything but what we were
carrying. Our ancestral womb was gone. *All* our home planets were gone. Our civilization was gone. Our *star* was gone.

There was no precedent for processing something like
that. No appropriate ritual. No traditional therapy.

Not one human religion had ever even contemplated such
a turn of events—not even the old, psychotically blood-
thirsty ones we'd had to eliminate. It upstaged Ragnarok,
dwarfed Armageddon, mocked Apocalypse, overshadowed
the Qiyamah, outdid the Kali Yuga, ruined the prophecy of
Maitreya Buddha.

The center of the universe appeared to be somewhere *else*.
The possibility had occurred to hardly anyone, ever.

By the time my 'doc decanted me for the second time,
forty-seven of my fellow colonists had committed suicide,
by an assortment of means.

That there were so few as that is a testament to the professional skills of Dr. Amy and her staff . . . and I think in equal
measure a testament to the regard in which she personally
was held on board the *Sheffield*. Several people told me later
they had wanted badly to leave, but decided in the end that
they could not disappoint her that way.

But I think it's fair to say that better than half of us still
warm were basket cases. Walking wounded. On my way back
down from the Infirmary to Rup-Tooey, at least four times I
passed adults who were just sitting on the deck, weeping.
Very few people I encountered acknowledged me, or even
seemed to see me. Nobody smiled or spoke. I went by a room
whose door was frozen open; its interior showed extensive
fire damage. There was a long line outside the Sim chamber,
and hardly anyone on it was talking while they waited. There
was an equally long line outside the ship's nondenominational chapel—but as I passed within fifty meters of it, a fistfight apparently broke out inside. I kept going, and a few

seconds later had to lunge out of the way of Proctors De-Mann and Jim Roberts to avoid being trampled. I did not go in The Better 'Ole, one of the two free taverns, but passed near enough to it to note that it too was packed, with a silent and morose crowd. The only thing audible was soft music. As I went by, Second Officer Silver lurched out into the corridor and began vomiting. It was not uncommon to see crew in colonists' country, but they tended to do their drinking among themselves. It was the first time I could ever recall seeing any officer drunk, and I realized that must have been a policy of Captain Bean's. Which nobody gave a damn about anymore.

IN RUP-TOOEY I found Herb, Pat, and Solomon, sitting around and bullshitting like students after curfew, though it was midafternoon. The moment I laid eyes on Solomon, it came into my mind that none of us were probably ever going to be able to bear to call him by anything but his full first name, ever again. Or at least for years to come.

He looked up and nodded as I came in. "Hey, Joel. How are you feeling?"

"Swell," I said. "You okay, Herb?"

"No," he said, with no more affect than if I'd asked him if he were left-handed.

"You going to be?"

"Yes," he said the same way.

I believed him both times. We nodded at each other. I wanted to put my hand on his shoulder, but knew he would hate it. It can be frustrating to care about people who hate to be touched, sometimes.

Solomon said, "I was such a big help the first time you woke up, I thought this time I'd leave you alone."

I put a hand on his shoulder, and squeezed. He reached up and squeezed my hand back.

"You want coffee?" Pat asked. "Or ethanol?"

"Yes."

Herb nodded, got up, and made me an Irish coffee. I pulled my desk chair over to join the group and sat. "Somebody bring me up-to-date on what's happened while I was out. Do we *know* anything, yet?"

"Everyone in the Solar System is dead," Herb said over his shoulder. "All other information follows at lightspeed. Sorry."

I wished I had asked anything else. "We're sure it wasn't just Ter—"

"Gene's twin sister Terry was behind Jupiter. She had time to know what she was seeing. Poor woman. The times match. Doom arrived from Solward at lightspeed. QED."

I'd forgotten I had already worked that out, back in the autodoc. Another ill-considered question, in any event.

Solomon said, "The specks of data we do have indicate that conversion of Sol's mass to energy was at least ninety percent efficient, and could have been perfect."

If there is an intelligent response to that statement, none of us found it.

"Is there a consensus guess what went wrong, even?" I tried finally. The smell of fresh coffee filled the room.

Solomon snorted. "First, we have to settle how many angels can dance their way into a pinhead."

"Solomon—" Pat began.

Herb said, "He's saying it's a religious question."

Pat looked scandalized.

"Exactly," Solomon agreed. "Everybody is going to end up with a firm opinion, based on intuition, but nobody's going to be able to defend his. The first scraps of actual hard data aren't going to catch us for years to come. And I doubt they'll settle anything. I don't think the question will be answerable in my lifetime. Except on faith."

"I just hate to even use the word 'religion' in this context," Pat said. "It makes my skin crawl."

"Occam's Razor," Herb said, bringing me my Irish coffee. He'd made one for himself as well.

"What?" Pat asked.

"We forgot Occam's Razor," Herb said.

"I don't follow." I could see that Solomon did.

Herb sat and drank some of his coffee. "The sky has always been full of things we can't explain," he said. "It still is. Anomalies always abound. Gamma ray bursts. Missing matter. Quasars. Dozens of things. Generations of astrophysicists have made careers creating different, complicated explanations for each of them—often brilliantly. But one explanation for *all* of them, a quite likely one, they have never once considered. Or at least, anyone who did propose it instantly lost all credibility."

"Oh, Herb, no!"

He nodded. "Intelligent design."

Pat tried to speak, but could only sputter.

"That's exactly why, too," Herb said. "For some reason, we let the god-botherers appropriate that term as a euphemism for their stupid deities, and let our revulsion for the latter cloud our understanding of the former."

Solomon spoke up. "He's right, Pat. Once you get over the baseless idea that an intelligent designer must necessarily be God, it gets easier to deal with. Nothing whatsoever except a lot of dead fools says an intelligent designer has to be omnipotent—just more powerful than us. He need not necessarily be omniscient—just smarter than us."

Herb said, "And God Himself knows there is no reason why an intelligent designer must—or even can—be omnibenevolent. He need not even be as *nice as* us. And we're swine with starships."

Pat's mouth hung open. Perhaps mine did, too.

"And finally," Solomon said, "nothing says there has to be only one—or even some low prime number."

"We found sentient life on Mars and Venus," Herb said. "But nothing at all outside the System. And the Martians and Venerian dragons were just so . . . irrelevant to us, it was easy to stop thinking about them. Even after we got bright enough to go out and look for ourselves, more than a dozen times in a row we found whole star systems containing nothing more complicated than a cat. For some reason, we concluded our star system must be unique. We got the notion we were the only sentients in the Galaxy. We should have seen how preposterous that was, and looked for more reasonable explanations."

"I really really really hate this," Pat told him.

"Exactly our problem. Hate does not add clarity."

I felt a powerful inexplicable impulse to put some music on. It would make us all feel better. I summoned up my library on my desk display and was going to choose one of my favorite old jazz records, a Charlie Haden/Gonzalo Rubalcaba collaboration that had never failed to soothe me when I needed it. But before I could start it, the album title sunk in. It was called *La Tierra del Sol*.

And every song on it had been written by a dead man, to whom it was a posthumous tribute.

I cleared the screen. So much for the power of music. I had thousands of other albums available, but suddenly I didn't want to hear any music by dead men. I wondered if the next time I picked up my horn, any sound would come out.

"Why *can't* it have been a natural occurrence?" Pat was saying. "It seems to me *that* would be Occam's Razor. Occam's Razor says don't multiply entities unnecessarily. Which is less likely? One single cosmic event we can't explain yet? Or a galaxy full of lethal monsters, hiding perfectly, explaining dozens of astrophysical mysteries at once?"

"What does Matty say?" I asked.

The silence told me I was still asking bad questions.

"Aw, *shit*—"

"Don't be mad at him, Joel," Solomon said. "He spent every minute of the last six and a half years praying to a God I happen to know he didn't even believe in that he was wrong, that nothing was wrong with the sun. But he knew he wasn't; that's why he came apart. The measurements he lucked onto as we were leaving told him something unprecedented and scary was going on. He was too good at what he did to be wrong. Having it confirmed was just too much."

He was right: Matty *had* hinted about this to me, more than once. Something about a perfect solar eclipse by Terra occurring as we'd left the System, and something wrong about the predicted displacement of some stars behind Sol. Whatever had happened—or been done—to our star had taken six or more years to finish happening. The few subtle signs had been visible only to someone outside the System. One day, our descendants might find that a useful clue. If we had any.

Oh, no wonder Matty had gone to pieces.

Not that he could conceivably have done anything to prevent the tragedy. With no one else in a position to replicate his data—until whenever the next starship containing a good astronomer was built and launched to a point where it happened to see a perfect solar eclipse from the right distance— he could not possibly have gotten anyone to listen to him in time to do the slightest good. At most, he might have created a disastrous System-wide panic.

"He probably had more people he cared strongly about back in the System than anybody else aboard," Pat said. "Except maybe Dr. Amy. No, no, she's all right," he added hastily, seeing my expression. "But she's hurting."

I closed my eyes for a moment. Might as well get it over with. "Who else that I know is gone?"

Another awkward pause. I should probably never ask another question again.

Solomon answered. "Balvovatz, for one."

"What?" I was stunned. One of the last people I'd have guessed would ever suicide was Balvovatz, that cynical, fun-loving old Loonie.

But then as I heard that last word in my mind, I started to understand. His tragedy was, impossibly, even greater than that of most of the rest of us. Everyone he cared about back in the System lived—had lived—in Luna. It was the preposition killing him.

All the other planets mankind had used, it had lived on the surface of. Even the Marsmen had been aboveground for over a century now. Only Luna was too small to terranize. Loonies had still lived almost exclusively underground. Some of them quite deep.

By now, if there were any solids at all among the particles expanding from the place where the System had been, they would probably be only a pair of smelted lumps formerly known as Jupiter and Saturn. Even they might not still exist, if the destruction had been as complete as Solomon believed.

But some Loonies might conceivably have lasted whole seconds, broiling in lava, before it became too hot for even lava to exist.

"Everyone you or I knew back home is surely dead," Herb said. "So is everyone Balvovatz knew. But his were among those who suffered worst."

I rejected the image, and the thought. I knew I was going to miss Balvovatz badly. I had liked him a lot. Loved him. "Okay. You said 'for one . . .' Who else is gone?"

"Diane," Herb said. "And Mariko."

Mariko Stupple was the girl I'd used for consolation for a few weeks after Diane Levy had taken my virginity, glanced at it, and returned it. I wondered how close Diane had come to achieving her goal of sampling every male aboard. I found that I hoped she had. "Anyone else?"

"Nobody else you know well, I think," Pat said.

"None of your lot, Solomon? Not even Kindred?"

"None of us has the luxury of that option," Solomon said dully.

"I don't follow."

"We have no way of knowing exactly what happened to Sol—so we must assume worst case: total destruction."

It took a second or two to hit me. If all or nearly all the mass of the sun had been converted to energy, a wave of lethal gamma rays was even now racing after *us*. Faster than we were going, or could go . . .

I said, "Sorry, Sollie. I am not doing at all well on thinking things through, today."

He nodded. "Happens to me, too, every time I've been dead."

If even one Relativist became incapacitated, sooner or later the ramjet was going to go out and stay out. The *Sheffield* would never make port. She could remain self-sustaining for a maximum of three or four generations—but that didn't matter, because we wouldn't have anywhere near that long to live. We were only traveling at $0.976\ c$ . . . and death was chasing us at c.

"Will we be able to outrun it, do you think? By the time the wavefront catches up, will it still be—are we dead?"

Herb gave me a baleful look. "How long is a piece of rope?"

"He's right," Solomon said. "Tell me exactly what happened to the sun, what percentage of its mass was converted to what forms of energy in what proportion by the explosion, and perhaps a horseback guess could be made, by somebody as smart as Matty was. But we know hardly *anything* beyond the bare fact of humanity's annihilation. It could easily have been a violent enough event to fry us even as far away as Bravo. Indications are it was. We may be as dead as those poor bastards in Luna—just on a longer string."

"Jesus Christ!" Pat said, at the same time I said, "Covenant!" in the same tone of voice. I'd never heard him say that before, and took it as a clue to why discussion of religion upset him. Diehard closet Old Christians in the family might even help explain what a man like him was doing on a voyage to nowhere in the first place.

"If the explosion *was* that powerful," Herb said, "we'll never reach Immega, will we? At no time will we exceed the speed of light, and the wavefront is only six years and change behind us—"

"*Ten* years and change," Solomon corrected. "We've been *traveling* for 6.41 years. But we passed half the speed of light in the first year, and by now we're making more than ninety-seven percent of it. Lorentz time contraction. It adds up."

"So will it catch us along the way, or not? I can't believe it's taken me this long to think of the question." I'd always prided myself on being quick on the uptake . . . but I decided to give myself a pass, this time.

Solomon shrugged. "I can't believe I don't have the exact answer ready for you. Al Mulherin's been crunching away at it, but I haven't checked since yesterday. We've all been thinking of other things than survival, that's all. Give me a second." He began tapping on a keyboard.

I tried to work it out roughly in my head. The *Sheffield* and waves of evil start out just under ten and a half light-years apart, then race. Us at a very high fraction of *c* which will get even higher, but will never reach one. Them at *c*. At what point will the second train catch the first? It seemed like a classic grade school math puzzle. But relativistic factor kept royally screwing up my calculations. And then I realized I'd forgotten to factor in deceleration ... I gave up and waited for Solomon. I knew my father would have closed his eyes for a moment and just known the answer.

"I think we're all right," Solomon said finally. "As long as the ramjet keeps ramming. We expect to reach Bravo after twenty years, our time, 90.4 years in Sol time." He winced slightly as the phrase left his lips, but kept going. "Assuming a lethal concentration of gamma rays is in fact after us, it will arrive at our neighborhood about seven and a half years later. With luck, we can get dug in deep enough to weather it out in time."

Herb stood up to his full height and clapped his hands together, loud enough to make all of us flinch. "Well, that is just the best fucking news in the fucking Galaxy," he said loudly. "That makes my fucking day."

He spun on his heel and went to get the Irish whiskey. Solomon and I exchanged a nervous glance. If Herb were to go berserk in this enclosed space we would have a serious problem. He turned around and caught us at it, and his booming laughter was as loud and almost as startling as his handclap had been.

"You dopes, I'm serious! The distance between one and infinity is *nothing* compared to the distance between zero and one."

I decided to assume he was not cracking up. "What do you mean, Herb?"

"Think it through. There's one and only one reason we know, for sure, what's happened behind us. Chance dictated that two of our three telepaths in the System were in blast shadow. For my sister, Hell didn't arrive at lightspeed, but at something closer to the speed of Terra's rotation. She had time—barely—to hear and comprehend what was coming at her."

Get him off this subject. "Okay. I don't take your point."

"How many other colonies do you think were that lucky?"

Oof.

"Prophet's *prick*!" Pat said. "I never even thought—"

"Telepath pairs were even scarcer on the ground in the early days," Herb said. "Most of the earlier colonies made do with two. And most of those that shipped three are down to two, now. Li kept up on such things."

"We've got to send a laser!" Pat cried, and started to get up.

Solomon caught his shoulder and pulled him back down. "Calm down, son. Captain Bean has already long-since notified the only colony we can help."

"But there are—" He frowned. "Oh. *Oh*. Shit."

Any laser or radio message we sent would travel at lightspeed. Only one human colony happened to even lie in the constellation of Boötes: 44 Boo, from which our destination had been discovered. Taking into account the offset (it was not *dead* ahead), it was something like thirty-five years ahead of us by laser . . . and doom would arrive there in forty-one years. That was the one and only colony we could possibly hope to warn, and we could give them an absolute maximum of six years in which to prepare. That had already been done.

Any other colony lacking a telepath whose partner had chanced to be in apposition at the moment of explosion, and thus needing us to warn it, was screwed. Hellfire was coming for them at the speed of light, and we were powerless to alert them in time.

Between us, the *Sheffield* and 44 Boötes probably now held the very last surviving fragments of the human race. All the rest would probably be gone within sixty-five years.

We *had* to get to Bravo. We *had* to survive. It was far more than just our own lives at stake, now. It was our species. We were The Last Of The Solarians.

I remembered a spiritual book Dr. Amy had had me read the year before, by a man named Gaskin. I had been easy to persuade because the farmer in me had resonated to its title, *This Season's People*. It turned out to derive from a famous saying of the Jewish mystic Shlomo Carlebach:

We are this season's people.
We are all the people there are, this season.
If we blow it, it's blown.

I was the guy who had been trying to run away from all responsibility. And found just that.

I often wish I could believe in a deity, so I could compliment Him or Her on His or Her sense of humor. And then go for His or Her throat.

How long, Sol?" Herb asked.

Solomon winced to hear his own name. "How long what?"

"Blue sky it with me, here. Optimistic assumptions throughout. I just want to get a vague sense of how far away the payoff is."

"I'm still not understanding you."

"Assume all goes as well as we can reasonably hope, from here on in. The folks at 44 Boo dig in successfully, and survive with zero fatalities. We make it to Bravo, dig in successfully, and also survive with no further fatalities. Round our numbers off to five hundred for convenience, and assume 44 Boo has twice that population by this point."

Sol nodded. "All right."

"The human race now numbers fifteen hundred, total, plus an indeterminate number of frozen ova. It's in two pieces, forty-odd light-years apart, with no telepathic links. That's our starting gene pool and situation. We have specs for virtually every piece of proven technology the System had when we left, 44 Boo nearly the same, and we'll both get better and better at making our own parts, so again let's simplify, and just say we'll be able to build new relativistic ships again in a single generation."

Sol was dubious. "That's a damn big simplification."

"On the time scale I'm talking about, it'll disappear in the noise," Herb insisted.

"Go on."

"Here's what I want to know, and I'll settle for a very rough approximation: how many centuries will it be, do you suppose, before we have rebuilt and protected our civilization sufficiently so that we can *track down those shit-sucking back-shooting baby-burning vermin and blow up THEIR fucking star?*"

His voice rang in the silence that followed. Standing there

tall with a fifth of whiskey in his hand and death in his eyes, he had never looked more like a Viking chieftain.

"How many generations?" Herb continued. "A lot, I know—but roughly how many, do you suppose? How far away were we ourselves from having the power to make stars go nova?"

"I repeat," Sol began, "I really think we should be careful not—"

"You're right, sorry," Herb conceded impatiently. "A nova is a natural phenomenon, and we know this probably was not. G2s don't nova. That *is* a point worth remembering. So: how far away were we from being able to make stars go boom? How far do you suppose we are *now* from being bright enough to reverse-engineer it, once we start getting some hard data on exactly what was done?"

"It won't even start to happen in our lifetimes," Solomon said.

"I *know* that. I'm not talking about me. I'm talking about the human race. It numbers fifteen hundred people, and it has only two tasks. Hide. And hit back. I'd like to try and get a loose sense of how many centuries it's going to be before there's likely to be any good news again. My intuitive feeling is, on the order of five hundred years. What's your guess?"

The idea was breathtaking, heartbreaking. I had vaguely understood that a very long, very hard task lay ahead of me. Until now I had not grasped that it probably lay ahead of my remotest descendants.

Nobody had an answer for him.

I stood up and went to him. "Unhand that bottle." He passed it over, and I topped up my Irish coffee, which had been down to its last inch. I tried it, and it seemed the right concentration for the moment.

"Damn it," Pat said. "Damn it to all hells at once. *We* managed to evolve beyond war. Why couldn't *they*?" He shook his fist angrily in the general direction of the hull, and the stars beyond it.

"We didn't evolve beyond war," Herb said. "Just beyond violence—and we've only been free of that for a whole whopping century and a half. You still know how to shake your fist. There was a trade war going on back in the System last week, remember? The first. Who knows how far it might have gone?"

"Even if that's true, we were getting *better*," Pat cried. "Are we really going to have to go back to thinking and acting like the Prophets, and the crazy Terrorist nuts and Cold War nuts before *them*? Just when we were finally starting to grow up?"

There was a truly depressing thought.

I remembered Solomon's dichotomy of the Thrilled and the Threatened. Was the human race really going to have to spend the next half a millennium or more being as conservative, as paranoid, as utterly pragmatic and cynical and ruthless as Genghis Khan, or Conrad of Conrad?

What is thrilling—if entities that can burst a sun want you dead? Anything besides simple survival itself?

Would any human above the age of six ever again look up at the stars in the night sky in simple wonder?

For that alone, I wanted revenge. Never mind billions of unearned deaths by fire.

I WENT TO the Star Chamber, alone. I couldn't talk any of the others into coming along. Solomon nagged me into taking a sandwich along. Autodocs feed you well but do not fill the stomach, he pointed out. I had to admit that something to soak up all the Irish coffee did seem like a good idea.

The Star Chamber might seem like a pointless waste of cubic, but few aboard the *Sheffield* ever thought so. Sure, the Sim illusion you get with naked eyeballs in that huge spherical room is nowhere near as convincing as what you can get while wearing the rig. How could it be? And there's only the single illusion.

But you can *share* it.

In conventional Sim, in a tiny cubicle, wearing all the gear, you can have people around you, totally convincing ones . . . but you never really forget they're not real. And only partly because the smells are never better than close.

But in the Star Chamber, you could look at the stars in the

company of other human beings. Just then, I could not have borne to look at them by myself.

As I'd expected, it was just as heavily in use as the rest of the Sim Suite. I had to wait awhile for a space to become available. An argument was going on behind me as I reached the head of the line. "I *know* G2s can't go nova, I never *said* it was a nova," someone kept repeating. "What I *said* was, and is, there could be some equally natural process, *other* than the nova mechanism, by which a star can explode. *Obviously* it would be an exceedingly rare event, I'm not a *fool*—"

It was only when a bystander interrupted, "You play one brilliantly, Citizen," that I realized the speaker was Robin. My oldest living girlfriend. "We all took your point the first three times you made it," he went on. "And I imagine my great-grandchildren will be both the first to know whether you're right or not . . . and the first to *give* a damn. But right now, and until the day they're born, could you possibly shut up?"

Some atavistic hindbrain mechanism caused me to consider intervening on her behalf. But I did much prefer the silence the stranger had produced.

Five minutes later it was broken—from inside the Chamber.

At first, all I could tell was that someone was yelling in there, very loud. But as they got him closer to the outer door, his tone and then his words became audible. I don't think it took any of us on line more than half a second to understand. He was screaming at the top of his lungs, with berserker rage. At the stars.

"—shit-eating piss-drinking pig-fucking goat-sucking maggot-licking baby-raping *well-poisoning* illegitimate spawn of degenerate diseased vermin-vomit"—he was shrieking as they forced him out into the corridor—"I'll pop your mutant eyeballs with your own—" and at that point Proctor DeMann came trotting past me, touched him gently near the base of the neck, and caught him as he fell. He stood there with the man in his arms, his breathing as slow and measured as if he'd been standing in line with me, and gestured with his chin.

"Next!" he said.

I nodded to him, stepped into the lightlock, waited for the outer door to iris shut, then opened the inner one and entered the Chamber, almost on the heels of the two people who'd ejected the screamer. I stopped and waited for my eyes to adjust, and for the self-appointed bouncers to resume their seats so I could tell which was the empty one. The experience of the room came on like a powerful drug rush.

There was nothing to the Star Chamber, in one sense. A spherical room that was cut into upper and lower hemispheres by a floor filled with sling couches—but seemed not to be because the floor and couch frames were transparent. That was basically it. Until it was powered up.

But then one of the *Sheffield*'s countless servers caused the walls to display the universe.

Not perfectly, as I said. But well enough to fool the subconscious. And the heart.

Not the unrecognizable mess we would have seen out of portholes, if there had been such silly things—but a corrected image, which removed the eye-wrenching distortions and displacements of relativistic Doppler effect. The universe as it actually was out there right now, for anybody who was not racing photons. As we would see it if somehow it were magically possible to instantly shed all our hideous inertia and decelerate to sublight velocity for a few moments. Well, obviously not as it was *right* now; there had to be some lag, and some assumptions made. But close.

It was quiet and still in there, now that the sufferer had been removed. By the time my pupils had finished adjusting, I saw that the room had been reprogrammed as I had expected it would be. Known it would be.

When humans sit together to look at the stars, they look up. It's way older than rational thought, possibly older than thought. So the Star Chamber was customarily programmed to place whatever part of the universe the Chamber's inhabitants found most interesting directly overhead. Most of the time, though by no means always, that had meant Immega 714 could be found at galactic high noon.

Today, Peekaboo was directly under our feet, and we were all looking at where Sol had been.

As I had expected, someone had explained to the computer that it could delete Sol from its permanents, now. To have seen it there still blazing in the sky would have been unendurable. I had vaguely wondered if they would attempt some graphic representation of the explosion, but of course they had had better sense. To watch that happening forever in slow motion would have been equally unendurable.

What was there was endurable—but only just. Only just barely. It was shocking, and . . . neither "pitiful" nor "humbling" even come *close* to touching it, but those are the two closest words I can find. It didn't matter in the *slightest* that I had fully expected it, that I understood it intellectually and had for all my adult life, that it was old news.

It was simply heartbreaking, mind-numbing, soul-chilling, to see, with my own eyes, what an incredibly tiny, insignificant hole the removal of Sol left in the fabric of the Galaxy.

If I had not known exactly where to look, and been thoroughly familiar with that particular degree of the sky, I'd have missed it. Anyone would have.

As I STARED, mesmerized, it came to me for no reason at all that the very first cinematic work to take starflight seriously had been titled *Star Wars*. The irony was mind-melting.

I thought I felt a great disturbance in The Force—as if millions of voices had cried out as one, and then were silent.

Millions, you say? Hell, son, suck it up and walk it off! For a second there, I thought you had a *problem*.

Try forty-seven billion.

THAT WAS WHY I had come here, I realized. I'd had to see it with my own eyes. Among other things, I needed to put my brain more in synch with my mind.

My mind understood all about the universe and its correct scale and mankind's terrible insignificance in it—intellectually. It always had. But my brain had always seen things differently. To it, the Solar System was practically everything there was, and tiny hypothetical little Brasil Novo was the rest, and in between the two lay nothing but a gap in the map—one *wildly* out of scale. Like a Mercator projection of a globe, it was a false representation of reality that was much more useful than the truth.

Until now.

For humanity, the whole universe right at this moment consisted of nineteen tiny colonies, at least two of them believed to be slowly dying, many of the rest doomed. All of them many many light-years distant from one another, communicating by laser or radio. Even if any of them should survive this, it would take us many decades, maybe centuries, merely to finish hearing what each of them would have to say about this shared catastrophe, when they found out, and as long again after that before we could possibly hope to hear a word of response from anyone to anything we might say.

To my personal brain, the whole universe now consisted of the *Sheffield*, and emptiness. Bravo was a fantasy.

To my mind, the whole universe consisted of Bravo. The *Sheffield* was now just an antechamber, with a timelock on the door.

But my eyes kept reminding me that neither was true. It was good to be reminded.

Because sitting in a chair spoils the illusion somewhat, the Star Chamber restores it and reinforces it by always *drifting* slightly, while keeping the focal star overhead. It works quite well. The universe as it actually is blazed all around me, and I floated in it, so convincingly I felt the first faint symptoms of psychosomatic dropsickness.

But it no longer held the beauty, the majesty, the grandeur, the glory that it had always held for me before.

For no reason I could name, my mind leaped back more than six years to the night of my prom. Jinny and I orbiting each other like halves of a binary star. Someone singing, *"It would not be so lonely to die if I knew/I had died on the way to the stars—"*

In my brain, I was no longer on my way to the stars. I was on my way *from* them, to refuge.

With more than twice the distance I had already covered still to go.

I felt and heard my own left foot start tapping spastically

on the deck. I needed my hand to make it stop. For some reason that made me want to cry.

Someone ahead of me and to my left stood up and cleared his throat.

There was a rumble of annoyance, and a woman behind me muttered, "Whatever it is, keep it to yourself."

But then he said, "I apologize for disturbing your *wa*," and there was general relaxation as his voice was recognized. Tenzin Hideo Itōkawa was well liked, even by those few who had problems with Buddhism—possibly in part because in over six years I had not heard him use the word once. He was also one of the gentlest and kindest souls aboard, and what he did best of all was listen. You make remarkably few enemies that way. And finally, of course, everybody knew that he kept the most popular man aboard, his partner Solomon Short, extremely happy. And not just because Sol kept mentioning it.

I'm not sure anyone else could have said what he was about to say, and finished saying it, before being hounded out of the room. So it's good it was him.

People face in any direction they like in the Star Chamber, but now nearly all of us turned our seats around to face Hideo, near the center of the room.

"I wish to tell you all something," he said, when stillness returned. As always, he spoke slightly slower than another would have, and slightly softer. It made you listen closer, and think more about what you heard. "I need to tell you. You need to hear me. But it will be hard to hear. *Shikata-ga-nai.* It cannot be helped. For this, too, I apologize to you."

"You go on and say whatever you got to, Hideo-san honey," said the woman behind me.

He bowed to her. "Thank you, Mary."

His next seven words were spoken the slowest yet. Two slow pairs and a slow triplet, with pauses two or three full seconds long between them. Maximum emphasis and earnestness.

"The time . . . for fear . . . is *past*, now."

Everybody spoke at once. Not all were angry, but everybody spoke at once. Have you been in an enclosed hemisphere when everybody spoke at once—a dome, perhaps?

People far away sound louder than the ones beside you. It's so weird, silence usually resumes quickly, and it did now. Then two or three tried to speak at once, and none would yield, so someone told them to all shut the fuck up, and the noise level started to go right back up again—

"*PLEASE!*" the loudest voice I had ever heard bellowed.

Instant silence.

Even when I was sure, it was hard to believe that much sound had come out of quiet little Hideo. He took his time replacing the air it had cost, in a long slow perfectly controlled inhalation. It was a good example. I began measuring my own breath.

"I promise I will hear what each of you wants to say," he said. "Until you are done speaking. Please wait until *I* am done speaking first. It may be that my meaning will require more than a single sentence to fully express."

He had the floor back.

"Some of you might become angry if I said Sol may have died of natural causes, so I will not say that. We all know that is theoretically possible, if most unlikely. But it is unsatisfying to think about. It leaves us nothing to do but mourn our colossal bad fortune.

"I believe what happened was *done*. I believe one day we will meet those who did it. We will speak with them. And for all we can know now, perhaps we may choose to prune them from the Galaxy. If we can acquire such power."

The crowd was solidly with him again now.

Slowly, he shook his head from side to side. "But I do not believe this will happen in my lifetime, or that of the youngest infant in the *Sheffield*. I suspect it will not happen in her grandchildren's lifetime. Everything we learned and built in ten thousand years of painful evolution was insufficient. It will take us many generations just to restore that, if we can."

Murmurings of dismay, argument.

Again his voice drew power from some unsuspected source, not as loud as his earlier roar, but enough to override the impolite.

"But of this much I am certain: we . . . *will* . . . *have* those generations."

Silence again.

"I have heard many of you express deep fear that our enemy might even now be hunting the *Sheffield*."

Pindrop silence.

"This is not rational. If it were true, there would be none to think it."

"They're six years behind us," a deckhand named Hildebrand yelped. "How do we know they're not hot on our trail?"

"Reason with me, Dan," Hideo said calmly. "If I build a machine that makes stars explode without warning . . . is it not certain that I must be able to reach stars other than my own? Had I but the one star, such a machine would have no sane function. Agreed?"

Hildebrand reluctantly grunted agreement.

"If I can travel the stars so easily that I develop reasons to blow some up . . . can I possibly be constrained by the cosmic speed limit humans must presently obey?"

"What? The speed of light is abso—"

"Name a method of slower-than-light travel by which you could so much as approach our general region of this galactic arm *without ever being detected by the Solar System*."

Hideo had him there. Fusion, antimatter, ramjet, all were pretty much impossible to miss.

"To have ambushed us so successfully," Hideo said, "they *must* be superluminal. By orders of magnitude, at the least."

He paused there. After a few seconds of thought, someone said, "Subluminal, superluminal—what's your point, Tenzin Itokawa?"

Hideo turned his hands palm upward. "*We* travel at less than *c*. They travel at some very high multiple of *c*. Perhaps an exponential. And we have just agreed that we are clearly visible to anyone looking."

"What, they didn't notice us leaving?" said Terri, one of the Healers.

"Perhaps. Perhaps they mistook our nature. Perhaps they don't care."

"Beg pardon, Tenzin? Why *wouldn't* they?"

"It is hard for us to think this," Hideo said, "but the annihilation of humanity may not have been their purpose in destroying our star. For all we can know now, it might be merely collateral damage which they deemed either insignificant or acceptable. As we accept the deaths of millions of microorganisms living on our skin and in our hair each time we choose to bathe."

He had silence again. He let it stretch, while the stars drifted slowly past his head.

"There are wise ones," he said finally, "who say that man cannot endure insignificance on such a scale. That if confronted by a species as far advanced beyond him as he is beyond dogs, his spirit must inevitably break. For an example they point to the original inhabitants of the North American continent on Terra, who so thoroughly internalized a perception of their own inferiority that they became all but extinct within one or two centuries.

"Somehow they miss the counterexample of the original inhabitants of the *South* American continent. Or of the Africans chained and sold by other Africans to the Europeans even then conquering both Americas."

"Where are you going with this?" Hildebrand demanded. "We know we're not going to fold up and die."

When Hideo replied, his raising his volume again startled me, but not as much as his words themselves.

"I have great anger in my heart."

That made everyone sit up a little straighter.

"I do not wish to. It may help my grandchildren one day, but it is useless to me now . . . here. And I do not have room for it in my heart. I need all the room for grief.

"The only way to deal with anger is to cut it at the root. The root of anger is *always* fear.

"I do not fear for the dead. It is too late. So I must be afraid for myself, and my friends here.

"There are only two things for us to fear, and I have just showed you that the first is irrational. I share it myself! Even now a tightness in my spine tries to warn me that the Star Killer could be drawing a bead on us right now, that I may not live to finish my sentence. But it is madness, not good sense. I can learn to make it go, and so can you."

As he spoke I was feeling my own shoulders start to lower, my lungs taking in deeper breaths.

"The second thing to fear is that we will fail the test. That we will not be good enough, strong enough, smart enough, to found a society which can grow to accomplish the things that must be done. Last week, the worst decision we could possibly make would have killed five hundred and twenty people, at most. Such a poor decision today would come very close to literally decimating the remaining human race. An unacceptable loss. Let me say this just right."

He paused and went inside himself. Nobody said a word. Hildebrand started to, and there was a dull thud sound, and he exhaled instead.

"Both fear and its cover identity, anger, are notorious for producing spectacularly bad decisions."

No actual words, but there were widespread grunts, murmurs, snickers, and harumphs, all of firm agreement.

"I will offer only a single example: the Terror Wars that led inexorably to the Ascension of the Prophet.

"Shortly after Captain Leslie LeCroix returned home safely from the historic first voyage to Luna, fanatical extremist Muslims from a tiny nation committed a great atrocity against a Christian superpower. Suicide terrorists managed to horribly murder thousands of innocent civilians. The grief and rage of their surviving compatriots must have been at least comparable to what we all feel now.

"Intelligently applied, that much national will and economic force could easily have eliminated every such fanatic from the globe. At that time there were probably less than a hundred that rabid, and by definition they were so profoundly stupid or deranged as to be barely functional. It was always clear their primitive atrocity had succeeded so spectacularly only by the most evil luck.

"We all know what the superpower chose to do instead. It crushed two tiny bystander nations, killing some dozens of actual terrorists, and hundreds of thousands of civilians as innocent as their own dead loved ones had been. The first time it was suggested that nation's leaders had perhaps known about the terror plot and failed to give warning. The second invasion didn't even bother with an excuse, even though that nation had been famously *hostile* to terrorists. Both nations were Muslim, as the nineteen killers had been: that was enough. The nation nearly all of them had actually *come from* remained, inexplicably, almost the only Muslim ally the Christian superpower had in that region.

"The generation of a large planetary web of enraged Muslim extremists was so inevitable it is difficult for us now to conceive of the minds that did it. They were some of the most intelligent and humane people in the history of the planet: What *could* they have been thinking?

"Of course they were not. They were feeling.

"They were a superpower, and monotheist. No one had ever hurt them remotely that badly, and they were utterly certain no one had any right to hurt them at *all*. They reverted to tribal primate behavior. Beaten and robbed of your banana by a bigger ape or a more clever chimp . . . you find some smaller, stupider primate, beat *him*, and steal *his* banana.

"So doing, they ignited a global religious war that threatened to literally return the whole world to barbarism. The only thing to do *then* was crush it under the iron and silicon heel of a slightly smarter barbarism, a marginally less bloodstained religion, the best of all possible tyrannies. Nehemiah Scudder became the Holy Prophet of the Lord, smote the false prophets, and darkness fell."

He paused and turned slowly around in place. He seemed to be trying to meet the eyes of each of us in the dark. "If we respond to our own unendurable grief and sadness in that same way they did—by looking away from grief and sadness, and seeking comfort in fixating instead on paranoia and rage—if we react with our own version of their Terror Wars—then we will probably lose this fight, and we will probably deserve to."

That produced rumbles, and he let them happen, and waited them out. No one voice chose to try and take the floor, but many small murmured conversations were held at once.

"Let us continue on our journey," Hideo said after a while. "Let us build the new world we planned. Only its very *longest-term* goals have changed. We hoped one day to be part of a great interstellar community with a radius of ninety light-years and a volume of three million. *That is still our goal.*

"We hoped that community would live in the peace and harmony we were just beginning to take for normal in our home System. That will not happen now. Defending that community and ending a war are new goals we've only just learned we have.

"We also hoped to communicate efficiently by telepathy through the Terran hub. That will not happen now either. And for that very reason, this war will be so lengthy that we cannot even begin ending it for thirteen more years, and will never live to see any progress whatsoever. We have the luxury of much time in which to make our decisions. Let us make smart ones from the very start.

"The smartest thing we can do is take hate from our hearts. There is nothing to *do* with it, no one to use it on but each other. Thus we must banish our fear, lest it grow cancerous tendrils around our hearts.

"When a child hits his thumb with a hammer, if he is alone, he will say to his hammer, 'Look what you have done.' If he is with another, he will say, 'Look what you made me do.'" A few parents chuckled. "When we become victims, we want to victimize. So badly that if no victim presents himself, we will settle for an inanimate object, rather than have *no one* to hate. It is nature.

"We *must* be wiser than that child. There are no persons here but ourselves. There are no inanimate objects here we do not need.

"Be *sad,* citizens. *Hurt.* Grieve. Go insane with grief if you must. But please . . . avoid the different insanity of rage. At the very *least,* until we locate the target that deserves it. Meanwhile, let us teach our children love and compassion for one another, as we have always done, by practicing it in our own lives for them to see. Let not this inhuman enemy have taken our humanity from us."

The applause startled him. But after a moment he sort of leaned into it, like a stiff breeze he was sailing through.

He bowed then, and headed for the door. People made

way. Some touched his shoulder or arm or face as he passed, and he acknowledged each.

When he got to the door he stopped and turned. We waited for his coda.

"Many of you know I am a student of Zen," he said. "All my life I have belonged to the Rinzai sect. Long ago it was the Zen of the Samurai. Warrior Zen." He took a deep breath. "I have changed my affiliation. As of today—as of now—I am a student of Soto Zen, like Hoitsu Ikimono Roshi, who discovered the relativistic engine. Soto is the Zen of the peasants. Farmer Zen." He looked around at all of us one last time, and made a small wry smile. "As of today, it is the more useful to me. And now you must excuse me, for my shift is soon to begin." He was gone; the lightlock cycled behind him.

The silence he left behind him went on for several minutes before anyone tried to say anything, and those who did were politely asked to say it somewhere else, and after that it lasted . . . well, I don't know, but at least until *I* left, a couple of hours later.

Word of what Hideo had said spread throughout the ship. The *Sheffield* had recorded every word, and he readily granted permission for its uploading. It was more words than he had spoken in the entire voyage until then. It didn't produce any miracles. But over the next few days, it gradually started to seem possible to us all that we might heal one day. Not soon enough, surely. But one day.

We had a shot, anyway.

IT SEEMED THAT way right up until four weeks after The Day, when Relativist Peter Kindred was found dead by suicide in his quarters.

He had taken massive lethal overdoses of a stimulant, a depressant, an analgesic, and a powerful entheogen, using care and a lifetime of extensive experience to time it so that they all peaked at once. I imagine he went out feeling just like the energy being depicted in Alex Grey's "Theologue," burning with universal fire. The first witnesses on the scene described his expression as "transcendent" and "blissful," until

Solomon Short arrived and caved in half his face with a looping overhand right that began and ended at the deck, blasting Kindred's corpse and the chair holding it two meters across the room, and breaking five bones in Solomon's hand. Despite the pain he must have been in, he stayed enraged long enough to find the suicide note Kindred had left, and delete it unread. By the time the proctors arrived, he was calm, docile, and dry-eyed, ready to be escorted to the Infirmary. Their relief was obvious. If he'd still been crazy enough to assault them, they'd have had to let him beat them up.

He and Hideo-san and Dugal Beader did their best for us, and managed to hold out for longer than anyone thought they could. The first time the drive went out, a week later, Hideo got it restarted in a matter of minutes. Four days after that it failed again, for the last time, on Solomon's watch.

Nothing we could possibly do would ever allow us to drop below ninety-five percent of the speed of light again, now. We were going to reach Brasil Novo at something ironically very close to the time we'd expected to—and sail right on past, too quickly to do much more than wave good-bye to our dreams.

In theory, we could then persist for another three or four useless, pointless generations. But a century after our departure from the Solar System, when we were 444 light-years from where it had been, the gamma rays from its annihilation were going to catch up and complete the job. Sterilize the *Sheffield*.

Mankind was down to *eighteen* scattered outgrowths. And we weren't one of them.

That old song was wrong. We were *going* to die on the way to the stars . . . and it was lonelier than I had thought it would be.

19

> We have learned now that we cannot regard
> this planet as being fenced in and a secure
> abiding place for man; we can never anticipate
> the unseen good or evil that may come upon us
> suddenly out of space.
>
> —H. G. Wells
> *The War of the Worlds*

Existence had lost all point.

For the first time ever, it was not hyperbole. It really had.

Fine. Tell that to the goats. *Their* existence had a point: being fed and milked. It seemed enough to them. Tell it to the rabbits. Their existence had all the purpose it would ever need: fucking. The chickens thought the point of existence is hatching eggs; the rooster held a different opinion; but both were convinced. The vegetables did not even dignify the question with an asking.

Being around that kind of naïve certainty was soothing. And I had made a deal with those critters. It did not contain an escape clause letting me off the hook in the event of solar disruption or even disappearance of local gravity. They had kept their end, so far, by living.

Also, I needed to be somewhere that was not Rup-Tooey. I had been sleeping like a baby there, lately. Alone, waking up wailing every few hours, wetting the bed. Not a good thing in free fall.

So I was on the Bravo Ag Deck. I'd thought of going up to the Horn and playing Anna for whoever was there. But I'd decided that if somehow I did succeed in blowing everything that was in my heart out the end of my sax, I might fail to inhale again. And so might my listeners.

By now I found the steamy smells of Bravo—or what we had imagined they might be like—conducive to inhaling. It would have been a terrific planet, if we could have gotten there, I remember thinking.

But of course, the smells were much less intense and local than I was used to. Now that the *Sheffield* was in free fall again, we were back on free-fall air-conditioning. That translates to constant heavy airflow in any cubic where humans spent time. It has to. In zero gee, unless the air is kept very well stirred at all times, the carbon dioxide you exhale tends to form a sphere around your head and smother you.

The mood I was in, I'd almost have accepted that to have the good Bravo smells back, rich in my nose again. But of course, I never would, now.

I was wearing the Zog's treasured old Japanese gardening shirts, which he'd picked up on a trip to Terra in his youth. Tiger Kotani owned a similar one. It was a PreCollapse garment, made in prerepublican Japan in respectful imitation of an even older style, cream with turquoise trim, covered with colorful images of samurai, peasants, beautiful maidens, pagodas, mountains, and tall Noble fir trees. Just wearing it made me feel I could talk to plants, and understand their replies. In zero gee it flapped around me like wings.

I had no responsibilities at the moment. Over a dozen of us had chosen to emulate Peter Kindred—so far—but fewer than half of those had left instructions to bury them. I guess if they'd seen any point in contributing to our ecosystem, they would not have opted to leave it. Those few who had chosen the oldest form of eternal rest had long since been tucked beneath soil. Admittedly it had proven more difficult without gravity to help keep the dead moving in the desired direction. I decided to see how the goats were doing in their improvised zero-gee enclosure. I had a pretty good idea I knew what the rabbits were doing.

"Citizen Johnston," the *Sheffield* said softly, "Captain Bean requires your presence on the Bridge immediately. Acknowledge, please."

Requires? Of a free citizen?

I thought about how much the Captain must be in the mood for backtalk, right about now. That he was still functional at all was a miracle. He had expected to carry the heaviest of responsibilities for another fourteen years. Now he had none. No further piloting was ever going to be needed.

"I'm on my way."

He's going to announce his retirement, and ask me to take his job, I thought. *Joel Johnston, Star Pilot! How old was I the first time I ever thought those words—six?*

It was the first even mildly humorous thought I could recall having in . . . some period of time. That couldn't be good, could it?

Along the way, I checked both the official news site, *Sheffield Steel*, and the barely tolerated unofficial one Jules ran despite Richie's help, *The Straight Shit*. Neither had word of anything unusual or even interesting. In fact, each had barely been updated since the day before Kindred had wasted us all. Who cared anymore if RUP-0 sector got their plumbing problem under control, or young Sparks Reilly succeeded in adding another thousand digits to pi?

I was surprised to note that one of the few headings showing new material at each source, besides obits, was the wedding announcements. The same news that had triggered fifteen suicides had also apparently inspired nineteen couples, one triad, and one quartet to get off the dime and make a commitment for the future. Since there wasn't going to be one, it seemed incredibly sad to me. What shall it profit a man if he gaineth his soul, yet he loseth the whole universe? How could you have children now?

Kathy's group, I noticed, had replaced a suicide husband with a new wife. Until then, I had not consciously realized I'd been toying with the idea of trying to get back together with her, in some way, on some basis. As soon as I did realize it, I knew it had been a bad idea—sheer loneliness, looking to get comfort without the trouble of pretending to get to know someone first. I'd already screwed up Kathy quite enough. I had come aboard this bucket of mildew loudly proclaiming my intention to die a bachelor—it was time to put my vast, useless money where my big dumb mouth was.

I had a momentary image of myself dying all alone. And suddenly I saw that the me in it was the same age I was now. Right then and there in the corridor, I became aware for the first time that if I continued as I was going, if I did not make some kind of drastic change, it might be no more than a week or two before the Zog would be planting *me*.

I would like to say I froze in my tracks, consumed with horror at this revelation, and resolved to race to Dr. Amy for help as soon as I'd finished whatever the Old Man had in mind. It did disturb me, but I didn't break stride. And I was pretty sure I'd already seen Amy's best moves.

Well, when you reach that mental state, about the only thing that can save you is for random chance or intelligent design or the Lord God of the Heavenly Host or whatever you want to call the source of all the irony in this universe to come kick you square in the ass with His almighty reinforced boot.

I got mine around the other side, that's all.

I HAD NEVER seen the Bridge. Not with my own eyes, anyway. But it looked much like it did in the Sim, even to apparent size and lighting. The main visual difference I noticed as I came through the hatch was that almost none of the countless screens, dials, or readouts were active, including the main display before the Captain's Couch. In Sim, everything was active all the time, and there was a constant faint undercurrent of metallic beeps, chirps, buzzes, and other technosounds. And the Sim had the scent all wrong; instead of electrical ozone, the predominant notes were stale coffee and an odd, hauntingly redolent perfume. I would never have taken Captain Bean for a perfume kind of guy, and while I didn't know the Second Officer, van Cortlandt, his picture hadn't made him seem like one either.

One other intangible was different. Here I was somehow acutely conscious of the stupendous thickness and weight and ingenious design of all that shielding above my head, and of the fact that our speed was so horrendous, some dangerous stuff was getting through anyway. The hazard was low, but I would definitely be safer when I got back down as far as the Ag Deck or Rup-Tooey.

Terrific.

All these things registered on the subconscious level in the time it took me to complete a preliminary census. Big as it was, one big open area, the Bridge Deck was considerably more crowded than I had expected it to be.

I counted fourteen people total, began ticking them off. Because of the higher than normal airflow, all were displaying a tendency to drift away from their handholds. A slight majority were facing my way, so I started with them, left to right.

Governor-General Cott and Perry Jarnell, both imposing as hell in full formal attire including ceremonial swords, and drifting tall arm in arm as if they were posing for a sculptor, Jarnell grasping a chair to anchor them in the steady breeze. Solomon Short, wearing only a dirty breechclout and an expression it took me a moment to be sure was a broad grin, since he was upside down with respect to everyone else. Second Officer David van Cortlandt, tall and portly, with a flowing white walrus mustache, a receding mane of white hair, and extremely well-developed smile wrinkles—which he too was exercising. Odd. Captain Bean, wearing the kind of pepper-and-salt Vandyke beard, heavy on the pepper with slight mustache twirls, that has been the most common choice of skippers since the age of sail, was more what I'd been expecting; his expression was the one on my mental picture of Magellan, the day he realized he wasn't going to make it home. To his left, Third Officer Bruce looked madder than a wet hen, ready to peck somebody and then lay a bad egg. Completing the array on my extreme right was, to my mild surprise, Paul Hattori, in his best business attire. I'd have thought he was now even more useless than the crew—whether we admitted it or not, we were now a de facto social collective, operating on the barter system, with no further use for money as long as the toilet paper held out. Yet his expression was the oddest of all; he looked . . . exalted, like someone in church, or a groupie backstage. He was gripping the back of a chair with both hands in such a way as to make it seem he was standing on the deck.

Those facing away from me took several seconds longer to identify.

I got no instant-recognition hits from size or body language, nor from clothes—in fact, there was something subtly not right about their clothes I was too busy to analyze. The seven of them broke down into two het couples and three singletons, two female, one male. Something about placement and stance gave me the idea the taller of the single fems might have deliberately interposed herself between the other two, but I couldn't be sure. Without exception, they all seemed to carry themselves with an air of enormous confidence, as if they were used to being listened to respectfully.

Nobody had noticed me enter. I hadn't identified any of the ones facing away yet, and some instinct or insecurity made me keep my handhold just inside the door until I had. So I went with my strengths. Four people were talking at once and none would yield; probably anybody else would have called the result noise. I chose to treat it as a quartet— and used my composer's ear to pick out the individual horns by their timbre and range rather than the mangled notes. Whatever they were saying could be repeated to me later; now I wanted to know who was saying them. The enhanced free-fall airflow worked for me, now, bringing me their voices with unusual clarity.

Three of the instruments I knew at once, would have even if I could not have seen them being played: Captain Bean, Jarnell, and Lieutenant Bruce, working as a trio, alto, trombone, and trumpet. That fourth horn doing the counterpoint, the baritone—

Damn, it was strange. It teased at the edges of memory. Long-term storage. Whoever he was, I'd met him briefly years ago, probably shortly after we'd left, and hadn't encountered him since. I hadn't liked him much for some reason. The penny resolutely refused to drop farther.

Another voice entered, causing the others to fall silent. A clarinet, but with the quiet authority of Goodman. This one I was sure I didn't know; its timbre was so unique I knew if I'd ever heard him speak I'd have tried to get him to sing for me. His couple-partner remained silent, contributing no harmonies.

He stated a brief theme. Captain Bean picked it up and restated it three times, changing it slightly each time. The third time, the clarinet joined in in unison, to tell him he had it right.

Lieutenant Bruce began a counterstatement, but had traded his trumpet for a kazoo; in compensation he blew so hard it broke.

The baritone entered again, but allowed itself to be interrupted by a cello in its lower register. I didn't know this voice either, I was sure of it. And I didn't much care for it. It had an undertone of menace, of unstated threat.

My strangeness meter was beginning to max. In a small town of less than five hundred, there can be one or two people you've just never chanced to run into. But *three* of them, that you're sure you've never even passed within earshot of? I had to be mistaken.

Captain Bean's alto reply started out softly, but built to a small angry crescendo, like the first harbinger of trouble ahead in Wagner.

The next voice, the tall singleton female, I knew at once, and started to relax. Her name would come to me in a second. I hadn't seen her in years, but had always liked her. This one was no horn, but a singer: smokey voice, like late period Annie Ross. Some sort of joke in her name. Miss Steak? Miss Fortune? Ms. Rhee? Something literary about the joke. Miss Elenius? An adolescent erotic undertone too, somehow. Something dirty . . . female honorific . . . last name that made it all a quote or literary reference . . . I was almost there . . . famous character? Title? *Title*. That felt right.

Oh, for Pete's sake, of course. *Les Misérables.* "Lay Ms. Robb." Dorothy Robb, sweet old lady, had been kind to me the last time we met. What was that funny job title of hers? Chief Enabler, that was it. . . .

Chief Enabler for Conrad of Conrad.

Given that context, I recognized the baritone at once. "Smithers." Alex Rennick, Master of the North Keep.

Well, *hell*. That was annoying. Clearly my wiring was

misfiring. Not that I blamed it, given the events of recent weeks. But I could not even override it—no matter how hard I assured my ears that they were mistaken, they both stubbornly insisted we were all hearing Dorothy Robb together. Slightly older, perhaps, but her.

All right, this did not necessarily mean I was losing it. People can have vocal doubles. I'd have remembered a colonist in her nineties, but it was not impossible this woman was imitating one for some—

Once while colossally drunk, Herb had spoken of himself as "hanging by my fingertips from my own anus, to keep from falling out." I was in that mindset, clutching for dear life.

Then from the couple with the cello female came the unforgettable, unmistakable, inarguable, utterly impossible voice of Conrad of Conrad, and I lost my grip.

BUT I WAS in zero gravity. I didn't *go* anywhere.

Naturally I felt instant fear. But not terror.

When the impossible happens—when a planet *moves* beneath your feet, and won't stop—when you look up on a gorgeous morning and see something huge fly majestically into the side of a tall building—when a man you buried shows up at your door with a six-pack—you're supposed to feel a primal terror, a superstitious dread. It's in all the books. You pass out, or vomit, or your bowels and bladder void, or you howl. If the universe is prepared to *cheat*, you're screwed, right? The only alternative is to decide it's all a bad dream or sustained hallucination and just go with it.

I didn't do any of those things. I can't say why not. Maybe I was simply too far gone. I'd been electroshocked so many times, they no longer had a voltage that would put me into convulsions. In a twisted way, it was almost starting to get good to me.

The fabric of the universe itself was coming apart? Fine—bring it. Fucking thing hadn't turned out that well anyway. The dead were rising, Time itself flowing back up over the dam? Great. Gee, if I unaged slower than normal because I was on a nearly luminal starship, I might finally get to meet my mom. Go on, disintegrating reality, give me your best shot.

It is *never* a good idea to say that.

It seemed perfectly clear to me that I had fried my operating system. Deep down, I *knew* I had. I did *not* believe in ghosts, never had . . . well, not since I was real little. No more did I actually believe in universes that cheated. Given the insistent evidence of my senses, I knew I was nuts—the kind of nuts hardly anyone ever went anymore. There seemed only one sensible response to that.

I roared with laughter.

In a timeless instant, I saw my life as a whole, saw the *shape* of it, and the flavor of it, saw that it led inexorably from hope and great promise to gibbering madness in a doomed can full of tragedies ten light-years from the hole where the human race used to be, haunted by the ridiculous shade of the evil old bastard who'd forced me onto this donkey ride to heaven in the first place—all because some nameless unknowable alien vigilante *other* had concluded that mankind was not a feature but a bug in the Galaxy—and there just wasn't anything else to do, not to do *about it*, but just to *do*, except to laugh my ass off. Part of me was aware the Captain had wanted my participation in an important meeting—but since he wasn't going to get it anyway, why *not* disrupt the silly thing? I didn't even try to hold back; I laughed like a buffalo, like a bull ape, like a brontosaur—they might all be extinct, but by God they were still funny.

Naturally everyone stared at me as if I had lost my mind. I thought I had, too.

Especially when the people facing away from me started turning around.

Yep, that was Dorothy Robb, older but still as vital as I remembered.

Yes, that was Smithers, his hairline strangely receded.

Yes indeedy, absolutely beyond question, the man in the center was Richard Conrad, Conrad of Conrad, and he *still* didn't look the part. He still looked like some sort of gruff lovable academic don, now well past retirement age but quite vigorous.

His companion was a short compact woman I had never seen in my life, and I was oddly grateful for that. At last, a hallucination with a trace of creativity! She seemed my age or a little older, remarkably fit, and as focused as a comm laser.

On Conrad's other side was another total stranger, about ten years older than me. This one was more interesting. His short stature, pale skin, and overdeveloped limbs told me he was a Terran. He had an overall air of sweet hayseed innocence, a gullibility based on intrinsic decency, which usually assumes itself in others. He wore a small dopey mustache like the one Jinny had once tried to get me to grow. But his eyes—his eyes had a contradictory quality I cannot express with words. I would have to show you a similar pair, and say, "Like those." I had only seen such eyes twice. My father had had them. And so had one of his best friends, who everyone knew should *also* have won the Nobel, and who I called Uncle Max. They were the kind of eyes that caused other great geniuses to drop their egos and just stare. I wondered what his field was.

I was giving myself creative credit for having finally produced a really intriguing hallucination, when the last two people present finished turning around.

Given the mental state and emotional shape I was in right then—and the seeming theatricality with which they had both turned so slowly—I was actually fully expecting one of them to turn out to be Jinny.

I was *not* expecting *both* of them to.

THE ONE FARTHEST from me, standing beside the man with kaleidoscope eyes, did not *look* like Jinny as I remembered her. What she looked remarkably like, I realized, was the mental picture I had always had of "fellow orphan" Jinny's imaginary "dead mother, Mrs. Maureen Hamilton."

This one was—convincingly appeared to be—the real, actual Jinny Conrad. If she were alive, she would have been about thirteen years older than when I'd last seen her. If this was her, she had apparently lied to me about her age. Despite excellent cosmeticizing, she looked thirty-five. That too would fit.

But it was difficult to focus analytical thought on anything at all, let alone a psychotic puzzle like this, because the *other* Jinny was *so* much closer to the Jinny I still carried in my heart's memory that it threatened to stop my heart. Jinny at eighteen or nineteen—an honest eighteen or nineteen—so beautiful it wasn't even fair, a perfect rose just unfolding. Jinny as I had seen her then—wise and smart and compassionate and strong and certain—transported through time. Looking back at me now exactly the way she had back then, with eyes that were lamps, whose pupils were black holes, calling me to fall in.

"Hello, Joel," they both said at once.

I HAD BEGUN to stop laughing when they both turned around, and finished a few seconds after they were done, with a last few "ha's."

But a split second after they both greeted me, I finally got it.

I may have been in ragged shape, an emotional basket case with a malfunctioning brain, belabored by too many impossible stimuli at once—but I had started the course with a pretty decent thinking machine. Presented with a series of clues that allowed only one rational explanation, I was bound to get there eventually. I was aware of the ancient dictum that if you're certain you've eliminated the impossible, whatever's left, however unlikely, must be the answer.

Once I got the premise, everything else made sense half a second later. I even had a pretty good idea who the two strangers were, and why they were present.

This time I laughed so hard I went into a tumble, and lost my vertical. I would have literally rolled on the floor laughing if there'd been any gravity to put me there. I had always thought it a hyperbolic expression. There was simply no position that could contain or properly brace my titanic mirth;

yearning to laugh even harder, I would curl into fetal position, then explode like a starfish, then punch and kick the air the way I'd learned in Tiger's dojo, desperate to force all the laughter out before it burst me.

The moment I could spare the air, I managed to squeeze four words into the outgoing message traffic, two at a time.

First: "Hello, Evelyn."

And then: "Hello, Jin."

TWO THINGS MADE my father special, and only one of them was that he could think better than practically anybody else.

The other was that he could think *faster* than practically anybody else.

That means more than just getting to the answer before anyone else can. It means you reach answers no one else will. The faster you can think, the longer a logic chain you can follow out before you get tired and decide to stop. In modern physics, that can be crucial. He told me once, "The universe is so simple, it takes very complicated thought to touch it."

I inherited a touch of his freak speed. It became clear quite early that I emphatically had not inherited Dad's gift for exotic mathematics—but it was just as clear that he genuinely did not give the least sub-subatomic particle of a damn about that, and maybe that indicates genius of another, completely different kind on his part. But I had mastered the alto sax at seven, playing with a speed that had literally frightened my first teacher, Francis Layne—who himself was called "Fast Layne." In my secret heart of hearts, I had always honestly believed I was one of the best composers alive, and one of the best saxophonists, too, although I had expected it to be decades before there was much agreement on that. Now, of course, I had it in the bag.

But I had also noticed quite early that I was usually faster on the uptake than most people. Unless the subject was me, anyway. I spent the better part of most conversations waiting for everyone else to catch up. Patterns form and combine in my mind like crystals reproducing at fast forward, sometimes so fast that even to me it seems like I skip whole steps in my logic process and just thumb to the back of the book for the answer. Telepathy is literally instantaneous; maybe sometimes other kinds of thought are, too.

I saw the people present, I knew who all but two of them were, and it seemed that the instant I got over disbelieving the evidence of my eyes, I knew who the two strangers had to be, and how all of them must have gotten here, and why each of them had come, and what their presence could mean. The actual deduction and induction itself didn't require genius, really—merely a willingness to think the unthinkable. I'd been doing that for weeks. I had most of it worked out by the time I'd stopped laughing.

JINNIA CONRAD, WHEN last seen, had been in the market for a new promising young genius-carrier.

Was there the slightest chance her grandfather would *not* have said to her, "This time, find one in some *serious* profession. No more damned *artists*," and made it stick? Selecting a sax player had probably been as close as she'd dared come to a gesture of rebellion against her dynastic destiny, tolerated only because of my father's pedigree.

What was the exact global opposite of a sax player, if not an experimental physicist? Okay, perhaps a financier, but Jinny wasn't a *pervert*.

Assume she repeated the pattern, found the male offspring of one or maybe even two of the greatest such tinkers in recent history, and assume that this lad *had* inherited the same *kind* of genius, the urge and ability to take the universe apart and put it back together in different ways with his own hands. He certainly had the eyes of a Tesla. And the naïveté.

Propelled irresistibly by Jinny's—oh, *horrid* pun—by her relative-istic drive, and funded by the unlimited resources of the Conrad Family—as if J.P. Morgan had been canny enough to simply find Nikola Tesla a wife who would keep him in harness—was there *anything* such a genius might not have accomplished?

Suppose he was interested in faster-than-light star drives? His grandfather-in-law would *like* that.

If he were, he would damn well have a ship equipped with one ready to test within five years, if I knew Jinny.

If he and it survived the initial tests, then the passenger list for its very first official shakedown cruise as a commissioned vessel, *long* before the rest of the Solar System was told of its existence, was absolutely and beyond question *going* to include at least two people besides the inventor-pilot: the pilot's wife, and her grandfather. This voyage would be not merely historic, but conceivably the most historic of all time—no possibility existed that those two names would not be in the first paragraph of the story.

They say luck is the residue of good planning. If the most paranoid man that ever lived ends up being the only one in a position to escape the end of the world with a few playmates for company . . . can you even call that luck? They must have been on the dark side of Terra, or some other large planet, when it suddenly began to glow around the edges.

If Conrad of Conrad was aboard a small vessel, a minimum of three others were, too.

First and most essential to that paranoid old villain, a very very good and very very very reliable bodyguard. She would be the one I had mistaken for a companion, the cello voice with menace in its undertones. No wonder she looked fit! She could probably fight us all with one hand, while using the other to hold a shield . . . over her employer. If you're compelled to try and screw literally everyone you'll ever meet, you need a strong condom.

Second, Rennick: pan-trained stooge, Speaker To Peasants, flapper, flunky, and designated fall guy should one ever become necessary. Don't leave the castle without one.

Third, Dorothy Robb: his walking desk, database, secretary, researcher, and necessary impertinent, licensed to sass him occasionally. She had the courage to be willing to pretend every day that she did not fear his terrible power . . . and the wisdom never to go so far that he began to suspect she really didn't.

Something about their respective positioning and zero-gee kinesthetics gave me the sudden insight that Jinny's mocking nickname for Rennick had indeed been aptly chosen. His loyalty to his boss was charged with, if not based on, suppressed eroticism. His body language said his subconscious absurdly considered even ninety-year-old Dorothy Robb a potential rival.

Given the not-terribly-surprising existence of young Gyro Gearloose—if any of them were here, he had to be—I fully understood at once the presence of Jinny, and her grandfather, and all three stooges. The one I had the most trouble explaining to myself was the person I still thought of as "little" Evelyn.

Little she no longer was—but it made little sense that she should be here. If the Conrad superluminal yacht had an extra seat, why hadn't it gone to some closer relative of Jinny's than a mere cousin? Why not one of her own parents—or if they were dead or the old man loathed them, Evelyn's?

All I knew was that her presence was the single most wonderful phenomenon in the Galaxy at that time. I was absolutely certain of that.

I'VE RECOUNTED THIS as if I examined each person there one at a time, and finished with Evelyn, because sentences can't happen all at the same time. It wasn't like that. Start to finish, she occupied a huge fraction of my attention and processing time. All the others I saw with peripheral vision—it was my day for clichés come true, and I literally could not take my eyes off her.

The resemblance to Jinny at her age was striking even given their kinship, enough to be eerie. But the *differences* were just as striking to me, now that I looked. And very dear.

This face was at least as strong as Jinny's, as determined, as proud. But it was not ruthless. Its eyes were fully as intelligent and alert—but nowhere near as calculating. It was every bit as heartstoppingly beautiful as Jinny's face had been at nineteen—and more, because it didn't care. It did not think of its own beauty as a tool, or a weapon.

For the first time I realized the imperfection in Jinny's

beauty that had always escaped my notice somehow, the missing note in the perfect chord: compassion. Evelyn believed other people were real, even non-Conrads. And *liked* them. Her eyes said in part that she had hurt others in her short life, and that she regretted more about that than the increased difficulty of getting them to accede to her whims.

As I was watching her, she did a little zero-gee move too complex to describe that caused her to look ridiculous for a brief moment, because if she had not, she would have bumped into Jarnell. She did it unconsciously, and I knew in a million years Jinny would never have done such a thing. Jarnell would have ended up apologizing to her.

This was a version of Jinny who could never play me the way the original had, no matter what the reasons.

As QUICKLY AS I absorbed all these things and reached all these understandings, I also saw just as clearly a couple of things that only two others present had fully realized yet, two of the most important facts in this whole equation.

Richard Conrad was not only still a very wealthy man, he was vastly wealthier than he had ever been, was now in fact without a doubt the wealthiest human being in the universe.

But his inconceivable fortune consisted of two assets.

And he only had one bodyguard.

20

**The butterfly counts not months but moments.
And has time enough.**

—Rabindranath Tagore

By the time I'd finally gotten the last of my laughter out, airflow had nudged me back within reach of the bulkhead I'd come through to enter the Bridge, and I used it to launch myself toward the meeting.

I tried to talk myself out of it all the way there. I guess I'm just not that big a man. When I reached the group, I used a deck chair to brake myself, and looked Conrad of Conrad in the eyes. For half a second.

"Hey, Connie," I said.

And turned away. "Dorothy, good to see you again. Alex, I see you again. Crave pardon, ma'am, we haven't been introduced, my name is Joel Johnston." I bowed as graciously as I had free-fall skills for.

"Alice Dahl," she said crisply. That was a scary cello she was playing, all right. She did not acknowledge my bow with even a nod, or offer to shake, even with her non-gunhand. Maybe she didn't have one. She was a golem.

Jinny said, "Joel, I'd like you to meet my husband, Andrew J. Conrad. Andrew, this is Joel."

He and I exchanged about a hundred thousand words by eye traffic in three seconds, and each put out a hand at the same instant. I liked the man. The mustache looked silly, but I knew it had not been his idea.

"It is an honor to meet you, Captain Conrad," I said. "Congratulations on your historic achievements. And I speak for the moment only of the latest ones. First man to exceed *c*. First master of a transluminal passenger vessel. First and only man ever to match orbits with a relativistic starship in transit." I thought of another one. "And one of only seven creatures we know of who've ever been in the close vicinity of an exploding star and lived to tell about it. Welcome to our covered wagon. We hope you'll find our technology quaint."

He didn't preen, or look smug, or sneer arrogantly, or try to pretend he didn't enjoy the praise. He nodded and said, "Please call me Andrew. Thank you, Joel. I'm glad to be here."

"You're welcome, Andrew."

"Jinny told me you're a quick study. I can see she was right; you seem up to speed. We're all lucky to be here." His face clouded. "And I can't hope to tell you how much I wish I'd built the *Mercury* years sooner. Centuries ago. Even last year. . . ."

"We all do, son," Captain Bean said softly. "Play the cards in front of you."

Andrew nodded. "Yes, sir, that's good advice."

Van Cortlandt spoke up, his voice a pleasant tenor. "How did you ever figure out what was happening in time to run?"

"We were fortunate enough to be in Terra's shadow when she lit up."

"And you're sure destruction was complete?"

"We reached Ganymede with a thirty-three-minute lead over the wavefront, and spent five minutes talking to telepaths on the ground there. They were just receiving information consistent with the annihilation of Terra. We jumped again, and thirty minutes later telepaths on Saturn confirmed the destruction of Ganymede, with timing consistent with a solar explosion. At that point, I gave her the gun."

"Andrew's quick reactions saved us all," Jinny said proudly, and his shoulders widened.

"What can you tell us about her drive?" I asked.

Solomon spoke up. "The subject came up, as you may imagine. Captain Conrad discussed the nature of the *Mercury*'s novel propulsion system frankly and forthrightly at some length, using short simple words, and continuing until the last of us lost the struggle to pretend we had the faintest clue what he was talking about. I myself gleaned only that its basic principle is—sometimes—called Drastic Irrelevancy. Have I got that right, Captain?"

"Drastic Irrelevancy Synergism, yes," Andrew agreed. "You see, it's . . . but then you don't. I'm sorry."

"Is there even a Sunday supplement shorthand version, albeit grossly oversimplified or crudely approximate, that you could give us?" Lieutenant van Cortlandt asked.

Andrew pursed his mouth in thought a moment. "I'm sorry," he said. "In a week, I could probably provide Relativist Short with enough tools to begin thinking about the first part of the answer you want. Uh, there are a lot of parts. Yourself, and a few others here, a month would probably do it. For sure," he amended, seeing van Cortlandt's expression.

Richard Conrad had put up with the unnatural state of being ignored for as long as he was prepared to. Ten percent louder than anyone had spoken so far, he said, "We've failed to cover this already. Can we for the love of privacy just accept for now that the *Mercury* is towed by a fleet of hyperphotonic swans under an enchantment, and move on?"

He was now merely a man like any other, without a multiplanet empire behind him anymore, and everyone in the room probably knew it. But he was also Conrad of Conrad, and had been all his life. We all flinched at his whip-crack interruption and fell silent, and the first one of us who felt capable of obeying him did so.

Captain Bean said to Andrew, "Captain, I have a confession to make. While I'm no mathematician, I've always thought myself capable of simple kitchen arithmetic, at least." Both his lieutenants made brief nasal sounds. "And ever since I received your hail . . . amend that: ever since I convinced myself your hail was not a hallucination, I've been using part of my mind to try and calculate what speed you were making. But there are a few more variables than I can handle, and I keep losing my decimal point. Curiosity trumps pride: Will you tell us your top speed?"

Conrad of Conrad—there were just too many Conrads present; I was going to have to start thinking of him as Richard somehow—started speaking at the same instant Andrew did, obviously trying to cut him off. I was surprised when Andrew didn't yield, then again when the old man did.

". . . not possible to answer your question, in the strictest sense," Andrew was saying, "but I'll do my best. You've traveled roughly 10.4 lights in a little over 6.41 years—your years, I mean. Thirteen years for us back home. We caught up in a little over six and a half weeks, by your clock." He sensed that he was taking too long. "But in the terms you're using, our equivalent of a maximum real-world velocity works out to be on the order of $19.6\,c$."

Several of us either sucked in air or expelled it noisily. You could almost hear a whining sound as many mental calculators began operating at full capacity.

How far away was Brasil Novo, at twenty c? I could make

a stab at it in terms of objective years, what Andrew had called "real-world" time, but when it came to how much time it would *seem* to take for a passenger, I lacked a basis from which to even guess.

Screw that: the answer was, a *hell* of a lot closer than it had been, whether you were speaking subjectively or objectively.

And real-world years, out there in the subliminal universe, had more than academic importance, too. They were the measure of how long we had to warn the rest of the colonies, before all their skies turned to fire.

AND WE'D HAVE been here nearly a day ago, if you people hadn't been silly enough to shut off your drive. We were lucky to find you at all."

Rennick's voice and ill-mannered irritation were like a cold-water bath. I saw Captain Bean, van Cortlandt, and Solomon all open their mouths to retort.

But Dorothy Robb beat them all to it. "Alex, if you actually believe anyone voluntarily shuts down a quantum ramjet, you're sillier than that would have been. None of these people have been rude to *you* yet." The hesitation between the last two words was perceptible, but so slight there isn't a punctuation mark subtle enough to render it.

Van and Solomon savored Rennick's facial expression, so it was the Skipper who spoke next. "Rennick, the *Sheffield* has had the great misfortune to lose three of her Relativists, the last just over a week ago. Heroic effort by the surviving three proved insufficient to overturn the laws of physics for more than a few days. Our drive shut itself off, sir."

"Mr. Rennick intended no offense, Captain Bean," Richard Conrad said mildly, and Rennick went from a blush to dead white.

There was a short silence, in which everyone tried to think of something to say or ask next that might not sound stupid in retrospect. It was pretty fast company; nobody was in a big hurry to be first.

I was mildly surprised at who turned out to be bold

enough. It was Paul Hattori who cleared his throat and said, "I crave pardon if this question is impertinent, but curiosity overwhelms my manners. May I ask the passenger-carrying capacity of the *Mercury*?"

Again, that ultrasonic whining sound, as a dozen minds radically shifted direction and then reaccelerated.

Richard Conrad spoke with maximum force. "Captain Bean, I must insist we adjourn this discussion to your quarters, or a place of equal privacy, *now*. I quite understand the natural curiosity of all present, have indulged it as long as I deem prudent, and will continue to address it as time permits. But there are matters that must be discussed first only in private, and among those of the highest rank. Matters of extreme importance. There is no time to lose." When the Skipper did not answer instantly in the affirmative, he forced the issue by rotating in place and launching himself toward the hatch. "Will you be kind enough to direct me," he called over his shoulder as he floated away, and I haven't given that a question mark because he didn't.

Most of the rest of his party began to trail him out of sheer instinct, like pilot fish who go wherever the big shark goes. Captain Bean was visibly angry, but he wasn't the kind of man who would make a scene for no better reason than to establish his authority on his own ship. This party was going to follow Conrad, and the only people who considered me of the highest rank were music lovers. I felt sharp dismay.

Conrad rotated to face us again on his way to the door. "Alex, ladies," he called, "perhaps *you'd* be willing to answer any questions the rest of our hosts may have, insofar as you are able."

Jinny, Rennick, and Robb were already in transit, but all three immediately rotated themselves so they could rebound and rejoin us once they reached the hatchway. Evelyn had not yet committed herself to a launch, and stayed where she was, using a large unused monitor for a handhold.

"Solomon, Van, Mr. Cott, come with me, please. Mr. Hattori, your input could prove useful as well." Bruce opened his mouth, but Captain Bean continued, "You have the con, Mister," and he closed it again. "The rest of you may remain here under Lieutenant Bruce's command until I return if you choose." Hattori was smiling like a musician who'd just been asked to sit in with Louis Armstrong.

The hatch irised open. Alice the bodyguard made Solomon and Andrew exit first, followed by herself, and then Conrad, with Hattori taking up the rear. She either rated the banker as zero threat or hoped he'd stop bullets.

LIEUTENANT BRUCE BEGAN a speech. I can't recall a word of it. It was flowery, trite, pompous, smarmy, obsequious, and self-aggrandizing, all at once. Jinny endured a sentence or two, and then said, without discernible reference to anything he'd been saying, "Thank you *very* much, Commander; you are gracious."

He was so pleased he shut right up. If she understood brevet rank, then she knew what a high-ranking fellow he was—which was all he'd wished to establish to begin with. "Very kind of you, ma'am."

"Yes. The last thing I would wish, Commander, would be to distract you from your heavy responsibility. I am myself married to a pilot." I did not catch her moving any of her limbs, but suddenly she was in motion, floating slowly away from him and us. "The other ladies and I can converse with Joel over at this end of the Bridge without disturbing you, I think, if we are quiet. And Mr. Rennick will keep you excellent company; thank you, Alex."

Both Evelyn and Dorothy had started moving on the third word. I was slower off the mark, so I got to savor the expression on Bruce's face. Rennick showed no reaction, and I savored that, too. "You'll forgive me, gentlemen," I lied, then picked a docking spot and jaunted after the ladies.

It was a short jaunt, but I'd done it slowly, so I had several seconds to think on my way. When I was near I said to all three, but looking at Dorothy Robb, "Time has been extremely kind to all of you."

One corner of her mouth turned up. "I love a liar," she said. She studied my face and raised an eyebrow. "You've had less of it, but I can see you used your time well."

I nodded. "I tried," I agreed. "Jinny, it is nice to see you again. You look wonderful."

Her eyes lit with pleasure at being addressed next—age before beauty. An instant later she realized second was not the optimal position in a group of three, and the light went out.

I noted it, but was busy with the sudden realization— maybe it was more of a revelation—that what I had just said to her was strictly accurate. It was nice to see her.

And that was all it was. Yes, this woman had chased me out of the System with a crushed heart, and yes, she had haunted my days and stalked me in my dreams. But not for five years or so, now.

"Evelyn, I can't tell you how good it is to see you again. Your letters have meant a *lot* to me. I knew you would be beautiful, but apparently I have a very feeble imagination. I hope you will let me play my saxophone for you one day." It felt awkward saying all that in front of Jinny, but I didn't have any choice.

"If I can sit in on keyboards," she said.

I stared with my mouth open.

"I have a new arrangement for 'Sol Keeps Shining' I want to show you. And a couple of other tracks from *Stars*."

Can an ego have an orgasm? *Something* made my heart pound.

"Perhaps we could postpone the soundtrack until the film is done," Jinny said coldly. "We do have *important* things to talk about, and little time. Grandfather doesn't have anything like the patience he used to."

"We do indeed," I said. "How many passengers *will* your husband's vessel carry?"

"Ten," she said.

"*Damn.*" I felt sharp disappointment. I'd been hoping against hope for some vastly higher number. Twenty-one *c* was definitely an impressive velocity, but even at that barely imaginable speed, Peekaboo was nearly four years away. I doubted we'd be able to get four hundred and something of us to Brasil Novo before the stellar shitrain arrived, even with a magic carpet to help.

I wasted a few seconds trying to work out how many of us could be saved, and how many would die of old age aboard the derelict *Sheffield* before a seat became available for them on the shuttle, and how they would be chosen. The maths were way beyond me, even if I'd known exactly how many of us were still alive. And so were the ethics.

It was not just a terrible letdown—it was also puzzling.

"What is it, Joel?" Evelyn asked.

How to put it? "I'm a little confused," I admitted finally.

"We're all confused," Dorothy said. "Which confusion troubles you now?"

If there was a way to say it pretty, I couldn't find it. "There really isn't any way you can be of much help to us with a ten-seater, even if it is twenty times faster than a speeding photon. Is there?"

Dorothy began to say something, but was overridden by Jinny. "There is a plan. As we speak, Grandfather and Andrew are discussing with your Captain Bean and his own advisers the feasibility o—"

"You're forgetting something," I said.

"What?"

"Jinny Hamilton," I said carefully, "you are one of the best. But I know exactly how you look and act and sound when you are lying."

Her control was excellent, but she could not stop her skin from reddening. She started a bluff but got only two chilly words in before giving it up and doing an instant one-eighty, so that the sentence came out, "How dare all right damn it, I was trying to keep this focused on the positive."

"That doesn't leave much to talk about," I said. "What I'm trying to understand is, since there doesn't seem to be any practical way to rescue us . . . why the hell are you here?"

"Joel!"

"There's damn little you can do for us—and for the life of me, I can't figure out anything we could possibly do for you."

"The whole Solar System just died!" she said. "Naturally we headed for the first—"

"If your grandfather just wanted company for comfort, why in Sol's name would he pick hundreds of doomed souls he can't help, with only a temporary ecology? It makes a million times more sense for him to make a beeline for someplace like Aradia or Hippolyte—they've both been thriving for decades. Or *any* of the self-sustaining colonies. Any technology we could possibly give you, any asset we could have aboard, you could get much better elsewhere, and without the social awkwardness of having to interact with dead people."

I stopped and waited for a response, but Jinny made none.

"It's a simple question. Why are you—"

Dorothy Robb said, "Joel, don't be dense."

I stared at her.

Neither of the others had anything to say. They were both just looking at me. As if I had two—

"Covenant's sake! We're here because of *you*, you idiot."

I LOST MY handhold and went free.

I wasted seconds uselessly fanning air as if to agree I was an idiot, and then gave it up, surrendered to free fall, and tried to get control of my breath.

Nobody seemed to have a problem letting me take as long as I needed to think it through, so I did, eyes shut tight. It probably took a good thirty seconds to slow my spinning mind down from dynamo speed to something more like the cyclic rate of a prayer wheel.

I opened my eyes in time to see a thick cable within reach and docked on it.

"I don't believe it," I said slowly to Jinny. "Are you seriously telling me that you came all this way, played with the hopes of all these people, all my friends . . . just to give me the finger, one last time?"

"*I* made them come!" Evelyn cried.

21

In my dreams
I can see, I can
I can see a love
That could be

—David Crosby,
"In My Dreams"

Evelyn, what—?"
   That was as far as I could go. I could not even form a
rational question.
   No, wait. Yes I could.
   "Evelyn, *why?*"
   She had just let me think over an answer for a good half a
minute. I gave her the same. So did the others. Jinny
watched her intently, with no expression.
   When she was ready, Evelyn said, "Joel, you were the first
person I *ever* saw defy my grandfather. You are the only one
I know who ever got away with it. You gave me the inspiration to become a musician—the only one in four entire generations of my family—in case perhaps that was the source
of your courage. And it was! You're the only man I've ever
known who thought it was a great thing to go to the stars—
and went."
   "But—"
   "Shut up. That's part of it. You were the very first adult I
ever met who took me seriously. Who did not talk down to
me, because I was small. You treated me as an equal with an
unfortunate height problem you were too polite to notice."
   "That was—"
   "I asked you to shut up. Because of that, you were the first
adult I *ever* allowed to have any faintest idea how smart I
was. Previous experiments had worked out badly. But it
didn't bother you a bit to need my help, or to get it. It didn't
even surprise you much."

"That's how my father always treated me at that age. I didn't know any other way to react."

"You were the first grown-up to remember my name the second time he saw me. And before you let me help you, you asked if it would get me in trouble."

I tried to remember. Was all this true? It had been a long time ago.

But then, it had been longer for *her* than for me: thirteen years to my six since we'd cannoned into each other in the corridors of the North Keep—how could she remember so much better than I?

"You didn't laugh at me." She hesitated, then went on more softly, "Even when I told you I was going to marry you." Then far more softly, "And you were engaged then."

Jinny snorted, but did not speak.

Evelyn made a small measured movement, and began to drift toward me. Snow used to fall at about that speed in the low gravity of Ganymede, once. She came with infinite grace, and her eyes seemed to get larger faster than the rest of her.

"Joel Johnston, you were the first man ever to write to me. You're the longest pen pal I ever had. You are the only man who ever kept writing to me after it was clear that I was not going to have sex with him. No one else of either sex, ever, has given me their attention without expecting *anything* in return. My letters ended up having to be a tenth the size of yours, and carefully edited, thanks to Gran'ther *Dick* . . . and yours kept on coming anyway. And you are the only man I have ever known in my life or expected to who did not care one single solitary molecule of a *damn* how much money I had!"

She gently collided with me, for the second time in six of my years and thirteen of hers. She was taller, now. Her eyes were only decimeters from mine, this time. So was her mouth. Both her arms were around me. I had both of mine around her. I must have let go of my handhold again. The room *literally* spun around us. She twined her calves around mine, completing the free-fall embrace. Our bellies touched, and we both discovered my waxing erection.

"I *bullied* them into coming for you," she said. "I said I

would space myself if they did not. They knew I meant it. Right now, Gran'ther would rather cut off his own feet than lose fifty percent of the universe's remaining supply of egg-laying Conrads." Her voice dropped so low then that even I needed to follow her exaggerated lip movements to know she was adding, *"But . . . he . . . is . . . going to."*

It wasn't so much any of the words as looking at her mouth that forced me to kiss her.

Very little coherent thought took place during that kiss. So it must have gone on for a long time, because I had time to think that no woman in my life had ever given me her attention for so many years in a row for *any* reason, let alone without reasonable hope of any possible return. That she had done this for years before she'd ever heard me play a note. That she had learned to play because of me. That she was far and away the best kisser I had ever met or even fantasized. And that it would be very convenient if our first two children happened to take to the bass and drums. Drums first, no doubt.

Then our faces were whole decimeters apart again, and there was a ship around us.

"You *are* coming with us, right?" she asked solemnly.

"I'm coming with *you*," I said just as solemnly.

We both grinned at the same instant. "This *is* insane, right?" I asked her.

"Believe it," she agreed.

"Oh, thank heavens. For a second there I was afraid I was going sane."

"Little danger of that," Jinny said from across the room.

I glanced over at her, found her expressionless. I realized that not once during that timeless kiss had it even momentarily occurred to me that Jinny was watching us. It made me want to grin even wider, but it seemed politer not to. The disease had come close to killing me—but the cure was now complete. Andrew, poor bastard, was welcome to her. I wished him well, hoped he was genius *enough* to hold his own with her. He had licked lightspeed; maybe he could.

My heart suddenly sprang a leak, and joy started to leak out into reality. It began to sink in that I had no clear idea what was going to happen next, what I was going to do now. Or how I was going to live with myself afterward. I wanted with my whole heart to go with Evelyn, wherever she might go. But how could I leave so many of my friends—any of my friends—behind to die in the *Sheffield*? If I stayed, I could save at most one other life—if it hadn't been for me, *nobody* would have lived—those and a dozen other rationalizations raced through my mind, but were of no help whatsoever.

Evelyn saw the change in my face. From her distance she could scarcely have helped it. "Joel, what's wrong?"

I sighed. "I really hate with my whole heart the idea of leaving anyone at all to die of old age in this bucket. I don't know if I can . . . I don't know how to . . ." I did not even know how to express my dilemma, even to myself.

Dorothy Robb spoke up. "Am I the only one here comfortable with arithmetic?"

Everyone turned to stare at her.

She was frowning mightily. "Admittedly, the math does become hairy. But surely *someone* must know how to operate a calculator."

"What do you mean, Dorothy?" Evelyn called.

She replied, "Joel, how many passengers does the *Sheffield* now carry?"

I wasn't at all sure. Too many deaths lately, no time to keep the figures current. "Can we call it four hundred and fifty for now?"

She nodded and closed her eyes, saying, "So: nine passengers at a time yields a total of forty-five trips, with a series of geometrically decreasing trip lengths beginning with seventy-five light-years—we assume zero turnaround time for convenience—" She stopped speaking, but her lips kept moving. We all gave her time. After a while she said, "Call it very roughly a hundred and fifty-one years."

My heart sank in my chest, but I nodded and kept going, needing to know just how bad it was. "How many could we transport in the first seventy or eighty years? You know, before we all die of old age."

Dorothy gave me the look a grandmother gives a child

who has just picked his nose in company. "Joel, Joel—those are a hundred and fifty-one *real* years."

"Pardon—*oh!*" My heart leaped.

"Since this ship is doing nearly ninety-eight percent of the speed of light, that works out to . . . half a tick, now . . . a bit under thirty-three local, shipboard years."

Blood roared in my ears. *We could all live!* Her figures assumed zero turnaround, zero downtime for maintenance, and a lot of other things—but it didn't matter: the thing was *doable*. Andrew had saved us all.

This changed *everything*. For the first time since the quantum ramjet had gone out, I started to feel real hope. With it came a phantom memory of an ancient film about a man struggling with Time, who said to a companion near the end, "It's not the despair—I can live with the despair. It's the *hope* that's killing me!"

Well, being killed beats being dead. I'd been dying for two dozen years now, since the moment of my birth. Another seventy-five years of it sounded very good.

If I could spend them with Evelyn.

THE HATCH OPENED and Andrew entered, as if invoked by my thinking of him. Herb came in on his heels, must have guided him there.

"Hi, darling," was the first thing Andrew said, I noticed, and then, "Hello, everybody. I hope I'm not—" He saw me and Evelyn. "But apparently I am. I should have tapped first; crave pardon."

"Don't worry about it," Herb told him. "That's the way I usually find him."

"Usually with his girlfriend," I agreed.

Evelyn turned to me, eyes twinkling, and we gave each other our best deadpan. She was good; I nearly lost it. "So I'm going about this backward, then?" she asked.

"I for one work best in that mode," I told her. "Come on in, Andrew—I can work with an audience. How goes the confabulation?"

He looked pained. "Well, they're still discussing what should be done to evacuate the *Sheffield* as efficiently as possi-

ble. Your grandfather's come up with the seed of a very interesting plan, actually. Several problems still to be solved, of
course, but ... look, could we talk about it on the way?
Richard sent me to tell you he'd be pleased if we all returned to
the *Mercury* right away, and began preparing for an immediate
launch. It's very important to lose as little time as possible, obviously, since every loss will cascade down through the whole
sequence, and he's determined to hit the ground running."

Evelyn and I exchanged a glance and adjusted our position until we were side by side, each with an arm around the
other's waist. "They're that close to agreeing on a plan?"
Jinny asked.

Her husband shrugged. "Your grandfather wants to be under way two seconds after the airlock shuts behind him. We
don't even know if all the provisions we were offered have
been loaded aboard yet, much less stowed properly."

She nodded. "I guess we can continue the conversation
there. Let's go."

"Wait a minute," I said. "Question."

"He just told you we don't have any minutes to spare,"
Jinny said sharply.

"I agree with Andrew. But that begs my question: who's
'we,' exactly?"

Everybody did a lot of blinking.

"Ten seats. Seven of you. If Evelyn has her way, I take
seat number eight. Who gets the other two?"

Very *loud* blinking. Herb looked less sleepy than usual.

Andrew cleared his throat. "As I was leaving, Mr. Hattori
had just agreed to join us."

"Really?" Jinny said. "Why?"

Andrew frowned. "To be honest, I'm not sure. It made
sense when Richard explained it."

"Hattori!" Lieutenant Bruce squawked, ruining his efforts
to avoid being caught eavesdropping. "Why in space should
he get one of the first berths? He's a *bean counter*!"

Jinny's stare basted him with superheated contempt, and
he withered. "I'm sure you would prefer to share your
Bridge with people *interested* in your opinions, Lieutenant,
so we will take our leave now. Your hospitality has been ex-

ceeded only by your courtesy. Shall we go, all?"

Evelyn turned her head to look at me. "Is there anything you want to pack, Joel?" One eyebrow rose slightly, copied accurately by the same side of her mouth. "Anyone you want to say good-bye to?"

I had absolutely no idea where we were going to go, or what we intended to do when we got there, or what if any contribution I could make.

I raised my voice a little. "Herb? Say good-bye to everybody for me, will you? You know how to say it pretty."

"If I don't get the tenth seat, sure," he called back. "Don't bother leaving me your porn folder; I hacked into it years ago."

"Captain Conrad?" I said at the same volume. "Would my baggage allotment aboard your ship accommodate a baritone saxophone?"

"Anna?" Evelyn asked.

I smiled. "You read liner notes carefully. Yes, my Yanigasawa."

Andrew called, "If it didn't, I'd tear out a couple of instrument panels or something."

He and I exchanged a look. "I'll meet you all at the airlock with my saxophone, then," I said.

Andrew pretended to clear his throat. "Joel, I hope you will forgive my presumption. I took the liberty of asking that your silver baritone be loaded aboard the *Mercury* shortly after our arrival. Evelyn said that was the one you'd want." His eyes went back and forth between Jinny and Evelyn twice. "It seemed the prudent course."

I knew what he meant. Jinny and Evelyn were twin forces of nature. If one of them said a man was coming aboard, the smart money said to save time and start loading his luggage. "I'm sure it was," I agreed, and a silent understanding passed between us. "Let's go, then. I'm eager to see your ship, Captain. I presume you docked down by the main passenger airlock?"

"That's right." He turned to Herb. "Mr. Johnson, will you accompany us? I can show you that thing I was talking about on our way up here." Herb nodded.

Bruce looked like he wanted to cry. Rennick looked like he could happily boil me. Dorothy looked like she wanted to suddenly extrude a judge's robes and marry Evelyn and me on the spot. Andrew looked as proud as a puppy who's learned some really amazing new tricks and is dying to show everyone.

And Evelyn looked like the rest of my life, smiling at me.

THE TRIP WAS nearly the whole length of the ship, and took longer than I had expected. We did not pass a lot of people I knew well . . . we passed few people at all; it seemed a lot of us were waiting in our rooms to be told what the hell was going on. But of the few friends we did encounter, there were none that either Herb or I could bring ourselves to simply float past without a word of personal leave-taking. We also wanted to make sure the news spread as quickly as possible throughout the ship that everyone was going to get out of this alive, sooner or later. I never did find a really satisfactory way to say it in a few sentences. Herb did much better, of course. All but one of the reactions I got were positive, supportive. The one—Richie—was just gaping at me, then turning and jaunting away without a word.

We had gotten all the way to the airlock antechamber before things started to shift around in my head.

I found myself thinking over everything that had been said since I'd gotten to the Bridge, and who had been saying it. Everything made sense, everything added up, except for a single term in the equation. It nagged at me. Gave me a faint sick feeling in the pit of my stomach that I could not seem to either justify or explain away.

I was so preoccupied I was barely paying attention to Andrew's eager babbling about his discovery, even though I did want very much to hear it. It was the genuine Secret of the Ages he was telling me. But I was distracted, and it didn't help that hardly anything he said conveyed much meaning to me.

Then all at once, three words leaped out of the noise, burrowed into my consciousness, and there exploded with great force. I lost my grip on my p-suit, and didn't bother jaunting after it.

"Andy," I interrupted rudely. "Did you just say, '. . . irrespective of . . .' a moment ago?"

He was struggling with his own p-suit, trying to get his feet in. He had the klutziness of the true supergenius. "Excuse me? Yes, Joel. Quite irrespective. As I was saying, the basis of the DIS principle—"

I stepped on him again. "Evelyn? Do you understand Andrew's drive? Has he explained it to you?"

She paused in her own suit-up checklist procedure. "He tried to," she said, puzzled but game. "It didn't take. I'm afraid I don't have anything like your background in physics."

I nodded. "Dorothy?"

She shook her head. "I was *handicapped* by my background in physics. It kept turning out that everything I thought I knew was wrong. I gave up listening at about the fourth sentence, when I seemed to hear him telling me that all mass is infinite in the first place."

"It is, in a sense," Andrew tried to explain. "You see—"

"Andrew, my new friend," I told him, "we don't. Very likely we can't. But I want to be as certain as I can be of at least one datum, so I'm going to ask you one more time. Have I just understood you to tell me that the DIS effect functions under any circumstances, *irrespective of mass*? Do those three words mean to you what they mean to us? Or is this some sort of semantic confusion?"

"No, you're correct," he said, puzzled. "Mass really is imaginary, you know. Like inertia. What you need to understand—"

I turned to Evelyn. "Do *you* get it?"

She was frowning hugely. Her own p-suit drifted away from her hands, forgotten. I saw understanding wash over her, like a wave of ice water. "Oh, no. Oh, *no*! Joel—"

Now the equation solved itself: the dubious term had been defined, and others adjusted themselves to match with the inexorable beauty of math working out.

"What are you talking about?" Jinny asked.

My stomach lurched. I turned and stared at her. "You *know*, don't you? Of course you do."

"I have no idea what you're talking about," she said.

"*What* does she know?" Herb asked me.

I could see from Dorothy's face that she got it, was thinking it through, and becoming as angry as I was. I could also see that Rennick had known all along, and was not even faintly surprised. He started edging toward the hatch that led back out into the rest of the *Sheffield*.

Uptake. Uptake was going to be important, now. I spoke quickly and in my loudest talking-to-the-audience voice.

"Everyone here has a mental picture of Richard Conrad. Can any one of you really picture him spending the next thirty-odd years rescuing a few hundred *farmers*?"

General consternation. Rennick made it all the way to the door and put his back to it.

"But he himself wouldn't—" Jinny began.

"Do you honestly think he believes that would be the best use for his one and only superluminal starship, during these next crucial empire-building decades?"

"He wanted to own the entire Solar System," Herb said. "Now he'll have to settle for what's left. But I think he would consider that the absolute minimum acceptable."

"My grandfather is with your own Captain this very minute, trying to—"

"Your grandfather is lying his aristocratic ass off at this minute," I said, "trying to persuade Captain Bean he's ever going to see him again after the *Mercury* leaves. That way he can consign more than four hundred people to death with an absolute minimum of harsh words or other unpleasantness. And we can all depart without Alice Dahl having to hold a gun on anyone."

"You're insane!" Jinny snapped.

"If he really wanted to help us, all he'd have had to do was order his grandson-in-law to unship his DIS drive from the *Mercury* . . . and install it in the *Sheffield*! Andrew just got finished telling us the silly thing *doesn't believe in mass*."

Jinny gasped in shock—but not as loud as her husband. "Coventry, what was I *thinking* of?" Andrew said, his face stricken. "I . . . I . . . I'd have to destroy the *Mercury* in the process, I guess that's why it simply never occurred to me, but—yes, damn it to seven hells, there's no real reason in the universe why I couldn't recalibrate and ramp it up to make the field large enough to enfold even a ship this large. I could have it done in a few weeks! I think . . ."

"Don't destroy the *Mercury*," Herb advised. "Just bring it aboard. It's about the size of one of our landing craft."

"That would work—"

"I heard earlier it took you five or six subjective weeks to overtake and match orbits with us," I told Jinny. "The *Mercury* was a private yacht on its shakedown cruise when Sol exploded. Even given Conrad family paranoia, I'd be surprised if she carried more than a couple of months' worth of provisions for a crew of seven. My guess is *your ship's just about out of food, water, and air by now.*" Andrew's groan told me my guess was accurate. "*That's* why the old bastard really let himself be talked into picking us for his first destination! He needs to be fully reprovisioned before he reaches an established colony planet, so he can deal from a position of strength. To him, we're no more than a supplies cache en route, disposable. We're the smallest number of people that stand between him and self-sufficiency."

"And the easiest to con," Herb said. "Because we're scared and tired and vulnerable. And we have evidence other than Conrad's word that Sol has been destroyed and hellfire is coming."

"Oh, *Grandfather*," Evelyn groaned. "Oh, this is awful!" She started for the exit. "Joel, you're absolutely right: we have to—"

Rennick reached into his blouse and produced the smallest hand weapon I had ever seen, the size of a stylus, waved it across us all once. "You have to stay right where you are," he barked. "Evelyn, I mean it! *Don't!*" He aimed his weapon at her, and I gathered myself to leap into the line of fire, and his head exploded into red mist, most of which boiled out of existence even as it formed. A few tiny drops made it all the way across the room and spattered my face and hands. His little weapon flew from his hand and started caroming off things.

Dorothy Robb had something even smaller in *her* hand. It looked like the smaller half of a stylus, with the pocket clip on it. As I saw it, she released it like a soiled tissue and let it drift from her. "I thought I'd get all the way out of this life without ever using that," she said thoughtfully, as if to herself, in the sudden ringing silence. "But it *was* worth carrying it, all these years."

I wondered how she'd gotten it past the Gurkhas back home. But then, Rennick had managed with a larger one. Maybe the Gurkhas had known—and just figured they could deal with it. "Thank you, Dorothy," I managed to say, wiping my face with my sleeve.

"You may always leave these little things to me," she said, making it sound like a quote. Then she brushed a hand across her face and made a sound of revulsion. "I would not have thought his brain was large enough to make that much of a splash."

Herb was instantly at her side with a pack of tissues. She thanked him gravely and accepted one.

The heat of the explosion had briefly been so intense, Rennick's massive wound had cauterized itself. Most of the red mist had already been dealt with by the *Sheffield*'s intensive zero-gee airflow, and the rest would be soon.

"They'll be here any minute," Herb said to me.

"I know," I said.

"You understand the problem. You've seen her."

I wished I didn't. "Yeah. I've seen Alice."

We shared a wordless glance that lasted ten seconds or more. He smiled suddenly. "I don't see another way. Do you?"

I thought as hard as I know how. Finally, reluctantly, I shook my head no. "Not with the tools at hand."

He nodded.

I retrieved Dorothy's weapon, glanced at it briefly, and tossed it to him.

"It's empty," Dorothy said urgently. "It was a single-shot."

Herb held it up. "Could you tell it's empty by looking at it?"

She made no reply, but her face said she understood now, and that the answer to his question was no.

A bounce took Rennick's weapon past me and I picked it out of the air. I looked around at the scene, studying it closely. Just behind me, beside the airlock hatch, was a large display showing data of several kinds. I found the right switch and powered it off. Then I stepped back, measured angles, and said, "What do you think?" to Herb.

"Good as it's liable to get," he said. "This is what a long time ago used to be called a Hail Mary play."

I nodded. "I *really* wish it was better," I said.

With infinite kindness in his eyes, he said *not* "Me, too," but "I know." Then he moved, to position himself just beside the hatch out to the *Sheffield*. Dorothy began gathering the p-suits we hadn't finished donning, and stowing them out of the way.

"What are you doing?" Jinny asked dangerously. "Damn it, what is going on?" Andrew couldn't decide which of us to gape at. He wore a look I could empathize with—a man re-arranging the entire contents of his brain, and heart.

"Can you handle her?" I asked Evelyn.

She looked me in the eye and said *not* "I think so," but, "Yes." Everybody was being very helpful to me today. I nodded thanks, and she left my side, jaunting over to dock beside Jinny.

"Cousin Jinny," she said clearly and firmly, "zip it."

Jinny was too shocked to respond, and before she could regroup, we all heard the sound of the party approaching the antechamber from outside.

"Joel—" Dorothy began.

"I think it'll be all right," I told her. "But stay alert."

She shut up, chose a spot well away from the hatch, near the air outflow, and tugged Rennick's body there. She held onto the grille with one hand, and held Rennick near it with the other. "Evelyn, over here, dear."

Evelyn looked to me, I nodded, and she joined Dorothy.

Herb and I shared one last long look. Nothing to be said.

* * *

THE HATCH IRISED open.

Alice Dahl entered first, and she was as good as I had presumed she must be. The instant she cleared the hatchway she sensed that something was wrong—body language? Blood scent the airflow hadn't finished flushing yet?—and went hyperalert well before she could have seen Rennick's body. She didn't actually kill anyone, but she was very ready to. And it was me she focused on.

Failing to notice, Conrad came in behind her, followed by Solomon Short. "All right, everyone," he was saying, "thanks to Captain Bean's insights, and Relativist Short's gift for lateral thinking, I think we've come up with a plan that will—"

It took him that long to see Rennick's drifting corpse and stop speaking. He must have been very tired. But he was still sharp, and quick. He didn't bother asking what was wrong.

"All right," he went on. "Everyone on board *now*. We will discuss this later."

"Gran'ther, how *can* you?" Evelyn asked him with infinite sadness.

He did not seem to understand her question.

"The race made a small mistake," Herb said. Alice's head turned to track him. "We did *finally* make some progress at stamping out war. But maybe it would have been better to start with greed."

"What's going on?" Solomon asked mildly.

"Conman of Conman here," I said, "was just about to depart, leaving behind a boatful of suckers who thought he'd be coming back to start a rescue shuttle."

Solomon caught on at once, and turned to glare at Conrad. "Really?"

"He also forgot to mention to anybody that with a little work, Andy's Magic Carpet drive will push anything you put it in, just as fast. Irrespective of its mass."

Solomon's face darkened even further. "I see. He had better things to do with it. Sure, he did."

"Sol," I said quickly. "It's *covered*. Okay? Watch out for green mist."

I saw him take my meaning. Stay out of the line of fire and await developments.

"Oh, for Covenant's sake!" Conrad snarled. "Jinny, *you* understand. Evelyn, dear, history is being made. Right now, by us. We need to form and consolidate the Confederation of Human Stars, get it organized. Ferry telepaths around until rational communication can take place, and then get busy and avenge our star. For all we know, a second wave of attacks is just about to happen——there is no *way* we have time to waste rescuing a bunch of losers from their own incompetence. Please try to be rational. You're a *Conrad*, for the—"

"I am a Johnston," she told him.

He rolled his eyes. "Young love. Oh, I love being old! Fine. I don't care what name you go by, as long as you get into that damned pressure suit and back aboard the ship, *now*."

She looked him in the eye and slowly shook her head. "I will not."

Conrad of Conrad sighed, irritated beyond endurance. "Alice."

Alice Dahl reached for her right hip, and Time slowed to its lowest possible velocity.

"Alice!" I shouted.

She was very good, gave me less than half her attention at first despite my shout.

That changed *fast* when she saw my hand holding the weapon I'd been palming all this time, though.

She was *so* good that in the fraction of an instant it took me to draw a dead bead on her center of mass, she had her own gun out and pointed directly at my left eye.

"If you kill me," she said calmly, "my hand will still kill you afterward."

"Probably," I agreed. Most of my attention was on my features, going for the best poker face of my life.

"Absolutely," she corrected.

Time was going so slowly now, I could actually see her discern some tiny flaw in my poker face. Her finger tightened on the trigger.

"Hey, Butch!" Herb bellowed at the top of his lungs.

She was still good. She turned her head *just* enough to pick him up in her peripheral vision. She knew he was bluffing, because she knew he was smart enough to know he could not possibly beat her—and still she checked.

And found Herb aiming Dorothy's tiny little weapon at her.

She identified it, must have realized it was much deadlier than the one I held. It didn't worry her a bit. The right side of her mouth curled up in contempt.

Faster than the eye could follow, she spun on her axis. Beating Herb was no more difficult than beating me had been for her.

And as far as Alice Dahl knew, nobody important wanted Herb alive. She shot him in his left eye, perfectly confident that shock and denial would hold a civilian like me frozen for the split second that was all she would need.

I was not in shock. I was not in denial. She died halfway back around to me, when my shot caught her square in the heart.

It was a far less gaudy death than either of the others that had happened in that room—but it was definitive. Rennick's weapon fired not a laser or projectiles, but something that relaxed muscles. All of them, completely. Her face went slack, her eyes became doll's eyes, her body went limp and derelict, and sphincters let go just before Solomon crashed into her.

My own nearly did the same. I had been more than half expecting to die myself, doing this. But I barely noticed; I was already in transit to Herb, just in case, knowing it was futile but unable to help myself. Halfway there I knew I was wasting my time, and started to relax and begin mourning.

An unexpected noise behind me scared the living shit out of me.

I wrenched my body around and just had time to realize Jinny had launched herself after me, hands curled into claws—when Evelyn slammed into her so hard her vector won the argument. They both drifted away from me, but only Evelyn was still conscious.

I collided with Alice's body myself, glanced off, and

grabbed a handhold. Now my attention was fully on Andrew.

He couldn't take his eyes off Jinny. He was staring at her as if she had just morphed into some loathsome insect, or perhaps a demon with fangs.

I felt truly bad for him. I knew *exactly* how he must feel. The same as I had, when *I'd* first learned she wasn't who I'd thought she was at all. That she wasn't who she had *told* me she was. That she was capable of enormities I could not have imagined, and would not have believed until forced to. Nobody that beautiful should be capable of that much guile: it was too unfair an advantage.

She was everything her grandfather had hoped for. And little else.

I decided he would probably live through it, too. He might even be able to deal with it, somehow, for all I knew. He *was* a supergenius. And a decent man down to his marrow. I would try and have a long talk with him, as soon as I could. A series of them.

Richard Conrad inevitably found his voice. "All right, now," he began.

Andrew Jackson Conrad cut him off. "Grandfather," he said, "shut the fuck up."

Richard stared at him, more confounded by this than anything else that had occurred yet. He groped for words, found none at all.

"If you say one more word," his grandson-in-law said to him, "I will come over there and shove it down your throat."

"*Way* too kind," I heard Dorothy murmur.

I saw it wash over him, and if it hadn't been so pathetic I'd have enjoyed it more. For the first time in his entire life, Conrad of Conrad found himself in a room full of people . . . not *one* of whom gave a damn what he did or did not want.

He had *always* been utterly alone—but had probably never even suspected it until now.

"Joel," Andrew continued, "I assume this ship carries proctors?"

"Good ones," I agreed.

"Will you summon one, please. This citizen requires re-straint."

"As a matter of fact," I said, "he'll be here any second. The ship calls him if it decides he's needed. As soon as he gets here, I suggest we all adjourn back to my quarters, and start making some plans."

"Good," he said. "Will you help me get my wife to your Infirmary first?"

"Not to worry," I assured him. "My place is much closer, more comfortable . . . and our Healer makes house calls. She is very good."

He nodded. "Thank you very much."

I told him he was welcome.

And then—*finally*—my obligations were over for the moment, and at long last I went to rejoin my Evelyn.

She was waiting for me.

We had been waiting for each other, for a long, long, long time. No matter what clock you used to measure it.

22

It's just beginning. Everything is always just beginning.

—Jakusho Kwong

That's essentially all I have to tell you.

Governor-General Cott's more formal account of the events of our voyage is vastly more complete, accurate, and factual. But it was felt that future generations will need more than facts. Too many of them make little or no sense without the subjective context. And it was decided that I was both best able to recount that story, from an insider's unique perspective—and the one least occupied with other, more pressing duties.

You have them, too. We all do, now. We need to know for

certain, just as soon as possible, whether our civilization has been crippled and nearly killed by stupendous bad fortune— of which there is certainly no shortage in the cosmos—or by enemy action. And either way, we need to figure out what needs to be done about that.

I do not doubt we will. But you must hurry. You have a limited time now to move yourselves and your entire civilization underground, including all the native and introduced flora and fauna you need to survive . . . before the wavefront of death arrives, from the very part of the sky you've always thought of as home. You will need to be at least several hundred meters underground when it arrives; several thousand would be even better.

Yours is the fourth world we have brought the news to. At each of them, I have been asked why I don't simply stay? I've done my shift, and more. Why not let someone else take up the torch? Having miraculously managed, against incredible odds, to set my feet on solid ground once more, why would I ever contemplate leaving it again? Evelyn and I have a child to raise now, after all.

The best I can explain it is, I've lost my taste for living on planets. It always was overrated.

The narrator of an ancient poem by Tennyson "held his purpose firm, to sail beyond the sunset." My wife and I—all of us—have actually *done* that.

It's going to get *interesting* now.

Afterword

This is an optional bonus: a sort of DVD Special Feature, "The Making of *Variable Star*," in which I explain how I ended up being the one to tell you the story.

Feel free to save it for later, or skip it altogether. Its principal purpose is to save me from having to spend the next few years answering the same questions over and over, and I already suspect it's probably not going to work.

I TYPE THIS in November of 2005, in my office on an island west of British Columbia . . . but for me, the whole thing began way over at the other end of the continent, in a New York suburb rightly called Plainview, fifty-one years ago in November of 1954, when I turned six years old.

My mother wanted to raise a literate son. But Mom also had a lot of resting she wanted to get done, so she came up with a diabolically efficient scheme for teaching me to read. She would start reading me a Lone Ranger comic book, and *just* as it got to the really exciting part, where the masked man was hanging by his fingertips from the cliff . . . Mom would suddenly remember she had to go wind the cat or fry the dishes. By age six I had taught myself to read out of sheer frustration.

On my birthday, she graduated me to the hard stuff. She drove me to a building called a "lie bury," and told me to go inside and ask the nice lady behind the desk for a book. I followed instructions. "Mom says gimme a book, lady." And the nice lady behind the desk sized me up thoughtfully, and handed me the very first book with no pictures in it that I ever read in my life: *Rocket Ship Galileo*, by Robert A. Heinlein.

Her name was Ruth Siegel. She changed my life completely.

It was the first of Robert's famous juvenile novels—and it was at least a hundred times better than the Lone Ranger! It was about teenage boys who were so smart they went to the Moon, and fought Nazis there, and there was nothing dopey about it, it all could have been true, practically! I finished it that night, and the next day I *walked* two miles to that lie bury and demanded to swap it for another one by the same guy. The same nice lady accommodated me, and the first *ten* books I ever read in my life were by Robert Heinlein, and they were *all* great.

When I tried other books, by other writers, it immediately became clear that some were good, and some were rotten. But it was just as clear that the ones in the same stack with the Heinleins—the ones that all had a sticker on their spine depicting a hydrogen atom inexplicably impaled by a V2— were *always* excellent, nearly as good as Heinlein himself. In 1954, science fiction was such a scorned genre that any sf actually published in hardcover—and then ordered by a public library—had to be terrific. I became a hard-core sf reader simply because that was where all the best stuff was . . . and so the whole course of my life was twisted.

Now THE STORY jumps ahead nearly a year—and yanks us halfway back across the country again.

On November 14, 1955, ten days before my seventh birthday, Robert Anson Heinlein sat down at his desk in Colorado Springs and wrote an outline for a novel he first called *The Stars Are a Clock*.

He later wrote in half a dozen possible alternate titles by hand, including *Doctor Einstein's Clock,* but never settled on one he liked. This was not unusual for him. *A Martian Named Smith,* for instance, was also *The Heretic* for a while before it was finally published as *Stranger in a Strange Land.*

His outline filled at least eight extremely dense pages: single-spaced ten-pica type with absolutely minimal margins on all four sides and very few strikeovers. He also filled fourteen 3X5 index cards with extensive handwritten notes relating to the book. And then, for reasons only he could tell us, he closed the file and put it in a drawer, and never got around to writing that particular book.

Now THE BIGGEST jump of all: less mileage this time, but nearly forty-eight years—to Toronto on September 1, 2003, where the World Science Fiction Convention, Torcon 3, was held that year.

I was Toastmaster for that Worldcon, the second time I have endured that honor, and it went *infinitely* better than the first time had, the Saturday night Hugo Awards ceremony this time fiasco-free. So I was pleasantly relaxed on Sunday morning when I showed up for my last obligation of the weekend, an appearance on a panel discussion about rare and obscure works by Robert A. Heinlein. Some remarkable discoveries of previously unknown Heinleiniana had been made in recent years, including an entire first book few had known existed called *For Us, the Living,* which Scribner's had just published for the first time. I was on the panel because I had contributed an Introduction to it—but what I wanted to hear about was the exciting *new* stuff I'd heard rumors about. Teleplays—screenplays, even! I was quite unprepared for what I got.

The star panelist was Dr. Robert James, one of the researchers busily combing through the country's libraries for RAH references, standing in for official biographer Bill Patterson who had been unable to attend. Robert is the man personally responsible for rescuing *For Us, the Living* from oblivion, and Bill had given him some terrific ammunition from the Heinlein Collection at the University of California at Santa Cruz to wow us all with. Those teleplays, for instance: most were based on known short stories . . . but not all of them. *There were Robert Heinlein stories we didn't know.* That room was packed to bursting with some of the world's most hard-core Heinlein fans, and we were electrified by the news that the Canon was not yet quite complete, after all.

And that wasn't all. . . .

There was, Robert said, an outline for an entire *novel* that no one knew about, that Heinlein had never gotten around to writing. What it read like, he said, was a classic Heinlein Juvenile, and indeed it had been dreamed up around the time he was writing them, and—

—and from the back of the room, a woman I could not see called, in a loud, clear, melodious voice:

"You should get Spider Robinson to finish that novel."

And there was applause.

One of the other people on that panel was Eleanor Wood, literary agent for the estate of Robert A. Heinlein—and also, as it happens, for *me*. Another was Art Dula, trustee for the estate and its half-million-dollar Heinlein Prize Trust (see *www.heinleinprize.com* for details) . . . and Robert's literary executor. Glances were exchanged. Immediately after the panel ended, words were exchanged.

I was, please understand, profoundly terrified that this cup might actually come to me. It was quite literally the most difficult and intimidating challenge that could possibly be handed a science fiction writer, a red flag to critics. It was like a musician being asked to write, score, produce, perform, and record an entire album based on a couple of John Lennon demo cassettes. In boxing it's called leading with your chin. But I was fifty-five years old, just in the mood for the challenge of my life. Most of all, I wanted to read a new Heinlein novel so badly, I didn't care if I had to finish it myself, didn't care what kind of grief it cost me to do so.

Once again, a woman I didn't know had changed my life.

I'm delighted to report that she did not remain anonymous. I sent this Afterword around to some of those mentioned in it for corrections, and one of them was David M. Silver, President of the Heinlein Society (*www.heinlein society.org*), who was also on that panel. He was able to identify my benefactress as a member of his esteemed society. Thank you from the bottom of my heart, Kate Gladstone!

SHORTLY AFTER I returned home from Torcon 3, I received Robert's outline, and permission to write two sample chapters and a proposal for Art Dula; if he liked them, the gig was mine. Wild with exultation, I fell upon that outline and read it three times with extreme care.

And then I began banging my head on my desk. Gently, at first.

You may recall I stated earlier that Robert's outline ran at least eight pages. It may have run fifty, for all anybody knows. What we *do* know is, seven of them survive.

They establish the ficton—Robert's term for the time-and-place in which a story is set. They create vivid characters and their back stories, especially Joel, Jinny, and her grandfather. They describe the basic antinomy that impels Joel to emigrate, discuss the economics of interstellar colonization, and sketch in some of his early adventures after he leaves.

And then they chop off in midsentence, and midstory.

My God, I said to myself, the first time I finished reading the outline, *there's no furshlugginer* ending! *It could go* anywhere *from here....*

God, this is great! I said to myself the second time I finished it, *I not only get to write a book with Robert, I get to pick the ending.*

Dear God, I moaned to myself after the third reading, *what the* hell *am I going to do for an ending?*

I holed up in my office for a week, and stared at those seven pages and fourteen quasilegible index cards and asked myself that question until beads of blood began to form on my forehead. Barring another miracle of forensic scholarship, this was going to be the very last Robert Heinlein novel ever. No ending I thought of seemed adequate. Twice a day my wife poked food in with a stick and retired to safety. I played my entire iTunes music library in search of inspiration, staring at its hypnotic visual display on my Powerbook screen, thinking like mad.

And one afternoon, iTunes finished playing the last Ray Charles album on my hard drive, and defaulted to the next artist in alphabetical order.

Robert Anson Heinlein.

Half a dozen short mp3 audio clips, of him being interviewed on radio in his hometown, Butler, Missouri, on its first-ever Robert A. Heinlein Day back in 1987, a year be-

fore his death. I'd listened to all those clips often. But the
first one in line made me sit bolt upright in my chair now.

There—in my GrandMaster's Own Voice—was the rest of
our novel, and the inspiration for its new title, in a single un-
scripted sentence. Two clips later, he said it *again*, in different words. Suddenly I recalled Robert griping to me once in a
phone conversation about a story he'd always wanted to tell,
that John W. Campbell had argued him out of writing. . . .

You have read both those soundbites. They were the
chapter-opening quotes for Chapters 17 and 18.

That quickly, the novel finished itself in my mind. All that
remained was the comparatively trivial business of writing
those first two sample chapters and a proposal, winning
Art's approval, marketing the novel, selling it to Tor
Books—oh, yes, and then typing 115,051 words, configur-
ing them in sentences, arranging those into paragraphs, and
separating them into chapters. Every waking moment of two
years of my life, tops.

TWO NOVEMBERS LATER, the task is completed, to the best
of my ability.

And well beyond. Fortunately I had help. Even more so
than any of my previous thirty-two books, I could not conceivably have completed this one without the generous and
patient assistance of many people far more knowledgeable
and intelligent than myself. We have come now, in other
words, to the closing credits.

My principal consultants and unindicted co-conspirators
were the gentlemen who have assisted me with all of my recent novels, the Vancouver Lunar Circle, particularly engineers Guy Immega and Ray Maxwell, physicist Douglas
Beder, and astronomer Jaymie Matthews. Once my colleague
and friend Allen M. Steele (*www.allensteele.com*) and noted
rocket scientist Jordin Kare had helped me decide what *kind*
of starship I wanted, Guy, one of my oldest friends, designed
the *Sheffield* with Doug and Ray for me, treating the Ikimono
Drive I handed them as a black box. Guy and his daughter
Claire created Brasil Novo together in the course of a bedtime story they spent several years telling themselves, calling

it "Jungle World," and latterly Jaymie added a few refinements to help it retain its atmosphere. Jaymie also figured out how to make its star satisfy the odd requirements I needed, and educated me about the destruction of my own star, its precursors and its consequences, as well as consulting on cosmology in general. Doug saved my bacon over and over, not only working and reworking complex relativistic computations in what appeared to be zero time, but continually suggesting ingenious ways to make the answers serve the needs of the story. And each of these Lunarians made invaluable comments on the work of the others.

Allen was also enormously helpful in helping me visualize what interstellar flight would actually be *like*, over a period of years, having devoted considerable thought to the matter for his own terrific Coyote novels. To help me imagine what a starship's farm that feeds five hundred might look like, however, I went straight to the man himself: Dr. Raymond M. Wheeler of NASA's Biological Sciences Office, who's designing the farm that will feed astronauts on their way to Mars; he gave generously of his time and special knowledge. The goat lore I acquired myself, painfully, a long time ago in Nova Scotia.

One more technical adviser must be thanked who, like Dr. Wheeler, had never previously helped me with a book, yet proved invaluable this time. Everything I know about the sax I learned by either listening to, watching, or questioning my friend Colin MacDonald (*www.crypticmusic.ca*), a composer, saxophonist, Soto Zen monk, and in his spare time (!) the keeper of my Web site *www.spiderrobinson.com.*

Nor will I ever forget the love and support of David Crosby, who gave me the chords and melody for "On the Way to the Stars"—not to mention the 1.67gHz G4 Powerbook on which *Variable Star* was researched and written. The music I listened to most often while I wrote was that of CPR, the band David and his older son James Raymond formed with Jeff Pevar (*www.crosbycpr.com*), and also the landmark 2004 *Crosby•Nash* double-album.

Numerous others also furnished invaluable ideas and insights, including Bob Atkinson, John Barnstead, Bill Patterson, Eleanor Wood, David Gerrold, Jef Raskin, Michael Lennick, James Gifford, Paul Hattori, Yoji Kondo, Herb Varley (who suggested the *Mercury* be powered by hyperphotonic swans), my editor Pat LoBrutto, and doubtless others I'm blanking on now. I hope they'll forgive me.

And *nobody's* input was more valuable or more profoundly appreciated than that of my beloved wife and partner, Jeanne, who read each day's copy when she woke up, and left extensive notes on my keyboard for me to find every night when I went to work; no one will ever suspect how many stupid mistakes she caught before anyone else got to see them, or how many neat ideas were really hers.

Once the story was complete, everybody named went over it looking for mistakes, misunderstandings, and problems, and then helped me repair them. So—crucially for my peace of mind—did my friends John Varley and David R. Palmer, both noted Heinlein experts, who went over the manuscript with great care and each made characteristically astute suggestions.

To all these people I give my deepest thanks. As always, any mistakes are my fault.

BUT IT TAKES more than just technical advice to finish a novel. Especially this one.

First of all, and last of all, I want to say that without Jeanne's boundless love and rock-solid support, I would never have even dreamed of starting such a nerve-wracking project, and would probably have finished it, if I did, with a massive dependency on Ativan, or worse. She is my invariable star, and our orbit is stable. Equally invaluable were the unquestioning love and sensible advice of our remarkable daughter Terri Luanna, both an advertising exec *and* a social worker in the toughest town on Terra.

Art Dula took a major weight off my shoulders right from the start, by telling me, "I do *not* want you to try and do the literary equivalent of a Rich Little impression of Robert Heinlein. I want you to take his outline and write the best damn Spider Robinson novel you're capable of." He also gifted me with Robert's own, many-times-hand-repaired desk dictionary. I had Robert Heinlein's personal box of words to dip into, any time I ran short of them—and still do. Thank you, Art.

A mainstay of my morale throughout was Robert and Ginny's granddaughter, Dr. Amy Baxter, M.D. Jeanne and I met her and her husband, Louis Calderon, M.D., at Torcon 3, two nights before I sat on that panel and learned of the existence of an unwritten Heinlein novel, and we hit it off immediately. When she learned I had landed the commission, Amy promptly sent me a pair of her grandfather's Polynesian cuff links to wear as I typed, and sent Jeanne some of Ginny's jewelry to wear for me. (I was startled and amused to discover that it was necessary to send one of my shirts out to a tailor and have it retrofitted to accept cuff links—apparently they stopped having them while I wasn't looking.) By the time I was steaming into the home stretch of *Variable Star* in summer 2005, I was wearing Robert's treasured, threadbare favorite gardening shirt as I wrote out in my office, and Jeanne was in the house, in her own office, wearing Ginny's kimono. Bless you, Amy.

Other moral support and/or morale support (sometimes inadvertent or unsuspected) was provided by Daniel P. Gautreau, Alex Morton, Anya Coveney-Hughes, Andrea MacDonald, Greg McKinnon, Bob Atkinson, George R. R. Martin, Parris McBride, Alex Grey, Joe and Gay Haldeman, Lawrence Block, Tom Robbins, Robert Crais, Donald E. Westlake, Amos Garrett, Gregg Carroll, Holger Petersen, Paul Pena, Seth Augustus, Moses Znaimer, Keith Hensen, Paul Krassner, David, Jan and Django Crosby, James Raymond, Graham Nash, Jens Stark, Gabrielle Morrissette, Rob Bailey, Kerry Yackoboski, Damien Broderick, James R. Cunningham, Brad Linaweaver, Robin W. Bailey, Steve and Lynn Fahnestalk, Will Soto, Evita Karlic, the Heinlein Society, Charles, Mary, and Jim Robinson, innumerable kind members of the Usenet group alt.callahans, and whoever I've forgotten to mention.

Finally, all the Portuguese names for Brasil Novo and its moons were furnished by my son-in-law, Heron Gonçalves da Silva, of Niteroi, Brazil—a classic young Heinlein Hero if there ever was one, who came to New York a few years ago without a dime, a reference, or a word of English, and is now studying electrical engineering at the same university I got my own degree from. *Obrigado, meu genro.*

WRITING *VARIABLE STAR HAS* involved more work, more pressure, more fear, and above all, more sheer *fun* than all my other books put together. I hope it will be given to me to write another thirty-three, but I doubt any of them will come close to this.

Every time I've ever sat down to write anything, I've had Robert looking over my shoulder, of course, because he is my first template for How This Thing Should Be Done. But this time around, I felt his presence far more powerfully than ever before. In general it had a calming effect.

Only twice did it actually get spooky.

The first time, I frightened my wife badly when she discovered me heading out to my office *with the vacuum cleaner*. She was vastly relieved to learn I was not going insane, but merely being haunted: in fact, she roared with laughter when I finally admitted that Robert had stubbornly insisted he was *not* going to work in that goddamn pigsty until I mucked the place out.

The second time, it was *me* who got the willies. A friend had sent me the URL for a particularly thrilling NASA Quicktime movie: a full 360-degree true-color view of the surface of Mars. (Google it for yourself.) I was mousing my way around in a circle in wild exhilaration, like a drunken dervish, intoxicated by what I was doing, thinking to myself how thrilled Robert would have been to see this. *Check it out, Robert!* I cried in my mind. *A robot on the Red Planet, named after Miss Sojourner Truth! I'm sitting at my desk, using my mouse to pan around* Mars, *can you believe this?*

Just then, I moused past a series of surface irregularities just odd enough to catch my eye: a string of roughly spherical depressions in the coppery sand, separated by intervals of about the same distance. I wondered idly what they were.

At that moment, I heard a voice—an actual, physically audible voice—the well-remembered, unmistakable Missouri voice of Robert Heinlein—say, I swear to you, these two words: "Willis tracks."

Well, those bumps in the sand *did* indeed look *just* like the tracks that might be left by a Martian bouncer such as Willis, the star of Robert's classic juvenile novel *Red Planet,* now that I thought about it. But I *hadn't* been thinking about it. The hair stood up on the back of my neck, and I nearly crushed my mouse. If you'll pardon the expression.

That is my only actual ghost story, I'm happy to say. And I admit I was not cold sober that night. Nonetheless, I report that from start to finish, writing *Variable Star* has left me feeling Robert's presence and spirit far more strongly than I had since he caught a starship for parts unknown back in 1988.

I sincerely hope it has done the same for you.

—Bowen Island, B.C.
24 November, 2005